P9-CEM-976

ENTER THE SPELLBINDING WORLDS OF

Anne Logston

Praise for her previous novels:

"Bright, cheerful, and charming, hotly spiced with magic and intrigue." —Simon R. Green, bestselling author of *Robin Hood: Prince of Thieves*

"A fun mix of magic, culture-clash, and fast-paced adventure that pushes all the right buttons." —*Locus*

"Highly recommended. Playfulness and pathos blend to form an entertaining and thought-provoking story." —*Starlog*

"Entertaining . . . plenty of magic, demons, and other dangers." —*Science Fiction Chronicle*

"Rollicking good adventure." —*Science Fiction Review*

ANNE LOGSTON

...has been steadily building a body of work that has earned a unique place in fantasy fiction. With the novel SHADOW, she created a fascinating medieval world filled with magic, humor, grit, and a feisty, unforgettable heroine, Shadow—an elvan thief who returned in the novels SHADOW HUNT and SHADOW DANCE. The adventures of Shadow's niece, Jaellyn—born of royal and elvan blood—are vividly portrayed in the thrilling novels DAGGER'S EDGE and DAGGER'S POINT. And her powerful fantasy epics GREENDAUGHTER and WILD BLOOD take readers deeper into Logston's fully drawn world—generations before Shadow was born. Her new novel, GUARDIAN'S KEY, is her most ambitious work to date, a magical journey of self-discovery that opens new doors of the imagination.

GUARDIAN'S KEY

Anne Logston

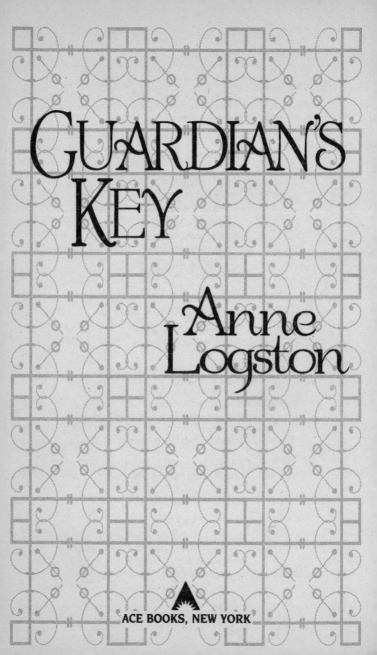

ACE BOOKS, NEW YORK

If you purchased this book without a cover, you should be aware that this book is stolen property. It was reported as "unsold and destroyed" to the publisher, and neither the author nor the publisher has received any payment for this "stripped book."

This book is an Ace original edition,
and has never been previously published.

GUARDIAN'S KEY

An Ace Book / published by arrangement with
the author

PRINTING HISTORY
Ace edition / May 1996

All rights reserved.
Copyright © 1996 by Anne Logston.
Cover art by Jeff Barson.
This book may not be reproduced in whole or in part,
by mimeograph or any other means, without permission.
For information address: The Berkley Publishing Group,
200 Madison Avenue, New York, New York 10016.

The Putnam Berkley World Wide Web site address is
http://www.berkley.com

ISBN: 0-441-00327-3

ACE®
Ace Books are published by The Berkley Publishing Group,
200 Madison Avenue, New York, New York 10016.
ACE and the "A" design
are trademarks belonging to Charter Communications, Inc.

PRINTED IN THE UNITED STATES OF AMERICA

10 9 8 7 6 5 4 3 2 1

To Joel
and the virtues of solitude

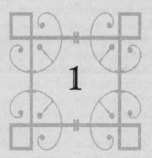

1

"**U**HH!" DARA FELL TO THE MUDDY
ground, one of her knees slamming into the
root she'd tripped over, her teeth clicking
painfully closed on the tip of her tongue. Dara collapsed
mutely, folding her arms around her stomach, shivering and
rubbing the frayed cloth over her elbows. Tears made wet
paths through the grime on her cheeks, but she did not sob.
She couldn't bear to hear her own voice echoing through
the mist and finally finding its way, hollow and distorted,
back to her ears. Even the sound of a crackling twig or
rustling leaf beneath her own boot soles was mysteriously
transformed into something sinister and directionless.

Surely, surely she must be nearly through this horrible,
ghostly fog. She'd been pressing on downhill as steadily
and straight as she could for what seemed like hours. It
wasn't fair, the mist had looked like such a narrow band
when she'd seen it from the ridge overlooking the valley.
It had made her shiver then, just looking down at the
strange mist. By now Dara was struggling to choke down
quiet moans of despair.

She'd felt so hopeful, too (if at the same time apprehensive), as she'd stared down into the valley at the Crystal Keep. This was a cursed place filled with unknown dangers—even the mention of it was enough to make men shiver around the hearth at night. And yet there were answers here, for those who were brave enough to ask the Oracle hidden within those crystal walls. Dara was not brave, but she had no choice.

The Crystal Keep. Journey's end, and still only the beginning for her. Dara had heard it rumored that the Keep was black; that it was purple; that it changed color every day; that you couldn't actually see it at all and had to walk right into it by chance; that it was guarded by a dozen dragons; that it didn't even really exist. Likewise one could find any description of the Guardian one liked, or of the Oracle itself, or of what one could expect when the doors of the Crystal Keep opened. The commonest and worst rumor was that the place was filled with fierce and horrible demons under the Guardian's command, all ready to eat or otherwise make away with unfortunate visitors. The only thing folk seemed to agree on about the Crystal Keep was that few dared go in, even fewer came out, and that it wasn't really a very good place to be if one could help it.

Well, the Keep wasn't guarded by dragons, not that Dara had been able to see from the valley rim. There were dense woods surrounding the clear crystal walls on three sides, but they were plain, wholesome-looking trees, gleaming green in the sunlight, their shade very inviting to a hot, tired wanderer. Dragons didn't live in forests, preferring remote mountainous country, and besides, dragon territory was blighted and flamed, littered with old bones and droppings, not lush and clean as the scene below. The whole delightful view from the ridge had made the Crystal Keep seem a far less ominous place than legend would have it.

But then there was the mist, a dark and impenetrable ring of it circling the valley in a snakelike band. It looked enough like an ordinary fog, if a dense one. But no fog made so perfect and neat a barrier, starting and ending so abruptly, and no fog would survive the hot afternoon sun. No, Dara knew enough about magic to be certain that she was seeing its workings in that uncanny wall of mist.

And whatever foreboding she'd felt looking at that barrier had been nothing to stepping into the horror of it. One moment she'd been walking in warm sunlight and a fresh breeze; in the next step, the sun had disappeared as if Dara had been swallowed—no other word conveyed the sensation so accurately—by the cold, damp darkness of the fog. The world narrowed to a dimly lit circle of vision no larger than two paces ahead or behind her, a nasty dampness clung to her skin and hair and quickly soaked her, and her ears felt oddly muffled. What had promised to be a simple hike straight downhill into the valley had become a confusing, frightening struggle to make any headway at all. Unexpected stone outcroppings reared up from the earth to divert Dara from her path, drop-offs appeared without warning to force her to backtrack, and every rock, bush, or tree she stumbled over looked, in the dense gray-white cloud, like every other. Even creeping along at a snail's pace, Dara had not seen the protruding root soon enough to avoid tripping over it, adding a bitten tongue to the pains of her hands and knees, already abraded from previous falls.

Now Dara crawled to the tree over whose root she had stumbled, pressed her back against the comforting solidity of its trunk, and pulled the stopper out of her waterskin with trembling fingers. She was wringing wet already, and her shaking hands owed as much to cold as to fear, but the very ordinariness of the gritty, iron-flavored water she'd dipped up from a muddy waterhole the day before was comforting in this frighteningly unordinary place. What she wouldn't give to feel Cav's hand on her shoulder and hear the familiar tones of his voice, even if all he had to say was to rebuke her for leaving.

Cav. Dara's mind seized on his image as a drowning man might seize on the rope to pull him to safety. How

Cav had argued against her making this journey, insisting that the open road, thick with brigands and other "ungentlemanly fellows," was no place for a simple serving maid who could neither wield a weapon nor cast a spell to protect herself. But that was the point, after all, wasn't it? Cavin might love her just as she was, but while High Lord Haranor and High Lady Alberta might possibly have borne the idea of an impoverished, magicless serving girl as their son and Heir's casual barn-loft tumble or even his luxuriously kept mistress, there simply wasn't a water-dragon's chance in the desert that they'd tolerate her as his bride. They might have forgiven her not being of noble blood, but there were few reasons why a daughter of so long a line of mages could not cast the simplest spell herself, and the most likely of those reasons was a curse of some sort. A curse she might pass on to her possibly equally magicless children.

Dara froze. *She* had not made that faint, furtive scraping, the sound of something hard rasping against stone. Her ears strained to pick out the direction and distance of the noise, but it bounced off the fog, seeming to emanate from all around her, both distant and nearby. Clenching her teeth to stop their chattering, Dara fumbled her belt knife from its sheath and clutched it hard. Weariness and pain forgotten, Dara levered herself to her feet and, as quickly as she dared, stumbled downhill through the mist.

She heard a low rumbling sound, like the roll of distant thunder or perhaps the growl of some gargantuan beast, again seeming to come from all around her or perhaps right under her feet. Dara whimpered deep in her throat and increased her pace, stumbling and righting herself, trotting downhill as fast as she dared.

The rumbling came again, and this time Dara was certain: It *was*, in fact, right under the soles of her feet, as the shuddering of the ground testified. Was it an earthquake, or was there some titanic creature there preparing to surface? Oh, gods, what she'd give for Cav at her side with his sword and his grimoire, no matter how angry he'd be at her for leaving against his wishes.

The memory of Cav gave Dara's weary legs new strength, and she took a deep breath and ran on almost recklessly now, jumping over small gullies and boulders as they materialized under her feet too quickly for her to dodge around them. There was a last thunderous rumble—surely this one came from somewhere behind her—and abruptly Dara emerged, sodden, exhausted, and chilled, into sunlight.

The sudden light was so dazzling that Dara could only stand where she was, blinking helplessly until her eyes adjusted. Her first realization was that the Crystal Keep was so close—only a short walk ahead, and nothing between her and it but grass. There was no outer wall, no moat, no other fortifications; if the keep had defenses apart from the unnerving wall of mist, they were invisible, or inside. That troubling thought, coupled with the very proximity of the fabled Crystal Keep, made Dara hesitate. It was far too late, however, to falter now. Dara shrugged and decided that least expected, least disappointed (as Lord Cavin IV, Heir to the throne of Caistran, always said, especially to her), and standing on the lawn would gain her nothing at all. And now there was the Crystal Keep ahead of her, no more than a few strides away, where all her answers lay. Dara squared her shoulders and stepped resolutely up to the door.

The walls of the Crystal Keep were indeed crystal, or as good an imitation as Dara had seen, although they were too thick to see through. The doors, however, were plain ordinary wood bound with iron, something that Dara found inexplicably comforting. These portals were closed tightly despite the midsummer heat, and there was no visible means of opening them; however, a large brass knocker in the shape of a gargoyle's face produced an impressive booming sound when Dara boldly employed it, and presently the thick doors swung slowly open before her. Taking a deep breath to calm herself, Dara leaned her head in to look.

Despite the almost oppressive summer heat outside, the air inside the Keep was still and quite cold, neither fresh nor stale, with no hint of either dust or dampness. A diffuse, wavery light filtered in through the translucent crystal walls, giving Dara the eerie impression of being underwater. There was no one to be seen in the wide, cold entry hall; only a wooden table with a chair behind it, a plain black stone floor, a few unlit lamps in wall sconces, and the otherwise featureless crystal walls. There were no other doors, no windows, no sound except that of Dara's still-ragged breathing.

Dara was surprised and somehow reassured by the very simplicity of the entry. It was wide, but still smaller than the entry of High Lord Haranor and High Lady Alberta's castle, and certainly less ornate. But why would such a magical place as the Crystal Keep be so barren? Wirin and Joraleen, Dara's father and mother, were powerful mages who commanded good fees, and even though Joraleen was only the House mage of Lord Evander, who held only a small territory, Dara's family had been able to afford to furnish their own small holding comfortably enough that any visitor stepping through the door would feel welcome.

But then, perhaps comfort—human comfort—had no place in the Crystal Keep. And perhaps nobody who entered the Keep was, in fact, welcome.

Dara shivered and stepped inside cautiously, then nearly jumped out of her boots as the door crashed shut behind her. Panicking, Dara whirled and ran her hands over the heavy wood. There was no lever or latch, no apparent means to open the door from within, only a keyhole framed in what appeared to be gold. Was this all some monumental trap? Was there perhaps a secret door concealed somewhere about? Dara pressed and pried at the wall around the door and the door frame itself, hoping to trigger some mechanism—

"Well, what is it?" an irritable voice demanded.

And turning around, she saw him at last.

* * *

She hadn't expected the Guardian of the Oracle to be so young; he seemed scarcely older than herself, although his eyes . . . well, his eyes knew something old. His long, wispy hair was black as a raven's feathers, with the same bluish sheen, and his clothes were of silk as dark, and his black leather boots were supple and shiny. His skin was pale, and his eyes were ebony like the night sky with no stars to light it. His features were so fine and sharp as to seem carved from crystal themselves, giving him an ethereal, sexless cast, rather like what Dara had heard of elves, but that delicate grace seemed at odds with the cold iron looking out of those old, old eyes.

When he spoke, his voice was as old and cold as his eyes, remote and empty as the featureless hall in which they stood.

"Name yourself and state your purpose here."

Looking at his rich and immaculate clothing, Dara was even more conscious of the road dust staining her patched, sodden trousers and tunic, the grime streaking her skin, the stray wisps of dirty brown hair pulling out of her lank and neglected braid.

"My lord, I'm—I'm Dara," she said, forcing the words out of a throat gone suddenly dry. "I'm a mage—I mean, I *should* have been a mage; I was born to a long line of mages. Actually I'm just a serving girl at High Lord—" She stopped, suddenly realizing she was babbling like a mist-witted fool. She squared her shoulders and looked the Guardian in the eyes. "I've come to ask the Oracle for my magic so I can marry the man I love."

"That isn't a question," the Guardian of the Oracle said contemptuously. "It's a wish. The Oracle doesn't grant wishes."

Dara's heart sank. "But I—"

"The Oracle only answers questions," the Guardian said scornfully. "Weren't you told that?"

Dara was silent for a long moment. She'd heard rumors

of a few who'd reached the Crystal Keep and been granted their heart's desire. But maybe their heart's desire had been the answer to a question. Maybe if she knew how she might make her magic work, even if it meant a quest across all the kingdoms—

"The Oracle only answers questions," the Guardian repeated, lightly polishing his nails against the silk of his tunic and inspecting them critically. "But *I* can grant a wish. One wish. And you've made two wishes: a wish for magical ability, and a wish to marry a man."

Dara swallowed hard.

"Then I can't have both?"

The Guardian smiled, a smile as cold as his eyes.

"You're lucky to be granted one wish, and you're ungrateful enough to complain because you can't have two? Choose."

Dara shivered involuntarily at that smile and struggled to pull her thoughts into some kind of order. She didn't really want to *wish* to marry Cav; that seemed somehow like cheating. She'd never asked that anything be simply given to her in her life, not since the night nearly five years ago when she'd quietly crept away from her parents' holding to make her own way in the world. If she gained Cav through a wish, maybe she'd wonder for the rest of her life if Cav really loved her, really would have married her on his own. But would wishing for her magic make Cav marry her for certain? She remembered uneasily the way they'd argued before she left.

"Then I wish," she said deliberately, "for *whatever* I need to win the man I love."

The Guardian was silent for a moment, staring at her with something very like amazement. Then to Dara's surprise, he threw back his head and laughed rather bitterly. That laugh banished the last of Dara's fear; *nobody* would laugh at her!

"You wanted to know my wish," she said stiffly. "I

made it. Or is that too much for the legendary power of the Guardian of the Oracle?''

The Guardian stopped laughing and gazed at her rather sharply. Dara fought the urge to shiver again; he seemed to enjoy her unease altogether too much.

''That's a large wish,'' the Guardian said lazily. He leaned back against the table Dara had seen. ''What will you give me for it?''

''Give you?'' Dara asked, surprised and dismayed. Nobody had ever said anything about a price. Why, wasn't leaving Cav and her place in the High Lord and Lady's household, journeying for leagues and leagues in search of the Crystal Keep, and making her way through the horrible mist wall price enough? And what else did she have to give? She'd been poor to begin with; after the necessary costs of her travel to the Crystal Keep, she had scarcely three Suns left in her purse, maybe enough to get her home, maybe not.

The Guardian settled himself more comfortably on the edge of the table, looking bored.

''Nothing comes without price; that's the rule of the Crystal Keep, a rule that was carved in the stones of this place long before I came. For value given there must be value received. Surely a humble serving wench has learned that lesson, at least. What is your wish worth?''

''Why . . . I don't know,'' Dara said confusedly. How could one put a price on another person, or on love? ''What do you want?''

The Guardian laughed again, coldly.

''How simple you are. You have no idea what you want, or even what value you place on it.'' Abruptly he rose from his perch and walked over to her. Dara forced herself to stand her ground, not flinching as he tilted her chin up, his grip uncomfortably strong, forcing her eyes to meet his. His hand was not cold as she'd expected; neither was it warm. Something in his touch, however, made her shiver again.

''You have,'' the Guardian said at last, ''most interest-

ing eyes." Just as abruptly, he let go of her face and returned to his seat, some indefinable expression crossing his
face.

"Turn about," he said, "and reach into the basin of the
fountain behind you, and draw out what you find there."

Dara turned around, then suppressed a cry of amazement. Where there had been only empty hall was now a
sparkling crystal fountain that seemed to glow with a cool
blue light of its own; bright water cascaded down into a
pool at the base. Dara peered into the basin; the water was
clear, but she could see nothing there except the water itself.

"But there's nothing in it," Dara protested, turning back
to the Guardian.

"Do as you're told."

Hesitantly, Dara reached into the water, which was
pleasantly cool but not cold. Her fingers touched the bottom
of the basin, then abruptly encountered a small, hard object.
She withdrew her hand and found her fingers clasping a
golden key, surprisingly heavy for its small size.

"That is the key," the Guardian told her in a bored tone,
"which opens the doors of my keep. Somewhere in the
Keep you may or may not find the Oracle. Find it, and ask
it the price of your wish. Return and pay me that price, and
the wish is yours. Or you may use that key to leave, whichever you like; it will fit the keyhole in the door by which
you entered. Having left, you will soon forget all you've
seen here and will never be allowed to pass the doors of
the Keep again; having lost the key, you may never leave.
Do you understand?"

How many had come into this keep and never left? Was
her magic really worth her life? But . . . Cav. Dara nodded
and clutched the key tightly.

"I would advise you," the Guardian said with a grim
smile, "not to tarry long about your task, or you may well
regret it. That advice costs you nothing; you'll find naught
else within for such a price.

"Well, go on if you will," he added impatiently, gesturing absently at one wall. To Dara's amazement, a large oaken door had appeared where only solid crystal had been before. Before her courage could fail her, Dara stepped to the door. Strangely, there were two keyholes, not one, but the upper keyhole was far too small for the key in her hand. Dara shrugged and tried the golden key in the lower lock.

The key fit perfectly. She turned it, and the door started to open, but Dara gripped the edge, halting its motion, and looked back over her shoulder.

"My lord—"

But the room was utterly empty, save for the table, the chair, and the sparkling fountain.

Dara sighed and opened the door.

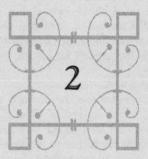

2

DARA BLINKED IN AMAZEMENT. SHE'D EX-
pected the door to open into a room of some sort;
instead, there was a long stone corridor lined with
doors on one side, strangely only a few paces apart—how
tiny the rooms must be!—and lamps in wall sconces on the
other. The floor of the corridor was completely covered by
a thick woven rug. What occasioned Dara's amazement,
however, was the ceiling—or lack thereof. There appeared
to be no roof at all; instead, although it had been bright
afternoon when Dara walked into the Keep, she now saw
a perfect night sky above, stars glittering but no moon visible. How could so much time have passed so quickly? And
the Crystal Keep *had* had a roof; she'd seen it herself as
she approached. Where had it gone, or was the starry night
sky perhaps only a magical illusion?

She peered suspiciously down the hall. There was no
end in sight, although she couldn't see terribly far because
of the darkness. Who in the world would build a keep in
such a strange way, all those tiny rooms on one side and
such a straight, long hall? And how could it be like that,

anyway? She'd looked down at the Keep from the valley rim, and it had been a rectangular building like any other. Shaking her head in wonder and perplexity, Dara stepped into the hallway to examine the nearest door more closely.

There was a solid *thunk* behind her, and Dara spun around to find that the oaken door had closed behind her. There was no latch or handle, just one simple keyhole. Dara reached out with the golden key, then slowly pulled her hand back again.

Having left, you may never return here. Had the Guardian meant the Crystal Keep, or perhaps this hall? If she opened the door, could she return? Best not take a chance; she already knew what was on the other side of that door, anyway. Reluctantly she turned to the first door on her left.

It too was a plain wooden door, bound with iron. At approximately eye level was a small hinged panel, now closed. Cautiously Dara opened the small panel and peered through; her eyes widened, and she gasped.

She'd expected to see a room (maybe a closet, judging from the spacing between the doors), or perhaps darkness if no lamps were lit inside, perhaps even another hallway such as the one she was standing in. What she saw, however, was a bleak, withered landscape with a gray sky, dead, gnarled trees, and a kind of ash covering the ground. Nothing was moving; no breeze stirred the powdery ash. Was it only a picture?

Dara gaped at the strange sight a moment longer, then looked up again at the starry night over the corridor. It was unchanged. She glanced through the panel again. Gray sky.

Puzzled, Dara moved to the next door, opened the panel, and peered through. Through this panel she saw open rolling hills liberally speckled with flowers, the light suggesting early morning. The next door showed dense forest at twilight. Nothing moved in each view; no breeze stirred grass or leaves; no bird sang or insect flew.

Were they indeed merely pictures? How could they be true places with nothing moving, no signs of life or even wind? And how could such different lands exist so close together? Was it a sort of Gate spell to send travelers to faraway places, or were the varied landscapes merely clever illusions? Wonderingly, Dara walked back to the first door and peered through at the desolate landscape.

Surely the Guardian wouldn't have sent her here to no purpose. He wanted his "price," and she couldn't pay it without finding the Oracle. She examined the door again; like the other doors she'd seen, there was only the keyhole and the small hinged panel; no latch or lever to open the door.

Dara glanced dubiously at the key in her hand. It was heavy, like real gold, but who would make a key out of soft gold? She chuckled to herself. Who but the Guardian of the Oracle, the master of a kingdom like this, which made no sense at all.

Slowly Dara slid the end of the key into the keyhole and turned it. Unseen tumblers turned smoothly and the door swung slowly open. Dara swallowed hard and stepped through.

And stopped in her tracks, coughing and blinking. The air was flying with grit as a brisk wind stirred the ashy ground. After a moment, the breeze died down, and Dara knuckled grime out of her tearing eyes.

What she saw was, indeed, the bleak and gray landscape she had seen through the hinged panel. Surely the Oracle wouldn't be in such an awful place.

"Nice and homey, ain't it?" a voice cackled behind her.

Dara jumped and turned quickly. To her amazement, there sat an old woman in tattered finery at a spinning wheel, the wheel turning briskly as the woman spun ashes into a silky gray thread. Just beyond the old woman was a plain oaken door with no visible structure around it, and only the ashy ground beneath it. The door she'd come through was slightly ajar; through the opening Dara could see a glimpse of the corridor she'd left.

"I do wish things would quit popping in and out," Dara said with a sigh.

The old woman blinked with indignation.

"Well! Don't know as Granny Good's been called a *thing* before, missy! And as for that, you rather popped in yourself, you know!"

"Oh, I'm sorry," Dara said quickly. "I was just—you know—unsettled a little."

The old woman cackled again, shaking unruly gray hair everywhere.

"And you'll be more so, missy, before the lord's done with you! I say," she said suddenly, her faded green eyes gazing at Dara sharply, "don't suppose you have a drop of water about you? This grit plumb dries out my throat."

"Of course." Dara held out her mostly empty waterskin—there she'd been, right next to a fountain and too stupid to fill it up—and watched as the old woman took a long swallow.

"Ah, that eases it," Granny Good sighed, nodding contentedly before giving the waterskin back. "And what may I give you in return, missy?"

"Oh, that's all right." Dara smiled at her. "It *is* dusty here."

"No, no, can't have that," the old woman scolded. "Value given for value received, that's the law of the Keep; you were told, weren't you? Can't take something for nothing here. What'll you have in return?"

"Could you give me some advice, then?" Dara suggested quickly. "I'm trying to find the Oracle. Could you give me any idea where to look? Those doors in the corridor just seem to go on and on forever."

"So they do, so they do, or nearly." Granny Good chuckled. "And so do we all here. So you're seeking the Oracle, hey, and what for?"

Dara sighed.

"I came to ask for my mage talent so I could marry the man I love," she said wistfully. "The Guardian said—"

"His name's Vanian, you know, the lord," the old woman told her.

"No, I didn't know. He didn't say."

"He wouldn't, at that," Granny agreed. "Well, go on."

"Well, the Guardian—uh, Lord Vanian—said that was a wish, not a question for the Oracle."

"That it is," the old woman cackled. "So why are you wasting your time looking for the Oracle, then, hey?"

"He said I was to find it," Dara explained, "to ask what price I should pay him for my wish. And he said I'd made two wishes, and had to choose, so I said that I wished for whatever I needed to win the man I love. And he gave me a key, so here I am." She shrugged.

"Oho! So that's the way of it!" the old woman said softly, as if surprised. "And that's just what you wished, eh, exactly that?"

"Yes, that's it, I think," Dara said, trying to remember her precise words. "Why?"

Granny had stopped spinning.

"Well, you won't find your Oracle here, and that's a fact," she said carefully. "But I'll give you a little advice, though I can't tell you where to look—the Oracle's a chancy thing, it is, sometimes you'll find the way to it here, sometimes there, depending on who's looking and how— and here's the first bit: When a thing's lost, it's always found in the last place you look, why's that?"

"Well, because you stop looking after you find it, I suppose," Dara said at last.

"That's right! That's right!" the woman said gleefully. "You're not so stupid as I thought. Now here's the second bit: What your eyes see and what your heart sees may be two different things, d'you see, but that doesn't mean either one is blind; and what your head knows and what your heart knows may be two different things, but that doesn't mean either one is wrong, do you understand?"

"No, not at all," Dara said exasperatedly. "How can two different things both be right?"

"They can't, but for magic, y'see, magic and love," Granny Good said, nodding sagely. "And this place is full of magic, isn't it, and you're here for love, aren't you? So you never know, you never know. Now here's the third bit of advice, and then I'll give you no more. Lord Vanian gave you a key, he did: Well, there's keys and there's *keys*, you see, and with the right key you'll open all sorts of interesting places, don't you know."

"He said this key opened the doors of the Keep," Dara volunteered, holding up the golden key.

Granny waved that aside.

"Well, that's a key, that it is, and a simple one at that; but there's other keys, d'you see, and other doors, and things as aren't even doors that are opened with keys of one sort or another, just as the sun opens the flowers in the morning. So don't you be thinking that that key in your hand'll put you every place you want to go, or that what's opened with it is all the doors there are! You've got to look sharp, d'you see, and find other kinds of keys, you know, to get where you're going." Suddenly she broke off and pointed with a gnarled finger. "There! Just grab that snake, will you?"

Without thinking, Dara reached down into the dust at her feet and grabbed a snake just below the head; then she stared in dismay at the thing in her hand, too afraid to move. She'd always been afraid of snakes.

"But what do I do with it?" she asked Granny, shivering but holding the squirming creature firmly nonetheless. If she let go, mightn't the thing bite her?

Granny chuckled indulgently.

"Well, hang your key on it, little fool, so you won't lose it."

"But how can I—" Dara looked at the snake in her hand and gasped, for now there hung a slender gold chain from her clenched fist, and no snake to be seen. Dara sighed resignedly, slipped the key over the chain, and fastened the chain around her neck.

"I do wish—Granny Good?" Dara turned around in a circle, looking in every direction.

Granny Good was gone.

"Oh, dear," Dara murmured, leaning gingerly against a large boulder, half expecting it to turn into something else as soon as she touched it. She sneezed resoundingly as a new breeze stirred the grit again.

"And how are you enjoying my keep?"

At the sound of the voice right beside her, Dara jumped away from the rock and turned. There was Lord Vanian, sitting cross-legged on top of the boulder, brushing irritatedly at the ash that clung to his feathery black hair.

"Well, I'm—" Dara stopped short. Why should she show him her confusion, when her strange task of finding the Oracle might well have been designed simply for his amusement?

"I'm enjoying it very much indeed, thank you, Lord Vanian," she said with dignity. "It's not nearly as dull as some castles I've heard about, though this particular part could use a little cheer."

His smile reversed into a scowl.

"Who told you my name?"

"Granny Good."

"That old witch talks altogether too much." Then he shrugged, although his gaze on her remained sharp. "What else did she tell you?"

Dara squared her shoulders proudly.

"With respect, Lord Vanian, that's between myself and her, and no decent girl would gossip about everything she's told. She didn't tell me where the Oracle was, if you're afraid she spoiled sport for you."

Sinuously as a cat, the Guardian leaped down from the boulder. His iron-strong hand seized Dara's chin again, hard enough to bruise, his black eyes staring piercingly into hers, yet his voice was mild.

"And you think this is sport for me, eh?"

"If it's anything else, Lord Vanian, you've only to say."

To Dara's disgust, her voice trembled; she steadied it, then stepped back, freeing herself from the lord's touch. "And it isn't polite to go about grabbing folks, not at all."

Some strange expression flickered across Lord Vanian's face, and he lowered his hand with a laugh.

"Well, you have some spirit after all," he said. "And I thought you were such a dull little quivering mouse at the beginning, at least to look at you. Here's a present for you." From nowhere he produced a fiery red ruby, as big as the first joint of Dara's thumb. He dropped it into her hand and folded her fingers about it. "And good fortune in my keep." Abruptly he gave Dara a terrific shove; she stumbled backward, tumbling through the doorway behind her.

Dara hit the corridor bottom first and yelped with pain, not only for her bruised posterior but for the sudden pain in her hand. She opened her fingers hastily; a glowing coal fell to the corridor floor, and her palm was beginning to blister.

Dara cursed furiously and stamped out the coal, glancing back at the door she'd just fallen through. It was still ajar, showing the bleak, desolate landscape, utterly still and devoid of life.

Anxiously Dara looked down, half expecting the golden chain around her neck to have changed back into a snake. Happily, the chain remained a chain.

Shaking her burned hand to cool it, Dara closed the door she'd just come through, then walked to the next and looked through the hinged opening. The same morning meadow was there. Well, that would certainly be a more pleasant place to put an Oracle—or at least a more pleasant place to look for one. Sighing, she unlocked the door and stepped through.

A gentle breeze carried the smell of flowers, and somewhere in the distance Dara could hear the sound of birds singing. Dara sighed with relief and sat down on the soft grass, admiring the variety of flowers adorning the hillside. She noticed a sprig of Painwort growing and chuckled a little bitterly. How many Painwort leaves had she and Cav picked on the hills near the city, Cav cutting his fingers with his dagger and demonstrating the simplest healing spell he knew again and again and again? How patient he'd been, never wavering in his faith that someday Dara would cast those spells successfully.

Wirin and Joraleen, too, had been patient with their daughter's failure for so long, although her lack was an embarrassment to the family. When Dara had been a child, they'd made excuses—she'd just gotten a slow start; those late bloomers usually were the most powerful; likely she'd shake the house down off its foundations once her courses started. Then when her courses had started, they said it was the unsettled energies of youth; she'd be fine once those errant energies calmed down. By the time Dara was fourteen they'd run out of excuses, and Dara had settled into what seemed a permanent niche as the family failure. What use was a girl like that? She couldn't follow the family tradition of service in the finest noble houses; she couldn't even manage simple tricks for some minor lordling's amusement, and no respectable fellow with a full set of wits would marry her when she might be carrying a curse—one that might well be passed on to her children.

Dara scowled and plucked the sprig of Painwort almost defiantly, sniffing the familiar aroma, then hesitated.

"Oh, why not?" she said resignedly. She murmured the short healing spell, put a couple of leaves in her mouth, chewed them well, and spat the pulp into her burned hand, rubbing the pulp well over the burn. To her surprise, the pain faded immediately, and when she wiped the pulp away, no trace of the blisters remained.

Dara sat still, rubbing her palm over and over, stunned. That spell had never worked for her before; in fact, *no* spell had ever worked for her before. Hesitantly she mumbled the simple levitation spell Cav had demonstrated so many times, picked a blossom, and tossed it up into the air. It stayed in place, bobbing gently in the breeze.

Dara swallowed hard. Had she gained her magery already, all at once? But why? Lord Vanian had said—or at least implied—that she wouldn't gain her wish until payment was rendered.

Maybe her magic would only function inside the Keep (if this place *was* somehow inside the Keep) or maybe even only inside this particular place. At least one thing was certain: If Lord Vanian could give her her magic, he could take it away again if he chose. If she didn't pay his price.

Wait, though; she *hadn't* wished for her magic; she'd wished for whatever she needed to win Cav. What if her magic by itself wasn't enough, and that's why she had gained it—because he was still withholding something else she needed? She couldn't imagine what that might be; Cavin had said himself that according to his parents, her lineage was good enough. There had been other Heirs who had married below their station. No, Lord Vanian must be counting on simply taking it away again if Dara couldn't fulfill her end of the bargain.

But if she had her magic now, even if only temporarily, she might be able to use it to find the Oracle more easily. Hmmm . . . a location spell needed water in a basin, or even a still lake or pool.

Dara ran excitedly to the top of the nearest hill and gazed about. Surely this place had some water, but she could see none nearby, nor did she see anything that looked out of place enough to be a magical oracle. And what *did* an oracle look like? Dara shook her head, banishing her doubt; she'd know the Oracle when she found it, or she'd find a way to recognize it. It couldn't be so impossible to find; others had found it. It was just a matter of patience and perseverance. Maybe the very next door, the twilight forest, was the one. At least there might be still water there. Hurriedly she hopped back through the door into the hallway, ran to the next door, and opened it.

Oh, bad. As soon as she'd stepped through the door she

began to feel that she'd made a mistake. The air positively quivered with menace. The forest, which had seemed merely cool and solemn through the opening in the door, loomed dark and somber now. Strange sounds, furtive rustlings, and querulous cheepings, very different from normal forest noises, filtered through the undergrowth.

It would be a simple matter to step back through the door, but Dara thought she could hear water trickling somewhere nearby, and there was a small footpath that seemed to lead in the direction of the water sounds. If there was a path, didn't that mean that people used it regularly, and if that was true, how dangerous could the place be? Besides, what if the aura of menace was just some kind of protection to keep people away from the Oracle, just as the ominous and confusing wall of mist had served a similar purpose for the Keep itself? Who knew what trials she might have to face to reach the Oracle; there was certainly no good in startling at every strange noise, or in being afraid of a bunch of trees! Dara stepped resolutely forward onto the footpath, carefully leaving the door open behind her.

The trail led deeper into the woods, and Dara quickly lost sight of the door to the corridor, which troubled her, but she could hear the sound of the running water closer all the time. Other sounds, however, less pleasant, were also reaching her ears—small titterings, the rustling of brush nearby, the crackle of small twigs—seeming to follow her through the forest. Dara walked a little faster, then increased her pace to a trot.

Suddenly the trail twisted and opened into a moderate clearing, and Dara sighed with relief. The clearing framed a small pool fed by an even smaller waterfall. The banks were mossy and inviting, just perfect for a noontime rest— if this twilight forest ever saw noontime, that is. A large plum tree grew by the water's edge, and huge purple fruit were scattered about. A few had split in their fall, and their luscious aroma perfumed the clearing. Aware of her few remaining provisions, Dara hurriedly stuffed her pockets and belt pouches with plums after sniffing one fruit more carefully to make sure it smelled right.

Dara sat down on the mossy bank and pulled her cup from her pack, filling it again and again until her thirst was satisfied. When she was finished, she composed her mind, reviewing the location spell. She had hardly begun the chant, however, when she became aware that the rustling she had been hearing seemed louder. Dara froze, holding her breath to listen more closely, then scrambled hastily to her feet as she realized that someone or something was approaching the clearing through the surrounding brush. Just as Dara drew her poor belt knife and considered a retreat down the path, the creature stepped out from the undergrowth, and Dara hesitated where she was, torn between laughter and flight.

The creature didn't appear very threatening. It stood almost two heads shorter than Dara herself on two small, cloven hooves. Its haunches and legs were thickly covered with coarse brown hair or fur that tapered off at the waist. From the waist up, the creature could have been any young boy except for the two curling brown horns emerging from the top of its head. A small crossbowlike device, apparently meant to fire darts, hung at its waist, but its hands were amicably empty.

"H-hello," Dara said nervously. Would advancing be considered a threat, or retreating a sign of weakness? She stood her ground, more out of confusion than courage. "I'm Dara. I'm only passing through your forest—ah, do you speak? Do you understand me?"

The creature gave her a friendly smile, cocked its head, and said, "Arbaggi drobble greep?"

Reassured, Dara stepped a bit closer. "I'm sorry. I didn't quite get that."

The creature also trotted closer, smiling in the friendliest way, and nodded its head. "Sinnog orgle obi!"

"Uh, orgle obi, right," Dara repeated. The strange creature's childlike air reassured her. She crouched down a little so she was eye to eye with it. "I'm Dara, you see? Dara." She tapped her chest. "Dara."

The creature raised bushy eyebrows and tapped its own chest. "Dararararara?"

"No, no." Dara gingerly took the small, callused hand and tapped her chest. "Dara. That's me. Hey—ouch!" she cried out as the creature suddenly grabbed her breast and squeezed it hard.

"Agibbi ogle fri!" it crowed.

As if on a signal, the brush parted and nearly a dozen more such creatures darted out toward Dara, who had pushed the first creature away from her and stumbled back a few steps. Every one of the creatures wore the same friendly smile as the first, but that friendly smile now seemed, to Dara, touched with more than a little malice.

"Maybe I'll do my location spell somewhere else," Dara acknowledged, edging around the pool toward the path.

"Grinnabi boggle eep!" one of the creatures announced, and several of the creatures surrounded her, advancing slowly.

"I—I really think this little gathering will go better without me," Dara said nervously, trying to edge away from those nearest her. "I don't think this is a good— yeow!" she yelped, jumping as a small hand pinched her buttock sharply. Suddenly there were dozens of small brown hands on her, pinching and groping, ripping at her clothing, reaching for her breasts, probing crudely between her legs. She struggled fiercely, but the small hands were surprisingly strong.

Desperately, Dara pulled a plum out of her pocket, muttered a short spell, and threw the fruit down hard at her feet, closing her eyes tightly. There was a loud *BANG*! and light flared through her eyelids, but the groping hands momentarily fell away, and one moment was all Dara needed. While the creatures were still rubbing their dazzled eyes, chattering angrily, Dara dashed headlong down the trail.

The spell didn't confuse her attackers for long, and soon Dara could hear dozens of tiny hooves pattering down the trail behind her. As she ran, Dara pulled out another plum, groped through her mind for the right spell—bless Cav and his patient repetition!—spoke it, and cast the plum behind her. She didn't look back, but was rewarded with garbled expressions of dismay as the pack ran headlong into a bushy plum tree. A moment later Dara was leaping through the door and then standing, panting, in the long corridor. She slammed the door shut behind her with all her strength, wishing she could somehow bar it, although a peep through the hinged panel assured her that the forest was utterly still once more.

Trembling, Dara assessed damages. She wasn't seriously hurt, although she could feel bruises forming where she'd been pinched and poked. Her tunic was nearly in tatters, and there were long rips in her trousers as well. She didn't have any more Painwort to do the healing spell unless she took the time to go back to the meadow, find more and pick it, and where was she to find clothing in this bizarre place?

And she was hungry, too, and so tired. She'd walked so far today; no wonder that mossy bank had been so tempting! It must be well into the evening now, although the forest door panel showed the same twilight and the meadow still showed early morning. But did she dare sleep in any of the strange landscapes? Who knew what other nasty creatures they might hide, even her pretty meadow?

Sighing and wishing heartily for a bath, Dara lay down on the thick rug in the corridor, using her pack for a pillow. After a good sleep, she could revisit the meadow for more Painwort, then maybe find a friendly room-world with some water where she could wash. Maybe she'd find someone around this strange keep who could trade or sell her some clothing. She thought wistfully that she'd trade every copper of her remaining purse for a clean undertunic.

What worried her more was her magic. Since she'd never shown any signs of being able to perform any spell at all, she hadn't really studied as she should have since she'd crept away from her parents' holding to make her fortune. She hadn't *planned* on ending up a serving maid in the High Lord of Caistran's household, but there it was, and she'd done her best with it—and a good serving maid didn't have much time for poring over grimoires, even if she'd had one of her own to study, which of course she hadn't. Cav, while eager to help, had limited his tutelage to the simplest spells, since if she couldn't master the easiest ones, why waste time on the more complicated rituals? Besides the few spells she'd already used, she knew only a handful more, and very little of what she knew seemed applicable to such a dangerous place.

And she was no fighter at all, although if she could defend herself by washing dishes or soiled clothes, kneading bread or sweeping floors, doubtless she'd do herself proud. The only flesh she'd ever cut with her belt knife had been cooked to a turn. Her knees and elbows had fended off the stableboy a time or two, but that was all; and in only three doors she'd already been burned, bruised, and nearly raped.

What would Cav do in her situation?

Dara laughed.

"He'd walk right out that door and be headed home," she said sourly to herself. No, Cav was feet-on-the-ground practical and, unfortunately, in some ways not very romantic at all. He wouldn't be found taking foolish risks for the sake of love; to be fair, as Heir to the throne of Caistran, he'd scarcely be allowed to do so. That, in fact, was why *she* was here; because however much Cav might love her, once he'd exhausted every reasonable solution he could imagine, that was that. He wasn't the sort to go chasing legends across the country in the faint hope that something else might be done; that left *her* to do it. And it'd do no good getting discouraged, unless she wanted to walk back to the city with her failure and watch Cav get married off to someone else.

No, Dara was the one desperate enough to clutch at faint hopes, else she'd still be back in her parents' household. The decision to leave her family and her home in order to make her own way in the world had, however, been easier than her decision to leave Cav and her place at the High Lord's keep to seek her magic. She'd always known she'd leave her family someday, after all, for one reason or another; and she'd believed, truly believed, that somewhere there was an answer, that someday she'd be a powerful mage just as she and her family had always expected. It had been harder to leave the High Lord's keep, where she'd at least been deemed competent and useful: harder still to leave Cav, the only person who'd ever shown unconditional affection for Dara the woman, rather than Dara the should-be mage.

But however grateful Dara had been when she found her position in the High Lord's household, she didn't want to remain a magicless serving wench forever, and Dara wasn't sure she'd be wise to wait much longer hoping for something miraculous to happen. She knew Cav loved her, but he was a practical sort, and one of these days he'd marry, her or someone else, for the good of the kingdom. He'd *have* to; otherwise his parents would simply arrange a match for him. Why, in this last year they'd been inviting any number of noble ladies to visit, hoping to tempt their son to make an advantageous match on his own. And lately Dara had noticed a whiff of expensive perfumes, the sort noble ladies wore, about him on occasion.

No, it was no longer a situation that patience might cure. Cav had done everything he could to help: paid great mages to come in from other kingdoms to examine her, consulted with great seers, and pored over voluminous grimoires, not to mention his own attempts to teach her. He'd relentlessly spent time, gold, and attention on Dara's "difficulty" far beyond the point his parents considered tolerable, and that defiance alone had warmed Dara's heart more than any gesture of affection Cav had ever made. But hers was apparently a problem beyond human solution.

Cav had been outraged when Dara had first suggested seeking out the Crystal Keep and consulting the Oracle. He didn't want her to go away, even for a while; he didn't want her to risk the dangers of the road and the Crystal Keep; he didn't want her to make such a long journey alone. But most of all, Dara feared, he didn't want to admit that she might succeed by herself where all his efforts had failed. It was a sobering thought.

But despite Cav's anger, despite everyone's doubts, and her own as well, Dara had desperately clung to that thin, threadbare hope that somewhere, somehow, there would be an answer for her. And she couldn't surrender that hope, for if she did, what did she have left? Nothing but dirty floors to scrub, turnips to peel, and silver to polish. Well, there was some value to desperation—after a while, it grew larger than fear.

Onward it would be, then, after a few hours of rest. Dara sighed resolutely and closed her eyes, concentrating on sleep that, despite the hard floor and her fear, soon came.

3

WHEN DARA AWOKE, SHE PULLED OUT ONE
of the plums she'd picked up and ate it, considering what to do next even as she relished the
sweet, juicy fruit. The next door in the corridor, judging by
the limited view afforded by its hinged peephole, appeared
to open into a dark cavern, but by craning around so a little
light from the corridor could shine through the peephole,
she could see the edge of a subterranean lake and knew
that cave water, flowing over rock, was usually clean. She
pulled her lantern out of her pack, shook it to test how
much oil was left, then sighed and lit it anyway. Thus prepared, she stepped inside.

The air in the cavern was unexpectedly warm and moist,
and Dara soon discovered that this warmth came from the
lake itself, which appeared to bubble forth from a warm
spring. Delighted, Dara pulled off her ragged clothes,
quickly gulped down another plum, and waded cautiously
into the pool. The bottom sloped quite gently and was very
firm, but she only waded out a few feet before she decided
merely to sit in the shallow water rather than dare a deeper

bath. Probably nothing lived in such warm water, but why take the chance?

As the grime of the past few days washed from her skin and hair, Dara noticed the bruises darkening her skin in various places and remembered with a shudder how she'd gotten them. Well, another trip to the morning meadow for more Painwort for the healing spell would solve that problem quite—

"I'd rather thought you would have given up by now," a familiar voice said.

Dara immediately sat back down in the water, folding her knees up and wrapping her arms around them to cover herself. Lord Vanian was sitting on a rock next to the pool, looking straight at her.

"It's not polite to creep up and look at people in their bath," Dara said indignantly, flushing hotly.

"Well, you're bathing in my keep, aren't you?" Lord Vanian sneered. "Do you often bathe uninvited in other people's lakes? Besides, I'm already impolite, aren't I, as you've so kindly informed me, so why should one more act of rudeness on my part trouble me overmuch?"

"With respect, Lord Vanian, as you make it so difficult to stay tidy in your keep, you may as well expect folks to clean up when and where they can," Dara retorted, "especially as you've failed to provide a bath for your guests. Would you be so kind as to toss my garments here?"

Lord Vanian laughed again and reached over, picking up Dara's tunic with a grimace of distaste.

"Are you *quite* sure you want this?" he asked, poking at the tattered and dirty garment.

"It's all I have."

Lord Vanian raised an eyebrow.

"That's rather poor planning on your part. Perhaps I should give you clothing."

Dara rolled her eyes.

"With respect, lord, if your other gifts are as fine as your last, I'd as soon you didn't honor me with any more.

Now *would* you toss me that tunic?''

His eyes challenging her, Lord Vanian dropped the tunic. "No."

Dara tossed her head defiantly, whispered the levitation spell, and quickly snatched the tunic as it floated to her. Turning her back to Lord Vanian, she gave the tunic a few sloshes through the warm water to rinse out the worst of the grime and then struggled into it. Although it clung wetly to her, it was long enough that she needn't try to levitate her trousers; besides, the Guardian had his foot on them.

Lord Vanian laughed. "You're learning," he said with grudging approval. "I see you're opening each door in order, so I'll spare you a bit of trouble: You may as well not bother with the next."

"Thank you for the advice," Dara said through gritted teeth, privately resolving to visit the next door as soon as possible.

The lord reached down for her trousers.

"Ah, what's this?" He lifted instead one of Dara's plums. "Where did you get this?"

Dara sloshed out of the pool, stopping cautiously just out of reach.

"From a tree in the—the room—before this one, a forest," she said defiantly. "Now are you going to scold me for picking your fruit as well, or am I merely expected to give you some outrageous payment for the plums I've already eaten? I'd say I paid enough in bruises for that fruit, although judging from the actions of its guardians, bruises weren't all they wanted." She held out her hand for the plum.

Lord Vanian looked at the fruit for a moment, then smiled slowly, a smile that Dara didn't like.

"Eat your plum," he chuckled, dropping it into her hand. "Eat as many as you please." Then abruptly he was gone, vanished as if he'd never been there.

Dara looked dubiously at the plum in her hand and hesitated, then bit into it defiantly.

"He'll not talk me out of anything," she declared. "Not the next door nor any other."

To her dismay, she had only two plums left, one of which she ate immediately to take her mind off the fact that she was nearly out of food again. She'd have to be pretty hungry before she'd risk the forest again, but surely there was other food to be found. She rinsed her trousers and pulled them back on with difficulty, then stuffed her feet into her boots and stepped out into the corridor to peep through the next door.

If Lord Vanian hadn't seemed to want her to avoid the next door, she'd have been sorely tempted to pass it by. The peephole showed a swamp, dreary and dim, festooned with hanging moss and other vegetation in various stages of decay. Still, if Lord Vanian troubled himself to tell her not to come here, it was worth Dara's while to see why. Slinging her pack over one shoulder, her last plum in her hand, Dara took a deep breath, used her key, and stepped through.

The place smelled as bad as it looked. Her hunger for the last plum disappeared as suddenly as Lord Vanian had, and she set it down on a nearby hummock. She fished in her pack for her waterskin, only to find the skin still empty. She'd forgotten, again, to fill it from either the cavern or the forest lake. Dubiously, she eyed the dark water of the swamp, then crouched beside one pool, dipped a finger in the water, and sniffed it. Ugh! No drinks here.

Suddenly Dara put the waterskin down beside the plum, peering into the murk. There was something . . . yes, there was definitely something shining purple on a hummock only ten or twelve man-heights out in the swamp. It was at least worth a try, although in some places the slimy water looked deep.

Cautiously Dara hopped to the first hummock; it gave a little, soggily, under her foot but seemed safe otherwise. Carefully, jump by jump, she proceeded onward. The stench of rotten vegetation and stagnant water was almost overpowering, but Dara's balance was precarious enough that she didn't dare rip loose a little cloth from her tunic to tie over her face. She jumped again, reeling a little, slipped, and her foot plunged into the slime up to her ankle. Grimacing, she pulled her foot out of the sucking mud and hurried on, holding her nose. At last, with a sigh of relief, she stepped onto the large hummock.

The shine came from an exquisite purple gemstone, large enough to fill Dara's hand. As soon as she touched it, a warm tingling spread through her fingers, and she nearly dropped the gem again.

Hmmm. Remembering how Lord Vanian's ruby had transformed and burned her, Dara hesitated to put the gem into the pack with her few precious supplies; instead, she wrapped the gem heavily with the cleanest grass she could find from the hummock and stuffed it into the front of her tunic.

Well, this was certainly no place to investigate the gem's possibilities; the stench was absolutely horrible. Dara hurriedly began picking her way back to shore. She was nearly halfway when something long and cold and very, very strong slid around her ankle and pulled hard. She had barely time to gulp down a hearty breath before lukewarm, fetid water closed over her head.

She couldn't see a thing in the turbid, churning water, although she could feel what seemed like roots closing about her legs. She kicked hard, downward and to the side, all the while trying to pull her belt knife from its sheath. As soon as she freed the knife, she cut as best she could at the confining bands—surely they *were* vines or roots of some kind—and was rewarded with a slight loosening of their grip; but now a tendril had worked its way between the pack and her back, and other vines were closing around her waist. Her lungs were beginning to burn.

Desperately Dara sawed at the vines around her waist, shrugged out of her pack, and kicked toward the surface with every ounce of her remaining strength, scrambling up onto the nearest hummock. Gray-green tendrils burst from the water behind her, waving blindly in the air, but Dara had already crawled rapidly through the slime and onto the shore, hopefully out of reach of the seeking tendrils. She lay still on the muddy turf, panting heavily, knowing that she could not move an inch to save herself if whatever-it-was were to emerge onto land.

It did not.

Gradually, as choking panic subsided, Dara became aware that someone was watching her. That someone was sitting on the hummock next to her waterskin, watching her with an air of unmistakable amusement. It appeared to be something similar to the southern monkeys Dara had sometimes seen at fairs, small and long of tail and covered with mud-clotted yellowish fur, but with a face rather more human than ape. It had blue eyes that twinkled with unmistakable intelligence, and that alone made Dara certain that she was being watched by some*one* rather than some*thing*.

"Ain't you the lucky one, girly," it said. "There's been a few go into that muck, but you're the first I've seen come out of it."

Dara wondered how lucky she'd really been. Her pack was gone now, with her little money and her few remaining supplies, and what was left of her clothing—nearly torn from her body in her struggle—was sodden with foul-smelling slime. Her ribs ached wretchedly where the thing in the water had squeezed her. She dully pulled herself to a sitting position, knuckling mud out of her eyes.

"What was that thing?" she asked.

"Garden variety fell-beast," the creature said with a shrug. "They're common enough in bad swamps to the west, or so I've heard told, but you can find just about anything here. Nothing I'd much want fondling me, I'd say."

"And what—I mean, who are you?" Dara asked slowly.

"Well, as to 'who,' the name's Gespry," the creature

said wryly. "And as to 'what'—" He looked down at himself with an expression of disdain. "Well, that's anybody's guess, truth to tell, but what I imagine I'd be is a demon."

"A d-demon?" Dara said slowly. She clutched her muddy dagger.

"I'd say so, girly, and you needn't scurry off like that." Gespry chuckled dourly. "Better get used to it, as you'll meet demons aplenty here, and like as not end up one yourself."

"How do you 'end up' as a demon?" Dara asked warily. "I thought demons were demons to begin with."

"Well, some are, and some ain't," Gespry mused. "To begin with, that is. Course, 'demon' is just a word, I reckon, but I always heard the Crystal Keep was full of 'em, and here I am, and I surely ain't human, so I figured I was a demon. But all of us as gets stuck here end up demons— or whatever you'd like to call us—in the Keep. If you lose your key, for example, or make a foolish enough wish, like I did."

"What did you wish for?" Dora asked, then added hastily, "if I might ask."

"Well, that you might," Gespry sighed. "I was a stupid fellow, past my prime and feeling winter in my bones; so I made my way to the Crystal Keep and asked to live forever, and so I ended up just as you see me."

"How horrible," Dara said sympathetically.

"Ah, 'tain't so bad," Gespry said, shrugging again. "Got my wish, anyway, as time don't rightly go on in here and it looks as if I might just live forever in fact. Might've been nicer if I hadn't lost my key and got stuck in this double-damned swamp. You didn't lose your key in the muck, did you?" he added with some eagerness.

Dara reached into her muddy blouse and found the chain still holding the golden key.

"No, I didn't lose it." A sudden suspicion made Dara add, "But I won't trade it."

"Well, I'd say not," Gespry said sarcastically. "But look

here: What'll you take to get me out of this swamp?''

"What, into the corridor?" Dara asked practically. "What will you do then? You couldn't even eat, or open any of the other doors."

"Well, you could put me into one of the better spots, someplace with food and water," Gespry suggested coaxingly. "Just about anything 'ud do."

"That's a rather large favor," Dara said, sighing. "What'll you give me in return?"

Gespry chuckled. "Learned that much already, have you? Good for you, girly. Well, what'll you be wanting?"

Dara considered while she wiped mud from her face. Granny Good had seemed to know a good bit about the Keep; maybe Gespry's knowledge, too, could be useful.

"Come with me for three days," she said at last, "or till I leave the Keep, whichever's sooner, and help and advise me as best you can, and I'll put you through whatever door you like."

Gespry grimaced.

"Now what do I want to go rattling about the Keep for? And it'll raise Lord Vanian's ire at me, that's sure and certain, if I go tellin' what he'd rather I didn't. Anyhow, ain't no way to measure days here. Can't you name something else?"

"Then from one sleep to the next is the same as a day. You might find an especially nice place while you're helping me," Dara said persuasively. "Someplace you'd like to stay forever." She shrugged. "Or you can stay here. Forever."

"All right, all right, three days," Gespry said crossly, but he'd given in so quickly that Dara realized disgustedly she probably could've gotten much more. "What're you looking for, anyway, the Oracle? It sure ain't in here, nohow; any fool could see as much."

"You've seen it?" Dara asked eagerly. "What's it look like?"

"Why, sure, I keep it in my pocket," Gespry said sarcastically. "Of course I ain't seen it. But whatever it looks like, long's I been here, I'd have seen it long since if it was hereabouts. I been all over this place. And there ain't no good in putting it in no foul hole like this, now, is there?"

"I know that," Dara snapped, a little irritated by his condescension.

"Well, then, why'd you come in here, if you know so much?" Gespry asked just as irritably.

"Because Lord Vanian told me not to," Dara admitted sheepishly.

Gespry stared at her a moment, then chuckled.

"Well, that's as good a reason as any, and better'n some," he agreed. "But we'd best move on to find a place with food—and water." He grimaced, glancing down at himself with some disdain.

Dara sluiced some of the mud off her ragged clothes.

"Well, you can have that plum if you like," she offered kindly, pointing to the hummock next to Gespry.

Gespry picked up the plum, sniffed it suspiciously.

"You didn't get this in the forest two doors back, did you, girly?"

Dara nodded absently, wringing out her hair as best she could.

"Well, you don't want to go eating these, then," Gespry said impatiently. He heaved the plum out into the swamp. There was a momentary churning in the waters where it fell, then stillness again.

Dara was still, staring after the plum as a hard knot of worry began to form in her breast. "Why not?"

"Make you forget things, these plums do," Gespry said, chuckling. "The more you eat, the more you forget. Better leave 'em alone if you—" He paused, gazing sharply at Dara. "You ain't had none, have you?"

Dara nodded. "Three," she said in a small voice.

Gespry shook his furry head.

"Not good, not good at all," he said sagely. "Well, what's your name? D'you remember that, hey?"

"Dara."

"And why you came here?"

"To get whatever I need to win the man I love," Dara said promptly, then sighed with relief.

Gespry squinted at her.

"And what's his name?"

"Cav—that is, Lord Cavin IV, Heir to the throne of Caistran," Dara said decisively.

"Well, sounds like you remember all the important things," Gespry said indifferently. "But three plums—that's not so good, girly. I've seen folks forget their own names on two."

"But what *did* I forget?" Dara begged.

Gespry shrugged again.

"How would I know? If you forget something, often as not you forget you forgot. When you run across something you should know but don't, then you'll know what you forgot."

Dara shivered, then reached into her shirt to draw out the grass-wrapped gem. Fortunately the grass had protected the gem, and it was undamaged.

"Do you know what this is?" she asked Gespry. "I saw it shining in the swamp and went after it."

Gespry hopped over and touched the gem with one fingertip.

"Magic, that," he said consideringly. "Who can say? I saw it shining out there, but I was too small to make the jumps, so I let it be. Likely that's what made the fell-beast let you go, though; can't take magic around them, or so I'm told. This thing, though, could be good, could be bad; you never really know around here. Still, if the lord didn't want you in here, chances are it might be something as he didn't want you to find, so likely it's something that'd do you good."

"It couldn't be the Oracle, could it?" Dara asked hopefully.

"What? That?" Gespry blinked at the gem dubiously.

"Could be, I suppose. I never imagined the Oracle to be a bit of stone, though. Ask it your question and see if it answers. Can't hurt, can it?"

Dara wiped as much of the mud off the stone as she could manage and cleared her throat nervously.

"Oracle," she said at last, "what price must I give Lord Vanian in exchange for my wish?"

There was no response.

"Well, that's not it, and a bloody good thing, too," Gespry said exasperatedly. "You don't know how to ask a question any better'n you know how to make a wish."

"It's what I was supposed to ask it," Dara retorted.

"Well, that question ain't asking nothing," Gespry told her. "Ask the real Oracle that and it'll just tell you 'equal value.' That's the law of the Keep, and we all know it, but it answers your stupid question, don't it? You have to ask a question that can only be answered one way."

"Then what *should* I ask it?" Dara snapped. "It seems to me everybody knows the rules hereabouts but me. I'm no mage, nor scholar; I'm just a plain serving maid, and nobody ever told me anything useful about oracles and magical keeps and demons. We've got a bargain, and you promised to advise me, so advise me!"

"Well, first off, you ought to see if you can't figure it out yourself, without asking the Oracle," Gespry said patiently. "Come on, let's get out of this stink hole while you think." He grabbed Dara's finger and tugged her toward the door.

Absently, Dara used the key, and they stepped into the corridor. The absence of the fetid swamp breeze was an immediate relief, although now that they were out in the fresh air, Dara was miserably aware that both she and Gespry reeked foully.

"I want to wash," Dara told Gespry. "There's a cave behind the last door that seems safe enough."

The cavern was exactly as it had been before, but now that Dara had lost her lantern with her pack, she was forced to leave the corridor door ajar to let a little of the dim torchlight in. Gespry perched on the same rock where Lord Vanian had sat, but even with the odd creature serving as a lookout, Dara could not help glancing over her shoulder every few moments while she pulled off her muddy, ragged clothes, to be sure the Guardian hadn't materialized behind her.

"What I don't understand is—" Dara turned around and saw Gespry staring at her. "Well, don't *look*! Can't a girl undress?"

"Sorry, girly," Gespry said, not sounding sorry at all. The creature turned to face away from the lake. "You were saying?"

Dara sat down in the warm water and sloshed her clothes about, wishing unhappily for soap.

"What I don't understand is how I *could* give equal value. I mean, unless Lord Vanian was in love with a woman and I had whatever he needed to win her."

"Well, you don't have to give him the *same thing*," Gespry corrected her. "Lord Vanian don't love nobody, nohow. You only need to give something just as valuable."

"But *whose* value?" Dara pressed. "I mean, this shirt would be worthless to most folk, but to me it isn't because it's the only one I've got. So how do I know how much value my wish has for Lord Vanian?"

"The lord don't value nothin'," Gespry said sourly. "So you'll have to go by your value, which is probably a pretty price if you're willing to go to this much trouble for the lout. Well, what'd you give to have this fellow—Cav, is it?"

"I don't know," Dara said slowly. "Anything, I suppose."

" 'Anythin', I suppose,' " Gespry mocked. "That ain't so. Would you give your life?"

"Well, if I gave my life, then I wouldn't have my wish, would I?" Dara retorted. "Because if I was dead, I couldn't have the man I loved, could I?"

"Then you *wouldn't* give 'anything,' " Gespry said patiently. "The trick's to figure out what you *would* give, see."

"But why would Lord Vanian want anything from me at all?" Dara asked. "You said he didn't value anything."

"It ain't Lord Vanian's choice," Gespry insisted. "Value given for value received, that's the law of the Keep, and he's got to obey it same as any other."

"But how can you put a price on love?" Dara said wistfully, scrubbing at her mud-caked hair.

"Everything's got its price, girly," Gespry chuckled. "And what's more, you know it; guess you thought it was worth a trip to the Crystal Keep, didn't you?"

"Well, I didn't intend to come here and ask for that," Dara told him. "Originally I thought I'd ask for my magic, since that's what's keeping us from marrying. But I ended up asking for whatever I needed, in case my magic wasn't enough."

"Weren't a bad change," Gespry said, nodding sagely. "Might get more for your wish, that way, as royalty always seems to want something special to come with the bride— lands or trade agreements or gold or such. Guess a serving maid hoping to marry a High Lord's Heir could use all the help she can get. That's the way of it, ain't it? Never aspired to royalty myself."

"Well, I don't want to marry Cav because he's the Heir," Dara protested.

Gespry chuckled wisely. "A mighty fine tumble, then, is he?"

"I don't—I mean, I'm not marrying him for his bedroom skills, either," Dara muttered, flushing hotly.

Gespry peeked over his shoulder at her. "Oho! A virgin, eh? Now, that's a rare thing, or was when I came here. Most virgins were withered old prunes when last I saw the world outside the Keep, and that's likely been a good while, I'll admit."

"It's none of your affair," Dara said defiantly. "And

I'm not a 'withered old prune.' But if I can't be Cav's wife, I'm not going to settle for being his mistress. And besides, as long as I'm a virgin, the High Lord and Lady can't argue that I'm of easy virtue or likely to bear a bastard child. So Cav and I agreed that we wouldn't—well, you know."

"Indeed I do, or used to," Gespry chortled. He peeked over his shoulder again. "And you ain't no old prune—not much!"

"Well, don't look!" Dara said angrily.

"Take pity, girly," Gespry entreated. "Ain't nothing else I *can* do anymore but look. You going to soak in that lake all day? I'm hungry."

Dara sloshed her tunic through the water again.

"You could use a bath yourself," she said irritably. "You smell like that swamp."

"Ain't surprising, after years, maybe decades making my home in it," Gespry said wryly. "Reckon my nose got used to it years and years back, and I figured that was a blessing. But tell me, my fine and dainty miss, if I can't even look at you and you seem likely to call that lake your home, how's a poor fellow supposed to wash in it so he don't offend your delicate nose?"

Dara pulled on her wet clothes and splashed out of the lake, grabbed the surprised Gespry by the scruff of his neck, and dropped him into the shallow water.

"There," she said exasperatedly. She sat down on the rock Gespry had previously occupied and picked up the purple gem. The warm tingle felt so good to her hand that Dara couldn't believe it could be harmful.

"I'd like to know what this is," she said slowly. "It might be helpful in some way. Maybe we should go back to the first door, the dusty place. I wonder if Granny Good wouldn't have some idea of what it is."

Gespry looked up from scrubbing his fur. "Granny Good? You met up with her? Lucky chance for you, girly!"

"Do you know her?"

"Aye, she pops in and out here and there," Gespry said,

returning to his scrubbing. "Stopped by the swamp to talk now and again. Wise old thing, she is, and no mistaking. You can bet whatever she told you was to the good. And I hope you can remember *that*."

Dara thought it over carefully.

"Yes, I remember, but I didn't understand it much. She talked about always finding things in the last place you look, and how things can be seen different ways and all of them right, and she talked about keys of one form or another." She contemplated the gem. "Could this be a key of some sort, do you think?"

Gespry shrugged. "Don't know. You're a mage, ain't you? Why don't you use your magic to find out?"

"I don't know much divination," Dara said thoughtfully. "But I suppose a variation of the location spell might do it. Hmmm, the lake is still enough water to"—her voice trailed off—"to—"

"To what?" Gespry said, not looking up from his ablutions. "What do you do?"

Dara swallowed hard. "I can't remember," she said very quietly.

Gespry stopped washing, his blue eyes narrowing. "Well, what spells *do* you remember, then, eh?"

Dara was silent a long moment, staring down at the gem in her hands. Abruptly she burst into tears.

Gespry padded out of the water and awkwardly patted her hand. "Now, there, it ain't all that bad," he said gruffly. "Spells ain't nothin', nothin' at all. You just sits down with the family grimoire and learns 'em again, see? Ain't nothin' but memorizing, not if your magic works in the first place, and you came here a good sight worse off, didn't you?"

Dara wiped her eyes and swallowed the sob that threatened.

"I suppose so. But I haven't got my family grimoire with me. The original's sixteen volumes long, and I never bothered to copy any of it because my magic didn't work anyway. Besides, even if I had it, I'd have lost it in the swamp."

"Well, so you wait till you get home, or use your fancy lord's grimoire instead," Gespry said, waving his hand negligently. "Who knows, maybe there's one to be found here, eh? Thought there was a library somewhere about, that I did. Things ain't so bad, see?"

Dara took a deep breath and nodded resolutely. "I suppose you're right," she said tiredly. "But it seems to me as if I don't have anything at all to give Lord Vanian, no matter what he wanted. I brought every Sun I owned with me, and now they're lost. I don't own a thing now, just my dagger and my key and this gem. Not even my spells to cast."

"Ain't likely he'd take any of that in trade, nohow." Gespry shrugged. "Unless that gem's somewhat more valuable'n we know. Guess you'll have to find something else, won't you?"

"But if something's in his keep, how can I trade it?" Dara asked slowly. "I mean, wouldn't it be his anyway?"

"Well, you're in his keep, ain't you?" Gespry said sensibly. "And *you* ain't his. So just take something, and maybe he'd trade to have it back, see?"

Dara scowled, running her fingers over the gem again.

"That doesn't sound like what Lord Vanian told me," she said thoughtfully. "He made it sound as if it had to be a fair trade, not—not stealing something and ransoming it."

Gespry shook his head and sighed with exasperation. "Fair don't mean nothing here. Play by Lord Vanian's rules and you'll lose by 'em, same as the rest of us," he said sourly. "Better learn faster'n that, girly."

Dara shook her head and sighed. "Nothing seems to make sense here," she said frustratedly. "I don't understand at all."

"Course not," Gespry said, grinning. "If you did, *you'd* be the Guardian, and no doubt we'd all be better off. Now,

I remember a nice little orchard a few doors down—what d'you think we stop in for a bite?''

Dara's stomach rumbled loudly in agreement, and she had to laugh despite her worries. She lifted Gespry to her shoulder—he was no heavier than a good-sized cat—and stepped through the door into the corridor.

Gespry directed her down the hall to one of the doors. The hinged peephole showed a neat, well-tended orchard, the trees heavy with ripe fruit. Dara hurried through, and Gespry immediately abandoned his perch on her shoulder to dart up one of the apple trees, where he fell unhesitatingly to gorging himself on the ripe fruit.

More cautiously, Dara picked a pear from another tree and inspected it closely. It looked and smelled all right, but then so had the plums. Carefully she lifted a small section of peel with her fingernail and touched her tongue to the fruit beneath. It tasted wonderful, but how could she be certain?

"Are you sure this fruit's safe?" she called to Gespry.

"Apparently not safe from theft, at least," a familiar acerbic voice said from behind her.

Dara had jumped at the voice, but this time she managed to suppress the impulse to whirl around to confront Lord Vanian. Leisurely she picked another pear, then turned. The Guardian was leaning nonchalantly against the trunk of a peach tree.

"So now I'm a thief?" Dara inquired. "Seems to me, though, as you'd given me the run of your keep without providing me any other food, you'd best expect me to take it where I find it."

Lord Vanian raised one eyebrow but made no argument. At last he observed, "Your clothes seem in greater ruin each time I see you."

"With respect, lord," Dara said sweetly, "your keep isn't kind to clothing. Or guests."

Lord Vanian laughed coldly.

"If you expect kindness, girl, you're in the wrong place."

"I certainly haven't been led to expect kindness," Dara acknowledged, meeting his gaze squarely, no matter how his piercing black eyes unnerved her. "At least not from you."

"Perhaps I might give you some clothing, at least," Lord Vanian said amusedly. "Although it might be entertaining to let you go without."

"I doubt I'd feel clever taking any more gifts from you." Dara bit into the pear. It was as sweet and juicy as it had looked.

"Perhaps a trade, then?" Lord Vanian suggested.

"With respect, lord," Dara said coolly, "I doubt there's anything you might ask that I'd care to give you at present."

"You're an ungrateful bit." Lord Vanian chuckled, apparently not the least insulted. "One would think you enjoyed looking like some impoverished peasant."

"That's quite a coincidence, lord," Dara said with exaggerated patience, "as I *am* an impoverished peasant. I know, though, that looks can deceive. You, for instance, dress like a gentleman."

Lord Vanian's smile remained, but his eyes narrowed. His voice was deceptively mild. "You'd do well to adopt a less disrespectful attitude," he told her. "You're not safely out of my keep yet, nor your wish granted."

A stab of fear made Dara's stomach jump, but she stood her ground.

"I can pander and toady to you as well as the next, I suppose," she said with dignity, forcing her voice to steadiness. "But if that's to be the price of my wish, say so now and be done with it. Otherwise I don't see as it's owed." She took another bite from her pear, although her throat had narrowed from fear.

To her amazement, the anger vanished from Lord Vanian's eyes and he burst out laughing, and her own anger banished Dara's fear.

"How delightful," he gasped. "You *are* an amusing bit. I've seldom been so well entertained by a visitor. I'll grant you this, girl: You've more fire than I credited you at first. I like that."

"Well, as I've given you such entertainment," Dara said defiantly, "I'm sure you can't begrudge me what little food and comfort I manage to find for myself. Scant payment it is in exchange for amusing so difficult an audience, and that's truth."

Lord Vanian stopped laughing, and his smile changed slightly.

"Yes, you do provide me entertainment," he said softly. "Perhaps sometime soon I shall repay you in kind." Abruptly he vanished.

"Pray, don't feel obliged," Dara shouted angrily at the empty space. "Not on my account."

"Shush, shush, you little fool!" Gespry's anxious face peered down from a tree. "Is he gone?"

"More's the blessing," Dara said sourly. "Have you been cowering up there all the while?"

"Aye, and I was wiser than you for all that," Gespry muttered, scuttling down to a lower limb. "Won't do to go insulting the lord like that, girly. You think you've had troubles already, you don't know what the lord can do to them as gets him soreheaded."

"I'd give him more than a sore head, given half a chance," Dara fumed.

"Shush, I say!" Gespry glanced nervously about. "Won't do no good to say such things, girly, not unless you've the power to back it up, and you don't, see? Otherwise you just make trouble on yourself, and that don't do you no good."

"I suppose you're right," Dara admitted reluctantly. She sat down with a sigh. "I'm just so tired."

"Well, might's well stay here as anywhere," Gespry

said. "It's a good enough spot for a sleep, and there's food."

"But it's not night yet," Dara said in surprise, looking at the sun, which was almost directly overhead.

"Why, that don't matter none," Gespry said, shaking his head. "Time's all funny hereabouts. It's always night in the corridor, come to that. Sun up or sun down, sleep when you want, that's the fact, don't make no matter what the sky says. It's Lord Vanian's word that's law here."

Dara grimaced, but stretched out on the grass, pillowing her head on her arms.

"Guess I'd give most anything for a bed and a pillow," she muttered.

"Watch what you say," Gespry warned her. "Or you may end up doing that very thing."

Dara merely sighed again, and slept.

4

WHEN DARA AWOKE, THE ORCHARD WAS dark—so time *did* pass here, in its own strange way!—and the air had taken on a decided chill. Dara shivered, sat up, and glanced around, rubbing her cold arms. Gespry was asleep on the wide branch of an apple tree, his long tail dangling so that she longed to give it a pull and see if he would tumble down. She chuckled at the thought and the odd creature awoke immediately.

"Had a long sleep, you did," Gespry said with a yawn. "Ready to move on?"

"I think so," Dara said. "But I want to find a way to carry some of this fruit along first." She eyed her tattered clothing disgustedly. Even if she could tear any off without leaving herself half-naked, the cloth was too dirty and full of holes to make a serviceable container for food. Then she had a thought.

"Gespry, Granny Good made me a chain out of—well, a snake," she said slowly. "If she's a—a demon, and you're a demon, too, can you do something like that?"

Gespry scratched his head with some apparent embarrassment.

"Now, you can't be going and comparing the likes of me with Granny Good," he said at last. "Been here a long bit, she has, and like as not she was something special before she ever even came in, and me nothin' but a cobbler. It ain't to say I won't be a fair hand in a century or two, but the fact is, girly, I wouldn't know how to begin to go about it. You're the mage, anyhow, not me."

"That's not much help, if I can't remember any of my spells," Dara said with a shrug. Then she shook her head. "But I didn't see Granny Good use a spell."

"Like as not she didn't use one," Gespry said after a moment's thought. "Magic of the Keep, that is. There's a trick to it, I guess, but it ain't no proper spell, or that's my guess. If I knew all of Granny Good's workings, you think I'd of let myself be stuck in that rotten privy of a swamp?"

"But if I'm not a demon, how can I use demonic magic?" Dara asked slowly, clutching the key on its golden chain.

"It ain't got nothing to do with that," Gespry said impatiently. "It ain't something in Granny or in me, see, it's in the *place*. And seeing as you're a mage, seems as you could use it, if you knew the trick of it."

Dara thought that over. Mages used magic by casting spells; demons used magic without spells because they were themselves magical creatures. Could a mage use magic even without spells? Well, somebody had to, in the beginning; some mage somewhere had created the first spells, after all. So perhaps it was only a matter of learning to focus the magical energies in another manner. She said as much to Gespry, who scratched his head thoughtfully.

"That might be so," he admitted. "Hadn't thought of it just that way, though. Tell you what, we'll see if we can't find that library and get you a grimoire, and see what's what then. But breakfast first." He scampered back up the tree.

Dara sat down on the grass and munched on a juicy pear while she thought. She picked up a few fallen leaves from the grass, stared at them for a moment, then bent one into a crude cuplike shape. She placed it on the ground, concentrating on trying to see the leaf as a basket. Dimly she could feel *something*, as if perhaps a long-disused muscle flexed weakly. After several long seconds, the leaf seemed to melt and re-form, immediately replaced by a basket— exactly the size of the leaf.

"Well, that's something," Gespry said encouragingly, hanging upside down from a branch. "Got the shape right, anyhow."

Dara's second try produced a bigger basket, but upon picking it up, she discovered that it was as fragile as the leaf from which she'd made it. The third try produced a stronger product, but the woven ends were not fastened and it fell apart. It took Dara nearly an hour and a blinding headache before she achieved a functional container, and it was sadly lopsided, but she was too tired and exasperated to keep trying. She filled the basket with as much fruit as it could safely hold, then carried Gespry on her shoulder through the doorway into the corridor. To her surprise, when she turned to look back through the door, the orchard had returned to its endless midday light.

Gespry directed her onward past dozens of doors. Dara unfastened several of the peepholes and gazed through at beautiful, frightening, or merely puzzling scenes, but when she might have stopped to investigate further, Gespry pressed her onward.

"Gespry, just how many of these doors *are* there?" Dara asked wonderingly as she walked. "How could there be so many in a straight line, and only on one side of the corridor? How could they all fit inside the Keep?"

Gespry shrugged amiably. "Who knows?" he said. "Ain't many as has been in more'n a few, far as I know, and ain't none as has been in 'em all, unless it be Lord Vanian. You might ask him—and see if he's in a mood to answer. There, that's the one you want.''

The peephole showed, indeed, a library, filled with tomes and scrolls of various ages and in various stages of disintegration. Dara hurried through.

''Goodness,'' Dara said, setting the clumsy basket on a table and plucking Gespry from her shoulder. ''This looks like Cav's family library. I've never seen such a collection of books and scrolls. Do you really think there's a grimoire in here?''

''I'd guess so,'' Gespry said, shrugging. ''Why not?''

''Well, I'll look down this way, then,'' Dara said, gesturing at one set of shelves, ''and you can go—''

''Now, wait, there,'' Gespry cautioned. ''I don't know nothing about no grimoires, and I can't read a word, see? Better not count on me.''

Look through all these books with no help at all? The thought made Dara's heart sink.

''Look, it'll be a thickish book, probably with a clasp,'' Dara said desperately. ''Inside it'll have drawings and diagrams. Just let me know if you find any books like that.''

Gespry shrugged.

''Guess it can't hurt, if I can lift them heavy books down,'' he said at last. ''All right, then.'' He scampered off among the shelves.

Dara wandered down the narrow lanes between tall cabinets, glancing at the dusty books with growing wonder. She'd never cared much for reading, even when her duties left her time for it, but Cav did, and so she'd made an effort to show some interest in scholarly pursuits when time allowed. These books were old, mostly, but they spanned every subject Dara could imagine and many she'd never dreamed of.

''I'll never find a grimoire in this,'' she sighed to herself. There were hundreds, maybe thousands of volumes here, many in languages she couldn't even read; she'd be weeks trying to puzzle the place out, if not months.

''Reckon this'll be what you're wanting,'' a cheery

voice said from the next aisle. Dara gasped in recognition and ducked quickly around the corner, almost shouting with relief as she saw Granny Good, rocking chair and all. The old woman was holding a thick, moldering tome.

"Oh, I'd been hoping I'd see you again," Dara said gladly.

The wrinkled old face lit with Granny's smile.

"Well, I'd say that's a sight better a greeting 'n I got last," she cackled. "Seemed to me you was overdue for a spot of help, mayhap, what with Lord Vanian teasing at you so. Pay him no heed, child, you're doing better than we all expected and no mistake. Oh, what you said to Lord Vanian was a joy and more. What a bother he's in now." She cackled again in remembrance.

"Gespry says I just made trouble for myself," Dara said wryly.

"Well, mayhap you have," Granny said slyly, "or mayhap you've done a bit of good, who's to say? And what've you learned, hey, these many days on your way, other than you should've brought three sets of clothes?"

Dara sighed.

"I've learned that I don't just go eating what I find," she said unhappily, "nor go bounding through swamps, nor take gifts from Lord Vanian. I did learn how to make a basket from a leaf," she added, brightening a bit.

"Well, then, seems you've learned a good deal to your advantage, child," Granny said comfortingly. "There's a price for your learning—always is, d'you see? But you paid it and you're doing fine, child, just fine. Don't look so sad. My, I'm hungry, aren't I? Don't suppose you've a spot of food about, hey?"

"I've got some fruit," Dara said happily, turning to run for her basket. Then she hesitated.

"You won't disappear, will you, while I'm gone?"

"No, reckon I'll just come along," Granny grinned. The rocking chair lifted from the ground and floated easily behind Dara until they returned to the point where Dara had entered. She was relieved to see the basket of fruit, Gespry beside it, on the table where she'd laid it.

"Granny!" Gespry exclaimed, his eyes lighting. "Good enough to see you, old woman!"

"Bargained your way out of the swamp, did you, little rat?" Granny Good chuckled. "Ah, I could've taken you out and long since, but a century or two more and you'd've learned the trick of it yourself anyway. Don't need a key but to leave the Keep, young idiot, once you learn to use the Keep's magic."

"All I have is this fruit," Dara apologized, offering the basket. "Will that do?"

"Fine, fine." Granny nodded, reaching a dry, gnarled hand to pick out two fine apples. "And here's my return, child, catch!" Abruptly she tossed one of the apples toward Dara, biting vigorously into the other.

Startled, Dara reached out to catch the apple and caught instead a bundle of cloth. It fell from her awkward grasp, unfolding into a tunic and trousers, and a pair of knitted stockings.

"Oh, thank you!" Dara said gratefully. Then she frowned. "But it seems like a poor trade," she said reluctantly. "Just an apple for those."

"Pshaw, 'tain't no trade a-tall," Granny cackled affectionately. "You'll do as much yourself after a bit of study; just gave you back your own apple in a different shape. 'Sides," she grinned, "I got the smile, too, child."

"Then she's still owed?" Gespry asked slyly.

"Hmmm—you're a wily scoundrel," Granny scowled. "All right, three questions. And no refund if'n I can't answer, or she asks wrong; and no help, either, little rat!"

"Gespry, don't offend her," Dara said quickly. "I've got plenty of fruit—"

"Tsk, child, the bargain's made," Granny scolded. "Ask on then, and make it count!"

"You said before you couldn't tell me where the Oracle was," Dara said slowly. "And I think if you could've given me any more help in finding it, you would have. So if I asked you anything more about the Oracle, you probably couldn't tell me.''

"You're thinking smart, child," Granny nodded. "Go on.''

Dara paused. "Granny," she said at last, "why is the lord so nasty and cruel?''

Granny Good's gray eyebrows lifted. "Eh!'' she said. "Of all the questions I thought you'd ask, that wasn't one of 'em."

"He seems to find me of interest," Dara said wryly. "And I've learned when powerful folk find amusement in tormenting those as can't do much about it, sometimes it helps to know *why* they take such a joy in doing it.''

Granny nodded. "Wisely thought, child, wisely thought. Well, to answer you full and proper I'd have to know Lord Vanian's heart, and there's none so wise as that; but I'll say you this: Lord Vanian's been so ever since he's been the Guardian. He's empty to the very soul, d'you see?''

"No, I don't," Dara said slowly. "I'd think he'd be happy with all this, the power and the Keep and—"

"Ah, but there's the trick of it," Granny said sagely. "When he's got all that, what's left to want? And if there's naught to want, what's to enjoy? Only love and death and freedom, and those three he can't have; so he uses his power to make others as miserable as he is, don't you see?''

"Well, he does that," Dara said wryly, but the thought was a new one. She'd never supposed Lord Vanian was miserable.

"But if he's set himself to torment me," she said slowly, "how can I defeat him? He's so powerful.''

"Why, child, you're well on the road to defeating him already," Granny chuckled. "And you needn't do a blessed thing; there's the beauty of it all. Now, that's your second question, child, and you've but one more.''

Dara drew the cloth-wrapped gem from her ragged tunic. Slowly she unwrapped it.

"Can you tell me what—no," she corrected hurriedly. "My question is, what are the magical properties of this gem? I found it in a swamp garden Lord Vanian didn't want me to visit."

Granny's eyes widened again. She reached out a shaking hand to touch the stone.

"Ah, child, child," she murmured. "That's a treasure, indeed, what you've found. What you hold, child, is somebody's wish."

"A wish?" Dara repeated.

"Aye, child," Granny said soberly. "You think all who visit here leave with their wishes granted? Nay, them as come but lose their key have no way to claim their wishes, so those wishes lie lost here and thereabouts. 'Tis somebody's lost wish you've stumbled upon."

"But then I can go," Dara said excitedly. "I don't have to trade Lord Vanian for my wish, I've found one, and—"

"Hold, child, nay," Granny warned, holding up a hand. "D'you know how to use that wish, eh?"

"No, but—" Dara stopped. No, and a good thing not. She'd made careless wishes aplenty since she'd found the stone.

"Aye, but, and but." Granny nodded. "No more do I, child. You'd leave with but a gem, pretty as it is, unless you found the way of it. Mayhap you'll find such a way, see? Ask the Oracle that, and mayhap you needn't make a trade. Or mayhap you'll learn yourself. I'd say no other knows save Lord Vanian, and he's not likely to tell you, y'see?"

"No, I suppose he wouldn't," Dara said at last. "Not without something in return, so I might as well save the trouble of asking. Well, I suppose I have to find the Oracle anyway."

"Don't look so downcast, child," Granny Good comforted. "You've found yourself a wish, and that's something, and a grimoire, and that's something else, and you've learned a bit more than you knew before, and that's best of all. So cheer up, young Dara; you're none worse off than before, and somewhat better.''

She reached over and patted Dara's cheek. "Study your spells, there's a clever girl, and learn to use the make-magic of the Keep, and you'll be a good bit better off. Now put your new clothes on, there's more of you showing than's hid.''

Dara glanced guiltily down at the clothes, rumpled on the floor; she'd forgotten them entirely.

"I'm sorry," she said. "I—" Then she stopped.

Granny Good was gone.

"Well!" Gespry rested his chin in one furry hand. "Taken a proper liking to you, she has. Ain't many as has seen so much of her. Usually she keeps pretty much to herself.''

"She was very kind," Dara agreed, picking up the clothes.

"Ha! Kind don't tell the quarter of it," Gespry said dryly, picking a peach out of the basket. "Don't be mist-witted, girly, she didn't need none of your fruit; Granny Good comes and goes as she likes. She could've gone to the orchard herself just as easy, or made herself food out of dust or whatever, just as she liked. She just made it look to be some kind of trade so's she could give you a bit of help and not break the rules.''

"I hadn't thought of that," Dara admitted. Of course, if Granny Good could go where she pleased, she could certainly find her own fruit; she hadn't needed the water, either, the first time Dara had met her.

"Gespry," she said slowly, "why would Granny want to help me?''

Gespry's eyes sharpened. "Now there's a question for Granny and none other," he said firmly. "Ain't for me to say, if I knew, and I can't say as I do. But if she's been a help to you, what's it matter why? Be grateful, girly, for she's a good one to have favor you.''

"I *am* grateful," Dara said quickly, just in case Granny

could somehow hear her. She hurried behind one of the bookcases and exchanged the new clothing for her rags as quickly as she could, half expecting Lord Vanian to pop in as mysteriously as Granny had. She almost left her soiled rags where they'd fallen, but after a moment's hesitation, she picked them up. If magic could create clothes when used by someone very skilled, such as Granny, perhaps it could mend clothes more easily, even when the mage was only a poor novice. Ducking back around the cabinet, she found Gespry poring over the thick tome Granny had left on the table, sitting nonchalantly on a page while he studied it.

"This here book looks to be a good 'un," he admitted. "Thick, at least, and full of drawings, like you said."

"Let me see." She pushed Gespry off the page and leafed through the grimoire. It was old and thick, written in a wonderfully ornate hand, the spellings archaic but legible. It wasn't as impressive as her family's grimoire, but that was several generations' combined research.

"It'll take me a long time to memorize anything," Dara said dubiously. "I'll have to take this with me, and look up every spell I want to use. That won't do me much good in an emergency, not till I learn some of the spells by memory." She shrugged. It was certainly better than her present lack of any spells whatsoever.

"Look, ain't no profit in staying here," Gespry said at last. "And besides, you got me only two days more anyhow, remember?"

"Yes, that's right." Dara sighed. "I suppose I'd better start looking for the Oracle again. Well, at least I can cast a location spell now. Shall we go back to the cave lake?"

"There's one closer'n that, and nicer," Gespry told her. "Two doors farther down, is all."

"Any still water will do," Dara told him. She bound the grimoire up with the remnants of her ragged clothing to protect it; with it, the basket, and Gespry, she was heavily laden and glad not to have to walk any farther. The door

Gespry indicated opened to reveal a wide, sweeping lawn around a clear lake, the whole fronting an impressively fortified castle some distance away. Dara stared in amazement.

"I thought we were somehow still inside the Keep," she said slowly. "But how can there be a castle inside a castle?"

Gespry chuckled. "If that's the strangest thing you see hereabouts, you're lucky, girly," he said.

Dara thought of the strange hoofed creatures in the first forest she'd seen.

"Does anybody live there?" she asked slowly.

"Only saw it inside once myself," Gespry told her. "It's a treat to get into—locked up tight, gates an' all, but that made me so curious I finally climbed the wall. Empty old place it was, but not dusty or cobwebby—fixed up nice, luxuriouslike, but so empty it give me the shivers somehow."

"But the Oracle wasn't inside?" Dara pressed.

"Not that I saw, not then, but that don't mean nothin'," Gespry told her. "That were years ago, girly, and as I hear it, the Oracle's sometimes found here, sometimes there."

"Hear it from whom?" Dara asked suspiciously. "You said you'd never seen the Oracle. How do you know so much about it?"

"If I knew 'so much about it,' I'd tell you everything, and then I'd be free of you and shut of my bargain," Gespry said irritably. "And what I've heard, I've heard of other folks as came and stayed for one reason or another. Granny Good you've met. There's others aplenty, wandering here and there. And as for the Oracle, if your spell can show where it is, then you know more'n me in any wise."

"All right, then." Dara leafed through the grimoire, praying there'd be a location spell. There was; although the form of any spell varied from mage to mage, simple location was such elementary magic that she doubted any mage (and hence any grimoire) would be without it. It seemed like a strangely elaborate ritual; she couldn't remember how she'd cast the spell before, but surely it had been more simple and straightforward than this. Nevertheless, Dara recited the spell, struggling with a few of the words, began the gestures—

—and abruptly found herself in a room.

Shocked to silence, Dara looked about her, wondering if this was one of Lord Vanian's tricks, or perhaps she'd miscast the spell. But surely no simple location spell, no matter how botched, would have the power of Gating a person from one place to another!

The room around her could have been any guest room at High Lord Haranor's keep. It was suitably luxurious, furnished in dark wood and velvet, with tapestries hanging on the walls to keep out drafts, soft furs warming the stone floor, and a brisk fire going in the fireplace. In front of the fire was a filled bathtub; the water was steaming. On the bed was a fabulous gown of rich red, looking to be about Dara's fit, complete to embroidered slippers and jewelry. Gespry and her belongings were nowhere to be seen.

Dara scowled at the bath and dress and glanced about the room. There was neither door nor window, nor did a careful search of the walls reveal any hidden passages. Despite the hospitable fire and heated bathwater, the room had an air of emptiness and long disuse that chilled Dara, but worse was the certain knowledge that Lord Vanian, or some other powerful influence, was behind this abduction. No matter how she might have miscast her spell, nothing she could have done would have created this place—most especially a room without doors or windows.

"I don't much care for this," she said aloud to the empty room. There was no response.

She glanced again at the bath. She'd never had the training to serve as a maid in the royal chambers, and her family, while proud and well off, had never been able to afford this extent of opulent luxury, but she knew this was the sort of room the High Lady herself slept in, the sort of gown the High Lady might find laid ready for her after her scented bath—the sort of gown and room and bath that she, as Cav's wife, might one day have.

Despite her fear, the warm water was tempting, and she could see soaps and scents laid out beside the tub. Dara glanced around again and shrugged resignedly, laying her clothes aside and stepping into the heated water. Whatever or whoever had brought her here—and the whole thing certainly smelled of Lord Vanian's work—Dara had no spell to take her away. Whatever the purpose behind her abduction, her abductor would have to put her back, and he would do that only when it suited him. She might as well take what advantage of her situation she could.

To soak in a hot bath with expensive perfumed oils and soaps was a luxury unknown since she'd left her parents' household, and the water was cool before Dara abandoned the tub. She wrapped herself in a silken bath sheet—the smooth fabric caught on the work-roughened skin of her hands—and inspected the dressing table, experimenting with the powders, lotions, and scents for some time, nibbling from a silver dish of candied violets. She debated between donning her tunic and trousers or the gown for some time, then finally drew on the gown at last. Her hair was another problem; she'd seen the styles at court but had no idea how to duplicate them, and judging from the number of maids Cavin's mother had to do her hair, Dara suspected she couldn't hope to create such masterpieces alone, no matter what her skill. Finally she simply braided her plain brown hair and pinned the long braid in a coil at the back of her head, donned the jewelry, and waited.

And waited.

"Well?" Dara said impatiently at last, feeling a little silly addressing an empty room. She'd more than half expected Lord Vanian to materialize while she was bathing.

A slight whisper of a breeze from behind her attracted Dara's attention. She turned and was scarcely surprised to see that a door had appeared quietly in the wall where there had been only featureless stone moments ago. Dara scowled, but walked over to the door and barely hesitated before opening it.

The door opened into a wide, long hall, lit by ornate hanging lamps decorated by bits of polished crystal that threw the light around the room in glistening shards. At the center of the hall was a longish table, laden with food, with but one chair at each end. Lord Vanian was sitting in the far chair.

"How like a fish you look, gaping," he said indifferently. "Shut your mouth and the door, and sit down."

Dara closed her mouth with a snap and shut the door behind her. It seemed a mile to her chair, and she felt awkward in the elegant gown, but at last she sat down. Looking about, she realized that the door she'd come through had disappeared, and there were no others. Well, then, she was here until Lord Vanian made up his mind to let her leave. She said nothing.

There was no sign of servants, but the crystal goblet in front of her quietly filled itself with ruby liquid.

"Do have some wine," Lord Vanian said. He sounded bored.

Remembering what Granny Good had said, Dara peered down the table at him. He didn't *look* miserable, just lofty and rather jaded, like so many other noblemen she'd seen.

"Why?" Dara challenged.

Lord Vanian raised his eyebrows.

"Why not? It's not poisoned, I assure you."

Somehow his statement failed to reassure her.

"That's not what I meant," Dara said. She gestured at her dress, the table. "Why all this?"

Lord Vanian shrugged. "At our every meeting you've criticized my hospitality," he said diffidently. "You've made complaint that I've failed to furnish you with food, bath, and clothing. So you should be delighted, as you now have all three in the finest form my imagination can furnish. So eat and drink, that my hostly duties be utterly fulfilled." He laughed mockingly.

"And what's the price of all this?" Dara said suspiciously. "Where are my belongings, and Gespry?"

"If by 'your belongings' you refer to the fruit and the book you stole from me, rather than your pack at the bottom of the swamp, those await you by the lake where you left them," Lord Vanian said with that superior smirk Dara found so infuriating. "And as to price—" He laughed again. "I'll settle for the pleasure of your company. My word, fair lady, I'll not so much as touch one of your precious belongings. Nor your pathetic little friend."

"Why should I trust you?" Dara challenged.

"Because if you'd bothered to ask, either your little pet or delightful, demented Granny Good," Lord Vanian said idly, "you'd have learned that no denizen of this place, myself with the rest, may speak an untruth to any visitor so long as they remain merely a visitor. It's one of the rules."

"You didn't tell me that at the beginning," Dara accused him.

"Nothing obligates me to tell you anything, then or now," Lord Vanian retorted. "I tell you now only to save myself the bother of convincing you that the food and drink you considered it my duty to provide are fit for you to consume. Therefore trust me or not, as you will, but as you can't leave until I permit it, what have you to lose?"

"Nothing, I suppose," Dara said, shrugging and reaching for the wine. If in fact Lord Vanian couldn't lie to her, that was something worth knowing; on the other hand, he could well be lying about *that*. To cover her confusion, she sipped the wine. It was finer than anything she'd drunk, even when Cav had given her some of the good wine in High Lord Haranor's household.

Servants or no, she was well cared for. One by one the platters appeared before her, and she helped herself as she pleased. Bones and scraps disappeared from her plate as soon as she dropped them there.

The food was so tasty, and it had been so long since

she'd eaten a well-cooked meal, that Dara realized embarrassedly she'd been gorging herself greedily for quite some time without even looking up from her plate. Peering down the table, she noticed to her mortification that although Lord Vanian had food on his plate, he wasn't eating, his dark eyes fastened on her and that utterly condescending half-smile on his lips.

"Am I that 'amusing'?" she asked. "I'd thought you found me rather annoying instead."

"As you may have observed," Lord Vanian said, "there is a shortage of good dinner company hereabouts."

"If I'm the best you can do, pity you," Dara said without humor. "I don't know the fine manners nor the polite things to talk about. I'm more acquainted with clearing up the dishes from feasts like this, rather than sitting at table eating with a lord."

"So you were a serving wench?" Lord Vanian asked, but his words lacked their usual acid edge. "Go on."

"What—you want to hear about me?" Dara asked disbelievingly.

Lord Vanian shrugged. "I hear nothing of the outside world," he said, and this time Dara could hear the trace of some undefined emotion in his words. "And nothing changes here. Ever. Any diversion is welcome."

"There's not much to tell," Dara said slowly. "I was— I'm a kitchen maid in the household of High Lord Haranor and High Lady Alberta, royal house of Caistran. My family were all mages, generations back, and I wasn't, so I ran off and ended up in the High Lord's household. There's nothing very special about me."

"Caistran," Lord Vanian repeated, as if searching his memory. "I've not heard of it."

"It's not a large country, and it's a long journey from here," Dara told him. "I traveled weeks getting here, and most of that by caravan."

"A long journey, indeed, for a simple serving wench,"

Lord Vanian mocked gently. ''This man must be worth a great deal to you.''

''Cav—that's Cavin, Caistran's Heir and a mage himself,'' Dara said. ''Yes, we hope to be married.''

Suddenly she flushed with embarrassment. She hadn't given Cav a thought in some time. Immediately a wave of guilt swept over her. Doubtless he'd been thinking of *her*, and worrying about her, ever since she'd left.

''So you want to be High Lady of Caistran,'' Lord Vanian mused gravely.

''It's not that,'' Dara said annoyedly. Why did everybody seem to assume she was marrying Cav for his position? She gulped down a swallow of wine to fortify herself. ''I'd marry him if he were a stableboy.'' In truth, she thought, things would be a good deal simpler if he were a stableboy, just as she'd thought the first time she'd met him. She chuckled at the memory.

''You laugh,'' Lord Vanian said, leaning forward. ''Why?''

''I was just thinking of the first time I met Cav,'' Dara said with a sigh. ''He was in the stables in old patched leathers brushing a horse. I wanted to find someone in the household to see if there wasn't a place for me, and I thought a stableboy would do just fine. I snapped at him, in fact, when he didn't come out of that stall fast enough to suit me.''

Dara sighed again. How handsome Cav had looked, even in his old soiled leathers.

''He never told me who he was,'' she said. ''Just escorted me straight to his mother and father and asked that I be given a place in the household. I was so embarrassed I thought I'd die. I almost didn't take the position out of shame. I hoped I'd never see Cav again, but he came to the kitchen the very next day looking for me. By the time he was finished talking to me, I was able to laugh about it.'' That afternoon had sealed Cav in her heart forever— his rather sober smile, his gentle voice, the way he listened so gravely when she spoke, even the casual way he'd sat on the table edge.

"How touching," Lord Vanian said, chuckling. His eyes glittered. "And yet you will be a High Lady if you marry this Heir, regardless of your noble lack of ambition. Do you see yourself as a good High Lady?"

Dara's jaw dropped. In all the time she'd fought against the obstacles between her and her life with Cav, never for a moment had she actually considered that eventuality—that if they married, Cav would one day be High Lord, and she, High Lady, partially responsible for ruling Caistran. Yet what had she expected? Cav was Heir.

"I don't know," she admitted. "I hadn't really thought about it, I suppose. But Cav wouldn't want to marry me if he didn't think I'd do. He'd never do anything against the good of the country."

"Such as marrying a magicless kitchen wench?" Lord Vanian scoffed. "How noble of *him*. And yet with his gold and his magic and his family to ease the way, it is you and not he who dared the dreaded Crystal Keep."

"Cav's done everything he could," Dara protested, taking another swallow of wine. "He has responsibilities; he can't just go running off as he pleases. His parents would never allow it. And he can't take such risks, either, being the Heir to the throne of Caistran. His parents don't have another child to declare as Heir if something happens to him."

"Of course," Lord Vanian said smoothly. "I see. But you're not eating. Have I once more offended you with my 'ungentlemanly' ways? Or do my questions unsettle you?"

"Not at all." Defiantly Dara helped herself to another serving of basted fowl as the platter appeared in front of her. "But I could say it's none of your concern. Why do you want to know all these things about me? You can't care what goes on in a little country leagues away from here."

Lord Vanian shrugged.

"Sometimes I like to imagine the world outside the Keep," he said. "Imagine how it's changed. And yet folk go on with their small, boring lives just as they did before. I suppose nothing changes outside, either, not truly."

"Then you *weren't* always the Guardian?" Dara asked daringly. "Why did you come here?"

Lord Vanian slowly put down his goblet and leaned forward, his eyes locking with hers. The expression in them was such that Dara swallowed heavily, involuntarily pressing back against the back of her chair. For a moment she thought he might blast her with some powerful magic.

Then the mask of indifference slipped back into place; when he spoke, his voice was cold.

"I came as you did," he said at last. "For love of one far above me. But to win her, I had to claim a kingdom—and in gaining it, lost what I had sought."

"I don't understand," Dara whispered.

"Indeed you do not." There was a noticeable edge to Lord Vanian's voice. "In any event, it pleased me to allow you to try for your foolish wish. And may your wish bring you more pleasure than mine did me. Enough!" He uttered the last word explosively, banging his hand on the table so that Dara jumped.

"Finish your wine," he said coldly. "Then come with me. I have something to show you."

Dara gulped down the last of her wine, grimacing a little at its strength, and rose. Lord Vanian strode to the far end of the hall, then stood impatiently waiting for her beside a hanging curtain.

Dara hurried over, stumbling a little over the unaccustomed length of her ornate gown. Inwardly she cursed herself. She'd never had the opportunity to drink such strong wine, or in such quantities, and she could feel it rapidly going to her head. But she'd have felt such a fool, asking for cider like a child!

Lord Vanian pulled a long silken cord, and the curtain flowed smoothly aside. Behind it was an oval mirror in a gilt frame, as tall as Dara. In its smooth surface, however, was no reflection at all, only a shifting white mist not unlike the one through which Dara had passed when she entered the valley.

"Your conversation has . . . amused me," Lord Vanian said smoothly. "Therefore I'll grant you a glimpse of your love. Think on him with all your mind, and look deep into the mirror."

It was all Dara could do to make her wine-befuddled wits behave, but her heart leaped at the thought. Obediently, she concentrated on the swirling mist, picturing Cav's dear face, the smooth white hands marred only by his sword calluses, his neatly trimmed, straight red-brown hair, the rich gilt of the braid on his robes . . .

Slowly the mist seemed to clear around a dim figure that rapidly became more visible. The familiar face looked puzzledly up, then smiled.

"Dara, love!" Cav said, his whole face lighting. "Where are you? How is it that I can see you like this?"

"I'm—I'm safe," she said lamely. "I—"

She glanced around her. The dining hall had vanished, as had Lord Vanian. She stood in a swirling mist exactly like that surrounding Cav on the other side of the mirror. Her head wobbled.

Cav had changed since she'd last seen him. He looked thinner and haggard, with dark circles under his eyes, as if from worry. His usually neatly combed hair was rumpled, as if from neglect.

"You seem so close," Cav murmured to her. "As if I could merely reach out and touch you." His hand reached toward the mirror.

So real was the vision that Dara's own hand reached to meet his—and suddenly her hand touched, not cold glass, but the warmth of flesh. A quick step, and she was in his arms.

Dara had feared that Cav was only a distant vision, but he was warm and real, his jacket smelling of the scent he liked, the softness of his hair beneath her hands, his lips firm and warm against hers. Dara clutched him tightly, shaking with joy.

"It's been so long," she breathed. "I wasn't sure I'd ever see you again."

"I've missed you so much," he murmured into her hair. "I've hardly eaten or slept since you left." His hands danced over the braid, freeing it from its clasps so that it fell down her back, then undid the braid so that her hair cascaded loose over her shoulders.

"But how fine you look," he said gently, stepping back slightly to look at her. "Fit to be a High Lady."

"I—it's not mine," Dara said awkwardly, smoothing her hands down the velvet of her gown.

"It doesn't matter." He folded her in his arms again, easing her to the softness of the deep furs beneath them, kissing her eyelids, her lips, until she was breathless.

Something about the furs stirred uneasily in Dara's mind, but how could she think with Cav's arms around her, his lips showering her with kisses, his hands clutching her urgently to him?

It was only when she realized that Cav was sliding the gown down over her shoulders, its fastenings already mysteriously undone, that she mustered a feeble protest.

"Cav, don't," she said weakly, fighting the wine and his overwhelming nearness. "We agreed—your parents—"

"I don't care what they think," he whispered against her lips. "You're mine. You'll always be mine. Nothing will ever keep us apart again."

This time the warning bell in her mind was weaker and easy to ignore. How long she'd waited, how long she'd wanted him—

His hands, his kisses, were warm and skilled, the furs were soft and luxurious, and the firelight itself seemed to stroke her bare skin. There was an instant of pain when he came to her, but he waited until it passed, then began again, very gently, until her pleasure could grow with his own, building until she gasped, staring up into his black eyes—

—black? Cav's eyes were blue, blue as the sky—

—and with that realization, Cav's face began to blur before her, the red-brown locks darkening, the glow of his cheeks paling, the features taking a form of horrible familiarity.

Dara had time for one single scream of denial as the world around her faded into blackness.

5

DARA AWAKENED SLOWLY. THERE WAS A rough hardness under her and an evil taste in her mouth. Pain made its way into her consciousness— a dull throb in her head, nausea threatening in her stomach, and an aching soreness between her legs. One of her arms had fallen asleep under her, and light stabbed a thousand needles through her closed eyelids.

Dara opened her eyes, gasped, and shut them again as her head spun. Gritting her teeth, she forced her arms to push her up. It was several long moments before she could bear the light enough to take in her surroundings.

She was lying, naked but for the chain and key around her neck, on the grassy bank of a still lake. Some distance away was her tunic and trousers, neatly folded as she'd laid them on the bed; on the bank of the lake was her basket. Beside the basket was Gespry, curled up tightly and snoring atop the grimoire. However fuzzy her knowledge of how she might have gotten here, though, her memory was crystal clear—too clear.

Slowly Dara tried to stand, but her head spun so that

she quickly gave it up and crawled across the grass to her clothes. Quietly she collected them, then crawled with them to the lake; even that short effort made her head ache horribly and her stomach threaten to expel its contents.

The water of the lake was cool but not cold; Dara managed to scoot into the shallow water, where, despite her aching head, she scrubbed herself vigorously with handfuls of sand from the bottom. Tears made shining tracks down her cheeks, but she made no sound, only scrubbing at her skin until it was red and stinging and every last trace of perfume adhering to it was gone. Then she washed her hair and braided it tightly, so tightly it pulled back the skin of her forehead and temples painfully, and sat on the bank, weeping silently, until she was dry enough to dress.

For a moment Dara thought longingly of the plums in the forest. At that instant, if she'd had a bushel of the treacherous fruit, she'd have eaten them all to the last drop of juice. In that moment, forgetting everything—even who she was—seemed a small price to pay to eradicate the memory of Lord Vanian's touch, the touch she'd believed to be Cav's, that she'd welcomed so eagerly. The mere thought of how her body had answered to his made Dara's gorge rise in her throat, and it was only by biting her tongue *hard* that she kept from vomiting.

She'd known two girls in the High Lord's household who had been forced by overamorous noblemen. At least they'd known what was happening to them, had the chance to bite and scratch and resist with all their strength. At least they had the knowledge that they'd fought as hard as they could. What had happened to Dara seemed somehow worse. Other girls she'd known had been seduced, plied by promises or, more honestly, by coins to abandon their virtue.

At least they'd had the chance to choose.

That thought threatened to bring on a new flood of tears, and Dara shook her head stubbornly, clenching her fists until she had herself under control again. Sobbing like a child wouldn't restore her virtue nor her pride, and there was nothing to be gained by sitting here pitying herself. It would be more to her profit to pull herself together, wake Gespry and reclaim her belongings, and put as much distance between herself and the horrible castle behind her—and hopefully Lord Vanian, too—as she could.

Dara pulled on her clothes and anxiously inspected the bundle of her belongings. The gem was intact, wrapped in rags as she'd left it—did Lord Vanian know she had it?—as was the book with Gespry on it. The fruit was still in its basket, apparently untouched. Gespry slept on, heavily.

Dara frowned and touched the odd creature, then shook him roughly. He stirred sluggishly, murmured something incoherent, and subsided again into deep slumber. Drugged, or bespelled?

For a moment disgust and hate warred in Dara's mind until she thought she'd either faint or scream. Desperately she put her head on her knees and willed her mind to clear. When she could think again, she dried her eyes and examined the ground around Gespry. No evidence that he had eaten or drunk anything; there was no smell of food or wine on his breath. Bespelled, then.

Dara carefully lifted Gespry off the grimoire and leafed through it. Yes, there was a spell for dissolving enchantments. For a moment Dara's stomach knotted—if only she'd had time to study that grimoire and learn that spell!—but she put the thought aside and began the incantation. As the last word was spoken, Gespry yawned and stretched, opening his eyes.

"Had me quite a nap, didn't I?" he gaped. "Well, found your Oracle yet?"

"No . . ." Dara closed the book, looking away. "I guess I bungled the spell. Maybe I'd better wait a bit and try it somewhere else."

Gespry scowled puzzledly at her puffy face. "Ain't all that bad, girly," he comforted. "Every mage bungles a spell or two, sometime, and you just a beginner, too. Ain't worth taking on so about it.''

Dara nodded mutely and wrapped the grimoire in its rags, her lips tight.

"Say, ain't nothing else wrong, is there?" Gespry pressed after a long moment of silence. "Didn't nothing happen while I napped, eh?"

"No." Dara stuffed the bundled gem back down her shirt and picked up the fruit and the book. "Nothing."

Gespry shrugged. "Just as you say, girly. Where to, then?"

"I need more water for the spell," Dara said, forcing her voice to calmness. "Another pool."

"Right, got just the thing," Gespry said, grinning. "Should put you in a better temper, too." He tugged the hem of Dara's tunic impatiently, waiting until she picked him up, and gestured her to the door. Once back in the long corridor, Gespry counted doors, indicating his choice. Too distracted to look through the peephole first, Dara simply opened the door—

—and stepped through into dazzling color.

For a moment Dara was nearly blinded by the play of light; it took several minutes for her tearing eyes to adjust. When they did, however, she gazed around her with a low gasp of wonder, her emotional upheaval for the moment forgotten.

They stood on the smooth floor of a cavern; however, unlike the first cave Dara had visited, this was a place of light and beauty.

Crystal stalactites of rainbow hues reached down from the ceiling to be met, in places, with equally colorful stalagmites. Even more brilliant formations grew from the distant walls of the cavern, apparently giving off their own light. Near Dara, a glistening fall of water arched out over a crystal shelf to fall, sparkling blue, into a waiting hollow beneath. The water was so clear that Dara could not gauge its depth, but at least it appeared pure.

"This will do." Dara nodded, cautiously comforted that at last *something* was going right in this horrible keep. She looked around until she found a crystal stalagmite with a hollowed top, then painstakingly carried water over in the cup of her hands until she had filled it. She reviewed the location spell in the grimoire, checking her pronunciation of the hard words, and knelt before the rock basin, confirming that there were no drips to disturb the water.

She began the chant, half dreading another interruption, but to her relief the spell completed with no difficulty. Clearing her mind as best she could, Dara bent over the still water. She'd have three questions; best make them count. She couldn't cast the same spell in the same body of water for three days, to allow the magical energies to clear.

"Show me the Oracle," she commanded.

The water appeared to ripple slightly. Abruptly the round pool became black as night. Dara squinted hard, but could make nothing out in the midnight depths.

She shook her head. Perhaps that was against yet another of the "rules" of the place that she hadn't been told. Dara blew on the water to clear it, waiting until her own reflection returned.

"Show me the place where the Oracle can be found," she said.

The water appeared to ripple slightly again, but nothing else happened; Dara continued to see only her own reflection in the still water. Exasperated, she almost surrendered the spell when she realized that she still had one question left.

Well, why not?

"Show me the thing I must give Lord Vanian in exchange for my wish," she commanded.

Again the water rippled, but the picture remained unchanged.

"Damn all!" Dara exclaimed. She plunged her hand into the water, breaking the spell, and splashed the cool liquid out of the basin. "*Why* isn't it working?"

"Don't know." Gespry shook his head over the grimoire. "Can't say as I can understand a word of it. Didn't seem like you was blocked, did it? The lord could be doing that."

"I don't know." Dara sighed and closed the grimoire. "I don't know how it feels to have a spell blocked. Until I came here, I never had one work anyway."

"Don't know why he'd trouble himself," Gespry said, shrugging. "He don't get his payment till you find what you're after. 'Sides, using magic ain't against the rules."

Dara was silent for a long moment, thinking of Lord Vanian's dinner conversation.

"But if he wanted me to fail," she said slowly, "wouldn't he just as likely show me a picture of the wrong place or thing, instead of nothing at all?"

"Can't do that," Gespry said firmly, shaking his head. "Can't even fib a little to visitors, let alone lead 'em astray. That's the rules, girly, for the lord same as any of us. He can keep mum as he likes, or let you fool yourself, but he can't tell you nothing that ain't true, same for all of us."

"But how do I know," Dara asked, "that you're not lying about *that*?" Or that Lord Vanian had been, of course.

"Well, if you want to waste time," Gespry said patiently, "I bet there's a truth spell in that book; go on and throw it at me and see what happens."

Cheered by the thought that at last she could be certain of *something*, Dara leafed through the book and spoke the simple spell; it confirmed that Gespry spoke the truth. Something about that nagged at her, but she couldn't quite decide what.

"Still can't make out why he'd block your spell," Gespry mused, munching on an apple from the basket. "And how come the water showed black the first time, and nothing a-tall after that? Why not black for all three, or nothing for all three? Odd, that was."

"Oh, these damned divination spells are always tricky, or so I was taught," Dara sighed exasperatedly, her brief happiness fading back into a sort of resigned despair. "Easy to muddy, and hard to get a straight answer even if you know to ask the right question." She sat down on the hard floor of the cave, burying her face in her folded arms, fighting to keep from weeping. At last she raised her head again.

"We'll stay here for a little," she said, suddenly so weary, body and soul, that she wanted nothing more than to sleep and never wake. But there was no time for sleep, not yet. "It's as good a place as any. I want to study the book and try a few experiments."

"Your choice, girly." Gespry shrugged, scampering up to a dry shelf and curling up comfortably, apple in his hand-like paw. Within a minute he was snoring.

Leaving Gespry to his slumber, Dara took some fruit and ventured deeper into the cavern, picking up odd bits of broken rock to use as raw material. When she was far enough away that she was sure her chants wouldn't wake Gespry—the one thing she *didn't* want was him looking on with his jokes and unhelpful suggestions while she fumbled—she sat down on the hard floor of the cavern and sorted her material into piles. Right now the effort of learning to understand the Keep's magic was as much her only comfort as it was her only hope.

Mastering the make-magic of the Keep was not as easy as Granny Good had made it look. It took concentration, plus a detailed knowledge of the desired end result. Her initial basket, Dara discovered, had been poorly done because she knew relatively little about basket-weaving. When she tried simpler items, things with which she was more familiar—simple cups and bowls, for instance—she was much more successful. Indeed, she even found it possible to transform rock or mud into food, although that took careful concentration on flavor and texture as well as appearance. She wondered if that was how Lord Vanian had come by his sumptuous feast, but if so, what was the purpose of the orchard?

Clothing she found much easier, as she well understood sewing; after a few hours of practice, she could wave garments into existence as easily as Granny had. That simple ability came as a great relief to her; there'd be no more filthy rags for *this* serving wench! For a few moments she played with creating sumptuous gowns, but at last abandoned them in favor of more practical sturdy trousers and tunics. Almost as good as the clothing were the wooden tub, hot water, and soap Dara conjured with a little practice. There'd be no more cold lakes and sand scourings, at least.

She wondered at the power of this raw magic. With it, she could produce many of the effects gained by much more elaborate and difficult spells in the grimoire, without the necessity of incantations or gestures and without drawing on her own magical energies as conventional spells did. Who knew what other applications there were of such magic? Small wonder Lord Vanian wielded such power!

That thought made Dara pause. Was it possible that Lord Vanian was only an ordinary person, albeit a mage, who had merely learned over time to fully use the magic of the Keep? Was it possible that the awesome power he displayed had its source not in him, but in the place itself? Gespry had implied as much, and Granny Good, apparently long of tenure in the Keep, seemed nearly as powerful as the Guardian himself. Obviously Lord Vanian had found no way to restrict Granny's assistance of Dara, however much he disapproved of it, or he surely would have done so.

But if that supposition was true, then Dara had available to her magical power equal to Lord Vanian's own! For a moment the knowledge was a fire burning hot and bright in her, fueled by rage; then Dara sighed and shook her head. *If*, in truth, such power was equally available to Lord Vanian and to her, it still made no matter. Dara could use only what magic she herself knew how to shape, while Lord Vanian had had some indefinable time to hone his own skills. Even assuming that the same raw magic was available to both of them—and there was no way she knew to be sure of that—Dara was the merest novice in its use and certainly a poor match for Lord Vanian, with little time to learn more.

After some concentration and several failures, Dara managed to create a knife of sorts, irregularly shaped and crooked, but satisfyingly sharp. For a moment she envisioned plunging it into Lord Vanian's heart, then shook her head again regretfully.

Revenge was a game played by those who had no better goal. If she tried to harm Lord Vanian, she'd likely as not end up dead, or transformed and imprisoned in the Keep like Gespry. And even if she succeeded, if she could at this very moment thrust her blade into Lord Vanian's black heart and kill him, it would afford her some satisfaction, but at a price—for then there would be nobody to grant her wish. No, Dara couldn't afford to let anger cloud her thinking; her purpose here was to find the Oracle, pay for her wish, and be gone from the place as quickly as she could. Indeed, what better revenge could there be than for the arrogant Lord Vanian to see her succeed where he, by his own words, had apparently failed? Her success would gnaw like a rat at his vitals, probably forever; and if Granny Good was right about the lord's misery, how it would twist in his gut, knowing that Dara would spend her life in happiness with the man she loved. She smiled at the thought and tucked the knife into her belt and, heart much lighter, hurried back to Gespry.

Gespry was playing in the water, sliding over the time-smoothed crystal falls to plunge ungracefully into the pool;

his laughter echoed off the walls in rolling peals. When he saw Dara, he abandoned his play and scampered out of the water, shaking moisture from his fur.

"Well, you look a sight better," Gespry said, grinning. "But I'd say you're about ready for a spot of sleep."

"I am," Dara admitted. "But some dinner first." She found a lump of crystal and concentrated, smiling proudly when it metamorphosed into two steaming bowls of stew, complete with spoons.

"Well, I'll say you've been busy while I slept!" Gespry chuckled approvingly. He tasted the stew cautiously, then dug in with a will. "Ain't that grand! Proper mage you've become, girly. Granny'd be proud of you, that she would."

"Thank you." Dara ate the stew with relish, for the first time since she'd arrived at the Keep utterly certain she could trust that what she ate was harmless.

When she was done eating, she turned an eye to the empty bowls. One became a straw mattress and the other a smaller cushion for Gespry; both were rather lumpy, but it was the best bed Dara had had in some weeks. She had not even time to conjure up a pillow or blanket before she was fast asleep.

Dara awakened slowly, luxuriously, so refreshed that she was momentarily surprised. Then she laughed. Why shouldn't she be refreshed? She'd slept long, on a full stomach, on the softest bed she'd had in weeks. For a brief moment she remembered the softness of furs beneath her body, and her laughter died immediately. Resolutely she pushed the thought from her mind.

"Slept a good while, girly." Gespry chuckled, peering around a crystal boulder.

"I suppose so." Dara yawned. "What've you been doing?"

"Ah, I was trying to conjure a bit," Gespry said disgustedly. "Figured if a—well, if you could do it, I could, too. Thought I'd pop up breakfast; ain't had no luck, though. Shows up fine, but all I can get is stuff as tastes like swamp mud.''

Dara laughed, but her mind was working furiously. This was her chance to learn just how available the make-magic of the keep was.

''Were you much of a mage before you came here?'' Dara asked, although she remembered that he'd already told her he wasn't.

''Nah, weren't no mage a-tall, just a plain cobbler,'' Gespry said, shrugging. ''My folk hadn't the magic for more'n a few simples, same as I learned—waterproofing shoes an' mending holes and the like. But you caught on so quick, being just a plain serving wench, I figured it must be easy.''

''Well, there you are,'' Dara said. ''You see, magic or no, I've spent practically my whole life studying to be a mage, in the hope that my spells would finally begin to work, so I've got most of the skills already—concentration, self-discipline, and so on. It takes training and practice, and Cav says they're just as important as having the talent for magic to begin with.''

''No fooling, girly. Ain't no different than any other trade, I guess.'' Gespry settled himself comfortably atop the grimoire again. ''You going to make us something, then?''

A well-rested mind and body and raised self-confidence showed; it took only two tries for Dara to produce a tray of bread and pastries.

''Sweets?'' Gespry scowled. ''Where's the bacon, girly, and the ale?''

''Sorry,'' Dara said, shrugging. ''I'm going to have to work at that. All the cooking I did was in the High Lord's house, and they didn't have bacon and ale for breakfast. My parents didn't either.''

''Huh. *You* try to do a good day's hard work on sweet cakes,'' Gespry retorted, stuffing a whole cake into his mouth. ''Better'n swamp vermin, anyhow, by a long sight. Don't know as how I'll manage on my own again.''

"You'll learn yourself," Dara comforted, but absently. Gespry's remark had reminded her that according to their bargain, today was the last day he must accompany her. After that she'd be alone again, and the thought was depressing and frightening, too. Although the odd little demon seemed of scant help, his mere presence, both as a companion and as an experienced denizen of the Keep, was comforting.

"Gespry, what do you think I should do?" she said at last. "I mean, apparently I can't locate the Oracle by magic, and trying every door in the hallway is going to take forever, especially if the Oracle moves about from place to place as you say."

Gespry sat back reflectively, nibbling on another cake.

"Well, as I see it, you got a few choices," he said after a moment's thought. "You could make somebody tell you, only that's against the rules; or you could try all the doors, only that'll take forever; or you can keep trying magic and hope you'll catch Lord Vanian unawares; or you can forget the Oracle and try to figure it out yourself; or you can forget the whole thing and just go home. Too bad you couldn't see what the Oracle looked like; otherwise you might not even know it if you found it, hey?"

Dara frowned. "Maybe I'm not being subtle enough," she said. "Maybe I should try something different. Hmmm. Gespry, hand me that piece of crystal, will you?"

Carefully Dara plucked three strands of her long brown hair and braided them into a slender cord. She took the crystal from Gespry, concentrating on it. This was different than changing one thing into another, harder in one way and easier in another—after a moment the crystal smoothed into a perfect orb, about an inch across, with only one small bore for the thread. Tying the orb to the thread, Dara suspended it from one of the many stalactites. She leafed through the grimoire until she found the spell she'd seen earlier.

"This is the very simplest divination," she told Gespry.

"Anybody with even a hint of magical talent can do it. Lord Vanian may not even notice anything as small as this. I hope not, at least." Closing her eyes, she composed her mind, then spoke the spell carefully.

"Answer me thusly," she told the crystal. "Swing from my left to my right for 'yes.' Swing toward and away from me for 'no.' "

"How many questions you got?" Gespry whispered.

"Nine," Dara murmured to him. "It's a *very* basic spell."

"First question," she began. "Is Lord Vanian blocking or interfering with this spell?"

The pendulum hung motionless for a long moment, then slowly swung toward Dara, then away.

"Good," Dara sighed with relief.

"Does the lord even know you're casting it?" Gespry said to her. Abruptly his eyes widened and he clapped his hand over his mouth, but too late—the pendulum had stilled and swung again, signifying negative.

"Thanks," Dara said exasperatedly. "You ruined my second question."

"Sorry," Gespry said sheepishly.

"Never mind." Dara shook her head. "Third question. Did Lord Vanian block the location spell I cast earlier in this cave?"

There was a pause; negative.

"Now, wait a minute—" Gespry began.

"Shhh! You'll waste another question if you're not careful," Dara said crossly.

"Well, ask on, then," Gespry retorted.

"Fourth question," Dara continued, ignoring him. "Is the Oracle in a dark place?"

The pendulum stilled, then began swinging side to side.

"That explains it," Dara sighed, relieved. "The spell *did* show the Oracle, or part of it, anyway. Fifth question. Have I already passed the Oracle?"

There was a long hesitation. At last the pendulum trembled uncertainly, but gave no answer.

"I must have phrased that badly," Dara said. "All right, have I already been through the same doorway through which I could find the Oracle?"

This time the pendulum's positive response was immediate.

"I don't know whether I wasted a question or not," Dara said, sighing. "Well, then—is the Oracle in the barren place with the blowing ashes or the forest with the plum tree?"

No.

"Is it in the dark cave or the orchard?"

No.

"Is it in the library or"—Dara hesitated, dreading the answer—"or the place with the lake and the castle?"

No.

Dara sighed with relief, then swallowed the spark of excitement she felt. It wouldn't do to jump to conclusions, not in this place.

"Last question, if I still have one left," she said. "Is the Oracle here in this crystal cave?"

There was a long pause; then the pendulum swung slowly toward Dara and away.

"No!" Dara exclaimed frustratedly. "How can that be? Those were all the places I've been, every one."

Then she stopped. Unless—unless the bedroom and the dining hall had not been, as she had assumed, part of the castle she'd seen near the lake, but were actually in another place entirely. If so, the Oracle could be in that place. But if that was so, how was she to get back there? And—could she bear to go back there at all?

"Only one way to learn," she said aloud. She untied the thin cord and put the crystal sphere in the meager parcel of her belongings. "Come on, Gespry. There's something I need to try."

"The hallway?" Gespry guessed. "You've been there, and it weren't one of them places you named."

"That's true," Dara realized hopefully. Perhaps she didn't need to return to the dreaded bedroom after all! Eagerly she scooped up Gespry and stepped back into the hall.

Her hope, however, was quickly dashed. There was *nothing* black in the hallway that she could see except the starry sky overhead. The rug on the floor was jade-green and brown, and the walls, save for the doors, were all plain gray stone. The lamp sconces were polished brass. Of course, no matter how far she walked, she still couldn't see the end of the hallway; it was always possible that the Oracle might be somewhere far ahead, farther than she could see.

Dara sighed. She'd hardly expected the Oracle to be sitting plainly in the hallway—much too simple, wasn't it?—but it had been a nice thought. Resignedly she retraced her steps to the lake and the castle.

"What you want in here?" Gespry asked as they stepped through the door. "Spell said the Oracle weren't in here, didn't it?"

"I know," Dara said. There was no chance at all she'd *ever* tell Gespry what'd happened. "I just wanted to see what's in the castle."

"And how'll you get in?" Gespry challenged.

"I don't know." She glanced at him. "You said you climbed the wall, didn't you?"

"Well, yeah, but I'm made for climbing, girly," Gespry said wryly. "You'd never do it. What're you wanting, me to go look for you, or just carry you up on my back?"

"Well, you could carry a rope up and tie it," Dara said patiently. *If* she could manage to make a sturdy rope that didn't break and let her fall; *if* Gespry could tie a knot that would hold her weight; *if* she could get across the moat in the first place . . .

"Was there anything in the moat?" Dara asked Gespry. "When you went across, I mean."

Gespry chuckled.

"Girly, moat wasn't *there* when I went in the first time.

And if you think I'm going to swim across and find out whatever Lord Vanian might have put in there, you're purely mist-headed.''

''All right, all right,'' Dara said. She gazed at the castle, then squared her shoulders. ''We'll just have a look, then.''

The moat might not have existed when Gespry had previously approached the castle, but it certainly *looked* as if it had always been there. There was no way of discerning how deep it might be; the water, if it could be called that, was greenish-black and utterly opaque. Occasionally ominous ripples indicated movement below the surface.

As Dara had feared, the drawbridge was drawn up; looking at the rust caking the iron chains holding the thick wooden slab against the castle and the worm-ridden state of the wood, Dara wondered if the bridge had ever in fact been used. It could all be for show. Assuming that Lord Vanian had made or at least used the castle, he could come and go as he pleased without benefit of the gates. Apparently he saw no need to allow anyone else entry. It was too much to hope, she thought regretfully, that the castle's defenses would be in the same state of disrepair. The wall certainly *looked* sturdy and well kept; there wasn't so much as a bit of moss growing between the blocks or bits of crumbling mortar falling out.

Dara was marginally comforted, however, to see that there was a narrow strip of dry soil around the castle on the far side of the moat. At least she'd have someplace to stand on the other side while she prepared to climb the rope, if she could find a way across.

''Maybe you could magic up a bridge,'' Gespry said, shrugging.

Dara thought about the idea for long moments, then shook her head disappointedly. She knew nothing about bridges, nothing at all, and ''nothing at all'' was likely going to get her dumped into the muck midway across the moat. The closest she'd ever come to bridge building was when she and her brothers had managed to topple a dead tree over a stream so they could play at balancing across it. Now if only a dead tree had conveniently grown next to the moat—

Now, there was a thought. She doubted whether she could build a usable bridge, but a log she could understand.

Dara had to walk almost all the way back to the lake before she found a few twigs to practice on; like all well-defended castles, this one had no trees growing nearby. There was a growth spell in the grimoire, but that was not precisely what Dara needed; in fact, the last thing she wanted was for the twig to root so she'd have to chop it down. Fortunately, as she'd already learned with the crystal sphere, it was much easier to change the shape—or the size—of an object than it was to change it into something else.

Gespry sat by impatiently while Dara experimented with enlarging the twigs. He did not share Dara's enthusiasm when she managed to transform a twig into a sturdy log.

"Don't see why you're so all fired to get into the damned castle, anyway," he grumbled. "Seems you wouldn't want to waste your time, since you know the Oracle ain't in there."

"Look how Lord Vanian's defended the place," Dara said evasively. "If he wants so badly to keep us out, mightn't there be something wonderful inside? Maybe more wishes. Maybe the secret of how to get from place to place without a key."

"Well, get on about it, then," he said, unconvinced.

Once Dara had mastered creating a log, she tried jabbing the twigs into the earth at the edge of the moat at a steep angle so that when she made the twigs grow, the log would fall properly across the moat to form the bridge she wanted. This, too, took several tries; Dara was both exhausted and jubilant by the time her efforts finally yielded a log sturdy enough that fell solidly across the moat. Then she remembered she'd need rope to climb the wall, and almost despaired.

When Gespry suggested that she try creating a wooden ladder instead of rope, Dara was dubious. She found to her surprise and relief, however, that after mastering logs, a plain wooden ladder was far simpler than conjuring hemp and, from there, fibers and a proper strong rope. She had to drag the heavy ladder across her makeshift bridge rather than carry it, but once that was accomplished, it was an easy matter to climb the wall.

From the outside the castle appeared to have a double wall, much like High Lord Haranor's castle did, and her view from the first wall confirmed this, although Dara was surprised to see that the inner wall was not substantially taller than the outer wall; nobody had built keeps with the shorter inner walls in a very long time. Fortunately the space between the inner and outer walls was dry, and although it would take some effort to haul the heavy ladder up and over the wall, passing through the walls promised to be an easy enough matter compared to what she'd done so far.

Both walls were as thick and sturdy as those she'd seen at High Lord Haranor's castle, crenellated and equipped with arrow slits and wooden shutters, although the shutters and the wooden hoardings had almost petrified, as if with great age, and the arrow slits were the old-fashioned vertical kind, not the modern cross slits to accommodate crossbows. The ground between the walls was thickly overgrown with weeds and brambles, without so much as a path to the inner gate. This gate, too, was locked and barred tight, with every sign of having been closed for ages.

When Dara had laboriously hauled the heavy ladder through the weeds and scaled the inner wall as she had the outer one, she was dismayed to see the castle courtyard in the same neglected condition. Of course, if this was indeed Lord Vanian's castle, he mightn't care much about the outside of the place, not if he merely appeared inside whenever he pleased, but still it seemed a poor way to run things. Why have the grounds and the courtyard there at all if they were only neglected and forgotten? And why have such elaborate defenses when the interior was let go to ruin?

To Dara's surprise, there appeared to be no windows to the castle and only the one door, and that as locked and barred as the gates. However secure the place might be kept, she'd never heard of anyone building a castle with no windows.

She turned to Gespry. "How did you get in?" she asked dubiously. "Did you climb to the roof? Is there a way in up there?" The thought dismayed her completely; her ladder wouldn't reach anywhere near that high.

"Huh! Not hardly," Gespry said sourly. "Nah, when I was here, the door was open a little. Just a crack, but a little thing like me don't need much. Guess things have changed. There weren't no moat then, like I said, nor the outer wall, neither."

Dara sighed exasperatedly. There were no windows, no door but the one, and that one closed up tight. Whoever built the place might well love his solitude, but must surely have a hatred of light and air!

Well, he might well have a hatred of guests, too, but Dara had no intention of letting that stop her, not after she'd gone through so much bother already. She thumbed through the grimoire and found a spell for opening locks. Almost as an afterthought, before casting the spell, she tried her own golden key in the lock, astonished when the lock clicked open. Gespry gaped openly.

"Now, if that don't beat all," he said, shrugging. "Never would've given a thought to using mine when I was here if the door hadn't already been open. Well, you're so bound to be in there; let's go!"

Cautiously Dara peered into the castle. The long main hall was lit by torches in wall sconces. The floor and walls were of the same dark stone Dara remembered. Shivering, Dara stepped inside.

The place was *cold*, and echoingly empty. Unlike the outer grounds of the castle, however, the inside showed no sign of neglect. The wall tapestries were fresh and seemingly new. Not so much as a speck of dust marred the stone block floor; no cobwebs stretched wispy silk in the corners. The echoing silence of the place was more chilling than the physical cold.

Dara didn't realize why the place unnerved her so much until she saw Gespry sniffing puzzledly. It was then that she realized what else was missing from the empty castle— all the smells she was accustomed to in High Lord Haranor's hall. There was no smell of food from the kitchens, oil from the lamps, dust or mildew or sweat or perfumes. There was no scent of strewing herbs from the floor or oil from the woodwork. There was not even a stale smell to the air, as she would have certainly expected; she could not even smell the burning wood and pitch of the torches. If it weren't for the familiar smells of the fruit in her basket, the old leather of the grimoire, and Gespry's slightly musty animal scent, Dara would have thought her own nose at fault.

Unlike the castle of her nightmarish evening with Lord Vanian, this castle at least had sensible doors and halls like any castle. At the end of the large entrance hall a door opened (without the slightest creaking of hinges) into the dining hall, and Dara was hard put to keep her reaction from her face. It was the dining hall she'd seen, or its twin; thankfully, the room was as empty as the entrance hall. The air held no memory of the smell of food or of the fire that had burned in the fireplace, and Dara wondered briefly if the whole dinner had been only a dream. Would that the rest had been!

A cursory search of the entry and the dining hall revealed nothing black in color, nothing that might be the Oracle, and Dara sighed regretfully. If this castle was indeed within the Crystal Keep, as she supposed it must be, she'd have to search the rest of the place.

Dara searched rather fearfully for the mirror she'd seen during her last visit, but there was no sign of it. Behind one of the tapestries, however, she did find a door leading to the kitchen. The kitchen was large and neat but otherwise featureless, but a small stairway led to a cellar pantry where they found, to Dara's astonishment and Gespry's delight, a good quantity of smoked and salt-cured meats and cheese and several casks of fine wine. Dara left Gespry rooting among the supplies while she continued her exploration.

A stairway led upward from the entrance hall. Doors on what Dara estimated to be the west wall revealed a number of rich suites. None of them held any particular interest. All were anonymous in their emptiness, no toiletries or clothes indicating occupancy, and Dara supposed they were guest suites. Starting back on the east wall, however, Dara hesitated, inexplicably reluctant to turn the knob of the door nearest the stairs. It seemed to tingle in her hand.

The room was exactly as she remembered it, from the velvet of the bed cover to the thick furs on the floor to the copper tub beside the fireplace. The copper tub, however, was dry and clean, and not so much as a speck of ash or shading of soot soiled the fireplace.

A glance around the room revealed nothing that Dara would presume to be the Oracle, but the room remained interesting simply because unlike the other rooms she'd seen, this one contained the cosmetics and jewelry Dara had seen previously, a selection of lovely gowns and slippers, the small dish of candied violets.

Another walk around the room, however, did reveal something of interest—or rather the absence of something of interest. Two of the wall sconces had been placed quite close together, and between them two small hooks had been driven into the wall. Dara had seen such arrangements in her own home and at High Lord Haranor's keep; generally a beloved portrait or perhaps a shield with the family crest was hung there on display. Had such a display been removed?

Could it have been the Oracle?

Well, if it had been removed, then it had been placed

somewhere else. Dara opened the second door on the east wall and found what might have been the lord and lady of the castle's suite, a larger set of rooms including a sitting room, a dressing room, and two bedrooms. But again, there was nothing of note to be found, and that left nothing but the last door, which presumably led to the tower Dara had seen from the outside. Resolutely Dara returned to the hallway and found the door open to the tower; it was locked, but her golden key opened it, as well as the door at the top of the curving staircase inside the tower.

The room at the top of the staircase was, if anything, larger and more luxuriously furnished than the one Dara had just left, and, like that room, showed signs of habitation. This room, however, appeared to be a man's room, judging from the suit of armor on a stand in the corner and the clothing she found. In fact, judging from the size and colors of the clothing, it might very well be Lord Vanian's room. The thought terrified her, and for a moment, heart pounding, Dara had to force herself to stand still and not flee; then she resolutely fought down her fear and resumed her inspection of the room.

She found what appeared to be a portrait sitting on the floor, turned toward the wall. It was the right size to fit the place she'd seen on the wall of the room below. Holding her breath, Dara turned it around, only to sigh with disappointment.

There was nothing black or even unusual about the portrait. It was the portrait of a beautiful young woman of regal air, with shining golden-brown hair and deep green eyes, with creamy pale skin. There was the faintest trace of a rather distant smile on her sweetly curving pink lips. Something about the portrait troubled Dara; then she realized that the young woman in the picture was wearing the same dress Dara herself had worn. Even the jewelry was the same.

"Dare I hope you were looking for me?" a light, mocking voice inquired, as Lord Vanian appeared abruptly in the doorway.

Dara's stomach lurched violently within her, but by dint of iron will she was able to keep her reaction from her face. She carefully lowered the portrait back against the wall and dropped one hand to her belt, where she could feel the comforting hardness of the knife there.

"Hope whatever you like," she said, surprised at the steadiness of her own voice. "That won't make it true."

"Ah, you wound me to the quick," Lord Vanian sighed, not sounding wounded at all. Then he laughed.

"Or would you prefer to wound me more literally?" he said. "Tell me, is that knife under your hand meant for me?"

"If I must," Dara said through clenched teeth. "Be sure that I'm prepared to defend myself."

"Why, my lady, was my lovemaking so inept?" Lord Vanian exclaimed, feigning hurt astonishment. "Indeed, I'd have thought otherwise from your response."

Dara felt her cheeks burn, and a mixture of anger and fear made her hands shake, but she said nothing.

"And what," Lord Vanian continued thoughtfully, "is your basis for comparison? I wonder. Since I'd swear you were virgin when you came to me, you must have had some adventure since. Have you been cavorting, then, with your furry little friend?"

Anger boiled up in Dara until the room seemed to swim, but she managed to keep her voice calm.

"My lord, if you must ever bespell maidens in order to seduce them," she said sweetly, "it seems that your love-making must be indeed insipid, and no doubt if I were to lie with swine I'd find it a favorable comparison. At least the boar pig comes by his beastly behavior honestly."

Lord Vanian's face clouded with an anger so cold that Dara shivered involuntarily. He leaned against the door frame.

"So now you seek honesty?" he jeered. "Truth, my

lady, I'd have vowed you came to my keep for love. Be warned, my innocent miss, that love and honesty seldom dwell in the same house, and then not harmoniously. And if you seek them both in the present, ask yourself if you've truly had them both in the past.''

"I've always been true to Cav,'' Dara retorted, "and he to me, or I wouldn't be here!''

Lord Vanian threw back his head and laughed.

"How delightfully naive you are!'' he exclaimed. "Answer me this, then, my lady who has all the answers: If an Heir loves the maiden but not the serving wench, and the maiden loves the man but not the Heir, then where is the truth in their love? And, in truth, will the Heir love the serving wench once he learns she's no longer the maiden?''

"Well, whose fault is that, I'd like to know!'' Dara retorted, although his words sent a spear of cold dread through her. She'd not allowed herself to think of what her lost virginity might mean to High Lord Haranor and High Lady Alberta—or to Cav.

"Ah, pardon me,'' Lord Vanian said, smiling coldly. "I'd quite forgotten my own beastliness! But in truth, while we speak of truth, your struggles against me were so feeble, your cries of refusal so faint, that clearly I missed them.''

"Because you deceived me—''

"That I did *not*,'' Lord Vanian said flatly. "As I told you, that simply isn't done. You deceived yourself, a common failing. Especially among lovers.''

"All right then, why did you do it?'' Dara challenged hotly.

Lord Vanian gave her a look Dara could not identify, then narrowed his eyes.

"Ah, lady,'' he said softly. "I shall answer your question—when you have answered mine.''

With that, he vanished.

"Damn all, I *hate* it when people do that!'' Dara shouted, stamping her foot. She was disgusted to find that she was trembling all over. She sat down on the bed; then she collapsed and wept helplessly.

"There, there, child," Granny's familiar voice soothed. A dry, gnarled hand patted her shoulder comfortingly. "Don't take on so."

Dara rolled over quickly, rubbing her eyes. Granny sat in her rocking chair beside the bed, and Gespry was perched on the edge of the mattress.

"How much of that did you both hear?" Dara asked crossly. Anger and humiliation rolled over and over in her mind until she couldn't tell which was which.

"All, or near enough," Granny admitted without shame. "I'd popped in to check on you, child, and this furry rascal thought you'd been gone a longish time. But don't take on, child, it does you no good and the lord no harm."

"Don't know what's got into the lord," Gespry scowled, shaking his head. "Had at you, did he? Guess it must've been a long time for him. Ain't like you're such a raving beauty—"

"Ah, begone, imp," Granny scolded as she saw Dara's eyes fill anew with tears. "This be woman's talk, and you're doing no good. Go back to your wine and be done!"

When Gespry was gone, Dara knuckled the tears from her eyes.

"He's right, though, Granny," she said slowly. "I'm no beauty; I'm nothing but a simple serving maid with no looks, no wealth, and no magic of my own. So he just did it to torment me, didn't he? Like you said, to make me miserable."

"Mayhap so, mayhap not," Granny said thoughtfully. "Best tell me the whole of it, child."

It was hard, but Dara obeyed, choking sometimes as she forced out the words but omitting nothing. Granny picked a cup of wine out of thin air and Dara drank it gratefully, this time glad of the relaxing effects of the drink.

"I suppose Gespry was right," Dara said finally. "I shouldn't have insulted him before and made him angry. I guess he got his revenge, didn't he?"

Granny thought for a moment, then shook her head.

"Not revenge, child. No, the lord's hard to fathom, but this ain't much like him, no, indeed. You don't know the full of his power, girl. Could've had you anytime he wanted, deary, if rape was to his taste—"

"Well, I guess it was!" Dara protested hotly.

Granny peered at her intently. "Ah, child, there speaks the blessed ignorance of a sheltered life," she said firmly. "Otherwise you'd know that rape can be a fearsome lot worse, and no mistake. You've been seduced, child, and fooled, mayhap; humiliated, we'll say that, too . . ."

Granny shook her head again.

"But it's beyond me, child, for it ain't like the lord a-tall; if that be revenge, he took it in a kindly way."

"Kind!" Dara said disbelievingly.

"Well, tell me this, child," Granny said patiently. "If you'd spent the first night in your man's arms, how much joy d'you think you'd have had of it? Or is he so practiced a lover, eh?"

"Well, of course he's not!" Dara said, flushing darkly. "Cav's never been with anyone else, of course—"

Granny cackled at that. "Now who's fooling who, eh?" She grinned. "Heir to such a kingdom, with fine ladies at his elbow at every meal and in his arms at every ball, all hoping to charm her way into the throne at his side? I'll wager your man's sampled a treat or two, and you none the wiser. But that's neither here nor yon. What irks me is this: If it were revenge, or even some odd whim, why'd he trouble with romancing you? Why'd he play the lover when he could've thrown you to the furs whenever he'd liked?"

"I don't know," Dara said embarrassedly, looking away. "I don't understand anything about him."

"No more do I, child," Granny sighed. "But doubtless he's got his reasons."

"Granny, how *did* he become the Guardian?" Dara said slowly. "I mean, he mentioned coming here himself, but—"

Granny Good was silent for a long moment, as if choosing her words carefully.

"From what you say," Granny said slowly, "I reckon he wished for just what he told you—a kingdom. I'd say he got it, didn't he?"

"But how did that make him the Guardian?" Dara pressed. "And why did he lose the woman he came here to win?"

"Well, he got his kingdom," Granny told her. "But to do that, he became the Guardian, and then of course he couldn't never leave, see? It were a foolish wish, child, foolish as most of us here've made."

"But what happened to the other Guardian, the one who granted Lord Vanian's wish?" Dara pressed.

"Oh, he went his own way," Granny said vaguely. "Here in the Keep, or outside if he'd chose. Soon's Lord Vanian became Guardian, see, he was free to go or stay as he liked—supposing he still had his key, that is, or could find one. Keep needs only the one Guardian."

Dara's eyes widened.

"You mean," she said, "that Lord Vanian can't ever leave here until someone else comes here and takes his place?"

"Ain't so terrible bad." Granny Good shrugged. "Don't get older, see, not in here, and there's plenty to see and do."

"But why did he lose his lady?" Dara asked.

"Well, he couldn't hardly go to her, could he?" Granny cackled. "And doubtless she wouldn't come here to stay forever, shut off from the world and her kingdom; what fool would? So to his way of thinking, he got his wish, but lost what he wanted."

"Oh, but that's awful!" Dara exclaimed. "No wonder he's so miserable and cruel."

She scowled. "But that doesn't excuse him," she said. "He may be miserable, but that's no reason to use such power as he's got to torment others."

"Ain't nobody to stop him," Gespry said, scuttling into the room with a full mug of wine precariously balanced on his head. He squatted in the corner and drank heartily. "Ain't nobody powerful enough."

"I'd think Granny could," Dara protested. "She seems to know as much about the magic here as Lord Vanian."

"Now wait right there, young miss," Granny Good admonished, shaking a gnarled finger in Dara's face. "*There* you step beyond yourself. You've a quarrel with Lord Vanian, but he's our lord, and this is our home. Ain't all of us loath to be here, either. Mayhap Lord Vanian could do a better job if he liked, but I don't much reckon *I* could. What'd you have me do, smack his bottom like a child?"

Dara sighed, understanding. Why should any of the inhabitants of the place challenge Lord Vanian? Unless they could physically send him from the Crystal Keep and take his power, it would become an endless war—and the Keep must have its Guardian. Besides, Dara doubted if Lord Vanian tormented the residents of the Keep as he did the visitors; why should he? Much more amusing to make life difficult for the defenseless visitors.

The only solution, of course, was that those visitors become *not* defenseless—as she hoped to do. And of course, that was what Granny had been saying all along.

All right, he'd seduced her, humiliated her, toyed with her—but she wouldn't fear him, no matter how powerful he was. She knew where his power came from now, and knew his bitterness, and she wouldn't fear him. Why, she came from an old and powerful family herself; all she'd lacked was her magic, and now she had that. Lord Vanian wouldn't find her such easy game from now on.

Granny smiled approvingly at the resolution on Dara's face.

"There you are, child," she said, nodding. "Go for what you want and if you meet him, why, meet him head on!"

"That I will," Dara said grimly, touching the comforting weight of the grimoire. "I'll learn every spell in this book if I have to."

Gespry scuttled a little closer, eagerness lighting his blue eyes.

"Say, there ain't a spell in there for putting a poor fellow like me back to his own shape, is there?" he asked hopefully.

Dara turned the pages, then shook her head. "There's the spell for dissolving enchantments, but if that would've worked, it would have changed you back when I took the sleep spell off you. There are more general transformation spells, but—but nothing just for restoring a transformed person," she said slowly.

"Well, couldn't you just use one of them transformation spells, or just *do* it, like you done the basket, then?" Gespry insisted.

"Gespry, did you see how many tries it took me to make the basket, and how the first ones looked?" Dara said exasperatedly. "It's not as though I have a dozen Gesprys to practice on till I get it right, and I don't even know what you looked like before. What happens if I try and get it *wrong*?"

"Oh." Gespry's voice was very small and quiet, and the strange creature shivered. "Hadn't rightly thought of that." Then he turned to Granny Good. "How about you? You don't seem to have no trouble changing things, eh?"

Granny cackled. "Wondered when you'd think of that, scamp that you are," she said, nodding. "And what'll you give for this favor, eh?"

"Ah, I ain't got nothing to trade, and well you know it, old hag," Gespry said, scowling. "And if I did, wouldn't be nothing you couldn't get yourself."

"There's one thing, little demon," Granny Good said thoughtfully. "For some reason Lord Vanian's got a powerful interest in this child—seems to be bound on making trouble for her. Now, he's cautious of me, seeing's I been here so long, and it could be I'd draw the lord's notice, too, and the child don't much need that; besides, I'm not as spry as you. So say you stay with this child and look out for her, just as you've been, till she's done here, or till she loses her key, and I'll do the trick for you then.''

Gespry groaned. ''See here, old witch, ain't I got troubles enough? I already agreed to three days of being dragged about, with Lord Vanian liable to turn me into something even worse if he took a mind. Now you say she's got the lord's attention, and so I'm to scuttle along after her while the lord sends dragons and earthquakes and whatever else suits him to plague us?''

''Well, that's my price,'' Granny said adamantly. Her eyes twinkled. ''Course, mayhap the lass will hone her spells sharp enough to do it herself, and she's a kindly thing—like as not she'd help you for some trifling price. But excepting you're with her, you'll never know, eh?'' Before Gespry could answer or Dara could comment, Granny was gone, only a last squeak of her rocking chair marking her departure.

''Ah.'' Gespry growled disgustedly. ''May as well give in as argue. Seems as 'tween the two of you and Lord Vanian I'll have no peace. Afore long I'll be wishing myself back in that swamp with worms and frogs to eat and fell-beasts for company.''

He turned to Dara, sighing resignedly.

''Well, seeing as you got me, I'd advise we get out of Lord Vanian's bedroom before he decides to come back,'' Gespry said wryly. '' 'Cause if he pops back in and sees you lying there on his bed, he might take the wrong notion, see?''

''Oh.'' Dara hastily slid off the bed, scrubbing tear tracks from her cheeks. ''Yes, we'll go. Gespry, what did you find in the cellar?''

Gespry shrugged. ''More wine, some good brandy, a few more hams and such, but not much else to eat or drink,'' he said. ''But what's it matter, seeing as you can make food anyway?''

"It's easier to make it out of *something* than nothing," Dara said patiently. "And it isn't ever *easy*. But what I'd really like is a lamp and oil—even candles. And especially weapons—a real dagger, or even a kitchen knife." She chuckled to herself with the realization that she certainly had more practice in wielding a kitchen knife or cleaver than she did a dagger. "Or maybe I can just bake a wonderful peach pie and poison him with it," she added, chuckling again.

Gespry snorted. "Remind me to stay away from your pies, then," he said, baring his sharp little teeth in what passed for a grin. "But as for daggers, what's the matter with that one?"

Dara glanced over to where Gespry was pointing. On the bedside table was a dagger in a sheath. Dara frowned; when she'd searched the room before, there'd certainly been no dagger there on the table. A little hesitantly, Dara drew the dagger from its sheath. She knew nothing of such weapons, but it seemed well made, straight and sharp, far superior to her poor makeshift knife. A gift from Granny Good, most likely; the other possibility, far less pleasant, was that Lord Vanian had placed it there. And especially if the dagger belonged to Lord Vanian, what would happen if she gave nothing in trade?

After a moment's thought, Dara sheathed the dagger and thrust the sheath through her belt, leaving her pitiful, crooked knife in its place on the table. If Granny Good had left the dagger, she'd appreciate the joke; if Lord Vanian had put it there, he *wouldn't*, and that was just as good.

Dara was even more eager to leave Lord Vanian's room than Gespry was, and she limited her visit to the cellar to the briefest of searches. As Dara had no experience with making wine, especially the fine vintage Lord Vanian had served, Gespry insisted that Dara fill and take a skin from the cellar; Dara, however, was more interested in the lantern and oil she found, plus the crockery bowl she took from one of the kitchen cabinets.

It was a pure relief to leave the chill, empty castle. Dara was glad to see that her ladder was exactly where she'd left it propped against the inner wall; it would be all too like Lord Vanian to have somehow taken it away. The time to climb both walls again, dragging the heavy ladder along, seemed gratifyingly short in comparison to the hours it had taken on the laborious journey in; of course, this time she didn't have to create bridges and ladders and open locks.

Despite Gespry's grumbling, Dara took the time and trouble to drag her ladder across the wide field to some bushes where she could leave it concealed. If for some reason she had to return to the castle (and she desperately hoped she'd never have to see the place again), the effort to hide the ladder was small compared to the trouble it'd probably take her to create another.

When she and Gespry reached the lake, however, Dara stopped, staring into the still water while she thought. Despite all her efforts, despite Granny Good's help and Gespry's, she was no closer to finding the Oracle than she'd been when she started. Why, she'd braved Lord Vanian's castle again for nothing at all—well, nothing but a dagger, a bowl, a lamp, and some wine and oil. Even her magic hadn't been much help.

Not yet.

Dara sighed and pulled out the crockery bowl, kneeling to fill it with water from the lake.

"Say, you ain't going to try that spell again?" Gespry grumbled, and Dara almost spilled the water in her surprise. She'd completely forgotten Gespry there on her shoulder. She laid the bowl down carefully and lifted Gespry from his perch.

"Gespry, what do you know about the Oracle?" Dara asked him thoughtfully. "How it works, how it moves, what it is?"

"Nothing," Gespry said, shrugging. "That's a question you'd better have asked Granny Good, mayhap."

"Well, there must be others," Dara pressed. "What

other demons would you think know anything useful about the Oracle?''

"Now, how am I supposed to know that, girly?" Gespry said patiently. "Ain't as if that swamp I was in was such a garden spot that lots of folks chose to visit, and I got into only a few other spots before I got stuck there. Lord Vanian's the one who'd know most about the Oracle, I suppose, and you ain't much going to ask him, eh?''

"Not much." Dara sighed again and leafed through the grimoire until she found the divination spell she wanted.

"That spell didn't do you much good before, did it?" Gespry said.

"You said you were a cobbler, didn't you?" Dara asked him. "If you were nailing a sole to a shoe and you used too short of a nail, would you blame the hammer when the sole came off? I just haven't asked the right questions yet. Living in High Lord Haranor's household and watching the nobles at court's taught me plain enough that sometimes you can't come at a thing straight on; you've got to go all around it sometimes and find the right side to sneak up on it. Magic's the same way. Now be quiet and don't spoil any of my questions this time.''

She cast the simple spell and thought carefully about her first question before she spoke.

"Besides Lord Vanian, Granny Good, and Gespry, show me what inhabitant of this keep can tell me most about the Oracle," Dara said.

The water shimmered and clouded, then cleared. Dara gasped at the picture in the still water, for curled around crumbling blocks of tumbled masonry was a dragon, its metallic scales gloriously rainbow-hued in the sunlight. Its gigantic wings were folded along its side and its tail twitched slightly in slumber like a cat's; abruptly its silver eyes opened and the creature raised its head, as if Dara's surveillance had awakened it. Dara hurriedly stirred the water with her finger, breaking the image.

"Show me the view from the door through which I must

pass to find this creature," she said, her voice shaking.

The water cleared again. The image showed the frame of the open door; beyond it was a sort of forest denser than any Dara had ever seen, luxuriant with strange, vibrantly green plants that grew so thickly together that Dara would have despaired of ever pushing her way through but for the narrow track leading into that growth. She remembered the place vaguely; it was one of the doors she'd marveled at when Gespry was leading her deeper into the Keep.

"Show me the object or service I must give this creature in exchange for his knowledge," Dara said. That was presuming, of course, that she could manage to bargain with the dragon before it killed and ate her.

The water cleared again, showing Dara standing before the dragon, extended hands offering the purple gem she'd found in the swamp. The water cleared again.

"All right then," Dara said, pouring the water out onto the ground. "Gespry, have you ever seen that door?"

"No, and I don't much want to," Gespry retorted. "Girly, that ain't no demon, that's a dragon! Your spell might've showed what you could give, but that don't necessarily mean that's all the dragon might *take*, starting with your legs and working on up! Now, I might not be worth the trouble, seeing's I wouldn't make even a mouthful for that creature, but that wouldn't stop me getting charred to coal while it was roasting you!"

"Then you don't have to come in with me," Dara said patiently, although the vision in the water had stunned her as much as it had Gespry. How could one bargain with a dragon? Dragons were animals—exceedingly dangerous, clever ones from what she'd heard, but animals nonetheless. Dara had never heard of anyone talking with one—for that matter, she'd never heard of anyone getting close enough to *try* talking to one, not while the dragon was still alive, at least. "You can stay far behind me, or even stay in the hallway, if you like."

"Oh, there's a good thought," Gespry said sarcastically.

"Then when you're dead and eaten and your key melted or swallowed, I'm stuck in the hallway, or stuck in there with the dragon."

Dara swallowed her irritation. If she'd been stranded in a stinking swamp for years—perhaps decades—she'd be just as eager to pursue any chance of freedom, and even more reluctant to endanger any such chance. She half thought of letting him keep her key until she finished her errand, but she banished that idea immediately. Whatever the laws of the Keep about equal value might be, that was simply too much temptation to put in Gespry's hands.

"All right," she said at last. "Tell me what door you want me to put you through and I'll leave you there until I'm done with the dragon, one way or another. That way if I'm killed, at least you're where you want to be. Granny Good will change you back to your human body then, and she said you'd learn how to get about without a key eventually anyway, didn't she? So what would you like, the orchard?"

"Ahhh." Gespry scowled. "Then I'll be sitting there wondering what's happening, half eating myself up with it. Guess I'll have to take my chances with you." He shrugged a little sheepishly. " 'Sides, guess I'd be breaking my deal with Granny if I let you go off alone."

Dara suppressed a smile. "You can follow behind me, then," she said. "So that if I get into trouble, you can come rescue me."

"Yeah, right," Gespry said, chuckling mirthlessly. "More'n likely I'll be just in time to be the dessert."

"Well, just between the main course and the dessert," Dara admitted, "I'm scared, too. But I can't think of anything better to try."

Gespry was still scowling, but he let Dara lift him to his usual perch on her shoulder.

"So now I've gone from a snack for a fell-beast to dessert for a dragon," he muttered darkly. "At least the cursed fell-beasts could be expected to stay in the water."

This time Dara ignored his complaints as she stepped through the door into the hallway. At least Gespry was going to be with her. Although Dara knew there was precious little the demon could do to help if the dragon *did* intend her harm, his mere presence was comforting.

Strangely the idea of confronting a dragon didn't seem as terrifying to Dara as it once might have. Warriors had faced dragons and survived, so she knew they were living, mortal creatures like herself; she'd certainly had no such knowledge of the Guardian of the Oracle when she came to the Crystal Keep, and despite his nasty tricks and all his power, Lord Vanian hadn't managed to kill her yet. And if this dragon was seeking something—something Dara could trade it—then it had nothing to gain by killing those who might be carrying the very object it sought.

Dara hoped desperately that the dragon had also thought about the advantages of such forbearance.

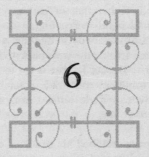

6

"**L**AST CHANCE," DARA SAID, TWISTING THE golden key between her fingers. "I can put you back in the orchard if you like, or the castle, or any of the others we've seen." There'd been a good few, too; it had taken Dara what seemed like most of a day of searching, opening the peephole on each door to find the one they were looking for. The search had given Dara a new sense of wonder at the Crystal Keep, as well as discouragement of her own quest; there were seemingly an eternity of doors, each opening on its own strange landscape, and any one of them could hide the Oracle.

"Last chance for you, too," Gespry returned. "You sure you want to trade that wish away? Might be you could figure out how to use it. Then you wouldn't need to bother with the Oracle or Lord Vanian or the dragon, neither."

"I've tried everything I can think of," Dara said, touching the hardness of the stone through its cloth wrapping. She had, too; she'd cast divinations until she was exhausted, asking the question "How can I use this wish?" in every possible way she or Gespry could imagine. She'd gotten no answer for her trouble. Either she still hadn't found the proper way to ask the question, or the proper spell, or, as Gespry suggested, perhaps such a question was "against the rules" and therefore her spell couldn't reveal what she wanted. Either that or perhaps, Dara suspected, Lord Vanian had a hand in preventing it.

"If I could think of a way to use this wish, I'd be gone as quick as I could find my way back to the beginning," Dara said wryly. "But as I can't seem to find out how to use it myself, I might as well trade it for knowledge I *can* use. If I actually can trade with a dragon, that is. I say again, do you want me to put you somewhere until I'm done bargaining?"

"Nah." Gespry scratched his head. "Curiosity's got the better of my good sense, I guess. I ain't never heard of anybody trying to talk with one o' them things. 'Sides, that dragon's sure to be something to see, hey?"

"I'd imagine so," Dara said with a shiver. "All right then." She inserted the golden key into the lock and turned it, opening the door; taking a deep breath, she stepped through.

Dara had been amazed in her divination at the image of the incredibly dense forest filled with such strange plants, but as soon as she stepped through the door the reality left her stunned and almost reeling, Gespry for once shocked to silence on her shoulder.

For one thing, nothing she'd seen had prepared her for the sudden oppressive heat, the thick, steamy air that seemed to clamp over Dara's nose and mouth like a hot, soggy towel to stifle her breathing. After she'd weathered that assault, there came another—an incredible clamor of sounds from birds, or insects, or beasts, or all three, that she'd never heard before.

"What sort of place is this?" Dara gasped, her chest heaving as she fought to breathe in the heavy, wet air. It was like being in a small bathing room after too many people had bathed in very hot water, and she wanted desperately to clamp her hands over her ears to block out the racket. "Gespry, have you ever seen anything like it?"

"Not hardly," Gespry said sarcastically. He, too, was panting in the heat, and moisture was beading on his fur. "Ain't like any forest I've ever seen. It's greener even than the brand-new leaves in springtime, ain't it?"

"Greener than springtime, but hotter than midsummer," Dara agreed. "Merchants from the far south coast talked about hot, wet places like this. Let's follow the path. If we're going to be killed and eaten by a dragon, let's get it done with before we have to bear too much more of this place."

Dara carefully stayed on the path, ducking to avoid the vines that frequently hung down. Before long she was slapping at insects, too, mosquitoes and midges and smaller biting insects she didn't recognize and, in fact, could barely see. Once a brilliant red snake slithered almost under Dara's feet, and she jumped and screamed. She'd never seen a red snake before, and who knew what poisonous creatures there might be in a strange place like this?

The trail seemed to go on forever, twisting among the strange plants like a snake itself, and the farther Dara advanced into the strange place, the more nervous she became. Dragons were dangerous enough, but who knew what other perils existed in such a bizarre world?

It seemed as though she'd stumbled along the twisting little path for miles before the dense growth opened abruptly into a clearing. Dara immediately saw what had held back the luxuriant foliage—she stood on the edge of a cluster of ruined block structures unlike any Dara had ever seen or heard of, and the ground was likewise paved by similar stone blocks that had tumbled from their places. A few enterprising vines had twined down around the blocks from the trees, and a few plants had pushed up between the paving stones, but otherwise the open area had remained relatively clear.

Dara cautiously edged a little closer until she could

climb up onto one of the stone blocks for a better look. The area of the ruins was larger than she'd thought at first; instead of a single group of tumbled buildings, there appeared to be several such groups interrupted by small stands of trees that had burst up through the blocks; likely the small groups of structures had at one time been a single plaza. Dara decided reluctantly that she'd have to venture deeper into the ruins, as there was clearly no dragon near her, nor any structure large enough to hide one. Now that she looked, she realized that nothing she saw looked much like the particular ruins that she'd seen in the basin of water.

She plucked Gespry off her shoulder, eliciting a yelp of surprise from him, and set him on one of the blocks.

"Maybe you should stay a little distance behind me," she said apologetically. "That way if the dragon or—or anything else is stirred up by my noise, you can duck behind one of these blocks. Besides, I'd hate to fall on top of you; I'm not very good at climbing."

"Nah, but I am," Gespry said staunchly. "I'm smaller and faster, too. Be smarter if I went on ahead and called back. If *I* stir something up, I can get out of the way quick—up into the trees if I gotta, and that'll give you time to duck down, eh? 'Sides, I can smell the critter already, and I can tell when we're getting close easier'n you can."

"Thank you, Gespry," Dara said gratefully. "That's very brave of you."

"Ah, ain't so brave when you can skitter out of the way as quick as I can," Gespry said, shrugging. "Got a lot of practice jumping around in swamps and dodging fell-beasts and other nasties. Just follow me, girly, and we'll see what we'll see."

After all his fear and grumbling, Dara was surprised to see how nimbly Gespry skipped from block to block, from tumbled heap to crumbling wall. When he reached the edge of the cleared area, he turned back around.

"Come ahead, then," he said. "But try to stay up on

them blocks, see? I seen a couple snakes down on the ground. Likely to be more there, basking in the sun.''

Dara shivered and followed Gespry more gingerly, careful to stay well up from the paving blocks. She quickly found that despite her much longer legs, she couldn't jump easily from block to block as Gespry did, and some stones, balanced precariously, rocked ominously under her as they had not under Gespry's lighter weight. Once she almost pitched forward from the weathered stone she'd jumped on a little too hastily; then she saw a swarming knot of green snakes below and yelped, overbalancing backward so she sprawled heavily on the rocking stone.

''A—a *couple* of snakes?'' Dara panted when she could speak again. ''That's a whole crawling nest of them!''

''Yeah?'' Gespry came hopping back and peered nonchalantly over the edge of the block. ''Guess you're right. Want to catch 'em?''

''*Catch* them?'' Dara gasped. ''Why?''

''Why, they're good eating, girly, snakes are,'' Gespry said. ''Better'n worms and swamp croakers, anyway.'' He snickered. ''But they ain't as good as your stew, nohow. Come on, or you want to sit in the sun all day, too?''

There was only one answer to that; Dara was already dripping with sweat and itching furiously from insect bites. She scrambled hurriedly after Gespry, giving the snakes one last glance as she did so. Snakes had always terrified her.

Once again Gespry skipped ahead, guiding Dara through the maze of ruined buildings, once or twice detouring to one side to avoid walls that seemed too ready to tumble down or, in one case, what appeared to be an empty well with seemingly no bottom. Dara stopped when Gespry disappeared from sight, but he quickly returned; to Dara's dismay, he was shivering.

''Found your dragon,'' he said. ''Bigger'n it looked, too. Lucky for us it's sleeping sound. Come on up and have a look.''

This time, after checking the ground ahead of her carefully, Dara preferred to wind her way along on the paved space between the fallen blocks, rather than jumping from stone to stone above. As dangerous as it might be to startle a dragon out of its sleep, she felt safer creeping more quietly along on the ground where she could take shelter behind the crumbling walls if she must—not that Dara had any illusions that the tumbled buildings would provide any shelter against a determined attack by a dragon.

The moisture and the overwhelming scents of the flowers and foliage had temporarily clogged Dara's nose, but as she crept closer Dara could detect a harsh, metallic scent that quickly overlaid the others. She'd smelled that scent before, when warriors had brought slabs of dragon meat to the castle for the High Lord's table. Terrified, but at the same time fascinated, Dara quietly peeped over the crumbled wall in front of her.

The dragon was there, just as Gespry had said, and its appearance utterly banished all thoughts of the heat, the insects, and even her fear from Dara's mind. For a moment of complete inner stillness, Dara could only stare in wonder at the marvelous creature before her.

The vision in the basin had no more than hinted at the incredible beauty of the glorious beast that lay half in, half out of the tall arched entrance to an unusually ornate and intact building that might have been a temple. From the portion of the beast shaded by the arched doorway, Dara could see that the dragon's scales were a gold as pure as a new-pressed Sun; where the sun's rays touched the bright scales, however, the scales threw back the light in sparkling rainbow hues as brilliant and varied as the gemstones in High Lord Haranor's crown. The huge wings, folded, heaved slightly with the creature's breath; Dara wonderingly realized that when unfolded, each wing would span a dozen man-heights or more. The long neck curved around snakelike so the huge head rested like a cat's on one paw. For the first time Dara realized the creature was male; female dragons, she'd heard, lacked the bony ridges that formed a sort of crest at the back of the creature's head. The dragon was snoring loudly, like the rumble of a wagon full of copper pots bouncing over paving stones.

"Stay here," Dara whispered to Gespry. "I'll go talk to it." Gespry nodded eager agreement.

Dara dug the purple gem out of her basket, leaving the basket with the rest of its contents behind the wall with Gespry. She'd approach the dragon with the gem in her hands. If the dragon saw that she had something it wanted, it might be less likely to flame her immediately. Dara climbed awkwardly to the top of the wall and sat there, one leg hanging down the back. For whatever good it would do her against an angry or hungry dragon, she could jump quickly down behind the wall if she had to.

The dragon continued its slumber undisturbed; at last, taking a deep breath, Dara cleared her throat loudly.

The dragon snored on.

Dara cleared her throat again, more loudly.

Snores.

Well, she was hardly going to jump down from her wall and tickle its nose with a feather. Dara picked up an egg-sized loose stone from the top of the wall and sighed resignedly. There were probably few better ways of getting a dragon angry than waking it from slumber by bouncing stones off it. Dara shrugged, sighed again, and tossed the stone as gently as she could. It bounced neatly off the dragon's nose, right between the slightly smoking nostrils. Dara might have congratulated herself for her aim, but the space was almost as broad as she was tall; it would have taken a poorer arm than hers to have missed.

The dragon gave one final snort and stirred drowsily, its silver eyes opening slowly. It yawned thunderingly and stretched, its tail stirring and knocking a few blocks from the top of the archway. Dara heard what sounded like cannon blasts, realizing that it was only the sound of the dragon's monumental joints crackling as it stretched. She shivered where she sat, aching to drop behind the wall and out of sight.

The dragon yawned again unhurriedly (the blast of warm air almost toppled Dara from her perch) and gazed unsurprisedly at Dara. It sniffed the air delicately, and the silver gaze flickered from the purple gem in Dara's hand back to her face.

"Brave child, to throw rocks at old Yaga and wake him from his slumber," the dragon rumbled lazily, his voice as sweetly musical as the finest wooden pipes. He flexed his claws; the rock groaned and cracked open beneath the massive talons. "Desperate child, to dare such a thing."

"With respect, Sir Dragon, I don't know that I can claim much bravery, but I suppose I'm desperate enough," Dara said. Strangely, she could feel her fear fading. She'd made her gamble; if the dragon wanted to kill her now, it would, so there was no profit in worrying too much about it. "I came to ask you to share your knowledge of the Oracle—what you can tell me, that is," she added hastily, "and whatever you can tell me about the Crystal Keep, too, would be welcome. And I've brought you this in trade." She held up the gem.

"Ahhhhhh." Yaga raised his head slightly until his eyes were level with Dara's. "And do you know what that is that you hold, desperate child?"

"It's somebody's wish," Dara said. "A wish that was never used. I tried to learn how to use it myself, but—"

The dragon threw back his head and made a trumpeting sound like boulders crashing down a mountain; the sound shook Dara's wall until she feared it would topple. She realized the dragon was laughing, and that realization made a hot rage rise inside her. Why, the oversize lizard could char her to an ember if it liked, or squash her under its foot like an ant, or swallow her whole, but she'd be pickled in brine before she'd sit here while the thing laughed at her! Without thinking, she grabbed another rock and threw it, this time as hard as she could. It bounced harmlessly enough off the dragon's neck, but the creature's laughter faded to a thunderous chuckle and it turned again to gaze at her.

"If you laugh at me again," Dara said in measured tones, "I'll turn you into a swamp croaker, and don't think I don't know the spell to do it." In fact she didn't; even if she had, such powerful transformatory magic would probably be far beyond her paltry skill. "I'm getting very tired of being laughed at."

"I beg your pardon, fierce lady mage," Yaga said gravely, swallowing a last chuckle. "You must forgive my poor manners. It has been some time since I entertained visitors and I fear I have become quite inexcusably rude. Pray do not turn your powerful magic against me. I was only . . . surprised, perhaps, that you did not realize that you can use, of course, no wish except your own. How could it be otherwise? I thought it was a jest you were making; else why bring it here to me?"

Disappointment and confusion shocked Dara to momentary silence. Well, *that* was why her divinations hadn't worked; the spell couldn't tell her how to use the wish if she could not, in fact, use it. But hadn't Granny Good said, or at least implied, that she could use the wish herself? Perhaps Granny hadn't known that Dara couldn't use any wish but her own, or perhaps Dara had misinterpreted Granny's words. Perhaps this trade with Yaga was the "use" she was supposed to make of the gem.

"If nobody but the one who made the wish can use it," Dara asked slowly, "then who would want to trade for it?"

"Why, any denizen of this keep who had never gained their wish, of course," Yaga said smoothly. "Such as myself. If that is my wish, then I can use it, and I will right gladly trade whatever knowledge I can impart for the chance to know if that is mine."

"And what if it's not?" Dara asked cautiously.

"Then I have lost nothing but a few hours of my sleep, and gained at least a momentary diversion," the dragon said indifferently. "And as I have little to do *but* sleep, and most generally lack for diversions, I am likely getting the best of the trade in any wise. So if the wish is not mine, you may take it with you when you go. Meanwhile, sit and ask what you will. Would you fancy a bit of boar? The meat is a trifle high, but all the tastier for it." He turned his head on his long neck and reached down for something over his shoulder; his head came back with a largish chunk of very smelly meat in his mouth.

"Ah, thank you, Sir Yaga, but I think not," Dara said hastily. "I've never been able to stomach boar. If you don't mind, I'll make myself something else—and would you object if I called my friend out from behind the wall?"

Yaga sniffed the air again and made a sound suspiciously like a chuckle.

"By all means, be comfortable, and your friend with you," he said politely.

It took some coaxing to persuade Gespry to leave his refuge, and even when Dara had retrieved her basket and climbed down from the wall, settling herself on a block near the dragon, Gespry stayed slightly behind her, not venturing forth even when Dara had conjured up meat pies and spicy seed cakes. The tempting aroma of the food somewhat countered the far less pleasant odor of the rotten meat that Yaga nibbled from time to time.

As they'd just settled down to dinner, and as Yaga seemed quite affable for a dragon, it seemed rude to get right down to questions about the Oracle. Dara tried to remember the polite conversation she'd heard in court.

"Have you been here long?" she asked at last. Most nobles liked to talk about themselves and their adventures.

"Long? Forever, or perhaps but a moment," Yaga said mysteriously. "What is time in a place where time does not walk? I came, and I remained, and I am."

So Yaga had been a visitor, then, like herself.

"Were you always a dragon?" Dara asked lamely. She couldn't imagine how a dragon could have fit through the door to the Crystal Keep, nor any of the doors inside. Too, Yaga's behavior was quite unlike that of any dragon she'd ever heard of; she'd never heard of one doing anything besides stealing cattle and flaming warriors.

"Was I? Am I?" Yaga mused. "An interesting philosophical question, that. Truth to tell, my child, I cannot remember. So perhaps it *has* been a long time."

"You don't remember how you came here?" Dara asked, surprised. Then she wondered if he'd perhaps eaten plums out of the forest with the strange, hostile boy-beasts. If he had, likely he'd forgotten that, too. At least he remembered his name. Hopefully he still remembered *something* of value to her. "Do you remember what you came for, what you wished?"

Suddenly Yaga thrust his head so close to Dara that she nearly toppled backward off the block on which she was seated. The strange silver eyes, each the size of her head, regarded her gravely.

"Indeed I do remember," Yaga rumbled. Hot breath rank with the smell of dragon and smoke and rotten meat blew Dara's hair back, and behind her, Gespry clung trembling to her tunic. "And that is one question, little one, that you will not ask and I will not answer."

"Naturally I'd never pry," Dara said hastily, praying that Yaga would pull back before she either fainted or vomited, either of which was likely to offend the dragon mightily. "It's none of my affair, of course."

Yaga did draw back, to Dara's utter relief, and settled himself again, half closing his eyes.

"I dream bedtimes of a fair land of silver trees and crystal waters," Yaga murmured, "where flowers perfumed the breeze and golden fruits hung ripe on the vine, where I danced in moonlight, following a song so sweet and terrible that it pierced my soul. It seems to me I came following that song, and when I tried to claim it as my own, found that it had moved beyond my grasp. Perhaps it was only a dream." He sighed, a sigh that made the earth shiver. "And perhaps it ever shall be only a dream."

Dara tried to picture a dragon dancing, especially in a grove of trees. Perhaps that was how clearings came to be made in the forest. Very *large* clearings. More likely Yaga had been a man once, or perhaps an elf—strange things were said of elves, although Dara had never met one herself and had heard that they lived in great cities, not near forests.

His eyes opened and focused again on Dara.

"But it is your dream, child, which has led you here to me. Tell me the tale of your journey, that I may know how to school you in finding your heart's desire."

"You sound just like a bard," Dara said shyly. It had been hard enough to tell Granny Good and Gespry, her friends, of all that had befallen her since she'd come to the Crystal Keep; it seemed almost more than she could bear to tell this ancient creature, so dignified and beautiful, of her humiliating and undignified adventures. But tell him she did, sipping wine to fortify herself, sometimes blushing, sometimes scrubbing tears from her cheeks, until she'd told him all. At the end of her tale she felt that indeed she *had* paid a price already for whatever he might tell her, and if her sorry story was the kind of "diversion" he sought, Yaga was far from the noble creature he seemed.

At the end of her story, however, she was amazed to see two great crystal tears roll from the dragon's eyes and splash onto the blocks below, splattering Dara with salt water.

"What sacrifices love demands," Yaga rumbled. "And what courage and strength it gives. I had forgotten the terrible beauty of it—how the gods themselves bow before its might. You are very like young Vanian."

"Like—him?" Dara said, wrinkling her nose. The very idea would have been laughable were it not so disgusting. "I don't see how I'm like him at all."

"I'd bloody hope not," Gespry muttered darkly from behind her.

Yaga eyed her gravely.

"He came here like you, bringing this richest of treasures, this most powerful of weapons, into the Crystal Keep, and yet called himself impoverished and unarmed. He walked in the light that dimmed the sun, yet saw only darkness. That was his downfall, and it will likely be yours."

"I don't understand," Dara murmured uneasily.

"Do you like riddles?" Yaga asked suddenly, and Dara frowned, confused and suspicious at the change in subject.

"Not very much," Dara said cautiously. Riddling with dragons was likely to be a dangerous pastime. Especially if she lost.

"These are simple," Yaga reassured her. "What is the coin which when spent returns a thousandfold, yet when kept, leaves you poorer than when you began?"

"Love, I suppose," Dara said slowly.

"Love is one answer," Yaga told her. "Hatred is another, for they are two sides of one coin. Here is another: What is the sword which, used to defend, makes you strong, yet used to attack, makes you weak?"

"Love—and hatred, I suppose," Dara added quickly.

"And here is the third," Yaga said. "What is the brightest light of all, yet casts no shadows?"

"Love and hatred?" Gespry guessed, peering around under Dara's arm.

"Only love," Yaga corrected gravely. "Yet glance away from that light for only a moment and you find yourself dazzled, stumbling blindly into darkness. When you walk with your eyes veiled in shadow, you can easily miss that dark and misty line separating love from hatred—but once you have crossed it, you will not easily find your way back again. Long ago Lord, Vanian strayed over that line from despair, just as your anger leads you ever farther into the shadows. Each time you act from anger and hatred, you take another step along that road. Follow your anger far enough and you, too, will be walking in darkness like Lord Vanian, calling his weakness power and his emptiness wealth because he cannot bear the truth—because for him there is no more light.''

''Were you—were you here when Lord Vanian came?'' Dara asked curiously. If Yaga had been here so long he'd forgotten who he'd been before he came, surely he'd been here longer than Lord Vanian. Unless, of course, he'd had a good bellyful of those plums!

Yaga chuckled. ''How young he seemed then, very unsure and full of dreams,'' the dragon sighed. ''In love, yes, and very much in love with love.''

''You met him before he was the lord?'' Gespry asked, hopping out from behind Dara to confront the dragon.

''Indeed I did,'' Yaga said soberly, ''as I was Guardian before Lord Vanian.''

''You were the Guardian?'' Gespry choked.

''Aye, for longer than I care to guess,'' Yaga said sadly.

''But how did Lord Vanian become Guardian?'' Dara asked Yaga. ''Did he—he didn't defeat you in battle, did he?'' The thought that Lord Vanian had been able to best a dragon and the Guardian of the Crystal Keep so long ago, even before he'd come to the fullness of his power, was terrifying.

''Defeat me?'' This time Yaga roared with laughter. The ground shook, and a couple of blocks tumbled from the wall where Dara had been sitting earlier. Gespry squealed and ducked back behind Dara. Yaga's great wings unfolded and fanned the air with his mirth, their sweeping length knocking limbs from nearby trees, and tremendous gusts of wind almost blew Dara and Gespry from their seat. Sunlight shimmered off glistening scales, and for a moment Dara was as awed as she was terrified. At last Yaga noticed the disastrous effect he was having and calmed himself with some difficulty, folding his wings back against his sides.

''Defeat me?'' Yaga said more quietly. ''If it could be termed conflict between us, I would name myself the winner, for he is Guardian and I am freed from that burden. Nay, he came to me wishing for the kingdom he said he must have in order to win the woman he loved, and my own kingdom was the only one I could grant him. I gave it to him right gladly, and in giving it I gained my own freedom and he lost his, for his kingdom and his power lies only within these walls. He raged against the limitations of his power, trying mighty spells to circumvent the laws of the Keep, but it was in vain, and then he learned that the noble lady he had courted had tired of the wait and wedded another. A sad tale, but I have seen many such in my time.''

Dara shivered. Yaga was right; if Lord Vanian had indeed wished for the kingdom he needed to win his love, it was very like the wish she'd also thought to make, for the magic she'd need to win Cav. Had she made that wish, she might well have had all the magic of the Keep at her disposal—and there she'd be, like Lord Vanian. But had the wish she'd actually made been any wiser?

''You mean he got to be the lord just by wishing for it?'' Gespry said disgustedly. ''Varak's chamber pot, guess I should've wished bigger!''

''Very few who come here think well on their wishes before they make them,'' Yaga said gravely, giving Dara a significant look. ''Oftentimes they find that what they wished for was not truly what they desired—or sometimes, to their surprise, that it was.''

''Did I make the wrong wish?'' Dara asked quietly. ''Lord Vanian laughed as if I had.''

''Did you?'' Yaga returned, just as softly. ''Only your heart or the Oracle can tell you that, young one, and you have not found the Oracle, and perhaps your heart is not yet ready to answer.''

''Well, what about the Oracle, then?'' Dara said eagerly. ''I don't know what it looks like, nobody's allowed to tell me where it is, and it moves all around. How can anybody ever find the Oracle, or do the ones who do just happen on it by luck?''

''There are those who court luck like a lover,'' Yaga told her, ''but I think they find her a fickle bedmate. And what is luck in this place, where all things are shaped by will alone? Is it luck that you found me? Is it luck that I am yet here to be found? To you it might seem so. To me it might not.''

That was true enough, Dara had to admit. She'd thought herself lucky to stumble across Gespry in the swamp, but doubtless Gespry wouldn't have called himself lucky to have been trapped there for so long.

"All right, but how do I find the Oracle?" Dara pressed. "Can you tell me what it looks like, at least?"

"Can I tell you." Yaga tilted his head contemplatively. "Yes is the answer, and no. There is no law that says I may not, if that is what you ask. But I cannot tell you what I do not know. I have seen the Oracle, yes, and it seems to me that perhaps I asked a question and was answered. Yes, perhaps. But what the Oracle was to me and what it is to you are not the same."

"You mean the Oracle moves around and it changes its shape, too?" Dara said despairingly. "How can anyone ever find it, then? It's impossible!"

"They find it," Yaga said sternly, "by asking themselves the right question—not how to find the Oracle, but how to look for it."

Dara fought down frustration. Was Yaga only toying with her as Lord Vanian seemed to so enjoy doing?

"All right then," Dara said as patiently as she could. "How should I look for it?"

"That I cannot tell you," Yaga said regretfully. "But I can help you tell yourself."

"Then help me, if you can," Dara said from between gritted teeth. Was this creature never done with its riddling?

"Who controls the Oracle?" Yaga asked her.

"Lord Vanian, I suppose," she said. "He's the Guardian, after all."

Yaga chuckled. "You truly believe that?"

"Well, who else, if not him?" Dara asked impatiently.

"Who else indeed. And who places the Oracle?"

Dara's eyes widened. "Why, Lord Vanian!" she said, startled by the thought. She'd understood that the Oracle moved, but she'd never thought it *was* moved.

"And where, then, and how would the Oracle be hidden?" the dragon asked gently.

"*I* don't know," Dara said crossly, more than a little tired of all this. "Where Lord Vanian doesn't think I'd look for it, I suppose."

"Mmmm. You have arrived near enough to your destination, though you chose a circuitous road." A little smoke drifted up from Yaga's nostrils. His eyes were sharp. "And *why* would the Guardian hide it, if indeed he did so?"

"Why, because—" Dara stopped. Why indeed? Because it was some law of the Crystal Keep? Because visitors' fumbling searches entertained him? Just to be cruel?

"I don't know," Dara said slowly.

Yaga nodded approvingly.

"Indeed you do not," he said. "But when you do understand why the Oracle is hidden, and how, then you will know how to find it. Or at least how to look for it."

Dara grimaced. The last thing she ever wanted to do was learn anything more about Lord Vanian, especially firsthand. But there *was* one other thing she did want to learn.

"That mirror, the one Lord Vanian used to show me Cav," she said. "Was that only a trick of his, or is there such a thing here in the Keep?"

"The mirror is real enough," Yaga told her. "I have gazed into it many times myself. But be warned. Self-deceit is simple and deadly in this place, as you have learned. The mirror is like the Oracle or the wishes granted by the Guardian—it grants you no protection from your own foolishness. The mirror will show you what you wish to see— and if you have already decided in your heart what that is, then that is assuredly what you *will* see."

Dara shivered, understanding all too well what Yaga meant. She'd been drunk and foggy, distracted by unaccustomed wealth and luxury, weary of her gritty and unpleasant adventures—all too anxious to see Cav exactly as she *had* seen him. His very appearance, however, should have given her her clue that all was not as it seemed. Cav was undoubtedly concerned for her, but he wouldn't have been gaunt and unkempt with worry. Likely he'd had the palace mage cast a divination from time to time to see how she fared, and knowing that she was alive and safe, he wouldn't have worried further. There was nothing he could do anyway.

"All right," Dara said at last. "I'll remember that. But where would I find this mirror?"

Yaga sighed with exaggerated patience.

"You do not need me to answer that," he said.

Of course, Lord Vanian had the mirror, as she knew very well. Dara nodded reluctantly.

"Y'know, though," Gespry said slowly, "there's no need for it, really. There's spells aplenty in that grimoire, ain't there, and anything you wanted to see in that mirror you could see just as easy with your own spell."

"He is perhaps correct," Yaga agreed, his eyes twinkling. "A great mage such as yourself, who could turn a dragon to a paltry swamp croaker, may have no need of magical mirrors."

"Well, maybe I was exaggerating just a little," Dara admitted. "I couldn't really have turned you into a swamp croaker. But I *can* cast spells if they're not too complicated." And it would be a considerable relief not to have to look anywhere near Lord Vanian for the mirror, or to bargain with him for its use if he had it.

"Perhaps you were exaggerating . . . just a little," Yaga returned, gently mocking. "But at one time Lord Vanian was no more powerful than yourself. With perseverance and determination you will grow strong; with patience and understanding you will grow wise. And if you remember the love that brought you to this place and do not wander too far into the shadows, you will remain fit to use the power you wield."

"You've been a great help," Dara said gratefully, although she was far from sure that she'd actually gained anything of any real value from the dragon's rather cryptic remarks. At least she felt that Yaga, unlike Lord Vanian, had genuinely *tried* to help her; he was simply too old and strange for her to understand completely. And there was really no knowing, of course, what limitations might be placed upon him—upon any demon in the Crystal Keep—to restrict what he could tell visitors. Whatever powerful magic had created the Keep, it had doubtless assured that the Keep's secrets would not be told.

"You've been very helpful," Dara repeated. She held out the purple gem. "Thank you."

Yaga dipped his head briefly in acknowledgment, then reached out with one gigantic forepaw. The very tip of one razor-sharp claw touched the gem with amazing gentleness. A long moment passed, while Dara held her breath, watching gem and dragon intently. Then Yaga slowly withdrew his claw, and Dara was once more spattered with salt water as two great tears splashed to the stones.

Yaga turned his head away and crept backward until almost all of his bulk lay within the shadowed archway of the building. He curled himself tightly there, resting his huge head on one paw, his face still averted.

"You may go," he said, his voice a mere whispering rumble.

Dara glanced down at the purple gem in her hand. At the moment it seemed a hateful thing, a deceitful, fraudulent bit of magic that promised hope and delivered disappointment. She stuffed it back into her basket and covered it with rags again, glad to hide it from sight.

"I'm sorry," Dara murmured, turning away. She picked up Gespry and her basket. Gespry was silent, too, as Dara made her way quickly back through the strange, steamy forest. Perhaps he was thinking of wishes lying scattered throughout the Keep, just waiting to be claimed. But then, they'd do him no good; Gespry had already gotten his wish, such as it was.

A thought struck her suddenly. Was her wish hidden somewhere in the Keep as this one had been? If she found it, could she claim it without paying Lord Vanian his price? She shook her head in frustration. That would have been a proper question to ask Yaga; now, of course, it was too late. She had nothing to trade for more answers, even if she could bring herself to disturb the sorrowing dragon again.

7

DARA STEPPED BACK THROUGH THE DOOR into the hallway, sighing at the sudden relief from the wet, oppressive heat. She realized disgustedly that she was dripping with sweat, her clothes and hair positively sodden with it, and she could feel tiny insects wriggling about inside her clothing over her wet skin.

"Look, girly, can't say as I've ever wanted two baths in as many days," Gespry said wryly, scratching vigorously, "but I'd be obliged if you'd make a stop at that there lake, or even the cave. I'm all acrawl."

"I am, too, and bitten half raw," Dara admitted. "All right, a bath it is, although after that hot air, I'd rather have cold water than warm. Let's find somewhere we can stop for a bit and I'll conjure up some soap." Soap, she thought wryly, was one thing she knew a good deal about from her serving maid days.

She'd seen another door with a promising-looking stream, when they'd been searching for Yaga, and it wouldn't hurt to fill one of her skins with fresh water while they were at it. Gespry might have a head for all that wine that they were carrying, but Dara certainly didn't.

Dara was wary and alert when she stepped through the door, remembering the forest where the strange hooved boy-beasts had lived, but although she had to follow the little stream into a forest before she found a pool deep enough for bathing, this wood had none of the ominous heaviness of the forest where she'd found the plums. This was a young wood in late spring, the trees slender, the leaves the bright, fresh emerald of spring rather than the tired, dusty green of late summer. The water of the stream was clear and sweet and very cold, apparently running down from mountains Dara could see distantly beyond the forest.

Dara conjured up a good quantity of soft soap in her bowl, and she washed her clothes thoroughly first, grimacing as tiny insects floated away down the stream. She hung her clothes over a bush to dry in the sun, then ventured into the cold water for her own bath, no longer worried about Gespry's occasional leering glances. Her former modesty seemed petty and stupid now; if Gespry couldn't even manage to escape his swamp prison alone, he certainly couldn't change his form to make himself any danger to her. It occurred to Dara belatedly that she might as easily have created new clothing for herself as washed the old, but somehow the idea of discarding perfectly good garments just because they were *dirty* seemed terribly wasteful, something Lord Vanian might do. That thought comforted her; whatever Yaga might think, Dara was *nothing* like the arrogant, cruel lord.

"Gespry, do you think my wish is just lying around somewhere?" Dara asked while she lathered her hair.

"Dunno," Gespry said, shrugging. "I don't reckon so. I mean, I figure them's just wasted wishes you've found—wishes folks didn't get, like Yaga. I got my wish, such as it was; I just made a lousy wish, is all. And you ain't lost yours yet. So I don't reckon they're there to be found."

Dara sighed. It had been a tempting thought, tempting

enough to keep her hunting aimlessly through the Keep forever. Then again, the Keep was full of such delightful self-deceptions, as well she knew, and she'd already paid a heavy price for one of them. She couldn't afford any more.

"Gespry, how many of the demons in this keep have you met?" Dara asked idly. Perhaps there were others who might not know as much as Yaga, but could answer her questions less mystically.

"Just a few," Gespry told her. "Granny Good, of course, and Lord Vanian, if you can count him. Kelara, she's the birdwoman, you won't get no sense out of her. Skivvit, he's one of them you met in the woods where the plums grow."

"One of those things?" Dara said, appalled. "And you *know*—him?"

"Well, things were a little different back then," Gespry acknowledged. " 'Sides, can't say I know Skivvit and his pals all that well. Not the kind of folks you exactly want to spend time with, if you catch my drift—not that they had the same kind of interest in a stringy ol' fellow like me, y'understand, as they did in a juicy bit like yourself." He eyed Dara's naked form appreciatively. "Can't say as I blame 'em too much. Ain't many women end up here, specially not young pretty ones. Anyhow, Kelara and Skivvit's all I ever passed words with. There were a couple of visitors came through the swamp, but they pretty much ended up dead before I ever made conversation."

"This birdwoman, was she here before you?" Dara asked.

"Reckon so, else I'd never have met her," Gespry said wryly. "Seeing as after I lost my key in that swamp and never went nowhere after that, and I'd only been through a few of the doors, too. But you won't get nothin' out of her. She don't even talk."

"Then how did you learn her name?" Dara said practically.

"Granny told me." Gespry scratched again, scowled, then hopped down to the river and dug a lump of soap out of the bowl, lathering his fur again and scrubbing vigorously. "*Three* baths in two days. You want to go see that dragon again, you can go alone."

Dara rinsed the soap out of her hair and glanced around suspiciously before she climbed out of the water and sat down in the sun near her clothes.

"I keep expecting Lord Vanian to appear," Dara said, sighing. "Ever since the first time he popped in while I was bathing in the cave, I can't stop looking over my shoulder."

"Well, talking about him and thinking about him's the best way to get his attention so he *will* show up," Gespry told her. "I'm surprised he didn't pop in while we were talking to that dragon, seeing as we talked about him so much. 'Cept maybe if Yaga was the old lord, he must be powerful enough to make Lord Vanian leave him alone if he wants."

"Granny Good must be like that, too," Dara said, hope flaring again. "Lord Vanian doesn't like it that she helps me, but he hasn't tried to stop her. Maybe he can't." She reached for the grimoire.

"What, you think there's going to be a 'Lord Vanian be gone' spell in there?" Gespry scoffed. "Think he'd have left the thing lying around the library if there was? Nah, if Granny and that dragon are too much for the lord, it's because whatever nasty sort of thing he can come up with, they can either stop it or do worse right back to him."

"That's a tempting thought," Dara admitted, leafing thoughtfully through the grimoire. There were powerful magics used in warfare; maybe the grimoire might contain such spells.

Then she hesitated. Her weak, new skill with magic was doubtless far short of what she'd need for great battle magics. Besides, she remembered uncomfortably what Yaga had said about the line between love and hatred, and how

Lord Vanian had been led into his own darkness. So likely she should concentrate on her quest—finding the Oracle so she could gain her wish and go home and marry Cav— rather than focusing on her anger at Lord Vanian.

But as Lord Vanian was the one with whom she had to bargain for that wish, and as he seemed bound to oppose her in her search, how could he not be a part of every decision she made? And how could she not feel anger, even hatred, after what he'd done?

Still, she couldn't easily discount Yaga's advice. If she didn't want to end up like Lord Vanian (although she still couldn't imagine how that would be possible), she'd best keep her mind off revenge—as far as she was able, at least. But a good defensive spell or two couldn't hurt on any account. That wasn't revenge; that was just plain common sense. And while there might not be a "Lord Vanian be gone" spell . . .

Dara thumbed through the grimoire and swore. She knew there were spells to block divination; there was one cast on one of High Lord Haranor's meeting rooms, so that any business requiring utter security could be conducted in confidence. But there was no such spell in this grimoire, which, admittedly, was rather elementary. Of course, Dara thought to herself, that was why Granny Good had given it to her in the first place. She wasn't up to much more than basics.

"All right," she said decisively, pulling her clothes from the bush. "I'm going back to the library. Do you want to stay or come?"

"What, y'think I want to stay here and take another bath, maybe?" Gespry said wryly. "I ain't much for books, girly, but seeing as you make the food, I'm best with you. Not that this mightn't be a bad place to stay," he admitted after a pause, "though it'd be a better spot in late summer or early fall, when there'd be plenty of nuts and berries and such. Still, it bears remembering, long as you don't go losing your key."

Dara shuddered at the thought. Imagine being trapped here for eternity, transformed into some hideous form, slowly losing her memory of herself like Yaga, or descending into outright savagery like Skivvit and his companions, all the while subject to the torments and whims of Lord Vanian!

Not that, Dara thought grimly, clenching her hand white-knuckled around the golden key. *Never that. I'd kill myself sooner.*

Dara rinsed and filled a skin with the sweet clear water, checked her belongings one last time, and carried Gespry back to the hallway. She was beginning to wish there was some way to mark the uniform doors; she'd passed so many that it was becoming difficult to find a particular one without going back to the beginning and counting each one.

The library was just as she'd left it, but this time there appeared to be no Granny Good to help her find what she wanted. She could only hope there was a larger, more detailed grimoire in the library, probably in several volumes. By now Gespry had a better idea what to look for and could actually be some help searching; however, there was another treasure Dara hoped to find here—a history of the Crystal Keep, perhaps journals left by previous Guardians. It seemed reasonable to believe that if such a book existed, it might be found here.

Several hours of searching later, Dara had located what appeared to be an extensive grimoire, although it was written in Almandim, a language of which Dara had a less-than-perfect knowledge. She'd have to find or make pen and paper and laboriously translate each spell she wanted; if she had to cast a spell hastily, there was no telling what catastrophe a single misspoken word might cause.

She'd found several books apparently concerned with the Crystal Keep, although they, too, were written in other languages, none of which Dara recognized. Inked pictures, however, on the pages of one book depicted scenes that

Dara found immediately familiar—the fountain she'd seen when she'd first entered the Keep, the golden key she herself wore, one of the hallway doors, and even a sketch of Yaga. She found one she could read, but by that time she was too exhausted to begin the thick volume. She'd sleep first, then start on the books the next day.

Dara hid the chosen volumes carefully behind other books on one of the shelves (just in case Lord Vanian didn't want her reading them and decided to take some action to prevent it) and set aside even the books on the Keep that she couldn't read; perhaps she'd see something in the drawings that could provide a clue.

By the time she'd finished her extensive search, Gespry was grumbling for dinner. Dara was so tired she could well have skipped food, but Gespry could hardly go pick fruit for himself in the library. She managed to conjure some rather tepid and lumpy porridge but lacked the energy or concentration for anything better; she didn't even attempt to produce bedding, but simply curled up in a corner with a book for a pillow. The hard floor didn't trouble her at all; she was asleep before she had time to notice.

Dara woke to the unmistakable prickling at the back of her neck that told her she was being watched. She stretched, unexpectedly comfortable, then opened her eyes—

—and bolted upright as she saw Lord Vanian sitting comfortably at a nearby table, his feet up, watching her amusedly. Dara gasped as she realized she was no longer lying on the bare floor; now she was sitting on a thick goosedown mattress over what felt to be a straw ticking, a warm woolen blanket over her.

Dara clutched the blanket around her protectively even though she was still fully dressed; steel armor wouldn't have seemed enough at that moment.

"Fair morn, my lady," Lord Vanian said smoothly. He removed his feet from the desktop, and a silver tray loaded with platters of food appeared in their place. Dara couldn't see the contents of the platters from her low level, but she could smell hot bread, bacon, and stewed fruit. "Something hot to break your fast?"

Dara's initial thought was to refuse indignantly, but of course that was what Lord Vanian was expecting. She laid the blanket aside reluctantly, ran her fingers through her rumpled hair, and stood with as much dignity as she could muster.

"Thank you," Dara said, turning to pull another chair to the desk. "Usually I like a wash in the morning before I eat, but today it can wait."

"You're everlastingly bathing," Lord Vanian chuckled. "Soon you'll know the location of every puddle of water in my keep."

Dara broke a piece from a steaming bannock and buttered it thickly.

"Cleanliness and clothing are two things that don't seem to last long hereabouts," Dara said, shrugging as nonchalantly as she could while stifling a dizzying mixture of fear and fury. Gods, had he somehow been watching her every time she bathed? "High Lady Alberta was like my mother—she insisted on a clean house and clean servants in it. Elsea, the old woman who ran the kitchen, used to look behind our ears and under our fingernails every day. She'd take us out back and scrub us with a stiff brush and harsh soap if we weren't clean enough to suit her."

"What was it like, being a servant?" Lord Vanian asked, a faint gleam of interest in his eyes.

"Not as nice as having them." Dara shrugged. "I suppose it depends whose household you serve in. Lord Haranor and Lady Alberta had a very strict, very formal household, but he was the High Lord—they had to keep up appearances. They were very kind and generous, too—saw that all the servants learned to read and write and that we had plenty of good clothes, and we ate almost as well as they did. They dowered the girls well, too, if they got married.

"Mother and Father only had a few of the village girls," Dara continued. "They didn't expect as much of them, but they didn't take as much interest in them, either. I don't imagine it's much fun anywhere, but it's better to serve than to starve." She sighed. "I suppose I've lost my place in Lord Haranor's household, just running out as I did. Lord Haranor and Lady Alberta would be glad to see me gone. They didn't like Cav spending so much time with me."

"Ah, yes, your noble paramour." Lord Vanian chuckled and nibbled at a thick piece of bacon. "And why did your lover not rescue you from your dreary world of chopped turnips and dirty platters?"

"That's none of your affair," Dara said firmly. In point of fact, when it became apparent that High Lord Haranor and High Lady Alberta might not soon consent to her wedding Cav, Cav had offered to buy her a house in the town and provide whatever she needed; he'd hastened to add that his offer was in no way contingent upon Dara giving him her favors in return. Dara had of course refused; she could no more bear to live like a leech on Cav's generosity than she could on her parents, and pride demanded that she earn her bread. She'd wondered afterward in some of her doubting moments whether Cav had made the offer only because he knew she'd refuse. Cav's parents certainly would not have stood for such an arrangement if they learned of it.

"Of course, you're no lordling's kept woman," Lord Vanian said gravely. "You prefer the dignity of your turnips and dirty pots."

Dara started to snap back at him, but controlled herself with difficulty. If Yaga was right, the two most valuable ways she could help herself were to master the make-magic of the Keep and to learn a great deal more about Lord Vanian. She couldn't afford to give way to her temper.

"Almost every member of my family, for ten generations or so, have served as mages to noble and royal houses," Dara said steadily. "I'll grant you that it's not the same as being a kitchen serving maid, but most times noble folk need a maid a lot more than they need a mage. I guess I'd never thought much about it before, but the High Lord and Lady of Caistran can't make it through the day without me and all the others. Why, High Lady Alberta wouldn't know how to draw her own bath. I've gotten by on my own for a good few years, and I can do for myself what noble folks need me to do for them. So maybe there *is* some dignity in turnips and dirty pots. Maybe more dignity than there is in rich nobles who don't know how to wash their own bottoms without a servant's help."

Lord Vanian's eyes narrowed. "Should I infer from your tone that you include me among your pitiable and helpless nobility, regardless of the small detail that I have not a single servant to wash my bottom for me?"

Dara put on her prettiest, falsest "sweet serving maid" smile and said with exaggerated humility, "Why, I'd never dare to speculate on such a subject when I know so little of m'lord's personal habits." Then she dropped the sweet smile. "And what little I know is far more than I wish."

For a moment Lord Vanian's brows drew down ominously; then his anger appeared to evaporate and he laughed heartily.

"A fair thrust, my lady, but I'll not return the strike. Have another pastry and tell me why you don't number your beloved heirling among the rest of us impotent nobility."

Dara was silent. Cav was the one subject she didn't want to discuss with the arrogant Lord Vanian; somehow the very act of talking about their love to the mocking lord would cheapen it. Lord Vanian would never understand what Dara had felt that first day when she'd stumbled in weary and dirty from the road and seen the handsome lad in his patched leathers currying his horse, her annoyance at his seeming impertinence, her humiliation when she learned he was the High Lord's Heir, her confusion when he'd approached her later.

Handsome young Heir; impoverished, naive young maid—Dara had heard that story, or variations of it, too many times not to be cautious, even though she wasn't beautiful enough to fit the usual description of the sweet young maiden. She owed it to her family—and to herself as well—to show better sense than to lose her virtue and possibly her hard-won position over the first handsome, well-spoken young lord who came along. But Cav had never been anything but gravely polite and friendly, without turning on her the dazzling easy charm she saw him display so often to the visiting noble ladies at official functions. He had, not surprisingly, heard of her family line and was interested in the tales of great magical deeds passed down through the generations. He was interested, too, and appeared impressed by Dara's adventures as she'd made her way to Caistran.

Cav had encouraged Dara, too, during those first hard weeks in the High Lord's household while her muscles protested the unfamiliar tasks of sweeping floors, scrubbing dishes and pots and tables and those same floors, and wringing wet laundry. The first night the fierce hard aching of her arms and shoulders had wrung hot tears from Dara's eyes even when exhaustion overcame pain and she slept. When Cav passed her in the hall the next day, he hadn't asked about her stiff movements and her red-rimmed eyes, and Dara had not complained, but when she staggered to her pallet that night, a jar of salve and a flask of a sweet blue potion had been tucked secretly beneath her pillow. By morning, when Dara woke deliciously refreshed and miraculously free from pain, she'd begun to love Cav, just a little. In retrospect she didn't know what had touched her more—that he'd cared enough to ease her pain, or that he'd respected her enough to leave her her pride.

In the days to come Cav often appeared when Dara would least expect it—taking one handle of the heavy pan of milk Dara was bringing back from the dairy, helping Dara thread the spit through a huge side of beef, or simply breaking the monotony of scraping mounds of turnips by sitting on the edge of the table and chatting with her, good-naturedly ducking the occasional paring that flew his way. The other servants whispered and chuckled knowingly, and most of them shunned Dara, but she didn't care.

Soon she was spending every free moment in Cav's company, when he wasn't busy with his own duties as Heir. They went riding outside the city walls (guards at a discreet distance), or walking in the gardens, or they'd simply sit in the library, Cav's favorite refuge, and talk. He'd made no overtures toward her until Dara had begun to feel rather disappointed; then as if divining her thoughts, Cav had led her to a secluded alcove in the sunset garden and quietly told her of his feelings for her, his wish to marry her. He'd kissed her work-roughened knuckles, then waited to read the assent in her eyes before he'd laid his second kiss on her lips. He would approach the High Lord and Lady privately that same day and win their approval of the match.

Cav's parents, to their credit, had not immediately ridiculed Cav's announcement that he wanted to take a plain, penniless kitchen maid to wife, nor had they banished Dara from the staff, as she'd feared. Neither, however, had they given their permission. Cav abashedly told Dara that they'd indulgently said that once they'd confirmed Dara's ancestry and a midwife had testified to her virginity, perhaps they'd discuss the matter. In the meantime Cav would be wise to put the needs of Caistran first and consider the advantages of wedding a young lady of his own station who would bring lands and alliances to the marriage.

Cav had told Dara solemnly that he would convince his parents of his resolve in time, and eventually they'd give their consent. If Dara could unleash her family's legacy of powerful magic, the prospect of bearing an heir with such a gift would surely sway High Lord Haranor and High Lady Alberta in her favor.

"Ah, such a scowl." Lord Vanian chuckled, startling Dara out of her woolgathering. "Is your fury directed as usual at myself, or must some other poor buffoon bear its sting this time?"

Dara sighed and put down her cup.

"I've told you a good deal about me," she said. "Why don't you talk about yourself instead? I've never known a lord who didn't like to do that."

"Ah, but you haven't met a lord who's had practically nobody but himself to talk to for the gods alone know how many years," Lord Vanian said lightly. "I already know about myself. Therefore I'd rather hear about you. Tell me, doubtless your precious lordling has wondered why the daughter of a family of mages had no magic herself. Have you never succeeded in learning why?"

Dara shook her head, suppressing her irritation as Lord Vanian once more found the most painful subject he could probe.

"Maybe that was the question I should've asked the Oracle," she sighed. "But I thought that even if I was answered, that didn't mean that the answer would solve the problem. Everyone's always rumored that it was a curse on my family. Powerful mages always make enemies."

"Rather a puny curse if it only affects you, and not the mage who incurred the curse," Lord Vanian chuckled. "And there are far worse curses, come to that, than to live without magic. Almost everyone does, after all."

"It's not that," Dara said patiently. "It *is* a small curse. That's why it's so bad. If Mother and Father, both powerful mages, couldn't detect and avert such a simple curse, how good can they really be? Mother lost her position in Lord Evander's court, where she'd been employed since before I was born, and not nearly so many people come to consult with Father since I came of age."

Lord Vanian chuckled. "And you?" he asked. "Do you think your family was cursed?"

Dara shrugged. "Maybe, maybe not. There are plenty

of mages' children who aren't mages themselves. But my father's line have all been mages as far back as anyone can remember, generation after generation. The story goes that one of Father's ancestors won the gift of magery for himself and all his descendants from a demon—a real demon, not the kind who live here—on a wager. They've always married powerful mages, too; it's almost a family duty. Everyone just assumed I'd be a mage, too, unless there was some reason why not." She sighed. "And I would certainly love to know what that reason is."

Lord Vanian leaned back in his chair, his eyes narrowing as he smiled.

"Perhaps I could tell you," he said. "Perhaps we could strike some bargain."

"How do you think you could do that?" Dara asked suspiciously. "Unless you're going to show me the Oracle?" she added hopefully.

"Why should I need the Oracle, when I've got my mirror?" Lord Vanian said casually.

Dara's heart gave a great thump, but she managed to calm herself before her surprise showed in her face.

"I don't know that I'd feel wise striking any more bargains with you," she said slowly. "Besides, if you could do it with the mirror, I could do it myself with a divination spell."

"Perhaps with the same degree of success you've had with your other divination spells," Lord Vanian said, chuckling. "You have power, my dear, but proper divination requires subtlety, skill, and experience that only time and practice can give. And obviously the answer has been concealed somehow, or your parents and your noble paramour would have learned it, wouldn't they? But the mirror is powerful magic, and *I* know how to use it properly," Lord Vanian said pointedly. "Of course, I could let you use the mirror yourself—" His eyes glinted mischievously. "But then would you 'feel wise' to dare my mirror again?"

"Meaning no offense, but not with you anywhere

nearby,'' Dara returned. ''Nor do I care to make any bargain with you, either. If my magic's what I need to win Cav, you'll have to give it to me when I've learned your price, and if it's not, then I'll just do without, won't I, and it won't much matter why I don't have it.''

''Ah, now there's a question,'' Lord Vanian said, obviously delighted rather than offended by her answer. ''Does it indeed matter or not? For instance, if your family *has* been cursed, will you pass that curse down to your children? Or perhaps even your husband?'' He shrugged negligently. ''But perhaps that doesn't matter either.''

Dara broke off another piece of hot bread to cover her confusion. What game was the lord playing now? For some reason he obviously wanted her to know the answer to her lack of magic; or more likely, he wanted her to *want* to know. That way he could torment her with her curiosity and try to manipulate her into some outrageous bargain.

But however little Dara wished to acknowledge it, Lord Vanian *had* raised a valid point. What if her family line *was* cursed? Dara had never really thought seriously about the possibility, mostly because everyone else seemed to make that blind assumption. She knew her parents were as fine mages as they professed to be; the chance that one of them might have been cursed and failed to detect and break such a curse seemed vanishingly small. But what if it was true? What consequences might she be bringing on Cav and, by extension, Caistran? What consequences might she be bringing on their children?

One thing was certain, however: She didn't trust Lord Vanian, not his motives nor his honor nor anything he might tell her, whatever the ''rules of the Keep'' might be about lying.

''I thank you for your kind offer,'' Dara said politely. ''But I'll get by on my own, I believe.''

''Of course you will.'' Now Lord Vanian's tone was almost unbearably smug. ''But in case you find yourself wishing for my company, take this.'' From nowhere he produced a small silver bell, ironically similar to the one High Lord Haranor kept at his place at the table to summon the servants. "Just ring it when you want me, and I would be delighted to answer."

Dara left the bell on the table; truth to tell, she didn't want to touch the thing.

"Thank you kindly, Lord Vanian," she said, "but I'd feel more comfortable knowing you *wouldn't* come if I didn't ring it than that you would if I did. Besides, it's hardly my place to go ringing for you like a lazy chambermaid. As I said, I'll get by as best I can on my own."

Lord Vanian smiled mockingly. "I'll leave you to it, then." This time Dara actually saw him disappear; in the merest second, he was simply gone.

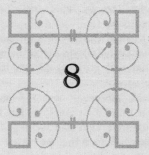

8

DARA SIGHED AND DROPPED HER EYES, THEN had to laugh. Lord Vanian had left his small feast behind, whether out of forgetfulness or, more likely, to show Dara his superior skill—that he could produce sophisticated dishes while she was confined to simpler food. He didn't realize, of course, that cooking for a High Lord and Lady had entailed learning to make the most luxurious dishes known in the country.

"Gespry?" she called, realizing she hadn't seen the odd little creature for some time. "Are you hiding?"

"And what else?" There he was, on top of one of the bookcases, peering anxiously down at her. "You can let your mouth get you into as much trouble as you like, missy. No bargain I done with you makes me eager to go getting the lord angry at *me*."

"I'm only trying to learn more about him, as Yaga said," Dara said patiently. "Come and have some breakfast. I haven't tried making anything this fine yet."

Gespry wasn't too frightened to scamper down from the shelf and stuff his mouth with the fine pastries and rich-flavored bacon. Dara resumed her examination of the books they'd found. The grimoire looked to be useful, in a tedious kind of way; Dara would have to copy each spell, and the time to do so was more time spent in the Keep and not searching for the Oracle. The other books, those she couldn't read, contained only one item of interest—somebody had tried to map the Keep, and had drawn a sketch of the corridor and labeled almost a hundred of the doors.

Of course, she couldn't read the labels, so it was more frustrating than helpful.

The other book, however, was far more promising. It was apparently a journal of sorts, undated of course, with no notation to identify who had written it, but from some of the entries Dara believed that the writer was either a past Guardian, or perhaps a visitor-turned-resident, like Gespry. Mostly it contained inexpert sketches of strange landscapes, some of which Dara had seen in the Keep, some not; there was a sketch of Granny Good, too, at her spinning wheel. The few entries were brief and disjointed as if the writer seldom bothered to open the book.

"Two new doors today. Does another come with each one?"

"No matter how far I go, the only end is the beginning."

"It was always within me. How could I not have seen it?"

"Searched a dozen doors since I've been here. Found nothing but despair."

"Once I prayed that this was all unreal. Now I pray it is real, for it is all I have left."

It went on like that for pages and pages, seemingly random ramblings of perhaps a lunatic mind. The last entry was on a page by itself.

"The only way out is deep inside. If only I had had the courage to open the final door."

"Gespry, what do you think this means?" Dara asked idly, reading the passage.

Gespry shrugged, peering at the book.

"Girly, in case you ain't figured it out, I ain't much the bookish type," he said wryly. "Reckon you'd know more than me. Just sounds mist-witted to me."

"It sounds mist-witted to me, too," Dara admitted. "But this whole place is sort of mist-witted, isn't it? Maybe you have to be mist-witted to understand it."

"Well, next time you see the lord you can tell him that," Gespry chuckled. "You done called him everything else I can think of."

"*I* could think of a few more names," Dara muttered grimly.

"Well, don't," Gespry said, glancing around uneasily. "Just eat the food he gives us, and if you can't be grateful, then I'd be much obliged if you'd be quiet before . . . somebody . . . hears it."

"Well, do any of these make any sense to you?" Dara said impatiently.

"Just the one about the songs," Gespry said, shrugging. "Read that one again."

Dara leafed back through the pages. The handwriting was the same throughout the book, but sometimes it was sloppy and hurried; at other times the writing was elaborate, as elegant as a scribe's.

"Here it is," Dara said. " 'Her songs are mad and maddening, celebrating grief.' " She shook her head. "You know what *that* means?"

"Nah, I know it don't mean nothing," Gespry said patiently. "Just that whoever it was met Kelara, the one I told you about."

"I thought you said she didn't say anything," Dara said.

"She don't, just sings, and no words, either," Gespry said. He glanced at Dara and sighed. "Guess that's where you're wanting to go next, eh, just like that, and I reckon you expect her to speak to you, even though she don't never say nothing. Girl, you just ain't got no sense, jumping here and there like a swamp croaker and expecting answers to hit you in the face."

Dara scowled and closed the book. Gespry was right. She'd simply been running here and there, snatching rather blindly at any new idea. She'd not outwit Lord Vanian that way, nor second-guess the Keep, either.

All right. The first priority was her wish. Lord Vanian had to grant that wish, and Dara had to ask the Oracle what price she must pay Lord Vanian—and pray that it was a price she was willing and able to pay. So she must therefore find the Oracle, which Lord Vanian would prevent her from doing if he could. Therefore her priorities remained the same—to increase her skill with magic, both defensive and divinatory, and to learn where Lord Vanian had hidden the Oracle. And to do the latter, little though she liked it, she'd have to understand how Lord Vanian thought.

Slowly Dara reached for the silver bell, picking it up very gingerly to be certain it didn't ring. She took a strip of rag from her pack and wrapped the clapper securely, then muffled the entire bell in a thick swaddling of cloth. The very last thing she wanted was for Lord Vanian to believe she had summoned him when in fact she had not.

"All right," she said at last. "You're right. But I still want to see this Kelara. If she's been here as long as you say, we could learn something from her even if she doesn't talk."

Gespry sighed. "If you say so," he said resignedly. "Least it's better'n sitting here while you squint over them books."

With "them books" added to the load, Dara's pack was quite heavy now, but she did not dare leave them behind; if Lord Vanian thought they might be of use to her, he'd most likely take them away.

Back to the hallway. Dara was surprised that Gespry led them not deeper into the Keep, but back to the very first door, the ashen desert where she'd first met Granny Good. When Dara would have stepped through the door, however, Gespry hopped down from her shoulder.

"I'll wait out here, if it's all the same to you," he said

wryly. "I'll just get all over grit, and be damned if I'm taking *another* bath."

"Well . . . all right," Dara said hesitantly, reluctant to leave Gespry behind. "If that's what you really want. I'll leave the pack here, then. It'd be hard struggling through all that loose dust with the extra weight, anyway. But the key goes with me."

"I don't doubt it," Gespry chuckled. "But it'll come out with you, too. Ain't nothing in there to do you hurt. Just go straight on back; can't miss the place. Take that extra waterskin, though, and fill it up if you get the chance. Go on, then, and when you get your curiosity's worth and come back, I'll be ready for some more of that stew if you can manage it. But I have to say I'm grateful you're leaving the wine here with me."

Dara laughed and laid her pack and the wineskin on the floor before she stepped through the door.

The bleak gray landscape was just as she'd left it, with powdery grit whirling in the wind; Dara quickly pulled a strip of rag from her pack and tied it over her nose and mouth, but her makeshift mask did nothing to protect her eyes from the flying particles. At last, as before, the wind died down, and knuckling her tearing eyes clear, Dara looked around.

This time there was no Granny Good to confront her, nor Lord Vanian perched on the rock, and Dara was able to pay more attention to the landscape itself. It was difficult to see far through the puffs of ash that occasionally swirled up at the slightest hint of a breeze, but Dara thought the land was not flat and featureless as she'd assumed before; off to the right (North? West? Who could tell?) there was what seemed to be a steep-sided hill. Maybe there were caves there; how else could anybody live in this horrible place? If not, at least she might get a better view from the hilltop. Why in the world had she been so impatient to rush in here when she might simply have asked Gespry for a better explanation of what to expect?

The swirling dust and dim light made the distance to the hill appear deceptively short; in fact, Dara found that the journey took what must have been hours over the soft, shifting dust that made walking twice as difficult.

When she finally reached the hill she found that it was larger than it had looked, too. There *was* an opening in the hillside, but nothing so natural as a cave; this was an archway constructed of white stone blocks ornately carved in strange designs. Dara had never seen an elf, but she had seen some pieces of their workmanship pass through High Lord Haranor's court, and she wondered if the marvelous elvan cities she'd heard described had been built of such odd-looking stuff.

In the dim twilight Dara saw that a pale green light flickered somewhere deep within the archway. For a moment she wondered whether Gespry's cheerful statement that there "ain't nothing in there to do you hurt" merely meant that he'd never found this entrance. But no, if he'd found this birdwoman she was most likely in a sheltered place like this. Nobody could live for long in the blowing grit without food or water, and why would anyone want to?

The wind was coming up again, driving fine grit even through the rag over Dara's nose and mouth. That more than anything else convinced her; she stepped up to the archway and peered cautiously inside.

A large tunnel hewn apparently from solid stone wound back into the hill, curving slightly so that Dara could not see far. There were no lamps or torches on the walls, but Dara could see the green light shining around the curve. She edged a little farther into the tunnel, sighing with relief as the dusty wind was almost immediately cut off. She drew her knife, comforted by the solid weight of it in her hand, and stepped along more confidently.

The tunnel curved again, and now Dara became aware that the light was increasing, and that the air was becoming moister as well, although not nearly as chokingly wet as in Yaga's strange hot forest. With the moister air came a sweet fragrance, a blend of floral scents.

Dara edged around the last curve, pressing herself tightly against the wall, and gasped as she peered around the corner. She was gazing into a huge open area apparently carved out of the inside of the hill, but to Dara's startled eyes it seemed more like a small enclosed world. The entire space was filled with trees, bushes, flowers, a summer scene that rivaled the lovely gardens around High Lord Haranor's castle. Flowers bloomed everywhere. Despite the fact that there must have been a cave roof somewhere overhead, the area was brightly lit with a green-gold glow that became greener as it filtered through the leaves. The faintest of breezes wafted through the area, stirring the leaves slightly and carrying the scent of flowers and fresh greenery to Dara.

As Dara watched, however, she became aware of one odd absence: Although she could see birds flitting from tree to tree, bees dipping into the flowers, she could hear nothing at all, not even the whisper of the breeze or the gurgle of the small stream she could see running through the middle.

As Gespry had said, there didn't seem to be anything to harm her, and curiosity drove Dara forward through the tunnel until she stopped again, this time abruptly.

She'd run into some invisible barrier or magical curtain, face first. It didn't precisely *stop* Dara, but it was . . . well, sticky, like putting her face into thick syrup. Dara pulled back, grimacing as the stuff seemed reluctant to release her skin.

What purpose could this invisible curtain serve? Obviously the breeze blew through it if Dara could smell the flowers, but why then could she hear nothing past it? Perhaps such a barrier would keep the birds and insects in, but would it keep a visitor out?

Even with the bright light of the enclosed garden behind the strange barrier, Dara could see nothing at all of it, not so much as a sparkle. She had to venture back out into the flying grit to find an old, dry twig she could experiment with, but she was encouraged to find that she could poke the stick through the invisible barrier and withdraw it with no apparent harm to the stick, although the gooey, sucking feel when she tried to withdraw it made her stomach flop. A stone tossed at the place neither penetrated nor bounced off; it slowed and seemed to stop in midair, then settled sludgily to the ground.

At last there was nothing to do but chance it; reluctantly she pushed first her hand, then her wrist, then her arm into the stuff. When she felt her fingers clear the barrier on the other side, she took a deep breath and stepped through.

Ugh—it was like pushing her way through a curtain of thick mud, queasily warm and noisomely clingy, but Dara braced her feet against the floor and shoved onward until at last she was through. She pulled free of the barrier, then stopped again, gaping.

There was plenty to hear now—the buzzing of bees, the rustle of leaves stirred by the faint breeze, and over it all the song of hundreds of birds, a great cacophony of birdsong. But somewhere in all that noise, not *under* the birdsong or *over* the fainter garden sounds, but weaving somehow through it all, was a delicate, sweet tone, darting up and down through the birdsong, weaving it somehow into a harmony as rich and rare as the blend of flower scents on the breeze. The sound tore through Dara's heart, piercing her to the very soul; Dara was sobbing even as the music was drawing her inexorably forward out of the shadows and into the light and warmth of this small summer.

Lush green grass was soft under Dara's feet, heavy flowering branches even softer against her cheeks as she brushed past them. The space inside the hill was larger than it seemed; Dara crossed any number of small paths winding through the garden, and it took some time working her way to the center. Now she could see where the bright light was coming from—the whole arching rock surface far overhead glowed with a brilliant golden radiance almost too bright to look at. But there was no stopping to marvel over these wonders; the song had her prisoner, bound fast in tendrils of silk and steel, pulling her onward.

Grassy paths wound through the greenery, gradually wandering inward, and Dara wandered inward with them. The flowers and birds and butterflies were beautiful, all right, but Dara found herself growing impatient, eager for something to happen. She was accustomed to noisy kitchens and busy households, not this idyllic, sleepy beauty. Even over the heart-wrenching music, the place smacked of idleness and apathy, two things she had learned to abhor.

Dara thought she was heading for some great confrontation at the center of the garden, but in that she was disappointed. Where the many paths converged there was indeed a grassy clearing, surrounding a pond cut apparently into the rock. Crystal-clear water splashed into the pond where a small waterfall had cut to join the wandering stream and the clearing. There was no one there, and other than the obvious construction of this strange and wonderful place, no sign that anyone ever had been there, but it was here and nowhere else that the music had drawn her, and she was as helpless to leave the clearing as a fly caught in a spider's web.

Not knowing what else to do, Dara sat down by the side of the pond, giving herself over to the music. It was a sound to break your heart—joyful and sorrowing all at once, strong and sweet and brilliant like the light until Dara wanted to plug her ears, to shut it out before she somehow withered under all that power.

The bushes parted without rustling, and Dara could only gape, tears running down her cheeks and a sob caught in her throat, as she stared at the figure that emerged from the greenery.

When Gespry had spoke of a "birdwoman," Dara had expected some fantastical creature, half woman and half bird—in this strange place, it seemed like the sort of thing one *would* see—but the white-robed figure who glided from the bushes seemed even stranger for the fact that it was no such legendary creature, only an ordinary woman of extraordinary beauty, golden hair tumbling like a waterfall down her back, slender arms as white as her silken gown, green eyes wide and warm and fixed upon some distant point, coral lips barely open as she sang. Then she stopped, and the abrupt silence was somehow more terrible than her song.

Dara was rocked by that silence, the sudden release from the spell that held her, but all she could do was scrub the tears from her cheeks and sit gasping, watching the strange figure. Was this one of the reclusive elves Dara had heard so much about? The woman's ears were covered by her hair, but Dara had heard that elves' ears were pointed at the tips instead of rounded. Certainly she seemed too beautiful, in an alien sort of way, to be human, and the cast of her delicate features, a strange sort of tilt to her eyes, was like nothing Dara had ever seen before.

The woman glided to the pond, kneeling while somehow not seeming to move, apparently oblivious to Dara's presence. She dipped her cupped hands into the water and stood again, the barest whisper of song trickling between her lips. Suddenly the air was alive with brilliant-colored wings as what seemed like a hundred birds settled themselves on her fingers, her arms, her shoulders, fluttering around her hands to drink the water she held out or around her hair to crown her in rainbow feathers. Dara almost held her breath, afraid some stray motion might startle the birds away, but they, like their mistress, seemed unaware or uncaring of Dara's presence. At last the woman turned and glided out of the clearing as mystically as she'd arrived.

Dara gaped after her. She could have understood it if the woman who could only be Kelara had either welcomed her or turned on her, driving Dara from her little summer kingdom, but not this seeming ignorance of Dara's very presence. Was there some special magic at work so that Dara was, in fact, invisible in this place?

Then the singing started again, and this time Dara pressed her hands desperately over her ears, afraid to hear that music again, afraid it would drown her and sweep away her soul in its wake. Hurriedly she tore little wads of rag and stuffed them into her ears; the sound faded down to a soft murmur that Dara could, if not ignore, at least overcome.

Crawling to the edge of the pool, Dara scrubbed the sticky tear tracks from her cheeks and took a quick drink to steady herself—the water was cool and wonderfully clear and sweet—then scrambled to her feet and hurried the way the birdwoman had gone, hoping she wouldn't become lost in the strange winding paths.

Fortunately the mistress of this summer kingdom appeared unconcerned with eluding her visitor and was nearby, sitting on a moss-covered rock and staring dreamily up through the leaves at the strange glowing rock ceiling overhead. Her lips were moving, and some of her song trickled past the rags in Dara's ears. Dara advanced very slowly as if the woman were some shy wild thing—come to think of it, she *was*—and stopped a short distance away. Once again the woman appeared not to see her, but Dara was having none of it; she positioned herself directly in front of the woman and stepped forward, then more, until Kelara had no choice but look at Dara or be bumped off her rock. The more Dara looked at the strange woman, the more she seemed somehow familiar, although Dara was mortally sure she'd never seen anyone so beautiful in her life. Surely she could never have forgotten such a person.

"Please," Dara murmured. "I don't want to frighten you. I don't want to hurt you. I just want to talk, anything you can tell—"

Kelara's green eyes dropped from the ceiling and slid past Dara's face, never focusing on it, and before Dara could stop her the birdwoman had flowed aside like water through half-open fingers. But in that brief moment Dara had seen what she had missed before—the cord, braided perhaps of long golden hair, hanging around the woman's neck, and the gold key it held. Dara was so stunned by this revelation that she made no move to stop the birdwoman as she slipped into the bushes again, faint tendrils of her song slipping past the rags in Dara's ears to stab at her heart.

This time Dara stood where she was, undecided whether she should pursue or not. If this strange creature still had her key, then she was here because here was where she wanted to be. And Dara had the thought, too, that whatever magic was here, the birdwoman was its maker, not its victim or its prisoner. And if she chose to be here as she was, and she chose to ignore Dara, what could Dara do about it? She was no rescuer; in this little garden of song, she was the intruder.

Slowly Dara retraced her steps to the edge of the vast cavern, not returning to the clearing at the center. No, she wouldn't so much as take the water to refill her waterskin. She had nothing to give here, and anything she took would be theft.

She left quietly the way she'd come, shuddering as she once more pushed her way through the invisible barrier. No, it wasn't there to keep the birdwoman in; it was to keep the birds and insects in, wasn't it, and the dust and debris out, to keep Kelara's little world safe and undisturbed. Did even Lord Vanian respect those borders? Dara thought perhaps he did—not because he'd respect Kelara's wishes, although she'd noticed that he seemed to avoid other residents of the Keep, especially those who had been there long enough to gather power of their own, but because Kelara's sweet and tranquil summer garden was as alien to Lord Vanian's nature as it was to Dara's, and he would be powerfully uncomfortable there just as Dara had been.

This time Dara remembered to tie a strip of rag over her nose and mouth before she stepped out into the billowing grit, but when she squinted out into the gray cloud, a sudden fear seized her. When the air had been relatively calm, it had been easy enough to see the tall hill and follow what she saw. But she'd closed the door to the corridor behind her when she entered this world. The wind was blowing the grit in a dense cloud that not even bright light could penetrate now, and Dara had only the remotest of ideas where the door was. In such a fog it would be an easy matter to pass right by the closed door, and how was she to find it if she couldn't see it? She certainly couldn't follow her trail back; every last hint of her tracks in the ashy dust was long gone.

Now she ground her teeth at her own foolishness. Foolish to close the door behind her; foolish not to think of some way to mark her trail. She could laboriously unravel some of her clothing and tie a thread to the rock to make an anchor, and then attempt to find the door, reeling the thread out behind her so she could find her way back to the tunnel, but if she stumbled once in the loose dirt the thread could easily break and she'd be lost completely. She could cast a guiding spell, or maybe even something powerful enough to calm down the wind, if she hadn't foolishly left the grimoire in the hall with Gespry. Why, she didn't even have the poor option of ringing the bell and summoning Lord Vanian, to humiliate herself by having to ask him to show her the way out.

Well, she'd simply have to wait and hope the wind would die down. So far as she'd already seen, these flurries seemed of short duration. Then she'd have to hope that she could spot the door to the corridor, or recognize the particular gnarled trees and boulders she'd passed on her way.

It was all so unfair. She was a serving maid and aspiring mage, not a tracker or forester or scholar or warrior or any of the other thousand things it seemed were expected of her in this place. And how convenient that this dust storm would wait until she'd gotten far away from the door to the corridor, and that this time there would be no Granny Good to offer help and advice. But, of course, likely it was no coincidence at all. Lord Vanian, in all his conjurings, would have no difficulty with a paltry dust storm in this place.

But did he control all of it? No, else he'd have kept her from meeting Yaga and Granny Good and maybe even Gespry. No, some things apparently remained beyond his control. And she meant to be one of them.

"Granny?" she said aloud, then called louder, "Granny Good?"

"Don't shout, child, or someone you don't intend to call may well answer," Granny said mildly, appearing beside Dara, just a little deeper into the tunnel entrance. "And step back out of all that dust, else you'll turn as gray as my own hair."

"Oh, it's so good to see you," Dara said, relieved. "This wind came up and I was so far from the door, I didn't know how I'd ever find my way back."

"Oh? And what is there about one knotty old woman that makes you think you'll get back now?" Granny Good said, cackling sharply.

"Well, I thought—" Dara stopped, confused. "I thought you wanted to help me."

"What I want don't hook the fish nor crush the grapes," Granny Good said sternly. "Value given for value received, that's the law of the Keep, missy, and well you know it. And if you ask my help, child, shouting as if I were a chambermaid late to her summons, what do you propose to give me in return? A drink from that empty waterskin I see hanging at your shoulder?"

Dara fought down a wave of hurt at Granny's words. What right did she have to presume that Granny would always make herself available for any help Dara might need? What right did she have to expect that Granny's aid would always be traded as cheaply as it had before? Dara shook her head in answer to her own question. That Granny would answer her at all, that she had given so much help so far, was more than Dara should have expected. But what could she offer the ancient woman that Granny could not have for herself whenever she chose?

"I used to be a fair hand in the kitchen," Dara said humbly. "I promised Gespry a good dinner when I came back. I could as easily make enough for three as two, if you'd help me find my way back there."

Granny Good's wrinkled face lit up in a grin.

"Now you're talking like a girl who's learned something here," she cackled. "I'll take your trade, missy, and thank you kindly. Now pluck me out three strands of your hair from the roots."

That was easy enough; the wind had pulled a good few strands loose from Dara's coil of braid. Granny Good took the strands and braided them together, her gnarled fingers surprisingly nimble, spat on the braided strands and tossed it out into the storm. A moment later a thick cable of rope, exactly the brown color of Dara's hair, came rolling out of the dust, the end stopping at Dara's feet.

"There you are," Granny Good said, nodding briskly. "You follow that right to the door out."

"Aren't you coming?" Dara asked, surprised. It seemed strange for Granny to insist on a trade and then vanish before collecting her due.

"I wouldn't miss my dinner, young one," she cackled. "But I'm gray enough now, thank you kindly. I'll just meet you on the other side." Then she was gone.

Dara sighed exasperatedly. If Granny was simply going to pop from here to there, why couldn't she have popped Dara with her instead of making Dara walk back through the dust storm? But no, that wasn't what Dara had asked for, was it? She'd asked for help getting back, not to be *taken* back.

"I'll never learn," Dara muttered darkly, picking up the end of the rope and pulling strongly at it. It seemed to be firmly anchored somewhere. "Never, *never* learn."

Since she had the rope to hold on to, she tied a strip of rag over her eyes as well as her nose and mouth, and began laboriously working her way across the soft, shifting dust. Although the relief from the flying grit in her eyes was considerable, walking blind, even with the rope to guide her, was slower and more difficult than she would have thought. Surely it hadn't been this far approaching the hill, had it?

At last, to Dara's relief, she collided with a solid surface that, when she pulled the rag from her face, revealed itself to be the door. When she turned her key in the lock and opened the door, she found Granny and Gespry waiting rather impatiently in the corridor.

"Thought you might've liked the place so well you'd decided to move in," Gespry complained. "I was just trying to argue this old hag into taking me someplace else."

"Sorry," Dara said, shrugging. She slapped at her clothes; clouds of dust formed their own dust storm in the corridor. Gespry scampered away hastily; Granny's chair rose and followed just as quickly.

"Missy, I'll thank you to leave that dirt where it belongs, for I'll trade you nothing for it," Granny Good said sternly.

"Sorry," Dara said again. She was tired and discouraged and hardly in the proper frame of mind for working magic, but Gespry had been waiting for his dinner and she'd traded Granny fairly. She sighed and reached through the open door only long enough to pick up two handfuls of dirt that she dropped into her bowl. Her concentration was off and it took her several tries before she was able to produce the rich mutton stew she wanted, the peppered meat buns and berry tart. Gespry would have shared his wine, but Dara and Granny preferred the cellar-cold cider that Dara was better acquainted with. For such a frail-looking old lady, Granny Good had a hearty appetite and she smacked her wrinkled lips as she wolfed down the food.

"My, that was tasty," Granny sighed, tucking the last meat bun into her pocket. "Time you want to make another such trade, missy, you give me a call."

"Granny," Dara said slowly, "why did you meet me in that place before?"

"Hmm. Mayhap I wanted a word with you before you wandered too far astray," Granny said. "Mayhap I thought you'd best see a friendlier face than Lord Vanian was likely to have shown you."

"You said the Oracle wasn't there, even though you didn't know *where* it was, or what it looked like," Dara said thoughtfully. "So far as you knew, it might've been in there, mightn't it? But you stopped me before I went any farther. It was because of Kelara, wasn't it?"

"Well . . . mayhap I didn't want you barging in where you weren't wanted," Granny admitted at last. "I have a particular fondness for that pretty one and I'd as soon see her left alone as she likes. But what I said before wasn't no lie all the same; you know that."

"Why did you go there?" Dara asked, turning to Gespry. "Were you looking for the Oracle then, too?"

"Something like that," Gespry said, shrugging. "I went there first, same as you, and I met Granny there and the lord, too. When I come to think about it later, seemed funny to me that they'd both show up so near the same place like that, so I went back snooping. Once I'd made it as far as the garden, though, I wasn't as eager to leave as you; figured I'd stay awhile with the fresh water and fruit, and fill up my game bag with some of them birds. Course, I had some hope of gettin' sweet with the lady, too," Gespry admitted. "That was back in my human days. I wasn't much to look at, but I figured the miss had been alone long enough it wouldn't much matter."

"I guess it mattered, or you wouldn't have ended up in a swamp instead of that garden," Dara said, chuckling a little at the thought. How insulting for Gespry if Kelara had ignored him as studiously as she had Dara.

"Don't know what it was irked her so, whether it was my hunting or just my staying around," Gespry said a little abashedly. "But them birds took to diving at me, pecking at my face or just splattering me with—well, you can figure. They'd drop it in a cup of water as soon as I scooped it up, on my plate while I was eating, in my face while I was sleeping—anyhow, I got the idea I wasn't much welcome, so after a while I moved on.''

"She's still got her key," Dara said wonderingly. "Why is she still here?"

Granny waved one hand dismissively.

"Missy, as I've told you before, not all of us are so eager to walk out the door and be gone," she said. "There's a good many still have their key. Some of us came here just wishing to stay." She turned to Gespry. "And you, scamp that you are, would you trade your immortality to go back and be a poor cobbler again, with winter creeping into your old bones?"

Gespry squinted one eye, then the other, then shrugged.

"Can't say I was so delighted with things as they was," he admitted. "If it weren't for being stuck in some stinking pile of swamp mud and looking like somebody's pet, I'd be happy enough here in one place or another. Maybe someplace like that castle, if Lord Vanian hadn't already made himself at home there," Gespry added with a wry grin.

"Granny, just how many doors *are* there in this place?" Dara asked suddenly.

Granny chuckled, her sharp eyes twinkling. "And why are you wondering that just now, missy?"

"This book I found." Dara rooted in her pack until she found it, then leafed through the pages. "Look here. 'Two new doors today. Does another come with each one?' Does that mean there weren't always so many?"

Granny cackled. "Seem so, wouldn't it? But what good's knowing that, eh?"

"Another—another door," Dara said slowly. "But what's 'each one'? Each visitor who comes to the Keep, it must be. But *why*? And how many are there?"

Granny shrugged. "I've never counted, myself," she said, but Dara thought she said it rather carefully. "Suppose you could, missy, given time enough. But again, why's it matter?''

"Because if there's a door here for each visitor," Dara said thoughtfully, "doesn't that mean that the last door came into being when I arrived? And mightn't that be a perfect place for Lord Vanian to hide the Oracle, in the very last door that I'd likely never get to?"

Granny's face relaxed in relief, but her sigh sounded almost disappointed.

"I suppose anything's possible, missy," she said. "I reckon if you went there looking for it, there's always the chance you might find your way to the Oracle there."

"Now, there's a thought," Gespry said, grinning. "My, wouldn't the lord look a proper fool if you just ran straight to the thing instead of fumbling around for years and years?"

Granny Good produced a ball of gold yarn and knitting needles from somewhere in her rags and began knitting busily.

"Be sure what you're doing, little girl," she said. "Be sure you're not just chasing another pretty illusion."

Dara hesitated. She'd trusted the old woman so far, and Granny had seemed to genuinely want Dara to succeed, but now she seemed to be discouraging her. And why *had* Granny intercepted Dara in that first place? To offer help, yes, but why sit there in the ash when she could have just as easily met her in the corridor? To keep her from trespassing on Kelara's hidden little world, right. Because she had "a particular affection" for Kelara. If there was anything else of significance in that place, Dara hadn't been able to find it, and Granny couldn't lie. The fact that Granny could tell her only the truth, however, didn't mean that she had to tell Dara *all* of the truth. Therefore—what? Did she trust Granny or not? Dare she trust Granny—or anyone—completely?

"What do you think I should do, if not that?" Dara asked Granny.

Granny shook her finger warningly. "Ah, ah, missy, our bargain was for help back to the corridor, not advice," Granny said archly.

"Yes, but you keep saying things, looking at me in ways, as if I'm supposed to make something of it," Dara insisted. "Why don't you just say what you mean, if you're going to say or do anything at all?"

Granny Good threw back her head and cackled, but when she looked at Dara again, Dara fancied she could see a hint of sadness in the sharp green eyes.

"Why, then, little girl," she said, "I'll say and do nothing at all." Abruptly she was gone, only crumbs marking the place where her chair had rested.

"Well, now I guess you've gone and done it," Gespry said resignedly.

"Oh, dear," Dara said, utterly wretched now. What in the world had she been thinking, rebuffing her only steady ally in this place besides Gespry? Even if she decided not to blindly accept any advice Granny gave her, even half-doubtful advice was better than none. And none was exactly what she'd have now, for she'd burned all her other bridges, too—likely Yaga was too sad and disappointed now to talk to her, Kelara bound to ignore her, and she'd done her best to thoroughly antagonize Lord Vanian. There truly was nobody now to stand by her but Gespry, and he was with her only reluctantly. Before the day was out she'd finish up making an enemy of him, too, most likely.

"Ah, don't worry too much," Gespry said, shrugging. "She'll likely pop back up again before too long. She's got an interest in you or she wouldn't have spent so much time looking in on you already."

Dara sighed miserably. She was far from being as sure of that as Gespry.

"Gespry, what do you think?" she asked. "Was it a bad idea, to check the last door?"

"Don't see why." Gespry shrugged again. "Don't know how long it'll take to get so far, but I don't see as how checking one door's any more foolish than another, and your thought was good enough. It ain't going about things the way the dragon said, though.''

"No, it's not." That troubled Dara, too, even more so as she wasn't sure exactly how to go about taking Yaga's advice even if she decided to heed it completely. "But I thought if a door was created when I arrived, I might know more about how the Keep worked. And if I knew that, I might know more about how to—how to start to look for the Oracle."

"Well, that makes sense, then," Gespry said indifferently. "'Sides, as I look at it, one place is as good as another, 'cept any of the places is likely to have more to eat and drink and more to see than this hallway, see? So let's do it, I'd say."

"All right then," Dara said, feeling a cautious sort of relief. Despite what Granny and Yaga had said to her, doing something, anything, was preferable to doing nothing, and nothing was exactly what she felt she'd been doing for some time now.

Dara repacked her bag and lifted Gespry to her shoulder before she set out confidently down the corridor. Surely it would be a long walk, and she'd want to sleep soon, but there was no harm in covering what distance she could before she stopped.

Brave sentiment, but Dara quickly found herself becoming both exhausted and discouraged. The hall seemed to go on forever, and Dara was increasingly reminded of one of those dreams where she'd find herself in some frightening cavern or long cellar hall, fleeing from some unknown creature behind her, while the tunnel or corridor stretched out more endlessly ahead of her with every step. Despite her weariness Dara was glad for Gespry's weight on her shoulder, his idle chatter about (of all the boring subjects) bootmaking. After what seemed like hours, however, Dara stopped with a sigh.

"I can't go any farther," she said reluctantly. "Find a likely door or camp here?"

"Better here," Gespry said with equal reluctance. "I haven't been this far down, so who knows what might be lurking around in any of these places? 'Sides, it's not as if we need a fire or anything."

Gespry was right, of course, but that didn't make Dara any happier about sleeping in the open and unprotected yet another "night." She'd slept safely indoors or under shelter all her life—at home, in High Lord Haranor's castle, even in or under wagons in caravans when she'd traveled. She didn't like sleeping under open sky in any of the strange worlds behind the wooden doors, and she didn't like sleeping under the starlight in this corridor, either. But the only enclosures she'd found so far were the library, Lord Vanian's eerie, deserted castle, and Kelara's cave, and none of the three seemed any safer than sleeping in the open. At least in the corridor there were walls.

Dara was itchy from the ashy dust of Kelara's world, discouraged from her lack of progress, and increasingly uneasy that Lord Vanian might take it into his head to pop in while she slept, and the latter fear, more than any other, made sleep difficult. Gespry had a good heart, but such a tiny creature wouldn't be much of a protector, especially if he went scurrying off in fear every time Lord Vanian showed up.

And what game was Lord Vanian playing now? His interest in Cav and in Dara's parents troubled her intensely. Could his power reach beyond the Crystal Keep in some way to threaten those she loved, or did he (more likely) merely hoard the knowledge to use against her in some way, perhaps something as intimate and horrible as the trick he'd played with his mirror? Who knew how far he would go for his "entertainment"?

Two things, however, were certain: She couldn't very well avoid Lord Vanian in his own keep if he wanted to find her; and as Gespry said, she wasn't much likely to find the Oracle running blindly after every idea that struck her. The answer to both problems was the same; she'd have to be canny and outthink Lord Vanian, as Yaga had told her. And that meant doing something other than what he expected her to do.

Dara sighed and turned over, irritably wishing she could stop thinking and sleep. But what *had* other visitors to the Crystal Keep done that Lord Vanian would assume she would do? Open the doors in order, methodically, as she'd been doing, of course. Trying divination, too, would be expected; surely at least some of the visitors had been mages, or had learned to use the Keep's magic. Well, that must be why her own divinations had failed; likely the Keep itself had some limitations on divination for that very purpose. Lord Vanian had implied as much.

Apparently his own mirror was free of such limitations, however; he'd said so, at least. But that meant making a bargain with Lord Vanian, which she was loath to do, or trying to find the mirror and use it without his knowledge—and by the laws of the Keep, would that be permissible if she gave nothing in return? What horrible fate might befall her if she did not?

It occurred to Dara that there was more to it than understanding how Lord Vanian thought. Some other had created the Crystal Keep, put in place the conditions under which it worked—grew, even. That someone had planned this place long before Lord Vanian had ever set foot inside the doors, that much was evident. There were rules and limitations that bound Lord Vanian as stringently as they bound her, and that implied that there was a power at work here greater than Lord Vanian. All well and fine to try and understand Lord Vanian, but she'd have to understand, too, the power that governed the Guardian (and it comforted Dara no end to know that *something* did). That power seemed rather more impartial than Lord Vanian himself; if only Dara had some way of knowing all these mysterious rules! Possibly one of the books she'd found held the key, but to find and cast a translation spell and then laboriously puzzle out the books would take a great deal of time, time Dara wasn't sure she could spare.

Dara turned over again, sighed, and sat up. Apparently she was doomed to sleeplessness unless she did something about it. There were herbal teas that aided in sleep, but Dara didn't have the herbs, nor did she know where in this place to find them; even if she could chant up a sleeping potion, it seemed too dangerous to take in case Lord Vanian should decide to pay a visit, and a sleeping spell would be no better.

Dara chuckled to herself. How long had it been since she passed a sleepless night? Probably nearly five years, that first night in High Lord Haranor's household, her muscles aching so fiercely, surrounded by the unaccustomed presence of the other serving girls sleeping in the room. It was Cav who had told her the herbs that would help her sleep; it was Cav who had given her some of them. Suddenly Dara's heart ached with missing him. One of the most wonderful things about Cav was the way he had of seeing the world as an orderly place that made sense—of making Dara herself see it that way, too. In Cav's world nobody would be sleeping on a corridor floor beneath a night sky, covered with dust from a world that couldn't exist, looking for an Oracle that changed location and appearance.

Disgustedly Dara reached for the wineskin and sipped at it until she began to feel dizzy, and between the wine and her weariness, she slept at last.

9

"**A**T LAST," DARA SIGHED. GESPRY SIGHED, too, but said nothing.

It had taken two sleeps to reach the end of the great corridor, walking as fast and steadily as Dara could manage. Dara hadn't paused to glance behind the doors she passed or count them, but she thought there must be thousands of such little worlds, and she was appalled.

How many visitors had come here seeking wishes granted, questions answered? How many of them had never left? More, obviously, than did manage to leave, or at least so the legends would have it. Were the rest of them all here now, perhaps transformed like Gespry? No, some surely had been killed, as she'd almost been. But surely that would leave a good many. Enough to people a kingdom, perhaps, but how scattered they must be, over all the worlds behind the doors. The visitors could have a little world all to themselves if they wished—but then so many of the strange worlds didn't seem like places one would, or even could, live.

The hallway had ended as abruptly as it began, finishing

in a blank stone wall. The last door on the left, just before the stone wall, was the one Dara presumed must have come into being upon her arrival. But why?

It was only a door, like the others, but Dara found herself reluctant to turn that key, to see what her arrival at the Crystal Keep had created, or at least precipitated. She touched the knob of the small latched peephole, but couldn't quite bring herself to open it.

"Well, go on then," Gespry said impatiently. "You wanted to see this, didn't you? Or would you rather just trot on back?"

That did it. Dara hurriedly turned the key and opened the door and, gasping, stepped forward.

For a moment Dara's mind refused to believe what her eyes saw. She stood in the courtyard of her family's own house, the familiar goats and chickens wandering about on the hay-strewn, hard-packed soil. The chimney of the large stone house was smoking and the sun was high, about dinnertime. A sudden lump of homesickness rose in Dara's throat until she could taste her own tears.

"Say, this ain't half bad," Gespry said, impressed. "Ain't no castle, though."

"Oh, no, it's my home," Dara said absently, lifting Gespry down from her shoulder. The house cats appeared from the barn and the house to twine about Dara's ankles as they had always done, and her pet goat, Dalmus, whom she'd raised from a kid, wandered over, too. Dara stood only a moment longer in shock, amazed at the spectacle; then she was running for the door, calling, "Mother? Father?"

The kitchen was warm with a cheery blaze at the hearth, but there was no pot hanging over the stove. The bins that Tabba, the cook, had had built were filled with onions, mushrooms, turnips, beans, garlic, parsnips, and fresh apples, but Tabba was not there at her worktable rolling pastry or dicing vegetables for the midday meal and no loaf was swelling over its pan in preparation for the hearth. There was no sound in that homey kitchen except for the crackling of the fire and the meows of the cats that followed Dara about. Dara scowled and left Gespry to putter about the kitchen while she continued her search.

The dining hall was empty, as was the main hall. A horrible suspicion had begun to creep into Dara's thoughts, and by the time she'd checked the sewing room and the maids' room, it had become a certainty. There was nobody here but Dara and the animals and Gespry. This was not her home at all, only a counterfeit, another deceit of the Crystal Keep. Dara tried not to be disappointed—what had she expected, that she'd been mysteriously Gated all the leagues home, or that her mother and father and the entire household had been Gated here?—but the blow was a cruel one nonetheless, and Dara's sleeves were considerably damper by the time she'd finished her exploration of the house and joined Gespry back in the kitchen.

"Pretty sweet little roost," Gespry commented, his eyes twinkling over the mug of cider he'd drawn from its keg. "Good as a castle to poor folk like me—better, even. Pretty fair copy, eh?"

"You knew?" Dara said softly. "I thought—well, I don't know what I thought."

"Well, what else could it be if you said it was your home?" Gespry asked, shrugging. "Nice kitchen gardens out back, too. Might be I'll ask you to put me back here when you go, if you don't care."

In a perverse way, Gespry's compliment comforted Dara. Yes, what could be a nicer place than this? High Lord Haranor's marvelous castle had been wonderful, but it was stiff and stuffy and expensive and mannered, not the sort of place Dara could call "home" with the same warm, comforting feeling she felt upon experiencing all the familiar sights and smells of home again. Even if it was not truly her home.

She stepped out the back door and looked past the courtyard. Here was a change, and one she'd have seen if she hadn't dashed immediately for the house; Lord Evander's keep, where her mother had once been in service, was not visible in the distance, although the hill where it had stood still swelled up from the fields. Beyond the late-summer fields of wheat and barley were the pastures where the sheep and cattle grazed, but Dara could see no herdsmen tending and protecting them. Dara leaned against the court-yard wall and gazed out, sighing.

"Quite the pastoral little paradise," Lord Vanian said, appearing beside her. "Yours, I assume."

"My home," Dara said stiffly. "Lord Evander granted Mother and Father the house and lands before I was born. Except for the time I spent in High Lord Haranor's house-hold, I lived here—there—all my life."

"Humble, but not without its comforts," Lord Vanian said with surprisingly little condescension in his tone. Then he smiled wickedly. "But here I am, invading your home without an invitation. Will you banish me?"

Dara swallowed a biting retort; as long as Lord Vanian was making an effort to remain polite, she had more to gain by doing the same than by angering him and perhaps in-curring his vengeance. She found, to her surprise, that his appearance did not fill her with the same sick fear it had before; but then, how could she help but feel at least somewhat safe within the walls of her own home, or at least its simulacrum?

"Well, it pleased you to show me the hospitality of your castle," Dara said a little awkwardly. "I suppose the least I can do is offer you a mug of cider and a pie in our dining hall. If you want it, that is."

Lord Vanian swept his arm around in an exaggerated bow.

"I thank you most kindly for your graciousness," he said grandly. "Whatever you deign to offer me, I'm certain it will be fine fare." He glanced toward the barn, where Gespry had scampered as soon as he had appeared. "Else that little pest would never have stayed with you so long."

"Gespry," Dara emphasized reprovingly, "has been a

kind and true friend." Then she hesitated. "You don't have to go in through the kitchen," she said awkwardly. Mother and Father would never have brought a nobleman into the house through the servants' entrance, but then no nobleman would have appeared in the middle of the back courtyard with the chickens and the goats. "We can go in at the front if you like."

Lord Vanian smiled again and inspected the sole of one boot, then the other.

"Too late, I fear," he said, so soberly that Dara didn't know whether to blush, laugh, or become offended. "The damage has been done already. The sight of your doubtlessly immaculate kitchen will do no further harm to my dignity."

When they entered the kitchen, however, Lord Vanian did not follow Dara out the other side, but wandered about the room, inspecting the bundles of herbs and sausages hanging from the rafters, sniffing at the spices in the pots on the worktable.

"So tell me, my fine serving wench," Lord Vanian said, glancing at her, "can you prepare my dinner with your own two hands?"

"If you like," Dara said warily, surprised by the request. Surely Lord Vanian would find it boring, waiting so long for such simple fare as Dara had ever been entrusted to prepare. "Do you want to sit in the hall? My parents have an extensive library, mostly on magic—"

"I believe I'll watch you instead," Lord Vanian said, and to Dara's amazement he perched himself on a stool in the corner, obviously prepared to do just that.

"All right," Dara said, feeling more awkward than ever. A quick check of the pantry and the cellar told her that there was an abundance of supplies, as she'd expect at harvesttime. A barley and dried mushroom sop in beef broth wouldn't take too long, and potted meat and turnips could be turned into a quick pasty, but whatever Lord Vanian might think of her, a simple pudding was all she could manage for a sweet; she couldn't stand there under his gaze and keep straight in her mind anything more complicated.

"It'll take a long time to bake bread," Dara said apologetically as she chopped the turnips. "At home Tabba baked three times a week, but would you mind—"

"Not at all. Allow me." Lord Vanian handed her a basket filled with steaming soft buns.

Dara chuckled to herself; such dainty rolls would dissolve to mush in the sop. Now she was glad of the practice she'd had, making food for Gespry; she was able to transform the buns into small sturdy loaves of good brown bread on the first attempt. To forestall any more "help" Lord Vanian might offer, she poured him a mug of cider.

"Do you know," he said, pulling his stool a little closer to the worktable, "I've never seen food actually prepared. I was never allowed in our kitchens. When I was a child I got the idea in my head that our cook just conjured our meals out of the air." He chuckled bitterly. "Which is, of course, exactly what I do here."

Dara stopped chopping for a moment to look over at him.

"But your castle," she said. "The cellars were full, and the pantry and the kitchen were stocked. At least with some things—the wine and brandy, the smoked and salted meats and the cheeses." Then she blushed; how shameless to admit that she'd been prowling about in his home without permission, even though he already knew.

Lord Vanian appeared not to notice her discomfort. He put down his mug and looked out the window, and for a long time Dara thought he wasn't going to answer, but at last he spoke in a low voice.

"When I—realized I was going to remain here, I was desperate," he said slowly. "Desperately alone, desperately unhappy. I knew I'd never again see anyone I knew, anyone I had ever—cared about. Yet there was the castle, Lord Esperon's castle where I'd been fostered, where I'd fallen in love with his daughter Marguerid. Having that was a comfort in one way, a torment in another. For a little while I gloried at least in my power here, and I thought, if the power of the keep could produce this place so exactly, why not the people I missed?

"So I created them all, exactly as I remembered them— Marguerid, the other fostered lads who had been my friends, the servants—all but Lord Esperon and Lady Helena, who had stood between me and my love." Lord Vanian fell silent.

"You . . . created . . . real people?" Dara asked, awed. If that were true, she'd terribly underestimated Lord Vanian's power. She'd never heard of any mage who could do that.

"No." Once again Lord Vanian was silent for a long moment. "I suppose they were only extremely potent illusions, or something like an homunculus, perhaps. They had the look of the ones I tried to create, moved like them. A few, those I remembered most clearly, even spoke a little. But they weren't real people, and when I stopped paying attention to them, they'd just stand there like statues. Over time they simply faded away slowly as my memory of the people I cared about faded. At last they were only formless shadows flitting about the castle, whispers echoing in the hall. Now there's nothing at all. The portrait of Marguerid, her room, her things—those stayed real, but parts of the castle I rarely use anymore, those have faded away, too. I've tried very hard to keep as much of it as I can, to keep that much of her memory."

Lord Vanian was silent again; then he abruptly stood and walked to the window, gazing out at the courtyard.

"So why did the Keep create this place," he mused, "do you think, instead of the grand castle where you work and where your lover lives?"

"I don't know," Dara admitted. In truth she'd wondered herself; certainly High Lord Haranor's castle was fresher in her mind than her own home had been. "I expect you'd know better than me," she added.

"Oh?" Lord Vanian turned back from the window and

smiled grimly. "So you believe this is yet another of my mysterious deceits, eh? And to what end? If I were bound to seduce you wearing your lover's face again, I'd more likely have done it in your lover's home and bed, wouldn't I? And how do you believe I'd know so detailed a description of your home as I'd need to construct such an elaborate illusion?"

"I don't think you did it at all," Dara said flatly. Then she realized how rude her words sounded, and she added hurriedly, "I only meant that you've been here far longer than I have and know much more about how this place works. You must've seen many of these doors come into being when other people arrived, didn't you?"

"For a while it was interesting, a welcome distraction to visit such strange and varied places as lay behind the doors, to talk to those at whose arrival such places came into being," Lord Vanian said absently. "But understand that at that time I didn't much care how it was done, or why, and in any event, what did it matter? It was but another unfathomable facet of a power I could never hope to master or perhaps even comprehend. Only another brick in my prison tower, as it were. One might well wonder at the marvelous architecture, but after the wondering is done, the tower is still a prison. And after enough unanswered questions and irrelevant answers, I ceased even to wonder."

"That's very sad." Dara turned away so he wouldn't see the interest in her eyes, setting the pasties to bake. If he knew that what he was telling her might be of use to her, Lord Vanian would doubtless say nothing further. "I wonder how elves manage."

"Manage?" Lord Vanian repeated.

"Well, they live for centuries and centuries, don't they?" Dara continued. "I wonder how they manage to stay interested in life over all those years. Cav always said they were rather cool and aloof, when anybody could manage to meet one, that is, but they're likely not that way among their own. And they're just as shut up inside their cities as somebody'd be in this place—more, I guess, since this place doesn't seem to have any end at all and hundreds and hundreds of little worlds inside it. I wonder how they manage to pass the time.''

''I would hardly know,'' Lord Vanian said wryly. ''In my time few humans, if any, had ever seen an elf. Nobody had yet managed to get any of them to leave their cities even to trade. Somehow it never occurred to me to use the mirror to look and see what's inside those mysterious cities. Perhaps someday I will.''

''You can't,'' Dara challenged. ''Mages have tried the most powerful divination spells known. The elves have shielded their cities with even more powerful magic. Father said their cloaking spells couldn't be penetrated by any human magic.''

Lord Vanian shrugged.

''Who knows?'' he said lightly. ''When I first came here, it was said in legend that magics existed inside the Crystal Keep that were unknown and unachievable anywhere else in the world. After the years I've spent here, I'm inclined to think the legends didn't more than half hint at the power of this place.''

''And you find that *boring*?'' Dara asked, honestly curious.

''I find it interminably boring,'' Lord Vanian corrected. ''After so many years, what's left to do?''

''What's left—'' Dara said blankly, utterly amazed that anyone could say such a thing. He was *bored*, and he'd never even seen somebody chop a turnip? Abruptly she thrust the bowl of pudding batter into his startled hands. ''*You* stir it, then.''

Lord Vanian stared down at the bowl as if it were some exotic creature. At last he gingerly grasped the handle of the wooden spoon and pushed it hesitantly through the batter.

''Stir it how?'' he said with a timidity that made Dara want to laugh. She swallowed the chuckle; it went down in a lump that made her throat ache.

"Like this," Dara said. She took the spoon from him and stirred a few times to illustrate, then handed the spoon back. "Just keep stirring it like that."

Lord Vanian stirred hesitantly, then more confidently; after a few moments, however, he glanced up rather impatiently.

"Well?" he said. "How long do I keep doing this?"

"Till the batter's light and fluffy," Dara said, vastly enjoying the sight of the arrogant lord sitting on his wooden stool and whipping a pudding.

By the time the preparations were finished and everything was set to baking or bubbling, Lord Vanian was rather less enchanted with the simple art of cooking.

"I never knew it was so much bother," he said a little irritably, brushing the last of the flour from his hands with a silken kerchief.

Dara laughed. "*This* is no bother," she said. "You should see the goings-on in the kitchen of a really fine household, like High Lord Haranor's. The cooking never seemed to stop, and it was fancier stuff that took longer to make, all those fine pastries and subtleties and rich gravies. And then on top of all the cooking, there was all the washing up, too."

"Surprising that you found time to dally with your lordling," Lord Vanian said wryly. "Somehow it always seemed *our* serving girls found time to put their bellies up."

"Well, I can't speak as to your household," Dara said saucily, "but in High Lord Haranor's household I wasted a good deal of time fending off arrogant lords who'd be delighted to throw a girl on their beds, willing or not, and put their bellies up for them. Sometimes after a big dinner my bottom would be all over bruises from being pinched and slapped by every lord at the table during supper. High Lord Haranor wouldn't let a pretty young girl serve as a chambermaid to any of the visiting lords, or she was sure to be mauled. So likely your serving girls shouldn't bear all the blame for their troubles.'' Dara bit back a comment that more than likely the lord's own loose morals had been responsible for the birth of many a bastard; as long as Lord Vanian, sitting in her home by her invitation, was troubling to remain civil, she could not bring herself to insult him.

''Whose library do you suppose that was, where you brought me the food?'' Dara asked idly. ''And is it only a library, or is there more to the place?''

Lord Vanian chuckled.

''What's this game?'' he said. ''Are you seeking to make me your own oracle?''

Dara's heart gave a great thump, but she fought to keep her anxiety from showing in her expression.

''I didn't bring you here,'' she said negligently. ''You came yourself. I thought you wanted conversation; you've said so before. Do you really want to talk about serving maids of light morals and how many eggs go into a pudding? I'd rather talk about something more interesting.''

Lord Vanian shrugged.

''Very well,'' he said. ''As you say, I came myself, and you did, after all, prepare my dinner—if it's any good, that is,'' he added, smiling slightly. ''No, the library is only that, a room full of books with no windows or doors. It appeared when a great sage visited my keep to ask the Oracle how mankind first came to be.''

''Did he find the answer to his question?'' Dara asked curiously.

''I believe he found the bottom of a gryphon's gullet,'' Lord Vanian said, chuckling. ''But I am grateful for the library. I'm not the scholarly type, but after so many years even a book is a welcome amusement. I admit I've learned rather more than I ever did from my old tutors, out of boredom if nothing else, out of desperation to find a way out of this place. So I've kept the place up.''

''Kept it up?'' Dara repeated. She remembered the dust in the library laying thick on the shelves, the cobwebs.

"Sometimes visitors brought books in with them," Lord Vanian said remotely. "I tried to save the books, if I could, for the library. That grimoire you stole wasn't a part of the library when it appeared. I simply placed it in the library when the owner . . . no longer needed it."

"Well, then, you can't say I stole it," Dara said practically, "since somebody else put the library there, and it was somebody else's grimoire, too."

"Ah, but the library is a part of my home," Lord Vanian corrected. "And that sage didn't *put* the library there; the Keep did, of which I am the Guardian. It wasn't his library any more than this is the house where you were born; it is merely an imitation formed by the keep. My keep."

Dara didn't like that thought; it gave Lord Vanian a sort of claim over this house, *her* house, that made her distinctly uneasy. If he thought everything in the Keep belonged to him, did he then believe that Dara belonged to him, too? Well, she'd just prove otherwise, if she had to!

"The pies are done," Dara said hurriedly. "I'm sorry, I've still got to get the dining hall ready."

"Not at all," Lord Vanian said grandly. "Here will do." He raised his eyebrows. "Do people eat in kitchens?"

Dara fought down another chuckle; how often she'd sat in this kitchen while Tabba fed her the nicest morsels from the pot. At High Lord Haranor's household the maids weren't allowed to eat in the kitchen except after supper; otherwise they had to take their bowls out back and sit on the steps to eat.

"You know," Dara said carefully, "I'm sure Gespry is as hungry as we are. I'll see if he'll come in."

Lord Vanian grinned.

"Do your best, if you really want that flea-ridden creature at the table with us." He laughed. "But I'm sure he won't show a whisker while I'm here."

Dara sighed; she was sure that Lord Vanian was probably right. She put a bowl of the broth, a meat pie, a few rolls, and some of the pudding on a tray and took it out the kitchen door, stepping down into the courtyard.

"Gespry?"

Gespry peered around the corner of the building warily, his eyes widening with relief when he saw that Dara was alone.

"He gone?" Gespry hissed.

"He's in the kitchen," Dara said, amused and a little annoyed by Gespry's cowardice. "Will you come in and eat? Or I brought you a tray if you won't come in."

"Tray's fine," Gespry said hurriedly. "It don't seem like a good idea, somehow, sitting there at table with the lord. Reckon I'll just sit out here."

Dara sighed, but there was nothing to be gained by arguing; Lord Vanian was waiting, and so was her own dinner. She placed the tray on the step and hurried back inside, where Lord Vanian was waiting with a less than patient expression on his face.

Dara ladled up thick bowls of the hot sop; that and the pies and bread, a wedge of cheese from the big wheel in the pantry, fresh apples and cider and the pudding, would make a dinner fit for anyone, she thought rather defiantly. Lord Vanian could have his swan simmered in almond milk; she'd cooked a good dinner and she knew it, and while he might wish for finer, he couldn't hope for better.

Somehow sitting in this kitchen, the kitchen of her own home, sipping barley in beef broth and nibbling meat pies that she'd made with her own hands, it was impossible to feel any fear of the lord who sat across the table on his plain wooden stool, slurping the broth from his spoon and licking gravy from his chin like anybody. Lord Vanian neither praised the fare nor complained, but Dara would have been utterly shocked if any compliment had ever passed his lips anyway. He ate heartily, and Dara thought that was praise enough.

All through the meal Dara wondered anxiously what Lord Vanian would want of her next. If he expected entertainment after dinner, he'd be disappointed; Dara could neither sing nor play any instrument, and she feared that whatever Lord Vanian considered "amusing" might not be equally agreeable to her. But she was both relieved and a little disappointed when Lord Vanian took his leave immediately after he'd finished eating—disappointed, because she'd get no more information from him until the next time she saw him, and she'd likely not meet him again on so nearly her own terms. Perhaps she should have tried to keep him there, to keep him talking so she could learn more, but—but—

"But I thought that would be asking too much of my luck," Dara said aloud, rather grimly. She'd been afraid, admit it, that through force or trickery she'd find herself in Lord Vanian's bed again.

Dara sighed and glanced at the dirty pot and bowls. The well was outside; she'd have to carry water in to fill the large boiling pan, then heat it up, then scrub the dishes, then haul the dirty wash water out back to dump on the ground. Dara stared at the dirty dishes and focused her concentration—

—and they were clean, as simply as that. Dara hugged her arms around her own ribs and shivered. Seductive, this power. It took a girl who'd spent the last year chopping turnips and scrubbing dirty pots to appreciate just how amazing such power was. No wonder her mother and father had made such a fuss about magic! Why, in their eyes she was as good as crippled or blind. Once having tasted the power of magic, how difficult it would be to lose it, how strange to imagine life without it. Poor Gespry—he'd never had a chance to use the make-magic of the Keep, but he'd seen it used often enough. Even if he could leave and return to the life he'd had before, how could he go back to the life of a cobbler after seeing someone wish a pair of boots out of thin air? And how difficult would Dara find it to go back to her pots and turnips now that she'd held that power herself?

"Well, I won't be going back to the pots and turnips,"

Dara said resolutely. "I'll be going back to marry Cav, and then I'll be High Lady of Caistran, and somebody else will be washing the pots." Her statement sounded shamefully callous in her own ears; unlike Lord Vanian, she'd never be able to forget that somewhere in and about her pretty castle, men and women were scrubbing the stone floors on their knees, mucking out stables, cutting the bad spots out of potatoes, emptying chamber pots. As a child, she'd never stopped to think that cheerful old Tabba might have resented her heavy labor, might have wished all day long she was doing something else. But now that she'd worked at those same tasks in High Lord Haranor's household for nearly five years, she couldn't unknow it.

Would she always feel guilty, knowing that others were earning a pittance doing the dirty, meaningless, monotonous work that she'd never again have to roughen her noble hands with?

Probably.

Dara ducked her head out the kitchen door. Gespry was nowhere in sight, but when she called he peeped around the corner again.

"Lord Vanian's gone, really gone, for now, at least," Dara told him. "I want to look around a little more, see if there's anything to be learned here. Do you think we could stay here tonight?"

"Don't see why not, if you want to be here that long," Gespry said, shrugging. "Seems a comfortable enough place, better'n I've ever seen, 'cept the lord's castle, I guess. You sure did whip up a nice spread for dinner," he added with a grin. "Food like that, reckon I could stay here as long as you liked."

Dara flushed proudly at the praise. Gespry didn't know that Dara had cooked his dinner with her own two hands, but Dara herself did, and suddenly she realized that she'd been wrong, terribly wrong, in what she'd thought about the men and women who served in the castle. Their work wasn't meaningless; her dirty pots and turnips weren't meaningless. The dinner she'd just cooked was good and filling and nourishing, and she'd made it with her own two hands; she had every right to be proud of the results of her labors. When she made a dirty pan clean and shiny again, when somebody ate her turnips and was nourished, she could be proud of a task performed well. Not so when she merely used the magic of the Keep to wish the pan clean or the turnips chopped; anybody could learn to use the magic to do what she did, and it wasn't even *her* magic.

Seductive, the power of the Crystal Keep, yes, indeed, but she'd have to remember that it was nothing more than a crutch for those who couldn't get by on their own skills.

Like servants for the nobility.

"Want me to check part of the place, too?" Gespry asked.

"That's a good idea," Dara said. What she really wanted was to find out just how much like her own home this replica was, and Gespry would be useless in that determination; but she felt the need to see it alone, without the constant interruption of his chatter.

Dara slowly climbed the stairs to the second floor. Mother and Father's rooms, the guest rooms, and the suites that her brothers Aidan and Erlien used when they visited were just as she remembered them, but so empty it made her heart ache.

She hesitated some time before she dared enter her own room, and when she did, she had to fight back tears. It was just as she had left it, and Dara wondered sadly whether her parents had kept it for her in case she should return, or whether the Keep had merely reconstructed it from her own memory. There were her second-best walking boots in the corner, the soles still caked with mud—she was forever forgetting to scrape them, and Mother and Father refused to hire chambermaids to coddle the family as if they were invalids—and there was the old cloak that Dara had loved to wear rambling through the woods and refused to part with although it was stained and a dozen times patched.

That memory made Dara pause, then hurry to her wardrobe. To her delight, the clothes she'd been forced to leave behind still hung on their pegs. Dara sighed with delight. She couldn't carry all the clothing with her, but the few garments she could take would save her the time and trouble of conjuring substitutes. She could even take Father's mule and saddlebags from the barn if she wanted, but after a moment's thought Dara decided she was wiser taking only what she could carry. Some of the places she'd visited weren't exactly the sort of places she wanted to try to get a mule through. Besides, she'd never learned to ride.

There was one load, however, that Dara was determined to carry away with her. She hurried down the hall to Mother and Father's rooms, where she found the keys in their hiding place under the hollow base of the flower urn, then down to the end of the hall to Father's workrooms, which she had to unlock. Father's consulting room, where he met with customers from the town, was neat and nearly empty, but the workroom connected to it was filled with jars and boxes of the herbs, spices, and other ingredients he used in his spells, powders, and potions, but Dara passed those by; they didn't seem actually applicable to the kind of magic used here in the Keep. Neither did the elaborate tools—braziers, wands and rods, bowls of different metals—seem necessary.

From what Dara had seen, Lord Vanian didn't even need to cast a spell, nor probably did Granny; they'd been using the Keep's magic for a long time and knew well how to manipulate it. But Dara had already seen that she herself fared much better when she used a spell, even only the incantation; that was probably because she herself had never had experience in working with magic and was new to the power of the Keep. The form of the spell was likely only a means of focusing her concentration properly, but if that was what she needed, that was what she needed. And if the Keep had made as complete a replica of her home as it seemed, here was the opportunity to find all the spells she would ever need.

She wanted the family grimoire.

Mother and Father never locked the thick volumes up beyond locking the door to the workroom whenever he or Mother left the room; nobody would bother to steal them. They were far too heavy and thick to carry away more than one or maybe two. Besides, nobody but a mage would have any use for them, and as any mage knew, it was dangerous beyond measure to try to cast a spell beyond her own level of learning and ability. That, of course, was why novice mages copied spells from the master's grimoire into their own as they learned them. Therefore the first part of any grimoire was always the simplest spells in the order in which they were learned.

Dara lifted down the first volume of the grimoire. She'd practiced most of the spells in it over and over, trying to make even one of them work, and if it hadn't been for the plums she'd eaten, she'd have many of the spells all but memorized.

Well, she'd simply learn them again. She'd have to. This evening she'd look through the other volumes, too, and see whether any of the spells might be worth copying before she left, in case she needed them later; Father always kept one blank volume for copying any new spells he learned. There was this to be said for the keep: Apparently there was no need for Dara to follow the slow, plodding progression from the simplest spells to the most complicated. It seemed to Dara that any spell she could learn, she could now use. Why, the basic pendulum divination she'd done had been no simpler to cast than the more complicated water vision. And now she'd find the most powerful divination spells in the grimoire and use them, too. Maybe she wouldn't need the Oracle or Lord Vanian's mirror, either.

She carried all sixteen volumes of the grimoire to the table in the workroom—and then opened one of the guest rooms for Gespry. She'd have time to leaf through some of the grimoire before suppertime, and more time tonight. A flask of brandy from the cellar would entertain Gespry to his fullest satisfaction, no doubt, and tonight she'd have the pleasure of sleeping in her very own bed once again.

By the time Gespry sought her out, complaining about his growling belly, Dara's eyes were sore and aching and her hand was cramped from copying. She gratefully put down her pen and followed Gespry back down to the kitchen. This time Dara was content to conjure supper into being; she felt vaguely guilty doing it after her earlier conclusions on the worth of self-reliance, but she rationalized that the time wasted in cooking could be better spent in copying. Besides, she might as well resign herself to making her food by magic; as soon as she left this place, there was no knowing when she might have access to a kitchen again, and she had to feed Gespry and herself.

Gespry all but inhaled the rich stew with dumplings, the salt-rising bread, mashed parsnips, and berry tart, praising each mouthful so extravagantly that Dara was embarrassed.

"I ain't eaten so well since I came to the Keep," he said, smacking his lips. "Come to think on it, don't know that I ate so well before it, neither. Course, I never had the coin for food like this. Don't know what I'll do if you make it out of here," he admitted wryly.

"Then you'll learn to do it yourself," Dara told him, ladling more dumplings into his bowl. "Granny and Lord Vanian do."

"Well, like as not they was mages before they come," Gespry said with a shrug. "And you at least studied magic. 'Sides, I wonder how many years it took *them* to learn? I'd starve in the meantime."

"Well, if you like you can stay here," Dara said, oddly reluctant to give the permission. It was like giving away her home. But what claim did she have to it, really? And besides, she'd be living with Cav. "There's plenty of food, a good clean well, and a comfortable place to sleep— everything you could want, really."

"Ain't a bad idea," Gespry agreed. "Presuming you don't go and get yourself sucked down some hole and your key with you before you get to bring me back here, or you lose your key and we can't *get* back here. Or your games with the lord gets us both turned into swamp croakers right back in the mud where I was."

"Well, I intend to get my wish and walk out of here and go marry Cav," Dara said positively. "And when I go I'll give you my key, and you can go anywhere you want. But if Granny says you can learn to get around without the key, you should learn," she added. "Or you might just lose it again someday and you'd be in the same fix you were before."

"Yeah, well, maybe if somebody was willing to teach me the trick of it, I'd learn faster," Gespry said wryly. "I'd be much obliged if you'd show me how to just make food."

"Well—" Dara hesitated. "The first thing to remember about transformatory magic is that everything in the world contains magical energies, but living things contain the most magical energy and so are the easiest to work with. Next are things that were once living, like autumn leaves or cloth or leather, and last are things that never had any life of their own, like rock or water. The other thing to remember is that all living things are made up of the same basic stuff and therefore has a very close affinity with any other living thing—"

"Girly, I don't understand a word of it," Gespry groaned.

"Well, think of wheat and bread," Dara said, spearing a dumpling and holding it up as an example. "You wouldn't look at wheat growing in the field and look at this dumpling and know that they're related to each other unless you knew about wheat, and threshing, and grinding, and cooking. So magical transformation is simply the discipline of seeing things in all their different forms and realizing that nothing is really very different from anything else in the way it's made up. So if you can look at this dumpling and see the wheat, you've made a beginning toward the kind of thinking that transformation needs.''

"You mean like looking at grapes and seeing wine?'' Gespry said cautiously.

"Just like that,'' Dara said, nodding. "And if you can make wine from cherries, too, then that means that grapes and cherries aren't so very different, doesn't it?''

"Yeah, I can see that,'' Gespry said after a moment's thought. "But it don't do me no good to change grapes into cherries when I ain't got no grapes.''

"Well, don't take what I say so directly,'' Dara told him. "For example, at High Lord Haranor's household I saw one of the cooks take sweetened almond paste and coloring and make that almond paste look like fruits, just like. You'd pick up what you thought was a strawberry and bite into it and find your mouth full of sweet paste. That seemed like a kind of transformation magic itself. For a while your mind refused to believe it wasn't a strawberry you'd eaten. But it's not so strange if you remember how much living things are basically alike. You learn to see that similarity, and at least here in the Keep it's just a matter of using the Keep's magic to make that similarity real. I don't think you have to have any magic yourself, just imagination and concentration.''

"How about going from one place to another, like Granny and the lord does?'' Gespry said after a moment's thought. "That work the same?''

"I don't know,'' Dara admitted. "Transportation magic was always left to the very powerful mages—Gates and the like. And why give visitors a key if they don't need it? Maybe only de—-I mean, maybe only folk who live here can jump about like Granny and Lord Vanian. As I see it, I'd just better not lose my key.''

"Well, couldn't you just make another, then, things being like you say?'' Gespry asked, his voice eager; Dara could well imagine that the next question was whether she could make a key for *him*.

"I could make a key," she said carefully. "Even a gold key, maybe. But this can't be an ordinary gold key. Gold's too soft to make a good key. It's likely that this key must have magical properties. I don't know anything about what magic's gone into this key, so I don't see how I could make another. A better chance would be copying my own key, but you can't expect me to experiment and maybe ruin my only way out of here. If I find a spell in my family grimoire that I think might do it, I'll try, but again, I wouldn't want to do that until I was sure I didn't need my own key anymore, so giving you mine would be just as good."

Gespry scowled and said nothing more, but he scampered off to the yard after supper, and Dara imagined he was probably experimenting with turning straw into wine. She wished him success; at least his occupation left her free to continue her copying in peace. Dara sighed and returned to the tedious task; if only she could wish her copy into existence as she could a loaf of hot bread!

That thought made Dara pause and put down her quill. Why couldn't she? She knew the process of copying the words and diagrams as well as she knew the process of baking that selfsame loaf. Maybe it *could* be done by magic.

To Dara's delight, a few experiments proved the spell simple enough—easier, actually, than the transformations she'd already done, since she could see the original as she was working. By the time she had copied what she wanted for the present, the blank volume was half full and her head was aching furiously, and her eyes were burning. Time to stop before she started making mistakes, a very dangerous thing to do when working with magic. Dara blotted her last copy meticulously, closed the book, and locked the workroom before she staggered down the hall to her room.

Even as weary as she was, Dara savored intensely the sweetness of sinking into her own soft bed, the pillow smelling wonderfully familiar with the scent of the dried herbs Mother mixed with the feathers for just that purpose.

High Lord Haranor's maids' quarters had been comfortable enough, Dara supposed, but when there were six maids to a room there was no space for anything more than narrow cots and no opportunity for privacy. To once again lie in a large, soft bed in a room to herself was an almost-forgotten luxury, so much so that she would have stayed awake to savor it if she could have managed to do so.

Tomorrow she'd copy a few more spells. Just a few more. She'd have time to pack clothes, too, and supplies— any supplies she wanted. Best to err on the side of too much; it was such a long walk back here that there might be no opportunity to come again. Best to copy all the spells she thought she might need, take everything she could carry. After all, what difference did it make if she had to stay here an extra day? It would be a welcome respite, a chance to rest, body and spirit, in preparation for the hardships undoubtedly ahead of her. What harm could one more day make?

Or two?

10

"ANOTHER CUP OF CIDER?" DARA OF-
fered. "Or maybe another slice of peach
tart?"

"No more," Gespry groaned, patting his swollen belly
gingerly. "Another mouthful of anything and I reckon I'll
just burst. Varak's boot soles, reckon I've et half my weight
again today."

Dara sighed contentedly and pushed back from the table,
leaving the soiled bowls and platters where they were. In
the morning they'd have mysteriously cleaned themselves
and replaced themselves in the cupboards, just as they had
every morning since Dara and Gespry arrived. The fire in
the hearth and in the bedrooms would be freshly laid, too,
the previous day's ashes gone, the chamber pots emptied
and scrubbed. Dara's clothes would be clean and fresh, and
the water in the jug on her night table would be replenished.
Even the flowers in the bowls and jugs throughout the
house would have been replaced with fresh, sweet-smelling
blossoms. Dara had wondered at this, but after all, she was
used to exactly such service from Mother and Father's own

servants, and if this place was modeled from her memory, then such invisible service wasn't really too amazing.

Between breakfast and dinner Dara would study the grimoire and practice the simple spells she was learning. Then it was back to the kitchen where Gespry would usually be waiting impatiently for his dinner. After dinner Dara gave herself a brief respite from her study to ramble about the lands, usually with Gespry for company, but then it was back to the workroom until suppertime, and after supper, until bedtime. She was, after all, here to learn.

And she was learning. How wonderful it was to speak the spells and see the results of her work made real, the more delightful for all the times she'd tried and failed in the past. Even her fumbling failures were encouraging; how wonderful to simply make a mistake and know it for the simple error it was! But she was progressing, with a gratifying rapidity, and such mistakes were becoming fewer.

It was only this encouraging progress that allowed Dara to justify the days they'd spent here. How many? Dara couldn't be certain that what she called day and night here were the same elsewhere in the Keep. They were happy days, but they were productive days, too, Dara excused herself, days of honing her skills and gathering the power she'd need to protect herself if necessary, to try to divine the location of the Oracle, to win her wish from Lord Vanian. So she'd stayed, and Gespry had stayed with her.

Not that Gespry was complaining. He did what he pleased all day, and what he pleased usually consisted of rambling about the house and the lands (''seeing to the place,'' as he put it). After dinner and his walk with Dara, the furry creature inevitably found a sunny windowsill where he'd curl up for a nap, and in the evenings he would inevitably perch himself in a chair before the fire with a mug of wine or brandy and Father's pipe.

Dara thought sometimes that neither of them had likely ever known such contentment in their lives.

Only the vaguest of guilt and frustration marred Dara's

peace of mind. She missed Cav, of course, and wondered how he fared (though what was there to worry about, when Cav was the High Lord's son and Heir, safe in Caistran?), but despite the most potent divination spells she tried she was unable to see him or learn anything of him. It was as if, for divinatory purposes, the keep was a world in and of itself, and nothing but perhaps the Guardian's mirror could reach outside. Dara worried now that perhaps the reverse was true, and perhaps nothing could reach from the outside in, either, including any divinations Cav or the palace mages had cast.

Likewise she had been unable to learn anything more of the Oracle, though she had wearied and frustrated herself trying. She was certain now that such knowledge was protected by a more powerful magic than anything she could summon up, and was that really so surprising, considering the magic that must have been used in building—if "building" was the right word—the Keep itself? Likely the entire Keep had been designed and created to protect the Oracle itself.

And this was the power against which Dara had decided to pit herself. Every time Dara began to worry that she should be resuming her search of the Keep and abandoning this pleasant reminder of home, her doubts of her ability to meet that power drove her once more back to the grimoires and her studies. That, and a nagging reluctance to leave even the illusion of home, the wonderful safety and comfort and familiarity of it all, to return to a quest that often seemed hopeless. Better to study the grimoires, to sit and think before the fire—

—to wait just a *little* longer.

On the seventh "day" of her stay Dara treated herself to a leisurely mug of cider on the steps after breakfast, and was considering a morning of wading in the stream before beginning her studies for the day. She'd been up late studying the night before, she excused herself, and she'd worked so hard for so many days; she deserved a bit of rest.

She had no more than dipped her feet into the cool water, however, when a familiar prickling at the back of her neck told her she was being watched. Dara turned quickly to find Lord Vanian lying comfortably on the bank, gazing at her with his usual air of rather condescending amusement.

"After all this time, and I find you playing in the water," he said dryly. "Imagine that."

Hurriedly Dara stepped out of the water, drying her feet on the grass.

"I only wanted a little rest," she said self-consciously, fumbling for her stockings and boots. "I've been working hard with scarcely a pause."

"Indeed you have," Lord Vanian agreed. "Knowing I would feel the sharp edge of your tongue if I visited your home without invitation, I was hard put to find a time I could visit at all, as every time I consulted my mirror you were hard at your studies. Studying great spells to kill me, no doubt."

"I wasn't—" Dara began, then stopped. Let him think her a danger if he wished. "I wasn't studying every moment," she finished awkwardly.

"Nor was I watching every moment," Lord Vanian said with a dismissive wave of his hand.

"You weren't?" Dara found the thought a considerable relief.

Lord Vanian laughed. "You think overmuch of yourself," he said. "Do you truly believe that entertaining as you may be, I have nothing else to do but watch you—that I have no other diversions, even no other duties? Far from it."

Dara sneaked a look at him out of the corner of her eye, but forced a casual tone.

"What sort of duties?"

Lord Vanian glanced back at her just as slyly. "Other visitors, for example."

"Other—" Dara hesitated, stunned. There were other visitors in this place? Immediately confusion took the place of her amazement. Well, why wouldn't there be others? The Crystal Keep was legendary. There had always been those eager to seek it out. Dara had heard of only a few who had gone before her, but then Caistran was only one small country and Dara had to some extent lived sheltered from the outside world—first in her parents' keep, and then in the service of High Lord Haranor and High Lady Alberta. Doubtless visitors came from all over the settled world to visit the Keep. Why, she could have assumed as much from the sheer number of doors and the vastly varied worlds they contained.

"There are other visitors here right now?" she said at last. "Besides me, I mean?"

"Perhaps a few." Lord Vanian shrugged. "If you think they'd be of help to you, you'd be wrong. They've had time to learn far less than you." He grinned. "And are far less entertaining as well."

They had arrived after she had, then. A horrible thought suddenly occurred to Dara.

"Cav didn't follow me here, did he?" she asked anxiously, yet a sudden wild hope flared in her heart. Had he come all this way, surely against his mother and father's wishes, to find her himself when his divinations could not? Had she misjudged him after all?

Lord Vanian smiled lazily.

"Do you know, I believe I'd best not answer that question," he said at last. "Of course, you could go from door to door in my keep, searching for your lover, as he'd be unlikely to have come this far. That could take some time, however, and you've already found that method yields precious little return, haven't you? Or you could use your crippled divination spells, the ones that have served you so poorly so far."

A great knot tightened in Dara's stomach; for a moment she thought she might faint.

"What," she said slowly, "do you want of me?"

Lord Vanian paused thoughtfully, as if considering the question, although there was no doubt in Dara's mind that he had been waiting for her to ask just that question.

"Five days," he said at last, drawing out the words as if they tasted sweet in his mouth.

"Five days?" Dara repeated, the cold knot of fear in her vitals tightening so she could hardly breathe. "Five days of what, exactly?"

"Oh, nothing like what you're doubtless imagining," Lord Vanian said, chuckling. "Although if you prefer such a bargain, I would be more than delighted to oblige you. No, I enjoyed our dinner a few days ago so much that I thought it might be pleasant to have a servant about the place again—a real kitchen maid to prepare my meals. And not by magic, either—with your own hands, just as you did. Five days of doing the work you know best. At the end of each of those days I'll allow you to ask one question of my mirror, but you may not ask the location of the Oracle until the fifth day, nor may you ask the mirror the question you intended to ask the Oracle. And you can't so much as set foot outside the castle without my permission until the five days are over."

He glanced at her and grinned again. "Well?"

It was tempting, so very tempting—all of her questions answered, even about the Oracle, no more plodding through the dangers of the Keep and wondering if it was even possible for her to find the Oracle. But five days in Lord Vanian's house—

Reluctantly Dara shook her head. "I don't trust you," she said flatly.

This time Lord Vanian laughed outright. "What a wise little miss. Very well, I swear that I will never attempt to take you to my bed either by force or deceit."

"Not good enough by half," Dara challenged. "Your

bed is all well and good, but there've been enough nobles try to put an honest maid on the dining-hall table or the dressing-room floor, or in a corner in the corridor, come to that.''

To Dara's surprise, Lord Vanian appeared neither embarrassed nor insulted by her statement. ''You *have* learned since you came here,'' he chuckled. ''As you wish, then. I swear that I'll not attempt any intimacy with you anywhere at all, either by force or deceit. Will that satisfy you?''

Dara hesitated again. It *did* seem the answer to all her problems, and likely it would have taken her a good bit longer than five days to find the Oracle on her own. And better yet, Lord Vanian hadn't put any time limit on his promise; it would bind him as long as Dara was in the Keep, and that safety alone was worth much. But she was very reluctant to grant Lord Vanian anything he might want; whatever purpose he had in asking such a thing of her, she could be sure it wasn't anything to her own good. Still, what if Cav was wandering the Keep, in danger of his life every minute? What if he lost his key?

''All right,'' Dara said after a moment's thought. ''I'll give you your five days, but with two other provisions: First, I may ask the mirror an additional question immediately; and second, if I learn where Cav is in the Keep, you'll bring him to us immediately and keep him safe there until I can leave.''

Lord Vanian smiled in a way that disturbed Dara, but she could not hide her relief when he nodded.

''Just as you say,'' he told her. ''You may ask your question as soon as we reach my castle, and if you find your lordling in the Keep, I'll bring him safely to you. Is it a bargain, then?'' He held out his hand.

Dara had to steel herself to touch him, but at last she reached out and gingerly clasped his hand. His fingers were cool and strong, but silky smooth; Dara was secretly delighted to note that despite the sword she'd seen in his rooms, he had no swordsman's calluses on his fingers. Cav was a fine swordsman.

"Very well," she said, although a deep, fearful doubt remained in her heart. Surely powerful mages must feel this fear when they summoned demons from the nether planes and struck terrible deals with them. "We have a bargain."

"Good." Lord Vanian stood quickly, brushing off his trousers fastidiously. "Gather your things, then, and your frightened little friend, and we'll be off."

"Right now?" Dara said in dismay. She thought she'd be allowed to walk back. That would give her time to slip up to the workroom and copy a last spell or two from the family grimoire before she left.

"I don't see why not." Lord Vanian's smile was gently mocking, and Dara was suddenly certain he had guessed her intent. "For the next five days you are my servant and under my orders, are you not?"

Inwardly Dara winced at the thought, but she stifled a sigh and bowed her head.

"Just as you say, m'lord," she said quietly. "I'll be ready as soon as I can collect my belongings and Gespry."

It took only a short time to stuff her clothes, the first volume of the family grimoire, and her half-filled copy book into a sack, transfer her other supplies from her makeshift basket to a sturdy pack, and roust Gespry from his drowse in the sun. When she told him of the bargain she'd made, however, Gespry groaned and clutched his head in dismay.

"Tell me you didn't never do such a mist-headed thing," Gespry said sourly. "Girly, sometimes you ain't shown much good sense, but I never figured you'd lost every speck of wits you ever had. And just what do you expect I'm to do while you're playing serving maid to the lord? You figured on that, eh? I'm stuck with you till you lose your key or get out. So what am I supposed to be doing in the lord's own castle, eh?"

"Well, I suppose the same thing you were doing here,"

Dara retorted a little impatiently. "Dozing in the sun or by the fire, eating the food I prepare, and drinking whatever wine or brandy you can find. You can do that just as well in the lord's castle as in my own house, can't you?"

"Well, that just depends, don't it," Gespry said patiently. "When you made your little arrangement with the lord, you didn't make no provision for me, did you? I'm bound by my promise, and so are you, but the lord ain't bound to give me so much as a crust of bread, is he?"

"I never thought of that," Dara admitted contritely. How could she have been so selfish as to forget Gespry and his needs? Then she smiled. "But I never promised I wouldn't provide food for you. He said I was to prepare his food with my own hands, but I'll conjure food for you if I must. Anyway," she added, "he expected me to bring you with me, so he must have known I'd go on providing for you."

Gespry was not reassured, and he grumbled to himself as he scampered along after Dara. Lord Vanian had politely stayed outside, and Dara was somewhat chagrined to notice that he was still standing where she'd left him in the courtyard, among the freely rambling chickens and goats. She made no apology, however, but mutely stepped to his side, slinging both packs over her shoulders with a grunt of effort. Gespry also said nothing, hiding behind Dara and clutching her leg.

"Ready?" Lord Vanian said almost pleasantly. "Very well, then—"

There was no sense of transition. One moment they were standing there in the courtyard; abruptly they stood instead in the cold entry hall of Lord Vanian's castle. Dara barely stifled her gasp of astonishment, but she could feel Gespry's small hands trembling as they grasped at her leg even more tightly.

"Well, I'll leave you to put up your things and make yourself presentable," Lord Vanian said, glancing at the comfortably old, patched tunic and trousers Dara was wearing. "I assume you can create an appropriate gown; otherwise I'll make you something myself."

"My lord—" Dara said, hesitating. She disliked to remind Lord Vanian that she'd entered his castle and searched it, especially when he'd politely respected the boundaries of the replica of her own home. "Where am I to stay?" she asked at last. "There's no servants' quarters here."

Lord Vanian sighed rather apologetically.

"Do you know, that's one of the parts of the place that has disappeared over time," he said. "I suppose it was only to be expected, since I'd never actually seen them and they had no importance to me. Well, no matter. Take Marguerid's room—the one you were in before," he added by way of explanation.

The thought of returning to that room, of sleeping in it, made Dara's stomach heave.

"My lord, that wouldn't be appropriate," she said desperately, "to put a servant in such a room. Surely there's someplace else—"

"There are the High Lord and Lady's chambers," Lord Vanian said sarcastically. "There are the guest suites. Take Marguerid's room. At least it's meant for a woman, and it's near the top of the stairs."

Dara started to protest, but then closed her mouth; she'd made a bargain, and it was not her place to argue with the lord's orders.

"What of Gespry, my lord?" she asked softly.

"Oh, whatever you like," Lord Vanian said absently. "Make him up a cushion in some corner, or if you're certain he's carrying no vermin, put him in one of the guest rooms. It doesn't matter." He turned and walked to the staircase, then paused and turned back.

"Whenever you wish to use my mirror," he said with a slow smile, "just come up to my room."

Dara sighed, picked up her bags again, and trudged quietly up the stairs, Gespry following silently. She opened the door to her room and laid her bags on the bed, shivering slightly as she glanced around her.

"Well, what now?" Gespry asked in a subdued voice. He was shivering, too. "Gonna put a cushion in the corner for me?"

"Oh, Gespry, don't be ridiculous." Dara's sudden wave of irritation did much to banish her fear. "I'll make up one of the guest suites."

"Nah, don't," Gespry said, to Dara's amazement. "Reckon I'd rather stay here, if you don't mind."

"Of course I don't mind," Dara said quickly. "But wouldn't you like a room of your own better?"

"Nah, not here," Gespry said, shivering again. "What's the good anyway? I can barely reach the door latch, and I ain't gonna leave the door open a bit like I did at your place, not here. If I got to be in the lord's own house, at least I'm staying well out of his way."

Well, there was sense enough in that. Dara tucked her sacks into the wardrobe, then took one of the gowns and experimented with turning it into a simple, sturdy gown for work. The dresses she'd worn in High Lord Haranor's household were recent enough in her memory that Dara had no difficulty transforming the finery into a sturdy broadcloth gown and apron and a scarf to hold back her hair. She'd worn finer, of course, the times she'd been allowed to serve in the dining hall at great functions, but to serve Lord Vanian alone, there was no sense in working in a hot kitchen wearing such clothing.

Dara washed her hands and face and tied the scarf over her hair, then reluctantly made her way to the tower. This time the door at the base was unlocked, as Dara had expected it might be, and Dara followed the curving staircase up to the closed door at the top. She knocked timidly.

"It's I, my lord," she said unnecessarily. Who else could it be?

"Come in." There was, as Dara had feared, considerable amusement in Lord Vanian's voice; this game was entirely to his liking, and he was undoubtedly going to make the most of it. It was, she thought miserably, likely to be the most wretched five days of her life. Even Cav's presence would be a mixed blessing; how wonderful to see him and know he was safe and by her side, but how awkward to have to play the maidservant to Lord Vanian before she could leave.

Dara opened the door and stepped into the room. The luxurious chamber was exactly as she had seen it last, except that the mirror she had once seen at the end of the dining hall—how could she ever forget it?—now hung on the wall of this room. Lord Vanian sat before the mirror, gazing into it, but the surface was that of a simple mirror now, reflecting only the room and its occupants.

"Come to claim your price, have you?" Lord Vanian said, a tone of surprising bitterness in his voice. "Come, then."

Dara timidly stepped up to the mirror, then hesitated.

"How do I use it?" she asked slowly. "Properly, I mean."

Lord Vanian shrugged. "The same as any other divination," he said. "Just ask."

Something in his tone made Dara more afraid than ever. Why was he playing this game? Why had he consented to her terms? Not knowing those answers could be deadly dangerous while she was bound under the terms of their bargain. But still—

Cav.

Dara turned resolutely to the mirror. "Show me where Cav is," she said firmly.

The mirror clouded as it had before, but cleared far more quickly—perhaps because Dara was far more clearheaded than she'd been. She immediately recognized the view reflected in the mirror. Why, hadn't she walked up that very hill to the High Lord's keep where it stood at the top that first day, the very day she'd met Cav? Yes, surely it was Lord Haranor's own castle sitting there on the hill, guards standing watchfully at the front gate.

"I don't understand," Dara said puzzledly. Had the Crystal Keep created a replica of High Lord Haranor's castle as it had of her own home? Had Cav somehow made his way past Dara to the end of the long corridor and into that replica, perhaps while she'd dallied in her home? But how could he have had time to learn to do that? And why would he have gone there to seek her even if he had learned so much about the Keep in so short a time?

Then something about the vision in the mirror made Dara turn again, take a closer look. Guards! Guards at the gate. And surely those were footmen at the door to the castle. But the Keep didn't duplicate—

Sudden realization made Dara turn from the mirror in fury. "He's not here at all!" she said, outraged. "He's still back at home in Caistran."

"I would assume so," Lord Vanian said in a bored tone. Then he grinned. "But as I recall, I never said otherwise."

Dara could have groaned aloud with her dismay. No, Lord Vanian had never actually *said* Cav was in the Crystal Keep, but he'd implied—

No, he hadn't. Now Dara almost wept as she recalled their conversation. Dara had been the one to blindly guess that Cav would have followed her to the Crystal Keep— and shouldn't she have known better? Cav would never have done anything so irresponsible. Lord Vanian had done nothing but fail to tell Dara that Cav was *not* there. She'd wasted her question to the mirror and bound herself to Lord Vanian's service for five days because she'd once more deceived herself, jumping to a conclusion without thinking it through.

Well, she hadn't deceived herself without help. Lord Vanian did everything he did out of some purpose that only he understood. He would never have brought up the subject of other visitors in the Keep if giving her that knowledge didn't serve his purpose. He'd *wanted* her to make the assumption that Cav was here, she realized, probably precisely so that he could tempt her into this bargain that she would otherwise never have accepted.

Well, whatever pleasure he'd gained from the success of his ruse, he'd not have the pleasure of seeing Dara weep and wail in front of him. Dara mastered her temper—how thoroughly she'd had to learn that skill as a servant!—and when she turned around, her expression and her voice was calm.

"Thank you very much, my lord, for the use of your mirror," she said quietly. "It's reassuring to know that Cav is safe at home. But what I really came for, my lord—"

"What, the pleasure of my company?" Lord Vanian chuckled, but to Dara's delight he did look somewhat disappointed at her composure.

"—is to ask the lord's preferences as to the time he wishes his meals served, and those dishes he prefers," Dara said demurely. "And to ask whether the lord would like supper served tonight, because if so, I should begin preparations immediately, even though I believe my employment doesn't actually begin until tomorrow—"

"Now, wait," Lord Vanian said warningly.

"—unless the lord is prepared to consider this partial day's service as fulfilling one of the five days of my obligation," Dara finished sweetly.

"All the gods forbid," Lord Vanian said sarcastically. "No, I will manage my own supper tonight, thank you very much, and you and your little pet may do the same. Unless you'd prefer to sup with me?" He raised his eyebrows challengingly at the last statement.

"Thank you kindly, my lord," Dara said calmly, "but I'd never dare be so above myself as to sit at table with the lord. If there's nothing further my lord wishes, I beg your leave to go." She stood quietly, eyes down, fighting hard to keep a smile from her lips.

"Oh, go, then," Lord Vanian said impatiently, waving a dismissive hand as Dara curtsied prettily.

Dara closed the door quietly behind her and almost

skipped down the steps. If Lord Vanian was hungry for
servants, for a pleasant, servile maid to bring him his food,
he'd have it—and not a crumb more. And may he have joy
of it, too, for once she'd asked her questions of the mirror,
he'd have no further opportunity to torment her; she'd have
her wish and be gone. Let him play what tricks he liked in
the meantime; she'd encountered his kind more than once
in High Lord Haranor's household and come away with her
pride and her virtue intact. She had no virginity to protect
now, but she still had her pride, and she meant to keep it.

Dara made her way to the pantry and the cellar, inspecting more closely the foodstuffs she'd seen there before, this
time with an eye to the absence, rather than the presence,
of certain staples. She left the pantry even more delighted
than she'd entered. The pantry and cellar had seemed well
supplied when she'd been here before, but in actuality Lord
Vanian had had only the vaguest of knowledge of the staples a lord's pantry and cellar should contain. There was
plenty of wine and brandy, and the smoked meats hung
neatly at the back near the round wheels of cheese, as any
casual observer in the cellar might have seen, but there was
nothing so humble as sacks of flour or meal, casks of butter
or rendered fat, braids of onions or bins of turnips, as Dara
had suspected. Lord Vanian had never likely seen most of
the foods he consumed every day in their most basic form,
so of course those humble supplies had no place in this
replica created from his memories. Likewise the kitchen
had no bowls of eggs or fresh fruits or vegetables, nor even
additional wood for the fire, although the hearth fire was
blazing at present as it had been when Dara had visited the
castle before. Dara chuckled and returned to her room,
where she conjured up honey-basted roast fowl stuffed with
apples, barley soup, and thick crusty rolls for Gespry and
herself.

It was difficult staying in that room, where every detail
reminded Dara of her humiliation. Dara put her things away
quickly, then, to Gespry's amusement, laboriously trans-

formed the rich bedclothes and hangings to different colors
and fabrics, the elaborate dressing table to a plain but sturdy
press, and the ornate wardrobe to a simpler one. Almost as
an afterthought she managed to even place two windows in
the walls; now at least she could look out, even if she
couldn't actually walk outside. Lord Vanian would probably be incensed if he found out Dara had altered the room,
and that in itself was a worthy reason for the change. In
any event, he could always change it back later.

There was a stout lock on her door, and Dara took considerable satisfaction in securing it when she retired. Then
she realized Lord Vanian must surely have his own set of
keys, and her composure vanished; she was debating pushing the heavy press in front of the door when she realized
that it was no use. Lord Vanian could just as easily appear
right in her room rather than bothering with the stairs, corridors, and doors.

Well, there was one precaution the lord couldn't prevent
her from taking; Dara hadn't spent all that time studying to
no end. Rather defiantly Dara conjured up water and salt
and sprinkled the corners of the room, the door frame, and
the windowsills, chanting the powerful warding spell she'd
found and copied. A pale blue glow sprang up on the walls,
ceiling, and floor as the wards came up, then faded quietly
from sight. Dara sighed with satisfaction, stripped to her
chemise, and crawled into bed. She was startled a moment
later to hear Gespry's voice from his pallet by the fireplace.

"Listen, girly," he said with unusual timidity, "you
care if I take a corner up there instead of down here?"

"All right," Dara said, surprised, flattered, and a little
dismayed at both the fear and the trust implicit in Gespry's
statement. "But you're really no safer up here than down
there. If the lord can come in through the wards, there probably isn't much more I can do to stop him."

Gespry made no reply, but Dara could feel the slight
pressure on the bedclothes as the little creature climbed
onto the bed and curled up in the corner at her feet. Once

more Dara wondered at the depth of Gespry's fear, and she suddenly realized she knew very little of the odd little fellow who had shared her travels. Had Gespry crossed paths with Lord Vanian before with an outcome so disastrous as to cause such terror? Dara would have thought not; Lord Vanian, in any wise, seemed to have no special concern over Gespry, and he'd seemed to turn his venom on Dara when irritated, not the little demon. No, more than likely Gespry was like some of the peasants Dara had seen as she was passing through High Lord Haranor's lands—overawed and simply fearful of the powerful folk who held authority over them. And like High Lord Haranor, Lord Vanian for the most part ignored his underlings, as if Gespry was of no consequence whatsoever.

Privately Dara wondered whether her wards were of any consequence either. If all her magic derived only from the power of the Keep, could her spells foil the Guardian of the Keep, whose power derived from the very same source? But there was no good in voicing these doubts to Gespry; she'd only frighten him needlessly.

She had, strangely, rather more faith in the power of Lord Vanian's promise. She was still far from convinced that everything a resident of the Keep said could be accepted as the flat and absolute truth, but she also believed that she knew Lord Vanian's manner well enough by now to be assured that he would not simply invade her quarters and rape her. Brute force wasn't the lord's style at all; he'd far rather let Dara fall into a trap of his making or, better yet, her own, so that he could chuckle and gloat over his own cleverness and Dara's foolishness. So as long as Dara was careful and thoughtful and did not let Lord Vanian provoke her, she should be safe enough. Still, the wards were a simple enough precaution to take, and if Lord Vanian had some means of detecting the magical protection, he'd either be insulted that Dara mistrusted his word, or impressed with her caution, or both. In either event, best that she keep the lord off guard and wondering—just as he'd tried to keep her. As long as *she* was the one provoking *him*, she had the advantage. And by the time Dara was done with him, he'd learn to respect the dignity of one humble serving girl, at least, turnips and dirty pots notwithstanding.

Dara chuckled to herself, nestled deeper into the warm bed, and slept.

11

"WHAT, BY THE TOENAILS OF EVERY DE-mon in this keep, is this?" Lord Vanian demanded irritably. He scowled down at his plate, where a few slices of plain boiled ham and a wedge of cheese sat alone. "Is this your notion of what a noble-man breaks his fast on?"

"I beg your pardon, my lord," Dara said innocently. "I thought perhaps this was what my lord preferred, as there was no other food in the pantry."

"Well, why didn't you make something else, then?" Lord Vanian growled.

"Again, begging your pardon, my lord, but I believe I swore I'd serve you only what I prepared with my own hands," Dara said, her eyes carefully downcast.

Lord Vanian sighed with exaggerated patience, those dark eyes probingly sharp.

"Very well," he said with cold deliberation. "We'll go now to the pantry and the cellar, and you'll tell me what you need, and I'll see that everything's stocked. Then we'll have no more of this foolishness."

Dara opened her eyes wide with apparent shock.

"Why, my lord, I'd be far above myself to ask the lord himself to bother about the supplies. In High Lord Haranor's household I'd tell the cook, and the cook would tell the pantler or the butler, and they'd tell the seneschal, and the seneschal would—"

"Well, as I've neither cook, nor butler, nor pantler, nor seneschal," Lord Vanian said from between gritted teeth, "you'll have to rise above your lowly station and deal with me directly, as the alternative would seem to be my starvation." He waved a hand at the plate of meat and cheese, which vanished. "Come, we'll do it now."

Dara struggled to keep a smile from her face as she followed Lord Vanian down the stairs of the tower, then to the kitchen, where she spent an entertaining morning infuriating Lord Vanian. She made a great show of ignorance and confusion, bustling from pantry to cellar and back again as she thought of just *one* more staple she'd need to prepare repasts suitable for a great lord. Then there were cooking implements that needed to be described at great length, as Lord Vanian had never seen them, and Dara steadfastly demurred when Lord Vanian impatiently demanded that she simply make whatever she needed.

At last, when Lord Vanian finally stalked angrily off back to his rooms, Dara waited a few moments before she scampered back up for him, innocently reminding him that she'd need water for the great kitchen cauldron if she was to make his dinner, and that—so sorry, my lord—that dinner would be delayed for some time, because as she was only just starting the water, it would take some time to heat enough for cooking, and preparing the food would take some hours besides. Lord Vanian's temper finally broke; roaring that he'd attend to his own dinner, he drove her out of his chambers, threatening Dara with the direst of fates if a proper supper wasn't prepared. Dara hesitated outside the door, wondering if she dared bother him again to remind him that he'd never told her when he'd want supper, but at last she decided she'd harassed him enough for one morning, and she joyfully skipped back down to the kitchen to start preparations for supper.

Once Gespry realized that the lord had shut himself in his tower and was unlikely to reappear, he scampered down to join Dara in the kitchen. They passed a merry enough afternoon, Gespry sipping ale from a mug and nibbling at whatever dishes Dara was preparing, Dara rolling pastry with more enthusiasm than skill and scattering flour far and wide, laughing helplessly even as they both sneezed and choked.

"Umble pie!" Gespry said with a sigh, watching longingly as Dara ladled the tripe, simmered in wine with onions and spices, into the crust. "Reckon I'd just about die for a slice of that."

"Well, you needn't die for it, nor the raisin pasty, nor the minted peas, nor the almond pudding," Dara said good-naturedly. "I've made a gracious plenty even for him and us, too. Cook never taught us how to make small batches, not for a High Lord's household. No doubt the lord will growl and moan because there's no bread, but goodness knows I haven't had time to fire up the bake house for a baking. Watch the pie, will you, while I go ask the lord whether he'll take supper in his rooms or the dining hall. Unless you'd go for me?" Dara added hopefully.

"Not a chance, girly," Gespry said firmly. "After the way you've riled up the lord—I could hear him even in your rooms—I wouldn't cross his path for all the gold I can imagine."

Dara sighed, but trudged up the stairs to the second floor again. She didn't relish bothering Lord Vanian now, either; after she'd angered him so this morning, he'd have had plenty of time to plan a suitable revenge, and she didn't doubt she'd more than pay for her brief satisfaction. Well, there was nothing for it.

To her surprise and dismay, however, she found Lord Vanian not in the tower, but standing in the open doorway to her own room. For a moment anger flared, but Dara quickly swallowed it. It *was*, after all, his castle, and the door hadn't been locked; likely, given Gespry's small strength, it had already been ajar. Dara cleared her throat quietly, but Lord Vanian did not turn; at last, Dara murmured, "My lord?" in a quiet voice.

Slowly Lord Vanian turned, and Dara was surprised to see not anger, but a kind of quiet sorrow in his expression before she remembered to drop her eyes and curtsy.

"You changed it," he said, rather remotely. "Her room."

"Begging pardon, my lord, but it was much too grand for a simple serving maid," Dara murmured. "I'll change it back if my lord says I must."

"No." Lord Vanian turned to gaze into the room again, and though his voice was quiet, Dara saw his shoulders slump slightly. "No. Leave it as you like it. Marguerid is gone. She'll never use the room again, so it hardly matters how it's kept. It was foolish for me to keep it. An unhappy reminder of a foolish dream long proved vain."

Dara was surprised to feel a pang of sympathy. Was her own dream of wedding Cav as foolish as Lord Vanian's dream had been? No, surely not, because Cav loved her as dearly as she loved him, and unlike Lord Vanian's lady, he'd be waiting when Dara returned. But she could certainly understand Lord Vanian's pain. For a moment she wanted to tell Lord Vanian that he should stay somewhere else, leave this place and its memories entirely, create a new castle for himself in another place if that was what he wished. Then Dara sighed to herself. It wasn't a simple serving maid's place to presume to advise the lord, not that Lord Vanian would be likely to welcome or heed her advice anyway.

Still, in the face of Lord Vanian's grief there was no pleasure to be had in Dara's game of passive rebellion, and she said only, "If you'd like to come down to the dining hall, lord, there's a nice hot supper almost ready."

Lord Vanian sighed again, but he turned away from the room, closing the door quietly. He glanced at Dara, and something in her expression must have comforted him, for he smiled rather wearily and said, "Yes, that sounds good."

He followed Dara downstairs, and Dara hurried to set the table in the dining hall. Her pie and pasty had turned beautifully golden brown, and Dara quickly filled bowls and platters and carried them to the dining hall. Then she had to trot quickly back for the wine.

"Beg your pardon I'm so slow, my lord," Dara said as she filled Lord Vanian's goblet. "I've never done the whole service, from cooking to pouring wine and clearing up. I was hardly ever let to show myself out of the kitchen when there were guests, and even Cook only let me make the simpler dishes. So I hope your lordship won't be disappointed."

"This looks fine," Lord Vanian said. He waved at the chair beside him. "Sit down and help me eat it."

Dara bit back her automatic retort, and instead said gently, "I'm sorry, lord, but I gave my promise to be your servant for five days, and if I behaved in such a presumptuous way I'd be breaking that promise."

This time a trace of irritation showed in Lord Vanian's expression, and he waved a hand impatiently. "If you're my servant, you're obliged to obey my orders, are you not?" he demanded.

"*Some* orders," Dara answered cautiously.

"And if I ordered you to sit down and eat supper with me?" Lord Vanian drawled, raising one eyebrow.

Dara bowed her head, but she could not quite keep a smile from her lips. "Then I'd have to do as you say, my lord," she said ruefully.

"Then I do so order you," Lord Vanian said, indicating the chair once more.

Dara sighed, curtsied, and sat down. Hopefully Gespry would have the good sense to go ahead and eat his own supper in the kitchen instead of waiting.

"Am I to eat from the platter with my fingers, my lord?" she asked gently, glancing pointedly at the bare table in front of her.

Lord Vanian chuckled with uncharacteristic good humor, and a setting identical with Lord Vanian's own appeared before Dara. Dara sat quietly while Lord Vanian filled her plate, but when she made no move to eat, Lord Vanian sighed.

"Do I have to order you to chew and swallow each bite?" he asked. "Or have you merely poisoned the food?"

"No, my lord," Dara said patiently. "But you're the lord of the castle. I can't eat before you."

Lord Vanian stared at her blankly, then to her amazement laughed delightedly, almost choking when he put a bite of pie in his mouth.

"By all the gods," he gasped, "it has been so long, I'd quite forgotten that. All the little niceties of court seem petty and useless when one dines alone day after day." His smile faded.

"A lord's true worth is shown by the strength of his character and his care for those under his protection, not the daintiness of his manners," Dara said soberly. "That's what Cav always said. Says."

"A fine and ethical lord, then, your paramour," Lord Vanian said with only a trace of bitterness. "Most lords I've known would fall far short of such stringent expectations."

"I beg your pardon, my lord, and hope you'll forgive me my impertinence," Dara said hastily, wincing to herself. He hadn't asked for conversation, especially such a bold comment as she'd made. It was possible that under the strange unwritten "rules" of the keep, her forward behavior could be considered a breach of her promise, and who knew what consequences might fall upon her then?

Lord Vanian waved her apology aside.

"I beg you, speak freely," he said with a somewhat

pained expression. "No—I order it. I've had little enough conversation of any sort in my time here, and little enough honest conversation in my entire life. I far prefer your sometimes irritating frankness to the petty and vicious little games we played at court."

Dara sat back, flattered and a little unsettled by his comment. Was that very frankness what had initially attracted Cav's attention? As a servant she'd quickly learned that life at court was far from the effortless and luxurious dream it had seemed to a naive young girl raised in a comfortable but sheltered country household, but Cav had never seemed troubled by the intricate dance of wit and etiquette among the nobility; in fact, he'd seemed to enjoy it. Still, he'd always chosen to spend his free time in her company, and he'd never made Dara feel clumsy or inadequate for her lack of courtly graces.

"You don't speak," Lord Vanian said, interrupting her thoughts. "Have I made you shy by speaking plainly as I did?"

"No, lord, but—" Dara hesitated. "If it's plain speech you want, then I'd ask you plainly: Why am I here? Why serving in your castle, why sitting at your table? If it's conversation you want, you said yourself there were other visitors. Likely you'd find them more pleasing company than me, as I seem to annoy you so."

Lord Vanian sipped his wine thoughtfully before he answered.

"There are many reasons," he said. "As little as you care for me, you're honest in your dislike. You're not afraid of me—or if you are, you've hidden it well. You're not especially clever, but you're persistent and determined. I respect those things. There haven't been many women who have come to the keep; usually only the men are that daring or that foolish, or both. I find it remarkable, all things considered, that you've done so well. You interest me; I suppose it's as simple as that, really."

It was far from that simple, and Dara knew it, but she

could see in Lord Vanian's smooth smile that he'd tell her no more. Perhaps it was simply that he'd lacked for female company and craved it. Goodness knows he'd have to be desperate to pursue and seduce her, and surely he'd scarcely bother with her if any fairer ladies were to be found hereabouts. Or perhaps he simply took a sadistic pleasure in his games, pausing in his torments only to throw her off balance with the pretense of a little kindness and courtesy. Or was it his cruelty that was the pretense? Cav had always told her that the more brash the exterior, the greater the fear it covered.

How was she to know?

To cover her confusion, Dara sipped a little wine, resolving she'd not finish the glass.

"You've hardly touched your pie," she said awkwardly.

Lord Vanian chuckled. "I'm certain it's a masterpiece, but I'm not fond of tripe."

To her disgust, Dara found herself flushing. "I asked—"

"My preferences," Lord Vanian reminded her. "I have no particular preferences. You didn't ask what dishes I disliked. For future reference, I also dislike apricots. Never mind. The rest will suffice." His eyes glinted mischievously.

Dara stifled a sigh and devoted herself quietly to her supper. Whatever had prompted his brief moment of kindness, the game was on again and Lord Vanian was already laying his traps for Dara's unwary feet.

After the pudding, Lord Vanian returned to his tower (although for all Dara knew, he might have vanished off for some other part of the keep as soon as he closed the door behind him). For Dara, however, there were the dirty plates and pots to wash, the scraps to dispose of—and how was she to dump those scraps, and throw out the dishwater, for that matter, when she couldn't so much as set foot outside the castle?

In the end there was nothing to do but haul buckets to the privy, and Dara swore under her breath all the time she did it. It was plainly ridiculous to expect one poor serving maid to handle all the work, from baking the bread to carrying away the waste; why, she'd have to get up long before dawn tomorrow to start the baking. Cook had had a dozen girls and lads in the kitchen besides Dara, just to assist with the simpler cooking—and that wasn't counting the real serving maids, the butler's staff, the under-cooks, or that fellow who specialized in the fancy pastries and subtleties. It seemed a hopeless task to try to accomplish so much alone—and how ridiculous that it should be so much work, cooking the meals for one lone man!

"Well, it's because he's a lord," Gespry said in answer to her complaints, trotting along cheerfully beside her while she carried her bucket down the hall. "Just cooking for the likes of me, see, that's still a job, as my missus could've told you when she was still alive, but simple folks like us find a rough pasty and a bowl of hot soup as good as a feast. Say," he said suddenly, "what are you going to ask the mirror tonight?"

"I don't know," Dara admitted. So many questions had crossed her mind, but she couldn't ask about the Oracle until her final night. She wanted desperately to ask to see Cav, but—

But. Dara could think of a dozen reasons to postpone that particular question, not the least of which was her reluctance to let Lord Vanian watch while she did so. Cav was safe at home; she knew that. There was no real need to ask to see him when there were other questions that might better serve her purposes here in the keep. There was so much she still didn't know, and she had only five questions.

If she was honest with herself, however, Dara would have to admit that she was afraid. Lord Vanian and Yaga had implied that the mirror could in fact be used as she'd thought she'd used it after her first supper in Lord Vanian's castle. She could choose not only to see Cav, but to speak to him, and to let him see and speak to her. And that was the most frightening thought of all.

If an Heir loves the maiden but not the serving wench, and the maiden loves the man but not the Heir, then where is the truth in their love? And, in truth, will the Heir love the serving wench once he learns she's no longer the maiden? Lord Vanian had planted that seed of doubt in Dara's heart, and Dara found to her disgust that it had taken root there. What *would* Cav say when he learned she'd lain with another man, no matter what the deceit that had sent her to his arms—and most especially when Dara appeared to him from that lord's bedroom, with the man himself possibly in view? And even if Cav still wanted her, what would happen when High Lord Haranor and High Lady Alberta learned that Cav's would-be bride was no longer a virgin?

Perhaps Cav would choose to keep it a secret from his parents. Perhaps they'd never ask. Perhaps—

But there were so many other questions to ask the mirror that were more . . . important. And so much less dangerous.

"I was going to say," Gespry said awkwardly, "if you didn't mind, you might ask where my key had gotten to, so I could go get it back. Any lost key in the place would do, come to that."

Dara hesitated, suddenly appalled at herself. She'd thought nothing of poor Gespry, as if nobody but Dara herself had troubles. Gespry deserved whatever help she could give him.

But—

"Gespry, that would be wasting one of my questions," Dara said patiently. "You're bound by your promise to stay with me till I'm finished here in the Keep, so that means you'll be with me when I find the Oracle, and you could just ask the Oracle where your key was. Anyway, you lost your key in that swamp, didn't you? Just because you might learn where it was doesn't necessarily mean you could still get it."

"Hadn't rightly thought about that," Gespry admitted.

"I guess knowing my key was at the bottom of the swamp with a fell-beast sitting on it wouldn't do me much good, would it?"

"No, it wouldn't," Dara agreed. "Besides, I told you that when I leave, you can have my key. I meant that."

"Well, what *will* you ask, then?" Gespry asked her.

"I don't know," Dara said at last. "I just hope I'll know the right question when I ask it."

When she'd finished cleaning and laid out what she needed for the next morning's baking, Dara made her way to the door to the tower, which was again unlocked. At the top of the stairs, Dara knocked on the door, entering on Lord Vanian's offhanded "Come in." Lord Vanian was exactly where he'd been the night before, sitting in front of the mirror and gazing into it.

"I suppose you want to ask me my preferences for tomorrow's meals?" he said, smiling mockingly.

"My lord told me he has no preferences," Dara said smoothly. "But if there is anything you would particularly like—or dislike—my lord has only to say so. But I came to ask my question of your mirror, if it wouldn't be inconvenient."

"I suppose that depends on what you'd like to ask," Lord Vanian said wryly. Then he shrugged. "Go on. Ask what you will."

Dara gingerly stepped up to the mirror. How could such a thing exist, potent enough even to overcome whatever magic protected the location of the Oracle? Or were they part of the same magic? It sometimes seemed she'd never understand the complex little world she'd entered.

Well, *there* was a question worth asking.

"Show me how the Crystal Keep came to be," she said.

There was a chuckle from behind her, but Dara didn't dare turn. The mirror was clearing.

The landscape Dara saw in the mirror was vaguely familiar; Dara realized gradually that what she was seeing was the same bit of land where the Crystal Keep sat, but without the building and probably long ago, judging from the size of the trees. A slender figure stood in the foreground of the picture; with a start, Dara recognized Kelara, the birdwoman. Kelara raised her arms and made a series of intricate gestures, her fingers moving in graceful patterns; Dara could see her lips moving, but heard nothing.

Slowly, block by crystal block, the Keep appeared. Kelara would sing for a while, then rest, then wearily rise to sing again—or was she chanting?—until Dara's own throat was sore just watching. At last, however, the great building was completed, and Kelara walked through the open doorway, which closed behind her. The scene faded from the mirror.

"You haven't quite gotten the knack of it," Lord Vanian chuckled. "Like making wishes or querying the Oracle, you must say *precisely* what you mean. But I'll honor the spirit of our bargain and give you what you want. Look there." He waved at the mirror, which immediately clouded again.

"It begins with an elvan woman named Kelara, a powerful mage," Lord Vanian said, and Dara saw the birdwoman again, this time walking in a different place. "She was better known, however, for her exquisite singing voice, and she journeyed here and there between the elvan cities, sharing her songs and her power with humans and elves alike as she traveled."

The scene changed, and Dara saw Kelara sitting by a fire, a circle of fair beautiful folk sitting around her. Kelara was apparently singing, stars falling from her fingertips as she wove illusions in the air.

"Doubtless many young men would have fallen at her feet," Lord Vanian said wryly, "but she took no husband, believing it her destiny to continue in her travels and take her magic where it was needed. She had a great hunger to know the truth of how magic came to the world, and dreamed of learning the ultimate source of such power."

Dara saw Kelara again, this time standing near the place

that would one day be the Crystal Keep.

"In her travels," Lord Vanian continued, "Kelara heard of a place of great power in the wilderness, where magic and even thought itself became a great power, and at the center of this place, a powerful oracle. Kelara searched the wild and unsettled lands until she found this place. She was determined to harness this power for the use of those who needed it, and she built by magic a great and beautiful castle where she could live in peace while she studied this magic."

The scene changed; now Dara saw Kelara bent over a book in which she was writing furiously. The change in the elvan woman was amazing; she had grown wan and nearly gaunt, but her green eyes burned with fervor.

"Kelara, however, became obsessed with her study of the powerful magic she'd found," Lord Vanian continued. "Days became weeks, and weeks became months, and while Kelara's magic grew, she felt herself fading slowly as if the very life was being drained out of her. At last she realized that somehow the magic of the place had seized upon her, upon her very soul, that it possessed her as much as she desired to possess it and she could no longer be free of it. Afraid that the power of the place would consume her utterly, and after her, others, she went at last to the very heart of the place and tried one final time to bind the magic of the place and to wrest herself free of the bond that held her prisoner."

Dara saw the beautiful woman speaking what would seem to be a spell of some sort, an expression of fierce determination on her face as swirling magical energies rose to surround and envelop her.

"She partly succeeded, but at a great price. She indeed bound the magic of the Crystal Keep to her command, but as her soul was bound to the magic, it was torn from her in her attempts to free herself. She had just enough power left to bind the Oracle as well, so that the Keep and the Oracle would stand ready for those who needed its power to come to use it, and those who would use such power for harm could never touch it. And she created a magical mirror—this very mirror, in fact—so that she could occasionally look out at the outside world, but she and her lost soul drifted farther apart, and as time went by she searched for it less and less, and she cared less and less. At last she built herself a small garden and sealed herself within it, and she wandered her garden remembering nothing of who or what she was.''

Lord Vanian fell silent, and the mirror grew dark. Dara waited, but when the lord said nothing further, she turned to him.

"But what happened *then*?" she asked. "What's the rest of the story?"

"That's all there is," Lord Vanian said, shrugging. "Kelara lives in her garden, singing her songs and grieving without knowing that she is grieving for herself, or why. She was freed of her bond to the Keep when the next Guardian took her place, but I doubt she even noticed; she no longer knows that there is a world outside the Keep, or cares to leave. And so it's been with each Guardian of the Keep—we rule our little kingdom with power greater than any High Lord has ever wielded, but we're bound to the Keep just as firmly as the Keep is bound to our will. And the keep exacts yet another price—that in time we forget. We all forget." He fell silent again.

The horror of it rocked Dara. What a terrible, insidious trap the Keep was, promising every wish, every dream, and luring in its victims to their death, or their eternal imprisonment—either as demons, like Gespry, or as the Guardian. How many centuries must Kelara have walked, mad and singing, in her beautiful garden of grief? How many centuries had Lord Vanian been a prisoner of his own kingdom? Dara thought of the hundreds, thousands of doors between his doorway and hers, and she shuddered.

And yet how much worse it might have been. The "rules" of the Keep, it seemed, were no part of the source of the magic itself, or of the Oracle; those limitations had been set by the bindings Kelara had placed. Without those bindings, without a Guardian to keep order in the Crystal Keep and oversee the use of the Oracle and the magic of the Keep—well, the Crystal Keep was remote enough, but not so remote that someone wouldn't have stumbled over it by now. Perhaps someone less wise or less scrupled than Kelara, who might ruthlessly wield such power for his own gain. Who knew what devastation might have been caused by the simplest misuse of the Keep's great magic? Indeed Lord Vanian had ''other duties'' to perform!

''Thank you,'' Dara said quietly. ''It was good of you to tell me the story after I botched the question.'' Especially, Dara thought to herself, as he'd given her information that she could use to her advantage, or could conceivably use against him. Why had he done it?

Lord Vanian shrugged.

''You could have probably learned as much with your own divination spells,'' he said. ''Or perhaps not—sometimes this place has a devious way of circumventing spells that pry into its secrets. I've often thought it has a life, perhaps a consciousness, of its own. Or perhaps it gains for itself what it takes from its Guardians.''

''But Kelara made this mirror with the Keep's own magic, didn't she?'' Dara asked. ''So why doesn't the Keep protect what's seen in the mirror?''

''Because the mirror belongs to the Guardian, and the Guardian protects the Keep,'' Lord Vanian said. ''I've never been less than vigilant about letting visitors use the mirror. Of course, I can't speak for the Guardians before me.''

Of course. He'd allowed her to see the *story* of how the Crystal Keep had come to be, but he'd been careful not to show her the Oracle or the actual magical source Kelara had discovered. He'd also let her hear nothing—such as the spell Kelara had used to bind the Keep's magical energies.

"Yaga must've been a good Guardian," Dara said absently.

"Ah, so you met the old growler himself," Lord Vanian said, chuckling. "I missed that, unfortunately. You *are* a brave little thing, aren't you, to walk up to a dragon?"

"Well, *you* must've done it," Dara said embarrassedly.

"True," Lord Vanian admitted. "But I was desperate." He glanced at her slyly. "But of course, so are you."

Dara refused to take that bait.

"Thank you for your help, my lord," she said politely. "If there's nothing else you need, I'll retire now. Unless you have instructions for tomorrow's meals?"

"All right, all right," Lord Vanian said hastily. "Don't start that bit again. Go on, then."

Dara curtsied and made her escape, hurrying back to her room. Kelara's story had raised more questions than it had answered, and before she slept, Dara planned to find some of those answers.

Gespry was waiting in her room, and he listened with unusual attentiveness while Dara told him what she'd learned. When she finished, he gave a low whistle.

"Weighty stuff, that," he said. "But what's it all matter, really? I mean, however the Keep was put here, here it is and here it stays."

"But now I know much better *why* the Keep works the way it does, even if I don't truly understand *how*," Dara said.

"You said you saw the birdwoman writing in a book," Gespry said. "Mightn't that be worth finding?"

"I doubt it would do me any good," Dara said regretfully. "Remember, she lost her soul before she ever discovered the secret of the magic that she was looking for, so the book would just be full of guesses. It wouldn't be worth the trouble of casting translation spells to read the Olvenic, let alone finding the book in the library—if it's even there, that is. If I were the Guardian, I'd have hidden such a thing well so no visitor could stumble across it, just to be careful. Besides, it would be five days before I could even go and get it, and I hope to have all this solved by then.''

''Well, then what're you looking for?'' Gespry asked practically.

''Just a hint,'' Dara said mysteriously. ''Something that Yaga said when we were talking to him.'' She quickly filled her bowl with water from her pitcher and cast her divination spell more confidently than she had in some time.

''Show me Yaga's appearance before he took the form of a dragon,'' Dara said.

The water rippled and cleared, and Dara saw a tall elvan youth, his hair so pale it seemed almost white. Dara knew little of elves, but she thought he seemed younger than Kelara; or perhaps that was only because of the open, dreamy expression on his face.

''Show me what he came to the Crystal Keep to find,'' Dara said, and she was not surprised to see Kelara's face in the water when it cleared.

''Show me what Yaga's wish was,'' Dara asked, but the water remained stubbornly clear. Apparently this was another forbidden question.

''Show me the view from the door behind which the stone of Yaga's wish is hidden,'' Dara said after a moment's thought, and this time she was rewarded with a view. When she recognized what she saw, however, Dara groaned; she was looking at the forest where she'd found the plums and the lecherous boy-beasts.

''Show me the wish and where it is,'' Dara asked, already dreading the answer; her fears were confirmed when she saw the large blue gem tucked into a neat stack of human skulls. The whole thing appeared to be sitting on a sort of shrine, built on a stack of bricks of what appeared to be gold, but it was difficult to see, as she seemed to be viewing it from the back. Disgustedly, Dara shook her head.

''Show me the person whose wish I carry in my pack,''

she said, and was even more dismayed to see one of the furry boy-beasts—maybe Skivvit himself, though they looked so much alike that Dara could not be sure.

"I shudder to think what sort of wish *that* is," Dara murmured, remembering all the hard little hands tearing at her clothes and pinching her flesh. Well, no question of bargaining there; in fact, she wondered whether she'd be doing good to let Skivvit or any of his ilk have his wish at all. She shook her head, but tried one last question.

"Show me the object or service I must give Lord Vanian in exchange for my wish," Dara said firmly, but her own reflection never left the still waters.

"Show me what I must have in order to win the man I love," Dara tried desperately, but the image remained unchanged. Dara swore, emptied the bowl, and flopped onto the bed.

"Thought you weren't supposed to ask them last two," Gespry said, chuckling.

"No, I never promised that," Dara returned. "Only that I wouldn't ask his mirror. And the last question wasn't what I'd planned to ask the Oracle, anyway."

"Well, I don't understand the bit about Yaga any better," Gespry said at last. "He followed Kelara here and wished for her to love him, eh?"

"I don't know," Dara admitted. "He came here to find Kelara, we know that much, but I don't know *what* he actually wished for. But I thought Yaga might be able to give us more help or information, and I wanted something to bargain with."

"Well, as you said, don't much matter, does it?" Gespry asked cheerfully. "After five days you'll be able to use the Oracle, and then you'll be gone, so you won't need his help, will you?"

Dara turned and stared at Gespry in blank astonishment. What was the matter with him? Didn't he care at all that Yaga had come so far, through so much, to find the woman he loved, that he'd been here so many years still dreaming of her? Dara could well imagine his frustration and longing; she'd certainly experienced those same feelings often enough in the years since she'd fallen in love with Cav. How could Gespry not care, not want to help Yaga if he could?

Then Dara sighed. Gespry hadn't come here for love. Immortality was a selfish sort of wish, and from what she knew of Gespry, she imagined he'd had no trouble absorbing the "value given for value received" philosophy of the Crystal Keep without any particular difficulty—at least when it came to Gespry receiving and someone else giving. He had, therefore, no particular interest in helping Yaga unless Dara—and by extension he himself—stood to gain by that help.

The sudden realization made Dara acutely uncomfortable, as it pointed to an even less agreeable truth—that all of Gespry's help, his apparent friendship with her, had been similarly motivated. The thought hurt.

"Gespry, whatever I can learn from Lord Vanian's mirror, it's no guarantee that everything will be solved by those answers," Dara said, forcing a light tone despite her disappointment. "Even if I learn where the Oracle is, I've got to get to it. Then I've still got to ask what I must give Lord Vanian in exchange for my wish. What if we need help? Yaga was Guardian before Lord Vanian, and the most powerful—uh—demon in the place besides Lord Vanian. We may need his help."

"Well, there's that," Gespry admitted, unruffled. "But how do you figure we're going to give Yaga his lady love when Lord Vanian, the Guardian of the place, couldn't give himself *his* own lady?"

"We can't," Dara said, more annoyed now. "I don't think anybody can give another person to anyone. If I'd thought different I'd have just wished for Cav to marry me. But evidently whatever his wish is, it's something he still wants, or he wouldn't have been so disappointed when the wish I found wasn't his. I don't know what Lord Vanian wants, but I do know what Yaga wants, and if he can still use the magic of the Keep, who knows? Maybe he can grant my wish just as well as the lord can.''

"Now there's an idea," Gespry admitted. "Can't much hurt to try, can it?"

Dara sighed and cleaned her bowl before she crawled into bed. Gespry was only Gespry, and she couldn't make him into someone or something he was not.

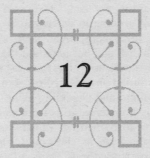

12

DARA ROSE WHILE THE SKY WAS STILL DARK, drowsily washed her hands and face, dressed, and stumbled down to the kitchen to start her baking. Despite her weariness, the delicious scent of baking bread cheered her, and she had to grudgingly admit that there were advantages to doing the cooking by hand. Conjured bread didn't fill a kitchen with the sweet yeasty aroma that set Dara's mouth to watering.

Lady Alberta had had a taste for hot tea in the morning, and Dara brewed a pot while she prepared the rest of Lord Vanian's meal. When it was nearly ready, however, Dara realized to her dismay that she'd have to go and wake the lord herself. The idea of approaching Lord Vanian in his bed and waking him filled her with apprehension, but there was nothing else for it; Gespry would doubtless refuse the errand, and Lord Vanian would only be angry if she let him sleep on while his food grew cold. Reluctantly Dara took a deep breath, mustered her courage, and stepped out of the kitchen—

—only to collide squarely with the lord himself. Unlike

Dara, Lord Vanian had apparently not satisfied himself with a hasty wash and hair-combing, and there was more than a hint of amusement in his expression as he gazed at the flour-dusted maid staring at him in blank amazement.

"Beg your pardon, my lord," Dara said hastily, stepping back. "I was just coming to wake you."

"The smell of baking bread and—" Lord Vanian sniffed the air. "Yes, and hot tea—did the job for you. I'll be in the dining room; bring the food on along as soon as it's ready." He turned and walked off, brushing flour from the front of his tunic and chuckling as he went.

Dara hurriedly transferred rolls from pan to basket, yelping as the hot bread burned her fingers, and scrabbled together a tray as quickly as she could. Opening the door while juggling the loaded tray, Dara yelped again and teetered precariously as she nearly stepped on Gespry, who was trying to enter the kitchen just as Dara attempted to leave it. For a moment she thought the tray would go crashing to the floor; then she got her balance again and stepped over Gespry with a murmur of apology even as she hurried on to the dining hall.

If Dara had hoped that her hours of hard work would elicit a compliment from Lord Vanian, she was still amazed when the lord sniffed at the tray and said, "That smells wonderful. Sit down and have some with me." He glanced mischievously at Dara. "That's an order, if necessary."

Dara had to laugh at his expression and at the ridiculousness of the situation; here was a great lord, Guardian of the Crystal Keep, ordering a flour-smudged and draggle-haired serving maid to sit down and break fast with him. Again she thought of Gespry and felt a pang of guilt, but he'd never poke so much as his nose tip in the dining hall while the lord was there, and besides, he could eat exactly the same food in the kitchen.

"So are you going to spend the whole of your day in the kitchen, as you did yesterday?" Lord Vanian asked her when they were finished eating.

"I've little enough choice, my lord," Dara said, "as your lordship forbade me to use magic and as I'm doing the work of a whole kitchen staff by myself."

"Then cobble together a cold dinner and put it in a basket," Lord Vanian told her. "After you tidy up, I'll take you to see some parts of my kingdom you haven't had a chance to visit yet."

"My lord—" Dara started to protest helplessly, then stopped. It wasn't her place to argue with the lord, she reminded herself sternly. If he wanted his servants to go picnicking instead of working, that was his right. Besides, by seeing more of the Keep, she could well learn something to her advantage.

"If we're going walking, my lord, might I change into something more suitable for the outdoors?" Dara asked, standing to leave.

"Whatever you like," Lord Vanian said, chuckling. "As long as it's clean."

Dara flushed, realizing that her present rumpled appearance was not all that different from the ragged and muddy condition in which Lord Vanian had usually seen her. Hurriedly she prepared a simple cold dinner and packed it in a large basket with a bottle of wine, then dashed back to her room, very conscious of Lord Vanian waiting in the main hall for her. When she told Gespry her plans, however, she was surprised and worried when Gespry offered, with obvious reluctance, to accompany her.

"Ain't as if I'd do you much good fighting if the lord took it into his head that he wanted some more of what he got before," Gespry said wryly, "but mayhap he mightn't take such a notion with an audience thereabouts. Sides, I promised I'd stay with you, didn't I?" he added hastily.

"Well, I don't think your promise meant every minute," Dara said, "else you'd have to follow me to the privy, wouldn't you?" She thought about Gespry's offer while she changed her clothes, but at last she sighed.

"I don't see there's much use in your going, although

it's kind of you to offer," she said. Gespry's offer had warmed her as much as it had astonished her; perhaps she'd misjudged him. "As you say, I don't know that there's anything you could do against Lord Vanian if he took it in his head to—to be ungentlemanly, and if he wanted you gone, he'd just send you back here or—" *Or do something worse to you*, Dara thought, but she left that idea unspoken. But the other thought she kept silent was that somehow in the last few days, an uneasy truce had been declared between her and Lord Vanian, a very precarious balance of goodwill, and she didn't want to be the one to upset that balance by showing her mistrust of the lord by way of Gespry's presence. Besides, she believed Lord Vanian's promise—not necessarily because he'd made the promise, but because there was more advantage to him in keeping it than breaking it, and because the awkwardness and struggle of rape, especially in the weeds and dirt, seemed far beneath the lord's dignity.

"Well, stay out of the wine, at least," Gespry advised her, seeming more relieved than sorry that she'd refused his company. "Get your head muzzied up again and who knows what you'd let yourself in for."

Well, that was true. Dara quickly checked to be certain that her freshly combed and braided hair and her clean tunic and trousers showed no smudge of flour, then dashed back to the cellar for a skin of cider that she watered before taking it with her to the entry hall where Lord Vanian stood rather impatiently now.

"I was afraid you'd taken my criticism too much to heart and gone off to bathe," Lord Vanian said a little irritably. "And how much wine do you think we'll drink?"

"Please forgive the delay, my lord," Dara said breathlessly. "And this isn't wine. High Lord Haranor didn't like his servants to drink too much wine unless it was well watered. I'm more used to cider anyway."

Lord Vanian took her hand without another word, and just as abruptly the entry hall of the castle vanished. Dara gasped and stumbled as her footing suddenly became unsteady; if Lord Vanian had not already been clasping her hand, she doubtless would have fallen.

The place to which Lord Vanian had taken her seemed to Dara's wondering eyes more amazing than anything she had seen yet in the Crystal Keep. Under her feet was fine golden sand speckled with pink-white flecks; it was the sudden softness of this footing that had made her lose her balance. Before them, however, stretched what seemed to be an endless huge lake of the purest gem-blue water, rolling onto the sand in great waves that made a gentle sort of roaring sound. Squint as she might, Dara could see nothing of the opposite shore of the lake, only the endless blue water, white at the tips of the incoming waves. To Dara's eyes it was more wonderful even than the rainbow crystal cave.

"I've never seen anything like it," Dara murmured. "What lake is this?" Then she remembered, and added hastily, "My lord."

"It's not a lake at all," Lord Vanian said loftily. "It's the sea, the great southern sea, most likely. Quite lovely, really. Especially at sunset."

Glancing at Lord Vanian for permission, Dara laid the basket on the sand and stepped forward, stumbling a little on the uncertain footing. As she approached the water, there was a band of sand wet by the waves, and there the sand was firmer. Dara gingerly edged forward a little more, until the foamy edge of the water was reaching for the toes of her boots as it slid up the sand. Dara bent down and dabbled her fingers in the surprisingly warm water.

"Go ahead," Lord Vanian said in an amused tone.

"Beg pardon, my lord?" Dara asked, inexplicably flushing as she turned back to look at him.

"Take off your boots and wade," the lord said, shrugging as if the matter was obvious.

"Well—" It was a wonderful idea, but Dara felt awkward doing such a thing when she was supposed to be Lord

Vanian's servant. "Only if you do." Dara raised one eyebrow in challenge.

Lord Vanian laughed, and to Dara's surprise he sat down on the blanket they had brought and unlaced his boots, drawing them off. Off came the stockings next, and Lord Vanian rolled up his trouser legs above the knee. He stood, hands on his hips, smiling back in response to Dara's challenge.

Dara flushed, but she could do nothing but return to the blanket and pull off her own boots and stockings. The sand was unexpectedly hot under her feet, rather unpleasant, and Dara hurried back to the cooler wet sand. She could not suppress a delighted laugh as the water foamed over her toes, and she waded out a little deeper before another thought made her hesitate.

"Is this dangerous?" she asked. "I mean, are there dangerous creatures in the sea, like fell-beasts in swamps?"

"I've heard tales of water-dragons and sea serpents," Lord Vanian said, joining her, "but only in very deep water. I've been here a hundred times at least, wading and swimming, and nothing has ever done me any harm."

"Swimming," Dara marveled. The way the water pulled at her feet, as if coaxing her out deeper, made swimming a tempting idea, but she'd never seen water that made such waves, higher than Dara's waist at times. Surely swimming in such a place would be dangerous, even if she was tempted to pull off her gown with Lord Vanian here— which she was not in the least. Daringly, she waded out a little deeper into the clear water and scooped up a handful. Surely such clear blue water must be sweeter than any other—

Dara coughed and sputtered, spitting out the mouthful of salty, bitter water.

"Oh, that's awful," Dara said hoarsely, spitting again and again to clear her mouth.

Lord Vanian laughed, but thankfully said nothing to ridicule her; instead he bent and picked up something from the sand and held it out.

"Look at this," he said.

Dara gingerly took the pale object he offered. She'd seen shells cast up on the banks of creeks and rivers, but this was rather different—oddly shaped and large enough to fill her hand.

Lord Vanian grasped her hand, and Dara started, her mouth going suddenly dry, but he only lifted the shell to her ear.

"Listen," he said.

It was hard not to focus on Lord Vanian's hand touching her, but Dara obeyed, and was surprised to hear what seemed like a quieter version of the sea roar, but from within the shell itself.

"Is it magic?" she asked.

Lord Vanian shrugged. "Not that I can detect," he said. "Keep your token and let's have our dinner."

Dara was loath to abandon her play in the water, but she obediently followed Lord Vanian back to the blanket. The plain cold food tasted good in the summerlike heat, and the cider washed away the last unpleasant taste of the seawater.

"What a wonderful place," she sighed. "I suppose I'll never see the southern sea—the real southern sea, that is."

"Don't feel too sorry for yourself," Lord Vanian shrugged. "I doubt if I will, either. And what you see here may be the best of it."

"Do you know who came in here and made this place?" Dara asked daringly. "Well, not made, exactly, but—"

"A common sailor," Lord Vanian said. "But he had a rather interesting wish."

"What sort of wish would a sailor have?" Dara wondered. "A ship of his own? Maybe the gold to buy one?"

Lord Vanian shook his head.

"No. On one of his journeys his ship landed at an uncharted island, and there he saw one of the fabled sea maidens, a creature like a lovely woman, but covered in glittering scales, her fingers and toes webbed like a fish's fins. He wanted to find and meet the lovely creature he'd seen.''

"Did he?" Dara asked.

"Indeed he did." Lord Vanian chuckled. "Unfortunately he never thought to speculate on the particular habits of his would-be lover. She pulled him deep underwater, where he quickly drowned. She probably ate him after that."

Dara grimaced. "How horrible," she said.

"Not so horrible," Lord Vanian said, shrugging. "He'd likely have gone through his life miserable, wondering about the vision of beauty he'd seen, forever dissatisfied. There are probably worse fates than dying in the arms of the love you've dreamed of."

"I suppose." Dara shivered, then quickly turned the conversation to another subject. "Lord Vanian, what door was it came into being when Yaga came here? Did you ever learn that?"

"Oh, you've seen it," Lord Vanian told her. "The forest, the one where you found the plums." He chuckled. "Delightful place, eh?"

"How could anyplace he came from be so awful?" Dara protested. "The place makes you shudder as soon as you step into it."

"I doubt it was always like that," the lord said with some amusement. "Just as my castle has changed over the years as my memories of it changed—as I myself changed, perhaps. That forest was probably a lovely place when he came here. Unfortunately it was likely an inviting place, too, and near the entrance, so it was frequented by almost everyone who came here—not to mention the gold, of course. For that reason a goodly number of them stayed there—lost their key, or for any of a dozen other reasons. I've no doubt that it was the nature of the tenants, rather than Yaga himself, that made that forest such a dismal place."

"I never got to see much of it," Dara admitted. "I thought I glimpsed a sort of shrine there, but I had to run before I got a good look."

"Ah, the shrine." Lord Vanian chuckled again. "It *is* an interesting sight. All that gold is amazing, isn't it?"

"I don't know," Dara admitted, grinning to herself. "I never got a good look."

"Well, then, you must," Lord Vanian told her. "I'll take you myself, if you're finished."

"Oh, I don't know," Dara said reluctantly, even while she rejoiced at the success of her ruse. "Those creatures who live there seemed rather vicious."

"Only to sweet young morsels like yourself," Lord Vanian said loftily. "They won't trouble me, so you should be safe enough."

Before Dara could say anything more, the sea and the sand had vanished, and they were sitting in a clearing in the forest.

"Best put on your stockings and boots," Lord Vanian said condescendingly. His own attire was perfect; had he done that somehow by magic? Dara wondered. She hurriedly pulled on her stockings and boots and stood, relieved when the blanket and basket simply disappeared. At least she wouldn't have to carry it back.

The forest had not lost its air of menace, and Dara wondered how it could ever have been a pleasant place, as Lord Vanian had suggested. She followed the lord down the winding paths, having to hurry to match his longer stride. She didn't dare fall too far behind him; Skivvit and his friends might not harm the lord, but there was no telling how far that protection might extend to others with him. She fancied she could hear rustling in the undergrowth; was it only a deer or squirrel, or something more sinister?

"There you are," Lord Vanian said, stopping suddenly so that Dara nearly collided with him.

Dara gingerly peered out around Lord Vanian's side. There was a small clearing, and this one appeared to be man-made, not a natural clearing, for Dara could see stumps where trees had been cut down. There was the shrine she'd seen, built of the gold bricks, with the mound of skulls on top.

"Is that real gold?" Dara asked, cautiously approaching the shrine.

"Indeed it is." Lord Vanian shrugged. "I don't know where these folk find it, but it seems to be plentiful enough. Likely a cave or some such."

Dara stepped up to the shrine, then glanced around.

"They aren't going to come here now?"

"Not while I'm here." Lord Vanian sounded bored. "Why? Do you want one of their bricks? Take it if you like. They've plenty more, I imagine."

Dara appreciated the irony in Lord Vanian's tone. What good was gold to him? What good would a mountain of gold do him? Or Dara herself, for that matter.

Dara walked around the shrine until she could see the blue gem peeping out from the mound of skulls. Trying to be unobtrusive, Dara gingerly plucked at the gem; immediately the stacked mound of skulls collapsed, scattering white bones far and wide. Lord Vanian, who had been strolling idly around the clearing, turned immediately, and his eyes widened, then narrowed when he saw the blue gem in Dara's hand.

"What do you think you're doing with that?" he said slowly, and Dara could hear a note of menace in his voice.

"It's a wish, isn't it?" Dara said hesitantly. She didn't want to tell him that she knew it was Yaga's wish, or that she'd come here expressly to claim it. But why had he seemed surprised? Surely he'd known it was here. "I just— I can trade it, if I can find the person who lost it, for help."

"No." Lord Vanian's expression was cold and closed now, and Dara began to worry. Perhaps she shouldn't have tried to claim the gem while Lord Vanian was with her. Perhaps—"It's Yaga's wish, and I want it. Give it to me."

Dara clutched the gem protectively. If Lord Vanian was

angry enough to inadvertently tell her that the gem was Yaga's wish, he was angry indeed, and she might be in real danger.

"You don't need it," she said, swallowing hard. "I do. I found it fairly."

"Give me that gem," Lord Vanian said coldly, holding out one hand. "You're my servant for five days and under my orders."

"Servants don't have to give up their property," Dara said, holding the gem tightly to her chest although her heart pounded hard with fear. She stepped back involuntarily. "It's not *your* wish. What do you want with it anyway?"

"He'll give anything for it," Lord Vanian said, and Dara fancied she could hear a note of desperate hope in his voice. "Anything at all. He'd even take back the Keep, become Guardian again, and set me free."

"Hasn't he suffered enough?" Dara protested. "Longer than you have. He deserves his freedom more than you do. Besides, I need the wish to trade for his help. You can already have anything you want here."

"Anything but my freedom, and that gem's the coin that's going to buy it for me," Lord Vanian said, advancing on Dara. "And you're going to give it to me. Or I'm going to take it."

Dara stepped back again but felt branches prickling against her back; she was at the edge of the forest and dared go no farther. She tried to remember some of the defensive spells she'd learned, but her panic-stricken mind could only remember fragments.

"You have to give me equal value for whatever I give you," Dara said, dismayed to hear her voice shaking.

"That gem itself is worth nothing to me," Lord Vanian said imperiously, his eyes glinting as he stepped closer. "Just as it's worth nothing to you. It only has value for Yaga, and he's the one I'll trade for it, not you. Now give it to me."

It was something in the arrogant tone of Lord Vanian's

last command that broke the hold of Dara's fear. Suddenly the memory of a spell flashed through her mind, and before she consciously decided to do it, her lips were shaping the words of the spell even as the fingers of her empty hand traced the glyph and hurled lightning at the angry lord standing before her.

As soon as she saw the ball of lightning leave her fingers, Dara would have called it back, but it was too late; Lord Vanian's eyes widened with surprise as white fire hurtled toward him. He raised his own hand just as the lightning enveloped him, and Dara heard him shout a single word before he was hurtled backward in an explosion of light.

For a moment Dara stood frozen where she was by the horror of what she'd done, her eyes dazzled to blindness; as her vision cleared, however, an even greater shock and relief stole her breath, for Lord Vanian was rising slightly dazed from the grass unharmed, the only fire visible in his eyes as he pushed himself to his feet.

Without hesitation, Dara turned and fled into the forest. Better to take her chances with Skivvit and his kin than the angry and powerful Guardian behind her. Let him come after her if he could. Perhaps he'd lose her trail in the forest. But even if he didn't, by the time he caught up with her she'd have time to better prepare herself to meet him.

Dara ran blindly through the forest, making no attempt to follow any of the footpaths she crossed. They'd make running easier and faster, but for Lord Vanian as well as herself, and Dara had spent more time (little as *that* was) rough in the woods than Lord Vanian had. Maybe, just maybe, he'd become lost enough or discouraged enough that he'd return to his castle to use the mirror to find her. That would buy a little more time.

Branches seemed to reach down to claw at her face; vines and brambles twined around her feet as if striving to trip her. Dara threw up her forearms to shield her eyes and pushed relentlessly forward; Lord Vanian would be acquiring just as many scratches in his own pursuit. She could hear him behind her, she thought, crashing through the undergrowth as clumsily as she herself was doing. He might have called out something, but by now Dara's breath was too harsh, the pounding of her blood too loud in her own ears to understand him.

She was losing speed now as she gasped for air, both sides knotting up tight, but still she stumbled onward, hoping that perhaps Lord Vanian had even less wind than she. Suddenly there was another clearing in front of her, and the abrupt relief from the vines and brambles tangling her feet did what the vines themselves did not: Dara stumbled and sprawled helplessly to the ground, curling instinctively around the gem even as she fell.

For an excruciatingly long moment Dara was too winded and stunned to do anything but lie there clutching the gem protectively and praying for just a moment, just another moment before Lord Vanian caught up with her; then she crept laboriously to her feet, her mind curiously clear and focused as she mentally paged through the spells she'd learned. If the lightning didn't stop Lord Vanian, what would? What could? Perhaps the strongest binding spell she'd found, but that needed more time than she'd have. No attack seemed more likely to work than the lightning she'd thrown, so that left only—

—only the Greater Summoning. Dara shivered; who knew what such a spell might bring forth in a place like the Crystal Keep, where so much power lay ready, so many doors stood open? But whatever it was, she prayed it was powerful enough to at least slow Lord Vanian down, to give Dara time to flee to Yaga's ruined temple. If she gave the gem to Yaga, surely he'd protect her from Lord Vanian's wrath. Grimly Dara thrust the gem into her pocket and began chanting the summoning, forcing down the quaver of fear in her stomach.

The sound of movement in the bushes. No time for wondering whether it was Lord Vanian approaching or one of the horrible boy-beasts; no time to think of anything but chanting the words of the spell.

More rustling, and Lord Vanian stumbled into the clearing from a place slightly to one side of Dara. Dara had no time to appreciate that Lord Vanian was scratched and cut by branches and brambles, leaves in his hair and his fine clothes rumpled and smudged with dirt; she dared not even look into his eyes for fear that what she might see there would shake her resolve. She chanted on, the air seeming to thicken around Dara as invisible currents of magic rippled across her skin.

Lord Vanian advanced, and Dara saw his eyes widen as he recognized the words of the spell she was weaving.

"You little fool!" he exclaimed. "You have no idea what could be unleashed! Stop now and give me the gem, and I'll—"

Dara shook her head and took a deep breath, then continued the chant. If only she could finish before he got close enough to—

Suddenly Lord Vanian's expression changed, and before Dara could finish the spell, he hurled himself at her. The chant was cut off abruptly as her teeth clicked shut on her tongue, as she was flung aside. Dara tried to catch herself, but to no avail; she slammed to the ground, the breath jolting out of her as exquisite pain blossomed in her bitten tongue. Dara rolled aside as quickly as she could, trying to scramble to her feet, wondering if she could even pronounce the simplest of spells with her bleeding and throbbing tongue.

To her surprise, Lord Vanian made no further move to attack her; in fact, he simply stood, swaying slightly, in the same place where Dara had stood. Then he staggered back a step, and Dara saw what she hadn't noticed at first glance—a feathered dart sprouting from his chest a little over his heart. He turned slowly to gaze at Dara, and his grimace of pain became a small, resigned smile. At the same time one of the boy-beasts stepped from the thicket where it had hidden, clutching a sort of miniature crossbow from which the dart had apparently been fired. Its eyes were wide, too.

Once again, Dara reacted without thinking, as Lord Vanian's knees began to buckle slowly, she was at his side, one arm around his waist, looping his own arm over her shoulders even as she dragged him back away from the hooved boy-creature approaching. Lord Vanian's hand clutched her shoulder spasmodically, and suddenly the forest vanished from around them; Lord Vanian groaned and collapsed to the stone floor of the entryway to his own castle.

Dara carefully rolled the lord to his back and gazed at the dart in consternation. Would she do more harm by pulling it out? Well, there was nobody to ask. Carefully Dara pulled the dart free of Lord Vanian's flesh; it was shorter than she'd thought and could not have penetrated very deeply, certainly not deeply enough to account for the lord's pallor, the shallow slowness of his breathing. Drugged, then?

Putting the dart in her pocket, Dara struggled Lord Vanian into a half-sitting position so she could slide her hands under his arms from behind. Grunting with effort and thanking all the gods for the years of heavy wet rugs, spitted sides of beef, and buckets of water that had strengthened the muscles in her arms, she laboriously dragged him up the stairs, a step at a time.

At the top of the steps she paused to rest. There'd be no getting Lord Vanian up the steep spiral stairway to the tower, and no reason to try. Her own room was the closest, and Dara dragged him there. Thankfully Gespry wasn't in the room; Dara was far from certain she knew how to explain what had happened.

Dara was panting heavily by the time she managed to pull Lord Vanian onto the bed. She pulled off his boots but hesitated over his clothing; at last she removed his tunic by simply cutting it away with her knife. The wound had not bled much, but the puncture was ominously dark, the skin around it red and inflamed. For the first time Dara began to wonder uneasily if the dart had not been drugged, but poisoned. Lord Vanian's color had returned, but he was growing flushed, and Dara could feel too much heat when she laid her hand on his forehead.

Hurriedly Dara turned to her grimoires and began leafing through them. Surely there was a spell of some sort—yes! Dara found what she wanted in the first volume of her family's grimoire, a general healing spell since she had no idea what might have been on the dart. No time to memorize it; Dara carried the book over to the bed and laid it on the covers. She felt her bitten tongue gingerly; it was bleeding and terribly sore, but she found that she could speak properly if she tried. She read through the spell, mouthing to herself the unfamiliar words until she was sure she could pronounce them all, then laid her hand on the wound and spoke the spell slowly but clearly.

When she raised her hand to look at the result of the spell, however, Dara was dismayed to see that while the small puncture had closed and healed, the dusky color under the skin remained, and Lord Vanian's fever appeared no less.

Was such a simple spell insufficient to neutralize poison, or was it only Dara's skill that was lacking? Dara paged quickly through the rest of the grimoire, then through her book of copied spells, but she knew she'd not troubled to copy any other healing spells, much less a spell specializing in the treatment of poisoning. Certainly there was such a spell in later volumes of her family grimoire, but she didn't know how to transport herself from place to place as Lord Vanian did, and it would take her days to walk back to the door to her family home—days in which Lord Vanian would lie here alone and untended and likely die.

If only she knew how to manipulate the Keep's magic without a spell! The ability to cure poisoning, or to transport herself, would be most useful right now—but it had taken her so many tries, so many failures, before she could even produce a usable basket or ladder, and she knew even less about healing or Gate spells. And given the likely consequences, she dared not try and fail.

Panic made her heart pound hard and her breath come fast. Dara took a deep breath to calm herself. All right, think logically and calmly. Lord Vanian was fevered and unconscious, but she could feel the strong, regular beat of his heart when she laid her hand on his chest, and his breathing seemed steady enough; he wasn't in any immediate danger of death. There was time to think, unless he suddenly worsened.

Dara leaned out the open door and shouted, "Gespry!"

"Down here." Dara could barely hear the response. "In the kitchen."

"Well, come up!" Dara shouted as loudly as she could. "Hurry!"

It seemed an eternity before Gespry scrambled up the stairs, a half-eaten bun in his hand and a scowl on his face.

"Whatever's the matter?" he said crossly.

"It's the lord," Dara said, picking Gespry up and carrying him into her room, where she set him down on the bed. "He's been poisoned, I think. Shot by a dart in that forest where the plums are."

Gespry whistled, leaning forward to look. At last he sat back, shaking his head.

"Reckon you're right," he said. "If it were just some kind of rot, it wouldn't've spread so quick. But I don't know nothing about poisons."

"What about Skivvit, the—the one you know?" Dara asked. "It's his people's poison. He'd know the antidote, wouldn't he?"

Gespry shook his head.

"That's a long chance, girly," he said. "Just because they hunt with a poison don't mean they ever expected to cure it—or would know how, or would have the makings, either. And even if I could find Skivvit without getting myself killed, and even if he had an antidote, why'd he give it to me to cure the lord when he—or one of his friends—tried to kill him in the first place?''

Dara bowed her head. "He wasn't trying to kill the lord," she said, forcing the words out. "He was trying to shoot me, and Lord Vanian pushed me out of the way, and the dart hit him instead of me."

Gespry whistled again.

"Don't know what to say," he said at last. "I doubt there's much chance getting an antidote out of Skivvit and his friends. What about Granny, though? She's a wise old thing."

"There's a thought," Dara said eagerly. She raised her voice. "Granny? Granny Good?" She and Gespry waited in silence, but there was no answer.

"This ain't a place I'd figure her likely glad to come," Gespry admitted.

"She came here before," Dara reminded him. "Never mind. I know another way to find her." She hesitated. "Gespry, would you watch over the lord, let me know if—if—"

"If he starts worsening, I'll come get you," Gespry promised. "You'll be in the tower using his mirror, eh? Good thought. Go on, I won't leave him 'cept he goes wild-headed and starts flinging magic at me."

Dara dashed to the tower door, surprised to find it locked. Of course, Lord Vanian wouldn't want Gespry to be able to get in. But Dara's key still opened the door, and the door at the top of the stairs as well, and thankfully Lord Vanian had not thought to take the added precaution of hiding the mirror again.

Dara composed herself with difficulty and said, "Show me Granny Good."

The mirror clouded. It began to clear, and Dara thought she could see forming a strangely familiar scene of flowers growing around a crystal pool; then the mirror clouded again, and Dara saw Granny's familiar figure, but with absolutely no background behind it, as if Granny sat in some featureless black void.

"Well, child, seems as if things have changed a mite since last we met," Granny said, startling Dara; she'd had no idea that Granny would be able to see *her*, although Dara had hoped that she might be able to figure out how to speak to the old woman through the mirror. "And how is it you come to be using the lord's mirror to find me, child, and why?"

Dara was secretly relieved that Granny would speak to her at all; she'd been frightened that the old woman was still angry at her.

"I need your help," she said humbly. "Will you please come? Please? It's very important."

"Well, as you ask so nicely, don't see as how I could say no," Granny cackled, disappearing from the mirror and appearing instantly at Dara's side. "Anyhow, I'm passing curious; didn't think I'd ever see you in the lord's chambers again, much less using his mirror. So what's your trouble, young one? The lord again?"

"Well, in a manner of speaking," Dara said hesitantly. "I think the lord's been poisoned."

"Poisoned!" Granny's eyes went wide. "Weren't you, missy, were it?"

"No, oh, no," Dara said quickly. "It was a dart shot by one of those creatures in the forest where the plums grow. I just wondered if you could—if you would help," she added.

"Hmmmp," Granny grunted noncommittally. "I'll have a look." She vanished as abruptly as she'd come.

Dara gasped—she'd *never* get used to people popping in and out like that—and ran down the stairs in a panic, half afraid that Granny would be gone by the time she reached her room.

To her relief, Granny was still there, her rocking chair beside the bed.

"You're right," Granny said, not turning to look at

Dara. "He's poisoned, no doubt of it."

"I know that!" Dara exploded, then hastily modified her tone. "I know that. I just—is there anything you can do to help him?"

"Help him?" Granny turned to look at her, the old eyes suddenly piercing. "*Help* him? Now, things have changed a mite, haven't they? Last we talked, seems you'd rather have seen him dead than alive, or I'm much mistaken."

"I've never wished anyone dead in my life," Dara said stoutly, although a pang of guilt made her words seem like a lie. No, she hadn't exactly wished Lord Vanian dead, but she certainly wouldn't have been sorry to see harm befall him, and she'd been more than ready to learn the most lethal spells to use against him if necessary. Why, the lightning she'd hurled at Lord Vanian might well have killed a man—a normal man. At that moment, Dara wouldn't have hesitated to kill Lord Vanian to protect herself. Was that very fact the cause of her guilt, the reason she wanted now to see him cured?

"Reckon she owes him," Gespry said before Dara could stop him. "He saved her from that dart."

"Oho!" Granny Good raised her eyebrows and turned back to Dara. "So you think you're in his debt, is that it?"

"I—I never thought of that," Dara said, unexpectedly feeling shy. "I didn't much stop to think of anything, to tell you true. I just—well, I couldn't just leave him to die, could I? Please, can't you help him?"

Granny looked from Dara to the unconscious lord and then back again. Then she sighed.

"Don't reckon as I can," she said at last. "Sorry, child."

Granny's answer sent a spear of panic through Dara's heart, and she twisted her hands together hard to stop their shaking.

"If you can't cure him," Dara said, "can you at least take me to the last door in the corridor and then back here when I'm done? My family grimoire would have healing spells, but by the time I'd gone and fetched them back—''

"It'd be far too late," Granny Good said, nodding. For a long moment she was silent; then she asked, "And what would you trade me, child, for such help?"

"Trade—" Dara fell silent, her mind racing. The mirror!

"Your wish," Dara said quickly. "I could find your wish for you."

Granny cackled again, but this time there was more bitterness than humor in her laughter.

"Ain't no wish to be found, child," she said, shaking her head. "Time was I could've made one, mayhap, but I didn't know it. No, whatever I might wish is beyond anyone's giving now. Sides, you can't trade what isn't yours, and that mirror isn't yours. You oughtn't even use it without his permission."

"I don't have anything else to give," Dara protested. She turned to her sack of belongings and riffled through it, tossing her possessions aside recklessly. "My grimoires, my dagger, the wish I found?"

"No value to me," Granny Good said firmly.

Dara patted her pockets absently while she racked her brain. Suddenly she stopped, pulling the blue gem from her pocket.

"There's this," she said slowly.

"Somebody else's wish?" Granny chided. "Now, child, what'd I do with that? And it's not a fair trade, something that's got no value to you."

"Trade it to Yaga for your—whatever you want," Dara said. She held out the gem reluctantly. "It's his wish. But it has value to me—I was going to trade it to him for his help."

At Dara's words, Granny became very still. Her eyes fixed on Dara's, and one seamed hand reached out shaking toward the gem. Then she reluctantly drew her fingers back and turned away as if she could no longer bear to look.

"Can't trade you, child," she said shortly.

"Why not?" Dara pleaded as panic threatened to over-
whelm her. If Granny couldn't—or wouldn't—help her,
who could? And what more could she do or say to persuade
the ancient woman? She had nothing else to give.

"There's rules how things is done here, and I can't trade
you," Granny said, not meeting Dara's eyes. "Trade it like
you planned and ask *him* for help, if you like. 'S all I can
do for you, child." Without another word, she was gone.

Dara stood where she was, almost paralyzed with dismay; even Gespry's jaw had dropped.

"Ain't never seen the old hag act like that," he said at
last, shaking his head. "You seem to send just about everybody awry, don't you, girly?"

"It certainly seems like it here," Dara said, near tears.
"Gespry, what am I going to do? I was so sure she'd help
me, at least take me to look through the other grimoires."

"Well, anything Granny could do, Yaga could do,
couldn't he?" Gespry suggested. "He used to be Guardian,
after all, and you know he'd trade you for the gem."

"But why wouldn't Granny trade?" Dara asked, confused. Value given for value received, that was the rule,
and certainly the gem had great value to Dara, even if that
value was indirect; why, her ability to trade it to Yaga
might be her best hope in gaining her wish.

"I don't know," Gespry said, shaking his head, "but I
reckon if you spend enough time worrying about it, it won't
matter none, 'cause the lord'll be dead. Best get on with
whatever you're gonna do, girly. Seems he's a bit worse'n
when you left him with me. Fever seems higher, anyway."

Dara pensively laid her hand on the lord's forehead.
Gespry was right; he was definitely warmer to the touch.
Dara filled her washbasin with water and concentrated; after
satisfyingly few tries, she was able to change the water to
ice, broken into small chunks. She poured water over the
ice and wet a cloth, which she laid on Lord Vanian's forehead.

"Keep the cloth wet with cold water," Dara told Gespry. "If his fever gets any higher, just wrap up some ice in the cloth and put it on his head." When Gespry hesitated, Dara added, "There's nothing to fear. I promise, he's in no condition to throw any spells at you."

"All right, then," Gespry said unhappily. "Don't suppose you'd let *me* go trade with Yaga, while you stay here and watch the lord?" he suggested.

"Lend you my key, *and* with the gem Yaga would trade anything for?" Dara said, half grinning despite her anxiety. "I don't think so. Believe me, I'll be back as soon as ever I can."

She took nothing with her but her dagger, the gem, and her key. It wasn't until she reached the entryway, however, and opened the front door that she realized that there was no Lord Vanian to transport her from place to place; she'd have to leave the castle on her own two feet, as laboriously as she'd entered it with Gespry. And her ladder was exactly where she'd left it, hidden in the bushes. On the other side of two walls and a moat.

Well, no matter. Dara had had a little more practice with magic now, and she was no longer reluctant to use it. Grimly Dara chanted her lightning spell, hurling one bolt after another at the walls until she'd made a hole in each, and simply stepped through. The moat presented no problem at all. Dara had just practiced turning water to ice; she simply froze the water in the moat and walked across. It took only a few minutes to dash to the doorway to the corridor, too worried to take pride in her accomplishments.

Finding Yaga's door took rather longer; she and Gespry had not marked it, and all the wooden doors were absolutely identical. It took a little searching before Dara opened the peephole and saw again the strange thick jungle where she'd met the dragon. Dara thought of the horrible, choking heat, the biting insects, and the snakes, and closed her eyes briefly while she mustered her courage; then she opened the door and stepped inside.

It was hard to run any distance in the incredible wet

heat, besides the need for caution to avoid the possibly poisonous snakes, and Dara was forced to a sporadic trot, pausing frequently to catch her breath. At last the ruins were ahead of her, and Dara doubted she had ever been so glad to see anything in her life.

As she had before, Dara climbed to the top of one of the blocks and hopped from stone to stone to avoid the paved floor. It seemed to take forever; but then again, the first time she'd been in no hurry, so the laboriousness of her progress hadn't troubled her. To her relief, however, the arched entrance of the temple was finally before her, with Yaga lying snoring exactly where he'd been before.

"Yaga?" Dara said, approaching cautiously. The dragon hadn't harmed her before, but he'd been so disappointed when she left. "Sir Yaga?"

Apparently this time Yaga was sleeping less soundly, for when Dara raised her voice his snores ceased, and gradually one great eyelid lifted, the huge silver eye gazing dispassionately at Dara.

"Well." Yaga yawned and stretched; the block Dara was standing on shook beneath her feet, but Dara was afraid to move for fear it might topple over. "So you've come again, young one. I welcome your company, but doubtless you have come for more than polite conversation."

"I—I enjoyed our talk," Dara said timidly, "but you're right. I came for more than advice this time. Do you know anything about poisons?"

"Poisons." Yaga rested his immense head on his forepaws and gazed at Dara steadily. "There are many poisons, most made by venomous insects or reptiles, but many from plants. Some, in order to be effective, must be eaten or drunk, while others, like the venom of snakes, must enter the blood of its victim." He sniffed. "And whom are you wishing to poison?"

"I don't want to poison anybody," Dara said hastily. "I want to cure someone who's been poisoned."

"Not yourself, surely," Yaga said lazily. "You have the

look and smell of good health.''

"No, not me.'' Dara ducked her head. "It's Lord Vanian who's been poisoned.''

"Indeed!'' Yaga lifted his head, a keen interest now showing in the sharpness of his silver gaze. "And you desire to help him? Why so?''

"Well, it's—it's rather hard to explain,'' Dara said awkwardly. "And there really isn't time—''

"If you wish my help,'' Yaga said gently, "then answer my question.''

Dara sighed. "All right,'' she said. "I owe it to him, in a way.'' She told him the story as quickly as she could, leaving out nothing she could remember—she didn't know what Yaga wanted from her story, but after he'd been so kind to her before, she'd not deceive him, even by omission.

When she finished, Yaga nodded slowly, his great silver eyes half closed.

"And so you wish to save him because you feel indebted, because he saved you?'' Yaga asked at last. "Only that?''

"Well—I'd try to save most anyone, I suppose,'' Dara said, a little confused by the question. "If I could. I'm not certain I understand what you mean.''

Yaga sighed, lowering his head to his paws again.

"Then it appears you are not yet done here,'' he said. "So you came to me hoping that I could give you an antidote for this poison? I can do so. And what have you brought to trade me for it?''

"This.'' Dara drew the gem from her pocket.

"Ah, another wish you've found for me to try,'' Yaga said, his voice sad.

"Not to try.'' Dara clutched the gem tightly as Yaga's head shot up from its resting place. "This one's yours. I used a divination spell to find it and went for it on purpose.''

Yaga's tail swished from side to side, toppling stones

from the archway. His eyes narrowed.

"Do not taunt me, child," he breathed. "Too many long centuries have passed me by without hope."

"It's yours, I promise," Dara said steadily. Then, more quietly, she said, "She's still there. In her garden."

A shudder ran through Yaga's immense body, and great tears rolled from his eyes, splashing to the stones and spattering Dara with salt water.

"Cruel, how cruel," he roared, shaking the ground and nearly toppling Dara from her stone with the force of the sound. "To give this to me now, now when I can no longer go to her. How can I bear it?"

"You can go to her," Dara said, her voice trembling. "What's stopping you?"

Yaga threw his head back and roared, a wail of grief and despair that nearly deafened Dara. She put her hands over her ears and crouched trembling on the stone until Yaga subsided again.

"How can I go to her in this form?" he groaned.

"You used to be the Guardian," Dara said cautiously. "You must know how to change your own shape. Can't you just change yourself back?"

"Too many years, too much forgetting," Yaga moaned. "I have forgotten myself."

Suddenly Dara realized what he meant. After so many centuries in the body of a dragon, he no longer remembered who or what he had once been. Why, he'd said as much when they first met. But—

"I can help you," Dara said excitedly. "All I need is some still water."

"Then you shall have it." A single gigantic claw dug into the stone block beside the one on which Dara was sitting, leaving a deep, wide furrow. Carefully Yaga rose from the stones and slid into the thick foliage, his every step making Dara's block rock and tilt ominously. When Yaga returned, his face was dripping; he spat a huge spray of water that soaked Dara thoroughly, but also filled the hole in the block beside her.

Dara was almost too distracted, between her worry for Lord Vanian and Yaga's antics, to manage the simple divination spell, but at last she succeeded, and Yaga gazed on in silence as Dara asked her question and the image of the young elvan man appeared in the water. Even after the image faded at last, for a long moment Yaga said nothing. Then another salty tear splashed to the stones, and the dragon rose once more to his feet.

"I remember . . ." Yaga said, and his huge outline began to blur as the image had done, slowly and painfully shrinking even as it blurred. At last the form of the elvan male, dressed in a tattered blue tunic and trousers, emerged from the shifting cloud of matter, and Yaga collapsed weakly to the stones, slender pale fingers clutching at the rock as if to assure himself of their reality.

Dara knelt at his side, laying one hand on his shoulder. Would he come to himself before Lord Vanian died of the poison? Should she have demanded payment before he changed?

"Are—are you all right?" she asked timidly.

"Yes. Yes." Dara could still recognize a hint of Yaga's tones in the melodic voice of the elf. He glanced at her through tumbled pale hair. "Better now than— " He pushed himself to his feet, Dara steadying him.

"By Alaster, I am myself again," Yaga breathed, trembling. "I am— " He glanced at Dara. "Forgive me. Your mission is an urgent one. Tell me of the poison."

"It was on a dart that—wait." Dara reached into her pocket and pulled out the dart she'd tucked away. "Here it is."

Yaga took the dart carefully and examined the pointed tip, sniffing at it, finally scraping at it with his fingernail and touching the scraping to his tongue tip. He spat hastily.

"A simple enough plant-based toxin," he said. "Perhaps it would not even kill the lord if he were strong and healthy, but—" He hesitated, glancing at Dara. "I doubt he much cares whether he will die or live, and that weakens him. The cure is a basic formula." A vial of clear liquid appeared in his hand, and he handed it to Dara.

"Give him ten drops mixed in a little water," Yaga said. "The fever should break quickly, but he will likely not wake for a day or two. Give him another such dose every quarter of a day until he wakes, and then half as much per dose until all is gone. He will have to regain his strength in his own time. Sleep and good food will do the rest."

"Days?" Dara asked, dismayed. Lord Vanian couldn't grant her her wish if he was unconscious; in fact, she couldn't even leave him to look for the Oracle, not while he needed constant tending.

"I know." Yaga's blue eyes were warm with sympathy. "I would help you if I could. But—"

"Thank you." Dara sighed. Yaga had his own concerns, of course. And why shouldn't he? He'd been waiting for centuries. A few days more would make no difference to Cav. She held out the gem. "Here's your wish."

Yaga gazed at the gem longingly, then sighed. He pulled off his tunic.

"Wrap it in this," he said. "I will not use it just yet."

Dara obeyed, confused. Why would he ever not want to use his wish now?

"Would you tell me what your wish was?" Dara blurted out. "I mean, in exchange for my divination spell?"

Yaga smiled a little sadly.

"That, I suppose, is only fair," he said. "So much of the tale you seem to know already. Indeed, I came to the Crystal Keep seeking Kelara. It took me the greater part of a century to find my way here to her. She was the Guardian when I came, but not a Guardian such as Lord Vanian. She had gone into her garden, and there she lived inside herself. There was but one other door then—it led to a fair forest filled with wonderful creatures and enchanting adventures. I stayed there for some time until I realized how much it resembled the enchanted wood Kelara had once sung of in my city, the song that had captured my heart. I wandered that place a very long time.'' Yaga sighed. ''But at last I found the Oracle, and I learned the truth—that when Kelara bound the energies of the Keep, when she turned the Keep's magic upon itself, Kelara's soul had in turn been turned upon itself, and was torn from her. In time without a soul she lost herself, as I had seen. So I asked the Oracle how Kelara's soul might be restored to her, and learned that I could ask the Guardian for my wish—provided I gave equal value in return. I thought my wish as good as granted, for what I wished was to benefit Kelara herself, and I left the Oracle behind me. I went to Kelara and wished that I would be able to restore Kelara's soul to her, and was dismayed when it was not immediately granted. Then I realized that I had wished only for the *ability*—that in order to restore Kelara's soul, I must first find it before that ability might be used, and I had no idea what form her soul might have taken. I returned to the place where I had left the Oracle, but it was no longer there.

''I wandered her garden, the barren lands around it, and my forest again, searching for Kelara's soul.'' Yaga sighed and shook his head. ''At last in the despair of my search I failed to remember all of the song Kelara had sung, and I sat down beside a clear pool in my forest and there found sweet fruit to eat—''

''Plums?'' Dara guessed.

''The same.'' Yaga sighed again. ''I ate my fill and slept. When I awakened I knew nothing of who I was or why I had come. I stayed alone in that place for some immeasurable time, for when I at last found the door and thought to use the strange key that hung around my neck, there were other doors in the corridor—many other doors. At last I came to this place. I caught a strange fever here— perhaps from the insects, or perhaps I was bitten by one of the serpents and never realized it. I stumbled about in my delirium and somehow lost my key. So the Keep transformed me, as it does all who become trapped here.

"Over the centuries—I can guess only vaguely how much time must have passed—a few scattered memories returned, vague bits of recollection that hardly made sense to me. I became the Guardian by simple virtue of the time I had been here and the power I had learned to wield; somehow, perhaps without even knowing it, perhaps because of my wish or because that power had no value to her at all, Kelara had relinquished that role to me. But like Kelara, I had never remembered *myself*, and though I found my key in time, even learned the form Kelara's soul had taken, the one memory that never returned was that of my own form, so there was no longer any reason to leave this place to seek out Kelara. Just as Kelara does not go and find her lost soul herself, though well she could; I think she does not even realize now—or care—that it is gone, for in her emptiness she has peace, even a kind of contentment, as I had."

He smiled.

"But peace and contentment grow tiresome after a time," he said, stretching his arms with a sigh of relief. "I think it is past time to set them aside."

He stepped into the darkness of the temple archway and emerged holding a familiar-looking golden key, which he slipped into his pocket. He smiled again, reaching out to take Dara's hand.

"I owe you much," he said. "I would grant you your wish myself if it was mine to give. It is not. But three more things I can give you, and I shall. The first is that I will not use my wish yet."

"How does that help me?" Dara asked, confused. Why, wouldn't it be better if Kelara was indeed made whole? Surely the creator of the Keep could—would—help Dara find the Oracle and gain her wish, especially when Dara had been instrumental in helping Kelara regain her soul.

"Trust me that it does," Yaga told her. He took the golden key out of his pocket, gazed at it a moment. "And now that this place no longer holds me, I can tell you something which I could not say to you before, and that is my second gift to you, and it is this: Remember that the final key is always within your own heart.''

"Please," Dara said desperately. "Please, no more riddles. Can't you just tell me what you mean?''

"And that is my third gift to you, the most difficult for me to give as it is for you to receive," Yaga said gently, squeezing her fingers. "And that is my silence. I will tell you nothing more.''

"If that's a gift, I'd rather not have it," Dara said, clinging to his hand. "Please, can't you just—''

"Good-bye," Yaga said warmly, and was gone.

Dara stood where she was, too stunned even to weep. How could he? After she'd done everything she could to help him, how could he simply give her yet another unsolvable riddle and vanish, deliberately withholding his aid? How could the laws of the Keep allow it?

But of course, he had his key and his wish. He was no longer a resident of the Keep; he was once more a visitor like herself, free to do and say—or not do and not say— what he would. And for all Dara had handed him his heart's desire, he'd chosen to repay her with silence and inaction.

Well, at least she had the antidote to the poison. Dara clutched the vial tightly in her hand. That was what she'd come for, after all. She carefully tucked the vial into the front of her breastband, then began to hop, block to block, back toward the door.

Returning to Lord Vanian's castle was easier than leaving it had been, since she knew where she was going and did not have to figure out a way over the walls; even the moat was still frozen fairly solidly. Dara trotted up the steps and found Gespry just as she'd left him, soaking the cloth in the bowl of icy water before returning it to Lord Vanian's forehead. Gespry sighed with relief when he saw Dara.

"Good to see you back, girly," he said. "He ain't gotten

too much worse, I guess, but he sure ain't no better."

"Yaga gave me a potion for him." Dara ignored Gespry's snicker as she fished the vial out of her breastband. She mixed the prescribed ten drops carefully in a cup of water, then wrestled the unconscious lord into a half-sitting position, propped up by pillows and her arm, so that she could give him the liquid from a spoon, sip by tiny, careful sip. At last, when he'd swallowed it all, Dara let him lie flat again.

"So what do we do now?" Gespry asked her. "Keep up the ice and water until the potion works?"

"*I* don't know," Dara said impatiently. "I suppose so."

"Ain't you never nursed a sick person before?" Gespry asked.

Dara shook her head. Her mother and father had been the mages, not she, and their healing had generally been of a quicker and more dramatic nature. Her father had administered potions, yes, but it had always been left to others to tend the patient through recovery.

"No, I never have," she said. "Have you?"

"Nah, but I been sick," Gespry told her. "Had a bad cough one spring, and the village midwife was a friend of mine." His grin told Dara just what kind of "friend" the midwife had been. "I was in and out sometimes, like the lord here, and she cleaned me up and fed me mostly broth and potions and put poultices on my chest."

"Well, he doesn't have a cough, and I don't know any poultices," Dara said, shrugging. "But I can make broth, and we have a potion." She hesitated. "But when you said she cleaned you up, you don't mean—I mean—"

"Yeah, just like a baby, I reckon," Gespry chuckled. "If he don't wake up, he can't make it to the chamber pot, can he?"

Dara involuntarily stepped back from the bed in horror. "But I can't! I couldn't possibly!"

"Well, then, he'll lie in it, I guess," Gespry said, shrugging. "I can't hardly roll him over myself, can I?"

Dara groaned and covered her face with her hands, but even as she shook her head, she knew she could not refuse. And even though there was nobody in the world she had ever hated with such a passion, nobody she would ever have been so happy to see dead, Dara knew she would do whatever must be done—postpone her search for the Oracle and wash Lord Vanian and tend him and feed him and watch over him. She would do this because he was the Guardian of the Crystal Keep and only he could grant her wish, yes, but also for a far more basic reason—because she *could* do it, and because he had no one else. It was as simple and as inescapable as that.

Wearily Dara trudged down to the kitchen and set a large pot of water to simmer over the kitchen fire with enough meat and vegetables to make a rich soup. She dipped up two buckets of warm water from the large cauldron kept on the hearth and trudged back upstairs.

Dara quickly found that it was easier to wash Lord Vanian in the bed, turning and rolling him as necessary, than to wrestle the heavy, limp body out of bed and into the tub and then carry upstairs all the buckets of hot water to pour over him. It was a nasty, awkward business, but not so frightening as Dara had thought it would be; she even felt a rather guilty satisfaction in seeing Lord Vanian utterly helpless, completely dependent upon her care. If she wanted to kill him for what he'd done to her, he could do nothing to stop her; why, she could in fact do nothing at all, simply leave him to his fate, and he'd die!

But Dara felt no real desire to take such vengeance now, though she might well have been tempted only a few days before. She remembered uneasily that Yaga had compared her to Lord Vanian, and what he'd said about walking in the shadows. No, Yaga had been right; blind anger made it all too easy to cross that line into darkness—why, Dara would never have believed herself capable of hurling lightning at another person, or even attempting a Greater Summoning that might bring the gods only knew what into the world. She could understand Lord Vanian's bitterness a lit-tle better now, how all the long, lonely years and the power of the Keep had torn from him his love and his freedom and robbed him of his ability to feel compassion, just as they had robbed Yaga of his memories and Kelara of her soul. Yes, Yaga had been right; best to concentrate on her purpose and be gone, not become embroiled in the Keep's dangerous game of give-and-get.

Well, the time spent nursing Lord Vanian would not be wholly wasted; Dara comforted herself with that knowl-edge. Why, she was serving him, just like she'd promised, and preparing his meals with her own two hands, so this time was fulfilling her part of their bargain amply, and she was entitled to use the mirror as Lord Vanian had promised. And however little the bitter lord might value his life, he'd owe her *something* for her pains, and that debt would serve her well, too.

Once she had finished washing the lord, Dara was re-lieved to find that his fever had already dropped, his flushed face resuming a more normal color. He breathed easily and his heartbeat seemed strong and steady, but slow; his fin-gers twitched occasionally, and expressions flitted across his face and were gone as suddenly as they had come. Dara wondered whether despite his lack of fever he was dream-ing.

When she had made Lord Vanian as comfortable as she could, Dara realized uneasily that she was faced with the choice of either leaving the sick lord alone at night, laying a pallet on the cold stone floor, or sleeping in the bed with Lord Vanian—and sick and helpless as he might be, that thought was unbearable.

"I'll stay in here," Gespry volunteered, startling Dara out of her reverie. "You can make up the next room if you want, and I'll come get you if he needs anything."

"Oh, would you?" Dara said, gratitude and relief mak-ing her feel suddenly weak. It seemed almost impossible that someone would volunteer to help her with no tricks or trades. Then she hesitated. "But he told me to stay in this room."

"Not really," Gespry told her. "He told you about the other rooms, too. Anyhow, that wasn't part of the bargain, and it'd be awful presumptuous of a maid to doss down in the room with a landed lord without him asking, wouldn't it?"

"All right, then," Dara said, sighing happily. "Thank you ever so much, Gespry."

"Well, I ain't exactly doing it for nothing," Gespry said hastily.

"Of course not." Dara tried to hide her disappointment. "What do you want in return?"

"Well—it's kind of special," Gespry said awkwardly.

Dara sighed. "What?"

"Venison pasty with leeks and gravy," Gespry said, grinning sheepishly. "And cherry sponge pudding with almond cream."

Dara had to grin back, the sudden warmth in her heart so strong that she thought, *Yes. I can bear this. This, and whatever else it takes*.

"I think I can manage that for your supper tonight," she said. "And while the lord's ill and you're staying in his room for me, I'll make you whatever you like for supper every single night. And dinner, too. Fair bargain?" She held out one hand.

"Girly, a bargain don't get no better'n that," Gespry said, grinning back as he grasped Dara's forefinger with his small hairy digits and shook it.

Dara conjured up Gespry's special supper, enough for both of them, chuckling a little as she filled a bowl with broth for Lord Vanian. How strange it seemed that she and Gespry, servant and peasant, should sup on fine fare while the lord got nothing but broth. But she'd prepared his meal with her own hands, as he had required, and she was tending him like a good servant would—well, better than any servant she'd ever known, come to that, for all that there was nobody else but Gespry to share in his care.

Dara fed Lord Vanian the broth, and then she and Gespry took their own meal sitting on the floor on pillows, enjoying the rich food in silence. After supper, Dara left long enough to tidy up the kitchen and move her belongings to the next room, but she returned after that to give the lord his next dose of the potion Yaga had given her. Other than the lowering of his fever, there seemed to be no change in Lord Vanian's condition, but then Yaga had said it would take days for the lord to regain his strength.

"Go on to bed," Gespry said, when Dara hesitated by the bed, smoothing out a last wrinkle in the covers. "I'll curl up here on the corner like always. Just leave the door ajar a bit, and yours, too, and if he so much as breaks wind I'll be right in there to wake you."

Dara obeyed, but she slept badly in the luxurious guest suite, dreaming unpleasantly that Skivvit and his companions pursued her through the forest while she recited spell after spell in vain, as all magic had once more abandoned her. Dara found herself up well before dawn, scrubbing her hands and face and dressing hastily, dashing out of her room and down to the kitchen as if she were late for her duties.

When she arrived at Lord Vanian's room with a bowl of broth for him and a basket of bread and fruit for herself and Gespry, Dara found Gespry still sleeping soundly at the foot of the bed, a corner of the cover pulled over his furry body. Lord Vanian slept on, more peacefully than he had the day before, not waking when Dara half lifted him to give him his potion and the broth. Gespry did not wake either, and Dara wondered uneasily whether allowing him to watch over Lord Vanian in the night had been a good decision. She'd let Gespry sleep a little longer before she disturbed him so she could wash the lord.

Dara left the room quietly, then found herself standing before the door to the tower. She hesitated for a moment, then opened the door. Why not? She was entitled to use the mirror once for each day of service, and she hadn't used it last night; she might as well ask her question of the mirror now.

Today there was no doubt of what Dara intended to ask; her dream of the night before had left one question burning in Dara's mind, and she intended to have her answer at last.

Dara sat down before the mirror and said firmly, "Show me why I have no magical ability of my own."

She had worried that perhaps since Lord Vanian had been absent from the room so long, the mirror might not work—it would have been a sensible precaution for Kelara to take when she'd created so powerful a device—but the mirror clouded and cleared obligingly.

Two figures writhed under rich woven coverlets, and Dara's cheeks flamed as she recognized her mother's dark brown hair spilling over the pillows. Why in the world—

But—but that room wasn't—

Then the couple rolled over, and Dara saw the man's face silhouetted in the firelight.

Lord Evander's face.

Dara gasped, turning hurriedly away from the mirror, her mind in turmoil as she fought desperately to deny what she'd seen. It couldn't be true! This had to be another trick of the mirror, another deception.

Even as she shook her head furiously, however, she knew that the only deception was the one she was trying to use on herself. She wasn't mist-witted with wine this time, as she'd been when she'd seen Cav in the mirror, and she certainly hadn't *expected* to see her mother in Lord Evander's bed. And, horribly, it made sense—her lack of magical talent, even her mother's dismissal from Lord Evander's service. Lord Evander's son and daughters were all younger than Dara; the last thing in the world he would have wanted was the scandal of a bastard child who might—failing other by-blows—have been his firstborn.

Dara hurried from the room, closing the door behind her. By all the gods, she didn't want to know what she knew.

It would have been better if she'd never asked, better to believe that possibly her family line had been cursed by some mage or demon. Did her father know? Surely not. But it would certainly mean the death of any hope that Cav's parents would ever consent to a marriage between her and Cav.

But then, how could they find out? Surely someone— her mother perhaps, or perhaps whatever mage Lord Evander had hired to replace her—had magically concealed Dara's illegitimacy, or it would have been revealed by one of the many prior divinations that her parents and Cav had had cast, trying to discover why Dara had not inherited her parents' magical ability. Only the powerful magic of the mirror would likely be able to pierce such protection as her mother could cast. No, nobody would know unless Dara herself told them, and she never would—except for Cav, of course; there could be no secrets between them. She didn't care how scandalized Lord Evander was, but there was no need to disgrace her mother now, so many years later, or to ruin her own chances of marrying Cav. She'd keep her mother's secret.

But of course Lord Vanian must know, or why had he seemed to encourage her to use the mirror to learn why she'd never shown any magical ability? Doubtless her story had made him curious and he'd used the mirror to learn the answer himself, and he thought it would be amusing to see her reaction when she learned the truth.

Dara leaned against the door to the tower, rubbing her eyes. No, she wouldn't cry. Whatever her mother had done, *she* had nothing to be ashamed of.

Gespry leaned out the bedroom door, looking up and down the corridor until he spotted her.

"Listen, you want to sit with the lord for a bit?" he said. "I found the food on the table, but I wouldn't mind a stroll outside in the courtyard, a bit of air, you know."

"I'm sorry, Gespry," Dara said distractedly. "Let me bring up some warm water and then you can go."

This time the disagreeable task of carrying the heavy bucket upstairs, undressing, washing, and dressing the unconscious lord was almost comforting in the distraction it provided. She couldn't even muster any anger at Lord Vanian. She *had* wanted to know why she'd lacked magical ability, after all; it wasn't surprising that her story had made him curious, too, or that he'd find the truth so amusing. She should have known better than to tell the capricious lord anything about herself.

Dara sighed and smoothed the covers over Lord Vanian's chest.

"What made you this way?" she said. "Was it the loss of the lady you loved? Was it all the lonely years shut inside the Keep? Was it the power that made you cruel, tormenting people just because you could? Or is it just that I still don't understand something, something important?"

There was no answer, of course. Lord Vanian was the helpless one now, while Dara had learned, at least to some small extent, to use the Keep's magic. Lord Vanian was as much at the mercy of Dara's whims as she'd been to his— more, for Dara had at least been conscious and able to act. And she'd had the choice to flee if she wished, to leave the Keep. Lord Vanian had lost that freedom a long time ago.

"Maybe you don't know how to care anymore," Dara said to him, although she knew he couldn't hear her. "Maybe you've forgotten how to feel compassion. But I haven't. And as well for your sake that that's true, isn't it?"

But whatever his reason, it was in part Lord Vanian's manipulations that had led her to consult the mirror, and she couldn't unknow what she knew now, any more than she could restore her lost virginity. And the question remained: What was Cav going to say when she told him about both those little flaws, as she must?

Nothing, of course, Dara told herself confidently. Cav loved her and knew she'd come to the Keep only so they could be together. Dara hadn't willingly gone to Lord Vanian's arms; she'd been tricked and bespelled, however Lord Vanian wanted to make it sound like her own fault. Cav would understand that. And the details of Dara's parentage made no difference, really, so long as no one found out. In fact, Cav might be reassured to learn that there was no curse that Dara might possibly pass on to her children.

Dara grimaced. She was deceiving herself again; it seemed to be something she was good at. Cav would have *plenty* to say in response to Dara's revelations. He'd blame her for losing her virginity simply because it had been *her* idea to come to the Crystal Keep. He'd heard the stories of how dangerous a place it was, just as Dara had; he'd certainly done everything in his power to persuade her not to go. She should have been more careful, or better yet, she shouldn't have gone at all. And her lost virginity, if discovered, would be something that High Lord Haranor and High Lady Alberta would have plenty to say about, too.

She didn't know what Cav would think of her illegitimacy. Bastardy carried greater stigma in some kingdoms—indeed, some families—than others. It really wasn't thought so unusual for a great lord like Lord Evander to father a child or two on the wrong side of the bed; the only strangeness was that Lord Evander would choose Lady Joraleen, a very powerful—and very married—mage, rather than some lissome young maid less known in the city and at court. The problem was that there was far less scandal in being a bastard than there was in a High Lord's son marrying one. If that fact were ever discovered, the consequences for Cav as High Lord of Caistran, and by extension the welfare of the country, could be terrible and far-reaching, and Cav took his responsibilities as Heir very seriously indeed. He would not treat lightly anything that could threaten the welfare of Caistran.

But surely he would agree that the secret of Dara's birth was likely to remain hidden forever. After all, the greatest mages in Caistran, using their most potent spells, had failed to discover it. No one would know but Lord Evander and

Dara's mother, and no one would be less likely to betray the secret. Surely Cav would agree.

Dara grimaced and shook her head. There was only one way to find out, and she didn't like it. That mirror had brought her nothing so far but confusion and grief. But . . . she had to know.

Dara glanced down at Lord Vanian, then gasped in surprise. His eyes were open, focused on her. Dara's stomach gave a great lurch, and she took a deep breath to calm herself.

"Hello," she said awkwardly, patting his hand. "It's good to see you awake." At the moment, however, she could only feel a most profound gratitude that he hadn't awakened while she was washing him.

Lord Vanian's eyes half closed, then opened again. His lips moved slightly, but no sound came out.

"You'll be well in time," Dara told him. "I—I found an antidote for the poison on the dart. Yaga said you'd have no strength, but that will pass in time."

Lord Vanian's lips moved again, and she could see the frustration in his eyes when he could not manage to speak.

"Don't worry," Dara said awkwardly, squeezing his fingers. "Just rest. You can tell me whatever you like when you regain more of your strength."

Lord Vanian sighed and his eyes closed again. Suddenly Dara was sorry she hadn't thanked him first, before she said anything else. He had likely saved her life, after all.

But then if Dara had been poisoned by the dart, surely Lord Vanian could create the antidote out of thin air just as Yaga had—if he'd wanted to, of course. But he must have wanted her alive, else why save her from the dart in the first place? Unless he'd simply acted without thinking, just as Dara had. Unless there was still some vestige of kindness left in him—just enough to move instinctively to save another from harm.

Dara sat quietly in a chair beside the bed until midday, when she allowed Gespry to take her place long enough for her to prepare dinner for Gespry and herself and warm more broth for Lord Vanian. The lord roused briefly while Dara was giving him his potion, but by the time she'd finished, he was asleep again. Dara was glad; after what she'd seen in the mirror, her thoughts were heavy, and she didn't really want to have to talk, even to Gespry. The strange little fellow seemed to sense that she wanted no company and left her alone for the most part, disappearing again after he'd claimed his dinner and not returning until nearly suppertime.

Dara conjured the roast boar with grapes that Gespry requested, but though the food was tasty, she had no appetite for it.

"You seem right down," Gespry observed bluntly after they had sat in silence for some time, Dara picking at her food while Gespry stuffed his mouth. "Been a bit off since this morning, haven't you? See something in the lord's mirror you didn't like?"

Dara nearly jumped out of her seat.

"Did you follow me up there?" she demanded, her heart pounding.

Gespry sat still and gaped, a piece of meat frozen in its journey from platter to mouth.

"Girly, you know better'n that," he said at last, putting down the meat. "I didn't even wake up till you came down. But it didn't take much figuring, 'cause you were coming out of the tower frowning like fury, and what else would you have gone up for?" He shrugged. "You don't want to say, ain't none of my affair, I guess."

"I—I'm sorry, Gespry," Dara said, suddenly ashamed of herself. How had she supposed Gespry would have opened the door to the tower or the door at the top of the stairs, both of which she'd closed behind her? And why had she even thought Gespry so careless as to leave Lord Vanian alone, or so sneaky as to creep up after her? "You're right. I did see something I didn't like, yes. I— I'd just rather not talk about it, if you don't mind. It was just something—well—personal."

Gespry shrugged again and reached for his third helping of honeyed cake and cream.

"As I said, ain't none of my affair," he said, but Dara thought she'd hurt his feelings nonetheless. "I just wondered whether I might use that mirror myself. I figure I'm owed, seeing as how I've been watching over the lord, see?"

Dara had to chuckle.

"I suppose you're owed, at that," she said. "But is that a fair bargain when you're making it without his consent?"

"Now, you know that ain't how it works," Gespry said patiently. "Bargaining ain't got nothing to do with it. Value given for value received, that's the rule. And I gave value, see, so as I figure it, I can take value, too. Don't cost the lord nothing, nohow, so it ain't much to ask."

"I suppose you're right," Dara said, but she wondered. The Guardian seemed as responsible for guarding the usage of the mirror as that of the Keep or the Oracle itself, and she was certain Lord Vanian would be quite angry to learn that Gespry had used the mirror without his permission and supervision. Still, it would be far easier to gain forgiveness than permission! "You can come up with me and ask your question after supper. In fact," she said, "maybe you can help me with my question, too."

Lord Vanian roused again briefly when she fed him his supper of broth mixed with Yaga's potion, and this time he seemed a little stronger and more aware, although he still could not muster the strength for speech.

"You seem to be doing well," she said as cheerfully as she could, wiping the last broth from his lips. "Better even than at dinner. Soon you'll be well. I'll take care of you as long as you need me."

She could not read the expression in Lord Vanian's eyes, but she thought surely he must find this situation utterly humiliating, to be at the mercy of her care after the way he'd behaved toward her, and what great lord wouldn't feel degraded at finding himself completely dependent on a lowly scullery maid? She took no satisfaction in the thought of his humiliation; in fact, the whole idea was rather embarrassing.

''You seemed interested in me and my family,'' Dara said awkwardly, sitting on the edge of the bed and wiping Lord Vanian's face with a damp cloth. ''My father was a mage like my mother, but he never wanted employment in a noble household; he liked working from his home, or taking the mule cart down into the village whenever somebody needed him there. He specialized in laying ghosts, lifting curses, banishing bogles, that sort of thing.''

She fancied there was a faint spark of interest in Lord Vanian's eyes, so she continued.

''Interestingly, the first work he had to do when he and my mother came to Caistran was to lay a ghost in our own house. Lord Evander—'' Dara had to force the name out, and she steadied her voice. ''Lord Evander gave my father and mother the house and its lands. It had belonged to a nephew of the seneschal who had moved out unexpectedly, apparently overnight, a few months before. Nobody knew how the ghost had come to be in the house, but it was there—hurled dishes about, made cold winds blow down the chimney to put the fire out, groaned up and down the corridors. Mother wanted to lay the ghost right away, but Father didn't want to until he could learn why it wasn't at rest.

''Father cast a divination spell and saw that the ghost was that of a young boy who had disappeared from the village almost a year before. The seneschal's nephew had enticed him up to the house and then knocked him unconscious, taken him to the cellar, and kept him chained there for weeks. The seneschal's nephew probably didn't intend to kill the boy, but the lad sickened and wasted away in that cellar. The nephew couldn't summon a healer, of course, so the boy died, and was buried in the cellar. Father had the whole cellar dug up until he found the boy's bones and had them returned to the boy's family. It worked, too; there was never any more trouble at the house. But nobody ever learned what became of the seneschal's nephew.'' Dara grinned. ''Maybe he came here and got what he deserved. If that's so, he was probably one of those lecherous boy-things in the forest, so he should have his fill of boys, eh?''

She thought she saw an answering twinkle of humor in Lord Vanian's eyes. Almost immediately that twinkle was replaced by another expression, less readable, and his lips barely moved as he tried to speak. Then his eyes closed slowly and he slept again.

This time Dara wondered what Lord Vanian wanted so badly to say. Surely he wouldn't try so hard just to thank her; gratitude didn't seem to be a part of the haughty lord's manner. Was he trying to give her some instruction? A warning? Well, it would simply have to wait. Likely tomorrow morning he'd be strong enough to speak, if he continued to improve as he had.

Meanwhile, Dara washed and dressed him quickly, afraid he'd wake again, but he did not. Gespry was waiting eagerly outside the door, but Dara would not go up to the tower until she'd hauled the dirty water, cloths, and dishes downstairs and cleaned everything. Truth to tell, she was more than a little reluctant to approach the mirror again. Gespry, however, followed her wherever she went, dancing from foot to foot in barely contained impatience, and at last Dara could think of no further excuse for delay.

Gespry approached the mirror as slowly as Dara, but his hesitation had an air of reverence rather than fear. He turned back to Dara.

''I got two questions,'' he said. ''That all right with you?''

Dara shrugged. ''It's not my mirror,'' she said. ''You don't need *my* permission. I won't say anything about it. But if the lord finds out you used it and he's angry—well, I don't know what he might do.''

"Well, might as well get blasted to barley for two questions as one," Gespry said resignedly. "So how's this thing work, eh?"

"Just ask it," Dara said. "But be careful, you'll get just exactly what you ask for."

Gespry nodded. "Didn't expect no different," he said. "All right then."

He turned to the mirror. "Show me how I used to look when I were twenty years old," he said.

The mirror misted and cleared, revealing a brawny youth, rather homely with a crooked nose and overstrong jaw, but not unappealing for all that, and the same blue eyes twinkled under sandy blond-brown brows.

After a time, the image faded, and Gespry sighed.

"Somehow I used to fancy myself better-looking back then," he said. "Good enough, though, and a fair sight better'n this." He turned to Dara. "You get a good enough look?"

"You think too little of yourself," Dara said comfortingly. "My brothers were no handsomer—why, Devan was downright ugly—and they married well. From the way you spoke, the village lasses didn't find you too homely, did they?"

Gespry grinned and shrugged a little proudly.

"Well, that time's long past," he said. "But what I figure, if I'm going to get changed back, why back to the way I was, all old an' wrinkled and joints aching? Why not back to a strong young fellow as might have a bit of a life if I ever get to leave, or at least a good strong body forever if I stay? Granny said she'd change me back, but I figure you know how I looked now, and you got your spells now, too; mayhap you could do it, or at least use one of your spells to show Granny how I ought to look, eh?"

Dara remembered the family grimoire. It would take her days to reach it, but Gespry's help *had* been invaluable, and she knew there were powerful transformation spells in the books. If only Gespry had thought of it, she could have copied one of them and saved herself the trouble of going back.

"All right," she said. "But it'd be safer to let me conjure an image for Granny. She seems to be a much more experienced mage than I am." Something about that statement caught in Dara's mind, but Gespry was still waiting to ask his second question, and she was agonizing over hers.

"Go on and ask your other question," Dara said, dismissing the nagging thought.

Gespry turned back to the mirror.

"Of all the gold keys that are lying around lost in the Keep," he said, "show me the exact location of the key I can most easily and safely get hold of."

"Oh, Gespry," Dara said, dismayed, "that'd be mine, wouldn't it?"

"Nah," Gespry said as the mirror clouded. "Yours ain't lost."

The mirror cleared, showing a view of the corridor. One of the doors opened, showing the beautiful crystal cavern to which Gespry had once taken Dara. The view wound down one of the passages, as if Dara was looking through a walker's eyes, and she heard Gespry muttering, "One right—one left—right—"

The view stopped in a small open area and focused on a skeleton lying on the ground. The gold key lay on the ground next to the white bones, the remains of the leather thong that had once held it now rotted away.

Dara fixed the image of the key, the skeleton, and the open area clearly in her mind. If Gespry wanted to go for that key rather than wait and gamble that Dara would still be able to give him hers, fine; but she'd cast a simple location spell so that Gespry wouldn't become lost and end up wandering through the cavern until he died of starvation. That was probably what had happened to the key's previous owner, after all.

When the image cleared, Gespry turned worriedly to Dara.

"What do you figure killed him?" he asked. "I didn't think there was nothing dangerous in that place."

"Well, the bones were whole, and they weren't scorched or chewed," Dara said encouragingly. "And there was only the one set of tracks, did you notice? I think whoever it was just got lost and died, probably of hunger, since there's plenty of water in there but nothing to eat."

Gespry shivered. "Reckon I'll have to take in some cord, or something to leave a trail," he said. He glanced at Dara shyly. "At least, if you'll let me through that door."

"Of course I will," Dara said, a little abashed at Gespry's straightforward idea. Why, a good long cord or even a sack of dark pebbles that would contrast well with the crystal were far more practical than a location spell, which would get Gespry to the key but not back, not without another spell. When had Dara started making the blind assumption that all difficulties could be, or even should be, solved by magic? It was a habit she'd best break, for when she left the Keep she'd be as magicless as she'd been before—unless that was what Lord Vanian chose to grant her. "We'll go there as soon as we can leave this place."

"It's not that I don't trust you to keep your promise," Gespry said hastily. "It's just if something were to happen to you, there I'd be."

"I understand," Dara said, and she did. "But, you know, you didn't need the mirror for these questions. One of my divination spells would have sufficed."

"Maybe so," Gespry agreed. "But then I'd've owed you for 'em, and I ain't got anything left to trade. The questions in the mirror I figure I'm already owed, like I said. 'Sides, I might's well use the thing. Ain't likely I'll ever get another chance." He shrugged. "What about your question? You said you wanted my help."

"Yes." Dara took a deep breath. "I want—I want to see Cav and talk with him, but I'm afraid my own feelings and expectations might warp what I see, like they did before, even though I'm not half tipsy now. I'd like you to ask for me. That way I'd be sure I'm seeing the real Cav, not what I wanted or expected to see.''

Gespry shrugged again. ''All right with me,'' he said. ''But if the lord don't like it, I don't get blamed for this question, right?''

''Right,'' Dara said quickly. ''It's my question; I just want you to ask it for me.''

''Right.'' Gespry turned toward the mirror, then back again. ''What's his right name again? I known a couple of Cav's in my time; 'spect you don't want to talk to any of *them*, even if they ain't long dead.''

''Oh, yes,'' Dara said hurriedly. ''Lord Cavin IV, son of High Lord Haranor of Caistran.''

''And you want to talk to him, right, and hear him, too, eh? Right, then.'' Gespry turned back to the mirror. ''I want my friend Dara here to be able to see, hear, and talk to Lord Cavin IV, Heir of Caistran, exactly as he is right now.''

The mirror clouded and cleared, revealing a sight that made Dara's heart sing—Cav in his dressing gown, sitting at the table in his room, poring over a thick book. She was seeing him from the back and one side, about where his dressing mirror stood in his room.

''Cav?'' she said timidly.

Cav jumped violently, as if he'd been poked, and looked around wildly. At last he seemed to see Dara, for his eyes widened and his jaw dropped satisfyingly.

''Dara?'' he said disbelievingly. ''How—where are you? Are you all right?''

''I'm fine,'' Dara said, warmed by the concern in his voice. ''And you? Are you well?''

''Of course. Of course.'' Cav waved dismissingly. ''But how, by the gods, are you appearing there in my mirror?'' He stepped forward, one hand extended, and Dara saw the skin of his palm flatten and spread, as if he'd laid his hand against an invisible but solid barrier.

Trembling, Dara reached out and touched the mirror where his hand rested. She felt only cool glass, and a pang of disappointment struck her silent for a moment. So she couldn't touch Cav through the mirror's power, as she had in the illusion. It was only a mirror, after all, a mirror with a powerful divination spell.

"It's complicated," Dara said. "It's part of the magic of the Crystal Keep."

"The Crystal Keep?" Disappointment was plain in Cav's voice. "I thought perhaps you'd solved your—well—problem."

"Almost," Dara said quickly. "I shouldn't be much longer."

Cav hesitated, then said, "I suppose I never really thought I would hear from you again. It's been so long, I thought—well, I thought something had happened to you."

"It hasn't been *that* long," Dara protested. Given the distance she had to travel to the Keep, and supposing it would take her as long to return, Cav shouldn't have had time to become too anxious just yet.

Cav gave her a puzzled look.

"How can you say that?" he said. "A year isn't long to you?"

"A year?" This time it was Dara's turn to gape. "But—but I only arrived at the Keep a few weeks ago. It took me only about three weeks to get here. It shouldn't have been more than maybe a month since I left."

"Eleven months and eighteen days," Cav corrected. "From the day you left. I sent messengers through all the neighboring kingdoms. I found the merchant from the last caravan you traveled with and learned you'd been safe and well when you left, but that's the last I was able to learn. That was months ago."

Months ago! Nearly a year! Dara's head spun, and she remembered what Lord Vanian himself had said when she'd first arrived at the Keep. "I advise you not to tarry long about your task, or you may well regret it.'' Did time pass more slowly inside the Crystal Keep than in the outside world? It would seem so! Was that what had happened to Lord Vanian—that by the time he gained his wish, so much time had passed in the outside world that his love had given him up for lost? How fortunate for Dara that Cav was more constant, had more faith in her!

"I'm sorry,'' she said. "I didn't know that time passed more slowly here. I tried to call you once before. But I'll be able to leave soon, very soon.''

"Well—'' Cav hesitated. "It had best be soon. Very soon.''

"What's happened?'' Dara asked slowly.

"I've been betrothed to Ariana, daughter of Lord Kanden,'' Cav said in his forthright way. "We're to be married in less than six months.''

"Betrothed?'' This time the shock of Cav's words left her stunned and shaking. "But, Cav, you—you promised—''

"Dara, what did you expect?'' Cav said patiently. "You'd been gone nearly a year. My best messengers couldn't track you, my best mages, casting their most powerful spells, couldn't find you. All I could think was that you were dead. How long did you think I could wait? When my father dies, I'm to be High Lord of Caistran. I owe my people an heir to follow me, and to give them that, I must have a wife. I didn't want you to go in the first place, you know that.'' He shook his head. "But it doesn't matter. You're alive. Come home quickly and I'll find some way for us to be together.''

Some way. To be together. Once those words would have lifted all fear and doubt from Dara's heart; was it her experiences in the Crystal Keep that had made her suspect the nature of such promises?

"You mean we'll be married?'' Dara asked cautiously.

Cav sighed. "Dara, you know I've done everything I could to make my parents agree to our wedding. But you're virtuous and of a good bloodline. If you return as powerful a mage as your parents, I think they'll consent.''

He thought. He *thought* they'd consent. But even those words were obscured by a single thought that repeated over and over in Dara's heart. He hadn't waited. He hadn't believed in her after all.

''And what,'' Dara said dully, ''if they don't consent?''

''They will,'' Cav said firmly. ''I'm almost sure of it. But I'll never abandon you, Dara. I'll always love you, always take care of you. You know that.''

Yes. She knew that. He'd take care of her—in a comfortable and very private house, with servants of her own, lacking no luxury she might desire. And he would love her—in secret meetings, while his private guards smiled knowingly and her servants chuckled. Of course, Cav would never insist that she grant him her favors, never ask that she repay his generosity. Never. But she loved him, and he loved her, and in time, when that love was all she had left to cling to—

''I called you because I wanted to speak to you personally,'' Dara said at last. ''To tell you—'' She gazed into his eyes. ''To tell you that I'm no longer a virgin.''

Cav's eyes darkened with fury. ''Someone forced you?''

Dara was not too bemused to appreciate that Cav immediately assumed that Dara had been taken against her will. But then, why would Dara willingly lie with another man when Cav, Heir to Caistran, was the man she loved?

''In a manner of speaking,'' she said. ''I was bespelled.''

''By the gods, who was it?'' Cav demanded. ''I'll cut out the swine's heart and feed it to him!''

Once such a vow would have melted Dara's heart. Now somehow it didn't seem to matter. Cav was only speaking from anger; if he wouldn't come after Dara, he'd scarcely journey to the Crystal Keep to draw his sword on the Guardian.

''You know that nothing could lessen my love for you,''

Cav said earnestly. "No one need ever know." He hesitated. "Unless the blackguard got you with child—"

Dara could have laughed. Could have wept.

"No," she said. "I'm not with child." At least she hoped not.

Cav stepped forward, flattened both hands against the mirror. "If only I could hold you, comfort you—"

Hold her, yes. Comfort her, indeed.

"There's more," Dara said deliberately. "I've learned that I'm a bastard." She had to chuckle. "Although my bloodline is likely rather improved by it."

Cav's eyes widened; whether at her announcement or her laughter, Dara couldn't be certain. But at least he didn't step back from the mirror.

"No one needs to know," he repeated. "Dara, why are you acting in this way? Did you think I'd turn away from you, hate you?"

"No," Dara said honestly. "No, Cav, I never thought that." *And I never thought you'd stop believing in me. But then, I thought your love for me was something more than what it was—something stronger than magic and kingdoms.*

"Tell me something, Cav," she said at last. "When was the betrothal?"

Cav's eyes widened, then flickered uneasily away from hers.

"Not long ago," he said at last. "Just a few—a few weeks."

Dara closed her eyes briefly.

"I have to go," she said. "I can't keep this spell up forever." Could she?

"All right." Cav touched the mirror again. "Hurry back. Don't forget I'm here thinking of you."

"No, I won't," Dara said. No. She wouldn't forget. Even if she wanted to.

The mirror clouded; when it cleared, only Dara, Gespry, and the room were reflected.

"Fine-looking fellow, that one," Gespry said cheerfully.

"Must think a good bit of you, too, if he'd rather have you over a lord's daughter, eh?"

"Yes, he must," Dara said dully. "Mustn't he?" Of course Gespry was right. She had the love of a High Lord's son, and he'd promised that he'd take care of her. That was more than a bastard scullery maid with no magic of her own had a right to expect, wasn't it?

Wasn't it?

"Come on," she told Gespry. "I don't much like it here anymore."

"I'd fancy duck with wine gravy, and sweet buns with currants, and honeyed parsnips, and brandied seed cake tomorrow for dinner," Gespry said as they walked down the spiral stairs.

"All right," Dara said listlessly. "Whatever you like."

Gespry glanced at her curiously as she closed and locked the tower door.

"What's gnawing in your belly?" he asked. "I'd've figured you'd be happy."

Dara forced a smile. "Sorry, Gespry," she said. "I'm just tired, is all." That was true; somehow she'd never felt so tired in her life. But she knew better than to believe she'd sleep now. "I'll sit with the lord for a bit and then go on to bed, I think."

"Good idea," Gespry agreed. "I'm gonna draw off a mug of brandy and sit down by the fire in the great hall for a bit, so you can holler when you want me." He grinned. "Might not be many more nights I can curl up in the High Lord's own chair for my evening sit."

"There might not, at that," Dara said. She certainly hoped not. At the moment she'd have given just about anything to leave this castle that seemed to hold nothing but grief and trouble for her. But she couldn't leave Lord Vanian alone with no one to care for him; that would be as good as killing him.

Besides, she'd promised.

Lord Vanian woke briefly when Dara gave him his medicine, but she was too tired and downhearted to talk to him; she merely smiled as reassuringly as she could and eased him back down to the pillows to sleep. Dara glanced at the chair, then shrugged and sat back against the cushions next to Lord Vanian. He was certainly in no condition to molest her.

Not that he'd have turned over and raped her if he was wide awake and well, not even if he'd found her there in his bed. At least she could say that much for him; his word was good, if not necessarily for the reasons he'd have her believe. And look how suspicious and untrusting a few days in the Keep had made her; the gods alone knew how the possibly uncounted centuries could warp someone trapped and alone in such a place. Kelara had lost her soul, Yaga his memory and will. It was not so surprising after all that Lord Vanian had lost his compassion.

It was all a trade after all, wasn't it?

"But it was a trade you didn't know you were making," Dara said to the sleeping lord. "The Keep took what it wanted and gave you what it wanted, too, didn't it? And you thought the game was yours."

There was no answer, of course, but Lord Vanian's brow furrowed as if he was troubled. Perhaps he dreamed.

"Are you dreaming?" Dara asked softly. "Am I? Maybe this has all been a dream. Or do you think it's the outside that's the dream? Did you ever begin to wonder that, what was the dream and what was waking?"

Dara shivered. Of course he had. But this place was his waking dream, where his every thought could become reality. What then *was* truth in such a place? And what was the price of unreality made real?

Come be my Guardian, that was the Keep's siren song. *Rule over all and be ruled by me. I will give you everything you have ever wished, all you could ever desire.*

And the only price is all that you have.

Dara shivered again. Had she done Lord Vanian good by saving his life? Perhaps he'd prefer to die. She would, in his place, rather than face the endless years alone. Perhaps all he wanted now was an end to it.

"You just can't give up," Dara mused aloud. "No matter what happens. Nothing really beats you until you give up." She glanced down at the sleeping lord. "I'll tell you that again sometime when you can hear me."

She sighed. Somehow it didn't seem worth the trouble to go fetch Gespry. Nor did she especially want to be alone with her thoughts.

"Don't mind me, my lord," Dara murmured, sliding down in the bed. She edged as far from Lord Vanian as she could, snatched a pillow, and closed her eyes.

If she dreamed—or woke—she never knew.

13

"**G**OOD MORN."
The words were barely whispered, but Dara
started violently, bolting upright. To her horror, Lord Vanian was awake and looking at her; worse, in her sleep she'd apparently grown cold and rolled over against the lord's side. In fact, she had the miserable suspicion that her head had been lying on his shoulder.

"I'm terribly sorry," Dara said hurriedly, scrambling off the bed. "I was so tired last night, and you couldn't be left alone, and Gespry was—"

"No matter." This time Lord Vanian's voice was a little stronger, and he turned his head to look at her. "You didn't disturb me."

Dara glanced out the window and saw to her chagrin that the sun was well up. With Lord Vanian unconscious and Gespry not an early riser, she'd grown lax.

"I'll make your food," she said apologetically. "It won't take me an hour. Maybe you can eat something solid today. But first, some more of your potion." She poured a cup of water and carefully measured the drops into it.

Lord Vanian was able to be of some assistance this time as Dara lifted his shoulders, and when he'd drunk the potion, she pushed more pillows behind him so he could half sit in the bed.

"Would—would you like Gespry to sit with you while I make your breakfast?" Dara asked timidly. "Or would you rather be left alone?"

"Don't go," Lord Vanian said tiredly. "Just make it here, if you would."

"But I prom—" Dara stopped. Servants didn't argue with a reasonable request from their master. "All right. What would you like?"

"Just some porridge," the lord said after a moment. "I don't think I could manage anything more."

Dara quickly created a bowl of hot porridge, rich with cream and sweetened with honey. Then she hesitated.

"Are you strong enough to eat this," she asked awkwardly, "or should I—should I help you?"

"I'll feed myself, thank you," Lord Vanian said irritably, and Dara hastily created a bed tray, too, so that the lord could balance the bowl more easily in front of him. But when she gave him the spoon, his hand shook so violently that the porridge merely spilled back into the bowl.

Dara looked away, hating the frustration and humiliation on Lord Vanian's face. She wanted to offer to help him again, but feared that that would make it worse.

"I suppose if I'm to eat, you'll have to help me," Lord Vanian said at last, very quietly.

Dara sat down and took the spoon, forcing a smile and a light tone.

"Well, you wouldn't find many lords as could talk their serving maids into feeding them," she joked. "I'll be expecting an extra Moon at the end of the year for my trouble."

Lord Vanian started to laugh, then choked on the porridge in his mouth. Dara hurried to pour him another cup of water, and at last the lord could draw breath again.

"A good servant," he gasped, "doesn't try to choke her master. It's a poor way to get that extra Moon at year's end."

"Sorry," Dara said. She hesitated. "Is there—anything else I can do for you?"

Lord Vanian was silent for a long moment, gazing into Dara's eyes. At last he sighed.

"I want to tell you something," he said. "That first night when you came here—"

"My lord, if you please, I'd rather not talk of that," Dara said hurriedly, her cheeks flaming.

"I let you deceive yourself," Lord Vanian continued deliberately, "so I could deceive myself as well. You looked into the mirror and saw your Cav, and I—I saw Marguerid." He gazed steadily at the ceiling. "I used you to give myself an evening's illusion."

Dara sighed. She'd tried hard not to think of that night. Somehow Lord Vanian's trick seemed pitiable now, an almost minor betrayal. Why should he have thought it any great wrong to deceive and seduce a simple serving maid, when everybody knew such girls were of easy virtue and not likely to dwell on such an event? Why, most of the girls Dara knew in High Lord Haranor's service would have shrugged the incident off and gone on about their lives; the more canny among them might have used the incident to their advantage, to extort coin or favors from the offending lord. If Cav, whom she had loved for years, could not believe in her, could not be trusted with her love, what should she have expected from a stranger, one who had been almost an enemy from the beginning? At least she could take pleasure in knowing that their coupling seemed to have troubled him as deeply as it had her.

But it all really had no importance anymore, did it? What was done was done, and couldn't be changed.

"It doesn't matter," she said quietly. "But thank you for telling me." She shook her head. "Are you comfortable? Can I get you anything else?"

Lord Vanian glanced at her, his expression unreadable, then gazed back up at the ceiling again.

"Leave me," he said, his voice tired and remote. "Just leave me be."

"Well—" Dara stood where she was, utterly confused. A good servant wouldn't refuse if her lord sent her away. But neither would a good servant leave her lord alone when he was weak and ill and couldn't care for himself.

"Leave me the water pitcher and a bell," Lord Vanian said irritably. "I'll ring if I need you between now and dinner. Will that suffice?"

"Of course, my lord," Dara said quickly. She placed the water pitcher and cup near him on the bedside table and conjured a bell that he could ring for her. As an afterthought, she picked up the chamber pot and put it within reach, too, but without saying anything. Lord Vanian could use it or call her or lie in his own filth, just as he pleased.

"Go on," Lord Vanian said impatiently, carefully not looking at the chamber pot. "And one more thing."

"Yes, my lord?" Dara said, hesitating by the door.

"My mirror," Lord Vanian said, not looking at her. "Leave it be. Stay out of the tower room entirely, in fact."

"With respect, my lord, the bargain was one question for each day I served you," Dara said, unaccountably irritated by his instruction. "And I've served you since we returned here."

"I said nothing of letting you use the mirror outside my presence," Lord Vanian said loftily. "And as long as I'm Guardian of this place you will not do so. You'll have your questions, never fear, but you'll wait until I'm well enough to return to the tower."

Dara sighed, but closed the door behind her and made her way back to the kitchen. What did it really matter, after all? She'd had only one question left, and that was the location of the Oracle. And she couldn't go in search of the Oracle until Lord Vanian was well anyway.

And now she was far from certain that she still wished

to ask the same question of the Oracle. She needed her magic if she was to have even a chance of wedding Cav, that was certain. She could think of nothing else that Lord Vanian could give her that would help. Her virginity? A legitimate bloodline? Dara chuckled bitterly to herself. Surely those things were beyond even the power of the Guardian of the Crystal Keep. No, her magic was all she had left to hope for. Could Lord Vanian grant it to her? Most likely. But what could she give him in return? That was the problem. She could make just about anything she wanted by magic, but anything she could make, Lord Vanian could make—and probably much more easily, too. But what did she have left to give?

Dara started a pot of stew simmering; surely Lord Vanian could eat that once the vegetables were good and tender. She drew off a pitcher of cider and took an extra cup, in case Gespry showed up, and took them back to her room, where she sat down and pored over the enigmatic journal she'd found in the library.

"Two new doors today. Does another come with each one?" That was simple enough; she'd already solved that particular mystery.

"No matter how far I go, the only end is the beginning." The beginning of what? That statement somehow reminded Dara of her first conversation with Granny Good in the ashy desert.

"It was always within me. How could I not have seen it?" That sounded like Yaga's riddling talk. What was it he'd said? "Remember that the final key is always within your own heart." What was she to make of that?

"Once I prayed that this was all unreal. Now I pray it is real, for it is all I have left." Dara read the passage aloud. It had a familiar sound. Was it—

"I've seen chickens bound for the block looked cheerier," Granny Good said, materializing suddenly at Dara's side. "Why so sour-faced, my girl?"

"Everything's so complicated," Dara said, sighing as

she poured a mug of cider for the old woman and one for herself. "When I came here I knew what I wanted, the magical talent that ran in my family. That was simple. I loved Cav and he loved me, and that was simple. Lord Vanian tormented me and tried to keep me from finding the Oracle, and I—I hated him, and *that* was simple. And now I look at all those things and wonder if any of them were ever as simple as they seemed."

"The world's a simple place to a child," Granny mused. "Why, go back far enough, and to a babe in arms the world's reduced to wet or dry baby rags and an empty belly or his mother's breast. But as you grow you learn that things aren't so simple. That's bad, I suppose, if you value simplicity above everything else. But love and hate are never simple; they only seem so from the inside, when you're blind with them and don't know any better. If you ever have a chance to step back and look from the other side, you'll see that just as love and hate are the most powerful forces there are, they're also the most complicated."

"Well, now that you've told me all that," Dara said crossly, "how does it help me?"

"It doesn't, if you want to go back to your mother's breast," Granny Good said blithely. "But if you want more than that, it's time to cast off your baby rags and grow up, child, and stop expecting a simple answer."

"I spoke to Cav," Dara said dully. "He was surprised I was still alive. He'd been betrothed to another woman, a lord's daughter. It must have been a long time ago, maybe right after I left, because when he said the betrothal was only a few weeks before, I could see he was lying. He told me if I came back with my family's mage gift, he was almost certain his parents would allow us to marry. And he said he'd always take care of me."

"Oh, child." Granny Good laid her wrinkled hand on top of Dara's. Dara was surprised to see the real pain in the sharp green eyes. "What will you do now?"

"I don't know." Dara shrugged listlessly. "Ask Lord

Vanian to give me the talent for magic and go back."

"Ah, but it's not the same, is it?" Granny asked sympathetically.

"Gespry said I should be happy," Dara said, shaking her head. "That a High Lord's son loves me and wants to take care of me."

"And what'll you do if the High Lord and Lady won't let you wed?" Granny asked gently.

"I'll go home, I suppose," Dara said indifferently. "Mother and Father would be overjoyed that I could finally learn the spells and become a proper mage like my brothers. For most of my life that's what I expected—what everyone expected—I'd do. It's all I've ever known, that and being a serving maid. And I don't think I could go back to being a serving maid again."

"A few days of peeling Lord Vanian's turnips and you've tired of it already?" Granny said, shaking her head wisely. "The magic of the Keep makes it easy, eh?"

"Too easy, I think." Dara sighed. "It gives you simple answers—or what you think are answers, anyway. Like this journal." She stared down at the page, at the passage she'd been puzzling over.

"Granny," she said slowly, "whose journal was this? Was it Lord Vanian's?"

Granny chuckled. "Figured that out, did you?"

"No, I was only guessing. Some of the entries in here sound like the way he talks sometimes. But what does it *mean*?" Dara demanded. "What do these things mean?"

"You're asking me what the lord meant?" Granny said, raising gray eyebrows. "Better ask him than me."

Dara groaned. "Granny, please, please help me—no riddles, no half answers."

"All right, child. I'll help you as best I can." Granny's hand on hers was warm again, her voice unexpectedly soft and sweet, and when Dara looked into Granny's eyes, she was surprised to see them brimming with tears.

Suddenly something in those green eyes, in that voice,

gave Dara the answer. How amazing. And how very, very sad.

"It's been a long time for you, hasn't it?" Dara asked softly. "A long time alone."

"Has it?" Granny said, just as softly. "I can't remember. Never could. That's a mercy, I suppose, all things considered. But what'll you trade me for my help, child?"

"Something nobody else can give," Dara said. "In fact, I've already given it. I gave Yaga back his wish, and helped him find the memory to use it."

Granny became very still, and two tears trickled down her seamed old cheeks. The withered hand resting on Dara's trembled slightly.

"Don't know as I can give you equal value, child," Granny said, her voice shaking. "There's so much I can't say. But there's one thing I can tell you. Go back to the beginning, just as the journal said. But you need another key to open the door you want."

"What door?" Dara asked desperately. "And where can I find the key?"

"The door you'll know when you see it," Granny said. "And the key you already have, if you know how to get at it. It's in your own heart, as it's always been." She shook her head. "But that's all I can say, missy. And it's not enough. Not near enough."

"Then do something else for me, if you will, and I'll call it a fair trade," Dara said after a moment's thought. "Take Gespry to the crystal cavern. There's a gold key there that he wants. Will you take him there and bring him back?"

"I'll do it now," Granny promised. "Where can I find the scamp? Never mind; I'll find him myself. That's the lord's bell ringing, if I'm not much mistaken." As suddenly as she'd come, she was gone.

Dara sat where she was, scarcely believing what had just transpired. Granny Good and Kelara, one and the same—why, she'd never have dreamed it! And yet the clues had all been there—Granny's appearance in the dusty land, her powerful magic, her great knowledge, even the careful distance the lord had kept from the old woman. But even the simplest of divinations would have revealed that link—if Dara had thought far enough beyond her own troubles to cast one.

"But I didn't need it," Dara said, suddenly proud. "I didn't need the magic. When I saw her eyes like that, I knew."

She sat a moment longer, then jumped to her feet as the ringing sound repeated from the room next door. Lord Vanian's bell!

When Dara hurried into the room, Lord Vanian was sitting upright in the bed, impatiently tapping his fingers. He'd piled more pillows behind him.

"There you are," he said irritably. "Where's my dinner?"

"I'm sorry, my lord," Dara said, confused. "But it's not midday yet." Why, he'd broken his fast less than three hours before.

"It certainly *is*," Lord Vanian snapped. "Or haven't you looked out the window yet today?"

Dara glanced at the window and groaned with realization when she saw that Lord Vanian was right. Of course, she'd slept late, and then she'd had to take time to prepare Lord Vanian's porridge, and then the stew—Gods, it was probably almost two hours past midday by now! It was easy to lose track of time in Lord Vanian's castle, where the only windows were the ones she'd created herself in this room.

"I do beg your pardon, my lord," Dara said, embarrassed. "I don't know what's gotten into me. But I've made a good rich stew for your dinner, and it won't take a moment for me to run down and fetch a bowl for you." She hesitated. "And I'm ever so pleased you can sit up yourself."

"Yes. Well, I won't be pleased until I can do a great deal more for myself," Lord Vanian said darkly. "But we'll start with the stew. Bring it quickly.''

Dara dashed down to the kitchen and filled a bowl with
the stew, then after a moment's thought filled another in
case Lord Vanian wanted her to eat with him. She eyed the
basket of buns, then shook her head; Lord Vanian would
be doing well if he could manage the stew.

Lord Vanian succeeded not only in eating the stew, but
in eating without Dara's help, though by the end of the
meal he was so exhausted that Dara barely had time to clear
the bowls away before he was asleep again. To her delight,
the chamber pot had been used; thank the gods she'd not
have to embarrass herself or humiliate him further by cleaning him again.

Lord Vanian napped until midafternoon; Dara had time
to wash the bowls and chamber pot in peace. She filled the
large cauldron with water to heat; tonight, if Lord Vanian
left her time, she'd enjoy a bath.

When Lord Vanian called her again, however, Dara was
surprised when he told her to bring in the bathtub and hot
water.

"This room reeks of sickness, and so do I," he said. "I
need to bathe, and then I'll move back to my own room in
the tower."

"Respect, my lord, but I don't believe you're strong
enough to bathe, much less go up all those stairs," Dara
said slowly.

"Then you'll have to help me," Lord Vanian said impatiently. "It'll be nothing new for you, or do you mean
me to believe that your furry little friend has been changing
my clothes?"

"As you say, my lord," Dara murmured. It took all the
force of her will to obey; however unnerving she found it
to touch the lord's naked body when he was sick and helpless, it was nearly impossible to conceive of doing it while
he was awake and aware of what she was doing. It only
slightly comforted her that the idea must be no less disagreeable to Lord Vanian himself. Or was this yet another

of his games, to force her to do something he knew Dara would find distasteful?

Lord Vanian tried to help as Dara wrestled him out of his robe, out of the bed, and into the bath, but his efforts exhausted Dara as much as they did him, and by the time she had brought the buckets of warm water to pour over him, he was mostly asleep again. Dara was profoundly grateful; it was ever so much easier to deal with the abrasive lord when he was unconscious.

Aside from the odd mumble, Lord Vanian did not wake again until she rinsed the soap from his hair; even then, he was so weak and tired he could only let his head loll back against the edge of the tub and gaze at her balefully.

"Good, you're awake," Dara said cheerfully, although her heart did a great flop and her hands shook. "If I help you up, can you hold on to the table and stand long enough for me to rinse you off?"

"By the gods, I will," Lord Vanian said grimly, but his will was greater than his strength, and Dara had to fairly hold him up while she awkwardly poured the clear hot water over him. At last she was able to wrap him in a clean sheet, and he toppled more than sat into the chair Dara had moved near the fireplace.

"Just sit there a bit and dry off in front of the fire," Dara panted. "I can't get you back up to the tower, but I'll at least change the bed linens and fetch you a fresh bed robe."

"I've never been bathed by a woman before," Lord Vanian said wryly.

Dara pulled the sheets from the bed and threw them to the floor, letting them sop up the bathwater that had gotten splashed on the stones. It would save her mopping up later.

"Well, how did you like it?" she asked.

"Not much." Lord Vanian grimaced, rubbing the back of his head where it had banged against the tub edge.

"Good," Dara said matter-of-factly. "No more did I. So get back your strength so we needn't do it again."

"Yes, I remember your contempt for helpless nobles who can't wash their own bottom without a servant's help." Lord Vanian chuckled, but Dara could hear a note of bitterness in his laughter.

"Well, I won't hold it against you, as you got your illness on my account," Dara said lightly. She put down the linens and stepped over to Lord Vanian's side, sitting on the stool beside his chair.

"I've meant to thank you for that," she said. Somehow it was hard to get the words out, and she felt her cheeks grow warm. "For saving my life."

"Well, you returned the favor and more," Lord Vanian said rather uncomfortably, gazing into the fire. "Believe that I never had any intention of taking that dart in your stead; that it happened testifies more accurately to my clumsiness rather than any admirable self-sacrifice." He shook his head. "I suppose you'll be wanting your questions of the mirror so you can go. You've served the five days you promised."

"I—I can wait till you've got the strength to care for yourself," Dara said shyly. "I couldn't bear my own company, knowing I'd left you in such a state. Besides," she added hastily, "it shouldn't be long, you've improved so quickly. And maybe you know spells to help you heal more quickly."

"Spells?" Lord Vanian glanced away from the fire for a moment, surprise in his eyes. "I know no spells."

"You weren't a mage?" Dara asked, surprised. She'd thought that at least the basic grimoire she'd found in the library had been his.

"Not the slightest hint of magical talent." Lord Vanian sighed and leaned back in the chair, closing his eyes. "Just as well. I was an idle fellow, never much inclined to study. Fortunately nobody expected it of me. The gift of magery was much rarer when I was born than it apparently is now, even among the nobles."

Dara sighed. "I wish I'd been born then," she said.

"Things might have been much simpler."

"Believe me when I say matters were no simpler then or in any age," Lord Vanian said, sighing, too. "Or there'd be far fewer doors in the corridor of my keep."

There was no reply Dara could make to that, so she simply turned away and finished making up the bed. Rather than go up to the tower and rummage through Lord Vanian's things, she simply created a new bed robe for him. It was surprisingly easy.

"Best get you back to bed, my lord," she said awkwardly. "You mustn't take a chill while you're still so weak."

This time Lord Vanian was so tired that Dara had to nearly carry him back to the bed. When she had settled him in comfortably, he was so nearly asleep that Dara hoped he would doze all afternoon; when she would have left, however, he caught at her sleeve.

"The mirror," he murmured. "Remember. Stay away from that mirror."

"I will," Dara said, troubled by his insistence. Why was he so determined that she not use the mirror outside his presence? Was it merely that he wanted to control what she learned, or did he take his responsibilities as Guardian that seriously? There was a third possibility, too, Dara realized—that there was some danger inherent in using the mirror that she did not know about, and Lord Vanian's duty was not only to protect the mirror from misuse, but to protect the user, too. Dara shivered. Perhaps she and Gespry had been more fortunate than they knew, to ask their questions, get their answers, and suffer no further consequences.

When Dara had dumped out the buckets of water, cleaned the bathtub, and returned to the kitchen, she was relieved to find Gespry there, sipping brandy by the hearth as usual. A gold key hung prominently around his neck on a piece of twine.

"There you are," he said, slurring his words a little. "Just having a cup in celebration." He patted the key.

"Granny took me right to it. Said she'd promised to see me changed back to my right form when you go, so she could stay around that long. Whatever that means. She figure some way out of the Keep? I always figured she could go if she liked, somehow."

"No, I don't think she can leave," Dara said slowly. "But what about you?" Somehow she couldn't bring herself to care. "If you still want me to do a transformation spell, you could go now. No need to wait. I'll release you from your promise."

"Nah." Gespry shrugged a little shyly. "I'll wait like I said I would. After what Granny said to me about going back to my old life, it got me thinking, and I ain't just exactly sure I want to leave the Keep and start heading on toward dying again, especially if I was walking out the door with not so much as a copper in my pocket. Anyhow, I'd never sleep nights if I didn't find out how this all comes out."

Dara forced a smile, although she felt only a faint weary gratitude.

"Thank you, Gespry," she said. "That's good of you."

Gespry peered at her over the rim of the mug; his bleary eyes sharpened slightly.

"Say, you look just about worn out, and you're all soggy, too," he said. "Why don't you go up and put on some dry clothes and then take an hour or two nap? I'll wake you up in time to carry up a bowl of supper to the lord."

"Thank you, Gespry," Dara said, this time with sincere gratitude. A short nap was just what she needed; after wrestling Lord Vanian into and out of the bath, she was as tired and sore as if she'd been beaten.

"Wait a minute," Gespry said as Dara turned to go. He thrust a small flask at her. "Drink this all down first. It'll help you sleep."

Dara took the flask and recklessly took a huge swallow, gasping as the brandy seared its way to her stomach. She nonetheless swallowed the rest of the flask's contents and stumbled up to her room, just managing the strength to pull off her wet gown before she collapsed on the bed in her light chemise. It seemed only a moment later that she opened her eyes with difficulty to find Gespry sitting beside her on the bed, a sheepish expression on his face.

"It's morning," he said contritely, nevertheless looking at her chemise-clad body rather than her face. "Sorry. I dozed off myself, and the lord never rang his bell. Guess he slept through himself."

Dara groaned in dismay and pushed herself upright with difficulty; she wanted nothing in the world more than a few more hours of peaceful oblivion. She crawled wearily out of bed, however, and made herself a clean gown before she staggered down to the kitchen. There was nothing prepared but the stew she'd left in its jar in the cauldron full of water, and over the course of the night it had cooked down to a thick sludge that she'd never be able to scrub out of the jar. Dara stared at the inedible mess and almost cried. It would take hours to prepare anything else.

Then she stopped, shaking her head. The five days were over. She wasn't obliged to cook with her own two hands anymore. Almost defiantly she conjured up a tray of the fanciest morning food she could imagine and carried it up the stairs.

To her amazement, Lord Vanian was up—not only awake, but dressed and sitting moodily before the fire. He looked up and gave Dara a small smile when she walked in.

"Good morn," he said. "I trust you're well rested after your long sleep."

"I'm sorry," Dara said, embarrassed. "I know it's late."

"You never came with supper," Lord Vanian said wryly. "When I woke last night I felt able to walk a little, and I saw you'd fallen asleep. I decided to let you rest. I drank the last of that potion this morning."

"I'm sorry," Dara repeated, utterly dismayed. He'd woken up and there she'd been, utterly neglecting her duties—and worst of all, Lord Vanian had seen her sleeping in only her chemise. Dara's cheeks flamed.

"It's all right," Lord Vanian said quietly. "You've worked hard caring for me." He glanced at the tray, then raised his eyebrows. "And even harder preparing my food, by the look of that tray."

"I—I didn't cook it myself," Dara said, now ashamed that she'd conjured the food instead of cooking it. "It was so late, and the five days are over."

"Are they?" Lord Vanian sighed resignedly. "I didn't know how long I'd been ill. Well." He shook his head. "But I'm recovered now, or near enough. So there's nothing further to keep you here. I suppose you'll be wanting to ask your other questions of my mirror now."

Dara hesitated. She didn't want to tell Lord Vanian that she'd already used the mirror twice while he was unconscious, but if she asked more questions than was her due, would that somehow void her bargain? Dara remembered her conversation with Cav, and a deep sadness filled her. Did any of her questions—or the answers to them—really matter, after all? Like virginity, trust, once lost, could never be restored.

"Listen to me," Lord Vanian said suddenly. "You needn't use the mirror again. You needn't find the Oracle. I'll give you the magical ability that you came here to gain, and I'll tell you the price."

Dara laid the tray down on the table.

"And what is that price?" she asked quietly.

Lord Vanian stood, and he met her eyes squarely.

"Come to my bed and lie with me once," he said. "Without tricks or illusions, without any self-deceit for either of us."

A great stillness filled Dara, a sense of standing at some monumental crossroads, or the edge of a cliff, perhaps. But her magic was the one thing that would guarantee that she'd survive—with Cav or alone. But—

"If that's your price," she said steadily. She reached for the lacing of her gown.

Whatever Lord Vanian had expected her to say or do, it apparently was not this. He reached out and seized her hand, stopping her before she could unlace her gown.

"No," he said, no anger in his voice, only a great weariness. "Don't."

He gestured and the room dissolved around them. Dara gasped; only Lord Vanian's grip on her wrist let her keep her balance. Another room formed around them; it took Dara a moment before she realized she was standing in the entry hall of the Crystal Keep. The fountain was gone now; there was only the plain wooden table and chair and the large oaken door through which Dara had once passed into the endless corridor.

Lord Vanian waved his hand again, and the bag of Dara's belongings appeared on the table; beside the bag was a very startled Gespry, a half-eaten pastry still clutched in his handlike paw.

"What's this? What's this?" Gespry squeaked, scuttling off the table and cowering under it, gazing fearfully up at Lord Vanian. "Begging your pardon, lord, I didn't know I was—"

Lord Vanian said nothing, his eyes locked on Dara's. He released her wrist, but took both her hands in his own instead. Dara gasped again, stifling the urge to pull free as a sort of cold burning shot from his hands into hers, flowing up her arms and down into her body. In a moment the sensation faded and Lord Vanian released her hands.

"Your books, your grimoires, are in your pack," he said remotely. "Whatever spells you haven't learned, I've no doubt you'll master soon. Go home to your lordling." He turned abruptly away, reaching for the door latch.

"But—" Dara was so stunned that for a moment her mind spun helplessly. "But you don't want anything in return?"

Lord Vanian stayed as he was, his back to her.

"For what I want," he murmured, "the price is too high." He turned to face her and gave her a small smile. "You saved my life. You cared for me when I was ill," he said. "That is enough."

"But you saved *my* life," Dara said, oddly dismayed. "Surely—"

"You gave me far more than the potion to save my life," Lord Vanian said quietly. "You gave me your kindness when you had every reason, every right, to withhold it. Therefore I'm in your debt." He shrugged. "Besides, I still owed you three questions from my mirror."

"Not really," Dara admitted. "I—I went to the tower and used the mirror twice while you were unconscious. You'd made me wonder why it was I hadn't had the gift of magery like my parents, so I asked—"

Lord Vanian sighed, and again Dara was surprised to see no anger in his expression.

"I'm sorry," he said at last. "I asked that question myself after we'd talked in the library. When I awoke and found you tending me, it seemed cruel to let you learn the truth." He sighed again. "At least you didn't have to seek out the Oracle. At least I spared you that pain."

"The Oracle?" Dara asked, confused. What did that matter? What difference would it have made if she *had* found it?

Dara's gaze was drawn suddenly to Lord Vanian's hand on the door latch. On the keyhole below it.

On the *two* keyholes.

The only end is the beginning, Lord Vanian's journal had said. *Go back to the beginning*, Granny had told her. *It was always within me. How could I not have seen it? Remember*, Yaga had said, *the final key is always within your own heart*.

"Of course," Dara said aloud. "I thought it was only another riddle."

Lord Vanian glanced down at the keyholes, then at Dara.

"You solved it, then," he said without surprise. "It took me much longer. And when I finally found it, it was from despair, not courage."

"I had help." Dara reached into her pack, drew out the journal, and handed it to him.

Lord Vanian took the journal, shaking his head as he thumbed through the pages.

"I was half mad when I wrote this," he said. "I'd only just realized how thoroughly I'd trapped myself here. I didn't even remember what I'd written."

While he turned the pages, Dara reached back into her bag. She pulled out the knife she'd found in Lord Vanian's castle. When she turned back, Lord Vanian was looking at her. His eyes flickered to the knife and back.

"Don't," he said quietly. "There's no need anymore."

Dara wanted to laugh. No need? He didn't understand any more than Cav had understood—that there was every need, now more than ever.

Drawn from its sheath, the knife was sharp and bright, like love—or hatred. Dara gazed at it only for a moment, and before she could lose her courage, she turned the point toward her and drove it into her heart with all her strength, ignoring Lord Vanian's anguished gasp and Gespry's cry of horror.

There was surprisingly little pain, only a brief flare of heat and a sense of pressure. But a sudden wave of dizzy weakness made Dara crumple to her knees, and it took all the strength of her will to turn the knife, pressing to widen the wound. She felt warm blood flow down her chest and belly, and even as she dropped the knife and reached into the gaping wound with trembling fingers, she wondered how it was she was still alive, still conscious.

Sickening warmth closed about her fingers, and her courage almost failed. But abruptly she touched something hard, and grasping it, she pulled it forth.

Under its coating of bright red heart's blood, the key was of crystal purer than the clearest water, brighter than the light of the sun. Weakness gone, fear forgotten, as alone as she'd ever been, Dara pushed herself to her feet and stumbled to the oaken door, sliding the crystal key into the small upper lock and turning it firmly.

Dara opened the door into light, a cold, clear light that for a moment dazzled her. Her eyes adjusted slowly, and as they cleared, Dara began to smile, then to chuckle, and at last to laugh.

She was gazing into a large empty space, perhaps a room with walls too far away to see. Like the entry hall of the Keep, it was cold and clean and almost featureless but for one thing: Just in front of Dara, hanging seemingly in empty air, was the large, ornate mirror from Lord Vanian's tower. Its smoothly polished surface reflected Dara's appearance, as if mocking her.

"Good golly," Gespry said, scampering to Dara's side and peering through the door. "All that trouble, and he had it in his tower all the time?"

"No." Lord Vanian stepped up beside Dara, too. "The mirror in my tower was Kelara's creation. Just a powerful magical object. The mirror is what you see because that's the image your mind, your eyes, makes of the Oracle. It doesn't exactly exist, I believe, until someone opens the door. It shapes your vision, and in turn your vision shapes the Oracle itself. If you'd opened the door, Gespry, you would have seen something different. Just as I saw something different when I finally opened the door."

Dara drew a deep breath and looked down at herself. The front of her gown was sodden with blood, and there was a gaping rent over her breast; when she hesitantly parted the cloth, however, she saw that beneath the thick slime of half-dried blood her skin was unbroken. Disbelievingly, Dara rubbed at the skin with her fingers, wiping the coating of blood away. There was no mark, no scar.

Gespry shook his head, looking, too.

"I'd never have thought," he admitted. "And if I had, I'd never have done it."

"You got your wish without it," Lord Vanian said. "But all you wanted was immortality—a petty, simple sort of wish. Some of us want more." He smiled a little sadly. "And we pay more to get it."

He turned to Dara.

"And what will you ask the Oracle?" he said. "You already have your wish as well."

"No." Dara felt again that utter stillness at the center of her being. Once more she stood on the edge of the cliff. She turned back to Lord Vanian.

"I didn't wish for magic," she said. "I wished for whatever I needed to win the man I love. But I didn't need to wish for that, because I already had what I needed. I just didn't know it, even though my divination spell had already shown me."

"It didn't show you nothing," Gespry protested. "I was there, remember?"

"It did," Dara said quietly. "It showed me my own reflection."

"Then what'll you ask?" Gespry asked her. "What you should give the lord?"

"No." Dara stepped back from the door and closed it slowly, locking it with her blood-smeared crystal key, which she then handed to Gespry. "You can keep it. I promised you my key, remember? I don't need the Oracle to tell me anything now."

She turned to Lord Vanian and lifted the cord with the golden key over her head, and jumped from the cliff's edge.

"I know what to give," she said, holding out the key, her eyes on Lord Vanian's.

Lord Vanian glanced at the key but made no move to take it.

"No." He sighed. "Go home to your lordling, Dara. It's been a long time—too long. I can't be the kind of person you want anymore—if I ever was. I've been alone too long, hating too long. I think I've forgotten how to love."

Dara shrugged. "I don't know that I'm that good at it myself," she admitted. "I've made rather a botch of it so far. Yaga once told me there's a dark and misty line between love and hate, and that if you weren't careful, you could cross that line from love into hate without knowing it. I didn't know you could cross that line from the other side, too." She shrugged. "I suppose we'll both have to learn about love the hard way."

Lord Vanian raised one eyebrow.

"That might take me a long time," he warned.

Dara shrugged again and glanced around. "We've *got* a long time," she said.

"There is that." Lord Vanian reached toward the key, then drew his hand back again.

"You know," he said, "I could just take this and leave the Keep."

Dara's eyes never left his.

"That's right," she said. "You could. If you didn't feel obligated to give me back equal value." She reached into her pack and drew out the little silver bell he had given her, pulling it loose from its wrapping with one hand. "Or maybe I'll just ring this so you'll have to come."

"Once I'm out that door," Lord Vanian said mockingly, "there are no rules. That might be a refreshing change."

"Have you gone mist-headed?" Gespry demanded, interrupting them before Dara could reply. "Girly, you got a High Lord's son waiting at home for you!"

"Somehow I don't think he'll wait long." Tired of holding the key out, she reached over and tucked it into Lord Vanian's pocket.

"Go on," she said. "If that's what you want."

Lord Vanian took the key from his pocket and weighed it consideringly in his hand. He strode to the door, and Dara's heart gave a great flop in her chest as he opened the door. Sunlight streamed into the cold, empty entryway, and Dara could hear birds singing.

Lord Vanian stood looking out a long time. Then he

drew back his hand and threw the key out as hard as he could. He turned quietly around and closed the door behind him.

"Satisfied?" he said, holding up his empty hands.

"Well, you didn't have to waste it," Dara chuckled, her heart settling slowly back into place. She had gambled—she had trusted—and, beyond all expectation, she had won.

"Yeah, you could've given it to me," Gespry said with a sigh. "I could've traded it to Skivvit for some of that gold, maybe."

"It'll be amusing to see whether anyone finds it," Lord Vanian said, chuckling, too. "Besides, I can make another anytime I like. I'm the Guardian, after all." He held out his hand; Dara smiled and took it. And this time, his hand felt warm.

"Well, you may not be for long," Dara said. "Once Yaga uses his wish, Kelara might prefer to be Guardian herself. She may still be bound to the Keep, you know. Unless you can set her free."

Lord Vanian laughed.

"I just may do that," he said. "I'm rather used to ruling the place, you know. So perhaps it'd be better to let her go if I can. For a suitable price, of course."

"Of course," Dara said with a grin. "Value given for value received. But I'm telling you, we're *not* living in that nasty cold castle."

"That's *my* 'nasty cold castle,'" Lord Vanian protested.

"No, it's not, it's High Lord Esperon's," Dara argued. "We'll stay in my house. And I don't wear anybody's gowns but my own."

"Well, what about me?" Gespry persisted.

"What about you?" Dara said. "You have a key of your own now. You can go wherever you want, or leave, if you want that."

"Well, I've still got to find Granny to change me back to somebody who could reach a keyhole," Gespry said wryly. "Then maybe I'll have a look at the rest of the Keep before I make up my mind. If I decide to go, might's well see what I can find to sell once I get out. Course, maybe I'll just show up a bit where I know the food's always good.''

Dara laughed. ''As long as you don't expect me to always cook it myself,'' she said. She glanced at Lord Vanian sternly. ''Or you, either.''

''Well—'' Lord Vanian appeared to consider. ''Perhaps not *always*. And why do you want to live all the way at the far end of the Keep when you still have to walk everywhere?''

''Well, I can't get about inside the Keep without my key, anyway,'' Dara said, smiling. ''Perhaps you'll teach me to pop in and out as you do.''

Dara paused before the door to the Keep, instinctively reaching for her key. She pulled back her hand when she realized it was gone, then waited for Lord Vanian—no, just Vanian now—to open the door. She'd have much more difficult lessons to learn than popping in and out, but so would Vanian; the hardest lesson, she feared, for both of them would be learning to trust again.

But they'd have time aplenty to learn.

''I could probably teach you,'' the Guardian said as he opened the door. ''And what'll you give me in return?''

''Oh, a far more important lesson than that,'' Dara said, taking his hand again. Beside her lord, she stepped into their kingdom.

''I'll teach you to peel your own turnips.''

Shadow Novels from
ANNE LOGSTON

Shadow is a master thief as elusive as her name. Only her dagger is as sharp as her eyes and wits. Where there's a rich merchant to rob, good food and wine to be had, or a lusty fellow to kiss...there's Shadow.

"Spiced with magic and intrigue..."—Simon R. Green
"A highly entertaining fantasy."—<u>Locus</u>

___SHADOW   0-441-75989-0/$3.99

___SHADOW HUNT   0-441-76007-4/$4.50

___DAGGER'S EDGE   0-441-00036-3/$4.99

And don't miss other Anne Logston adventures...

___GUARDIAN'S KEY   0-441-00327-3/$5.99
In Crystal Keep is an all-knowing Oracle hidden within the walls and an all-powerful Guardian who challenges those who dare to enter, even a young woman in search of her own special magic—and her own self.

___GREENDAUGHTER   0-441-30273-4/$4.50

Payable in U.S. funds. No cash orders accepted. Postage & handling: $1.75 for one book, 75¢ for each additional. Maximum postage $5.50. Prices, postage and handling charges may change without notice. Visa, Amex, MasterCard call 1-800-788-6262, ext. 1, refer to ad # 493a

Or, check above books   Bill my: ☐ Visa   ☐ MasterCard   ☐ Amex _____
and send this order form to: (expires)
The Berkley Publishing Group   Card#_____
390 Murray Hill Pkwy., Dept. B   ($15 minimum)
East Rutherford, NJ 07073   Signature_____
Please allow 6 weeks for delivery.   Or enclosed is my: ☐ check   ☐ money order
Name_____   Book Total $_____
Address_____   Postage & Handling $_____
City_____   Applicable Sales Tax $_____
                                           (NY, NJ, PA, CA, GST Can.)
State/ZIP_____   Total Amount Due $_____

World Fantasy Award—winning author

PATRICIA A. McKILLIP

*"There are no better writers than
Patricia A. McKillip."*
—<u>New York Times</u> bestselling author Stephen R. Donaldson

__THE CYGNET AND THE FIREBIRD

0-441-00237-4/$5.99

"Finishing a Patricia A. McKillip novel is like waking from a
dream. There are the same lingering images, the same sense of
having been otherwhere..."—<u>New York Review of Science Fiction</u>

__THE BOOK OF ATRIX WOLFE

0-441-00211-0/$18.95

Horrified after unwittingly bringing destruction to his land, Atrix
Wolfe fled to the seclusion of the mountains. Now the Queen of
the Wood summons the mage to find her lost daughter and
reunite the kingdom of Faery—a quest that could finally free
Atrix Wolfe from his pain. *An Ace Hardcover*

__WINTER ROSE

0-441-00334-6/$19.95

Wild and free-spirited Rois Melior roams the woods bordering
the abandoned Lynn Hall. When Corbet Lynn returns to claim
the estate, memories of his grandfather's curse are rekindled. Rois
is drawn into a world beyond her own, where love can nurture the
soul—or poison the heart. *An Ace Hardcover Coming July '96*

Payable in U.S. funds. No cash orders accepted. Postage & handling: $1.75 for one book, 75¢
for each additional. Maximum postage $5.50. Prices, postage and handling charges may
change without notice. Visa, Amex, MasterCard call 1-800-788-6262, ext. 1, refer to ad # 556a*

Or, check above books   Bill my: □ Visa □ MasterCard □ Amex _____
and send this order form to: (expires)
The Berkley Publishing Group   Card#_____
390 Murray Hill Pkwy., Dept. B   ($15 minimum)
East Rutherford, NJ 07073   Signature_____
Please allow 6 weeks for delivery.   Or enclosed is my: □ check □ money order

Name_____   Book Total $_____

Address_____   Postage & Handling $_____

City_____   Applicable Sales Tax $_____
                                       (NY, NJ, PA, CA, GST Can.)
State/ZIP_____   Total Amount Due $_____

KATHERINE KURTZ
DEBORAH TURNER HARRIS
Novels of
THE ADEPT

"Kurtz and Harris have created a charming and
unusual detective." —*Locus*

"An unusually adroit duo." —*Publishers Weekly*

Through countless lives and eras, the Adept has fought the powers
of Darkness. Now, as psychiatrist Adam Sinclair, he leads a secret
brotherhood against supernatural evil in all its myriad forms.

_THE ADEPT	0-441-00343-5/$5.50
_LODGE OF THE LYNX	0-441-00344-3/$5.50
_THE TEMPLAR TREASURE	0-441-00345-1/$4.99
_DAGGER MAGIC	0-441-00304-4/$5.99

A drowned body bearing a German *Kriegmarine* flag leads
Sinclair and his companions to a radical cult that mixes magic
with sinister Nazi teachings.

Payable in U.S. funds. No cash orders accepted. Postage & handling: $1.75 for one book, 75¢
for each additional. Maximum postage $5.50. Prices, postage and handling charges may
change without notice. Visa, Amex, MasterCard call 1-800-788-6262, ext. 1, refer to ad # 557a

Or, check above books Bill my: ☐ Visa ☐ MasterCard ☐ Amex	
and send this order form to:	(expires)
The Berkley Publishing Group Card#_____	
390 Murray Hill Pkwy., Dept. B	($15 minimum)
East Rutherford, NJ 07073 Signature_____	
Please allow 6 weeks for delivery. Or enclosed is my: ☐ check ☐ money order	
Name_____	Book Total $_____
Address_____	Postage & Handling $_____
City_____	Applicable Sales Tax $_____
	(NY, NJ, PA, CA, GST Can.)
State/ZIP_____	Total Amount Due $_____